Divi

There was the sound of a footstep behind me. I said, "Hey, how deep is this pool?"

The answer was quick in coming; somebody tried to hit a home run with my head. I had just readjusted my body into a kneeling position so the bat or whatever it was bounced off my shoulders for a bunt instead of a base hit. I tumbled off the walkway and into the cold water. I must have gone down around six feet before I realized I was no longer breathing air. I did a submerged somersault that wouldn't have impressed Esther Williams in the least, kicked my way to the surface and coughed a couple of gallons of water out of my lungs. The lights had gone out in the test room. I probed the darkness, wondering where I could pull myself safely from the water. I decided to strike out for the edge of the pool and take my chances.

I had taken one stroke when the pool lights blinked out. The blackness was now total.

I treaded water a few moments, trying to decide what to do.

Once more I started to swim and once more I stopped.

Twin lights had snapped on in the water below me like a tiger blinking its eyes open. The lights began to prowl in lazy circles, spiraling higher with each circuit until they neared the surface. They caught me in their beam. The ROV hovered a dozen feet away about a yard below the surface, examining me. It waited. I waited. I didn't have to wait long. There was an angry whirring of electric motors.

The damned thing was headed straight for me.

Bantam Books by Paul Kemprecos

COOL BLUE TOMB
NEPTUNE'S EYE

NEPTUNE'S EYE

•

Paul Kemprecos

CRIME LINE ™

BANTAM BOOKS
NEW YORK • TORONTO • LONDON • SYDNEY • AUCKLAND

For Jeff and Carol

NEPTUNE'S EYE

A Bantam Crime Line Book / September 1991

ISBN 0-553-29353-2

Published simultaneously in the United States and Canada

Bantam Books are published by Bantam Books, a division of Bantam
Doubleday Dell Publishing Group, Inc. Its trademark, consisting
of the words "Bantam Books" and the portrayal of a rooster, is
Registered in U.S. Patent and Trademark Office and in other
countries. Marca Registrada. Bantam Books, 666 Fifth Avenue,
New York, New York 10103.

PRINTED IN THE UNITED STATES OF AMERICA

RAD   0 9 8 7 6 5 4 3 2 1

The author wishes to acknowledge the invaluable assistance of the following people: Wreck diver and photographer Brian Skerry of the Boston Sea Rovers; Jim Jalbert of the Marine Systems Engineering Lab, University of New Hampshire; Peter Zentz of the Benthos Corporation in North Falmouth; Jeff Madison of the Gay Head, Martha's Vineyard Wampanoag; Henry Keatts, author and U-boat expert, Joe Bangert, and Eric Goodkind in the office of Congressman Gerry Studds. Special thanks to Chester Robinson, Jr. Any errors of omission or commission are the sole responsibility of the author.

"By their own follies they perished, the fools."
Homer—*Odyssey*

PROLOGUE

•

1945

The sound of doom was remarkably prosaic.

It came as a muffled metallic crash, like a firecracker going off inside a distant rubbish bin. In the control room at midship, the commander took his eyes off the dial of the depth gauge he'd been studying and cocked his head to listen. He frowned in puzzlement. The noise was like nothing he had ever heard in years at sea.

A second explosion reverberated through the boat's pressure hull, louder this time. Even as the echoes faded, another followed. The bearded helmsman and the equally bewhiskered hydroplane operators turned to the commander and watched his lined and weary face intently, waiting for instructions. There was alarm in their eyes. The commander calmly reached for the microphone hanging from an overhead cable and barked the order.

Close all watertight compartments.

The whole procedure, from the first explosion to the commander's directions, took about ten seconds. It might just as well have been ten years. As crewmen from one end of the boat to the other raced to follow orders, a

1

deafening blast, louder than any that preceded it, rocked the pressure hull.

The deck lurched violently. The commander was thrown off balance. He wrapped his arms around a vertical conduit pipe attached to the arched bulkhead and kept his footing. The crewmen grabbed onto the controls to keep from being flung from their seats. The boat shuddered and listed toward the stern. The diesels died. Forward motion came to a halt. Water had entered the engines.

They were sinking.

The commander called for battery power to keep the boat moving.

The control room went dark. Water in the electric motors.

The auxiliary power system came on, bathing the control room in a dim red glow. The commander glanced around at the hellish scene. Incredible. A minute ago they had been peacefully cruising at snorkel depth, recharging their main batteries. All was calm. All was secure. All was routine. All organized. Now this. Within seconds. Pandemonium.

He responded coolly. He had a reputation for a methodical go-by-the-book attitude that bordered on the phlegmatic. It was the reason he had been picked for this important mission. He ordered the crew to dump ballast. Compressed air hissed into the main ballast tanks.

The boat continued to sink stern-first.

They blew water from all the tanks. The added air should have been more than enough to restore buoyancy, but the boat plunged further.

The nose-up angle of descent became sharper. The emergency lights went out. Anguished shouts of panic in the darkness. Thuds and crashes. Bodies and objects smashed into the steel bulkheads.

The commander slid down the pipe and sat on the floor. Crouching in the dark, strangely detached from the bedlam around him, he knew it was over. He wondered briefly about the steel box in his quarters, if its contents were worth the end of his fine new vessel and its young crew.

Water was pouring in from the stern, surging from compartment to compartment, lapping around his feet. Strangely, instead of fear, the commander felt a serenity he had not known since the madness began in his country.

Die decently, the higher-ups had said. What a laugh. As if men could be ordered to go with dignity when they were gagging under tons of seawater. He twisted his mouth in scorn. And moments later, when death finally found him, his lips were still frozen in a rictus of contempt.

CHAPTER 1

•

The telephone call that launched me into the search for Leslie Walther came on a delicious Cape Cod morning in late spring. Sunlight bathed Pleasant Bay in a soft buttery glow and the sea-cool air was sweeter than strawberry wine. From time to time the breeze freshened and a perfume of salt spray rose, sedge and beach-plum blossoms wafted onto the boathouse deck where I lounged, half-comatose, with Kojak the Maine coon cat stretched out beside me. The boathouse was part of a large estate before I bought it and moved in. The old place isn't what it used to be. The roof leaks in a rainy southwest blow, and I have to crank the wood stove up to red-hot when the cold winter winds sweep down from Labrador. But the view of the misty barrier beach with the dark Atlantic beyond is a visual mantra, and I like to sit outside, gaze off at the ocean rim, and pretend the world is flat.

I was trying to sell my flat-earth theory to Kojak, who wasn't buying it. He was pretending to listen while he stared cross-eyed at a muscular ant struggling under the weight of a tortilla chip. I was at the part about the world being balanced on the back of a gigantic turtle when the cordless phone on the driftwood coffee table rang. I snagged the phone, stuck it in my ear, and managed a drowsy hello.

"Mr. Aristotle Socarides?" a man's voice said.

"Speaking," I answered, keeping an eye on Kojak, who had hoisted his bulky body onto all fours for a stretch. I lip-synched: Hey buddy, don't go away. He yawned and licked one black paw.

"My name is Winston Prayerly," the man said in an English accent. "Would you be available this afternoon or early this evening? My employer, Mr. Frederick Walther, would like to discuss the possibility of retaining your services."

I sat up at attention. The prospect of a paying job stirred me from my lethargy. My last case was three months ago. A Wellfleet quahogger hired me to find a stolen outboard motor. He suspected his estranged wife who told me she took it but said she'd bought the damn thing so the lazy bum couldn't use a busted motor as an excuse to stay home and loaf. She showed me the check to prove it. The quahogger refused to pay me because I hadn't delivered the goods, but the story had a happy ending. The shell-fisherman and his wife joined a Pentecostal church, renewed their wedding vows, and the last I heard they were taking a second honeymoon in Cancún.

I said: "I'll have to check my schedule, Mr. Prayerly. Could you tell me where Mr. Walther lives? That would have a bearing." Kojak sauntered toward the kitchen door. I tried to grab his scruffy tail, he bolted, and I fell out of the aluminum-and-plastic chaise longue.

"Not too far, Mr. Socarides. On Merrill's Island in Chatham."

I scrambled back into the chair. "In that case, I can fit you in after lunch, Mr. Prayerly. How about one P.M.?"

"Perfect. Let me give you directions."

A minute later I hung up and remembered what Homer said in the *Odyssey*, that our destiny lies on the knees of the gods. Or in my own less elegant metaphor, life is a crapshoot and somebody else is throwing the dice. Prayerly's call proved Homer's point nicely. My private detective work is incidental to my job as a commercial fisherman. I fit my investigations around the migratory patterns of groundfish, never forgetting that my success at catching cod, not crooks, is what pays my bar-bill tab. Ordinarily, it was the time of year when my fishing partner, Sam, and I would have been hooking cod from his line trawler. But Sam was in Florida with his wife Millie, enjoying a trip to Disney World and Epcot on a VFW raffle ticket I bought them. Sam had been reluctant to go. I don't think he's been off-Cape since Cal Coolidge was president. I told him the codfishing could wait and he agreed it was cheaper to take a vacation than to settle with Millie in divorce court.

I went into the boathouse and rummaged through the refrigerator for lunch goodies. The best I could do was two slices of fried bologna, rare, one egg over easy, and a stale Pepperidge Farm oatmeal raisin cookie for desert. As I dined on the health-food special I thought about Winston Prayerly's accent. His speech had been brushed with a layer of culture, but his diction needed another coat of paint because the flaws showed through. If you listened carefully, you could hear him rough up a vowel or manhandle a consonant, like an East Boston tough trying to talk Back Bay Brahmin.

After lunch I shaved, showered, exchanged my jeans and gila-monster sweatshirt for a pair of tan Levi's corduroys, a button-down blue oxford cloth shirt, and a brown Harris tweed jacket I had picked up for $1.50 at the Catholic church thrift shop. I hadn't seen lapels that wide since my father wore them, and if the Al Capone look ever came back, I'd be right in style. I had haggled the thrift-shop ladies down from two dollars. They weren't happy about selling the jacket at a discount, but it had been a slow day.

Sliding behind the wheel of my 1977 GMC pickup

truck, I murmured a prayer and turned the ignition key. The engine coughed asthmatically and blue smoke billowed from the vibrating exhaust pipe that rattled against the frame like a machine gun. The truck is in the advanced stages of decrepitude and it's a toss-up which will go first, the body or the engine. The pickup started on the fourth try, a good sign. I offered thanks to the high god General Motors and the miracle mechanic at the Sunoco station who keeps the truck on life-support systems and then pointed it toward the half mile of sandy drive that leads to the main road.

Merrill's Island is a twenty-minute ride from my boathouse. Shortly before 1:00 P.M. I drove over the causeway that links the island to the mainland. The road is flanked by a shallow cove on one side and salt marsh laced by tidal creeks on the other. On Merrill's Island itself, the rough natural beauty bordering the access road gave way to lawns as smooth as golf greens, as verdantly close to Astroturf as chemical science could make of living grass. A half-dozen houses have been built on the shoulders of the island, an oblong hill about a mile long. They're great sprawling edifices as big as imperial mausoleums, owned by people who like privacy and can afford to pay for it, hidden from the world and from each other by uninviting thickets of trees and sharp-thorned shrubs.

The Walther house was slightly smaller than a dirigible hangar. It sat at the southerly tip of the upland, surrounded like a game preserve by a high spiked stockade fence. The place was built in an English baronial style, rare on the Cape, where people like their houses faced with white cedar that weathers to silver, and would put shingles on their mattresses if they weren't afraid of splinters. The house had Tudor timbers exposed in beige stucco and small windows with diamond-shaped panes except on the Atlantic Ocean side, where huge expanses of glass faced easterly onto a wide veranda. The view must have cost a thousand dollars a square foot, and it was probably worth every cent of it.

An olive-green Mercedes sedan with Maryland plates crouched in the circular gravel drive. I pulled in behind it, walked up onto the wide porch, and rang the bell. The thick door was opened a few seconds later by a man about my height, just over six feet. He had balding black hair that could have been slicked back over his large meaty ears with two slices of buttered toast. His pale skin was as smooth as a salamander's and it looked even whiter because of the contrast with his clothes. He was dressed like a paid mourner. Black blazer, black turtleneck, black slacks, and black Chinese rubber-soled slippers. I was sorry I hadn't brought flowers and a message of condolence for the dearly departed, whoever it might be.

"Please come in, Mr. Socarides." It was the same soft-spoken voice with the English accent I had heard on the phone.

"Mr. Prayerly?" I stepped into a large circular lobby with high, beamed ceilings and a massive crystal chandelier.

He nodded. "Wait here, please." He went up a wide sweeping staircase. I strolled over to examine the exposed machinery of a tall grandfather clock. I was checking out the date on the face when Prayerly said, "Mr. Walther will see you now." He was standing a couple of yards behind me, looking as if he had caught me trying to stuff the grandfather clock in my hip pocket. A quiet one, Mr. Prayerly. He led the way up the stairs to a spacious landing and into a drafty oak-paneled room several times larger and a lot neater than my boathouse.

You could die happily in any one of the plump brown leather chairs after checking your blue-chip stocks in *The Wall Street Journal*, giving a loud harumph, and smoking a fat Havana cigar. A log fire crackled in a walk-in medieval fireplace large enough to roast an elephant with an apple in its mouth. Ancient volumes filled the bookcases lining the walls. It was a room with a theme. War. Old war, fought at spear's length. Shiny suits of armor stared vacantly out from each corner. Shields and halberds and flintlocks and paintings of battle scenes with soldiers dressed up like fancy-ball ushers hung from the walls. Someone had worked hard to make the room a shrine to the manly art of legalized murder, but it looked like the haunted house set of an Abbott and Costello movie.

Near the fireplace was a billiard size table. The green-and-brown baize top swarmed with hundreds of tin soldiers. Bending over the table was a slender man wearing a gray herringbone tweed jacket that wasn't half as natty as mine. He turned and smiled, then walked smartly over to me, and giving a quiet click of his heels, he shook my hand. His bony grip was strong. He looked about sixty but was probably ten years older. His silver hair was cropped Prussian close to a long firm-jawed Nordic head. His thin lips were as bloodless as two strips of liver. His face was all hard planes and angles, not a soft or a curving line on it, like one of those ice sculptures they chisel for winter carnivals. If he stood near a stove long enough, he'd simply melt.

His cold blue eyes focused on a spot six inches behind my head. "A pleasure to meet you, Mr. Socarides. Please have a seat. These Cape Cod spring days still have a nip of winter in them, don't they. How about some brandy?" It was a cultivated voice, not much louder than a whisper, with no particular regional accent I could place. I was wondering why everybody in the place spoke in a whisper. And why I wanted to do the same.

Winston Prayerly poured us two snifters of Grand Marnier. "Thank you," Walther said, "that will be all." The valet disappeared, quickly and quietly. Walther lifted his brandy. "To your health." We sat in facing leather chairs, sipping the brandy in appreciative silence. The only sound the snapping of the fire. Walther put the glass down on a side table. "You're probably wondering how I happened to call you."

It had crossed my mind. People who live on Merrill's Island don't exactly ring my phone off the hook.

"Most of my cases are referrals," I said, which was true, because I don't advertise.

"Just so. You were recommended to me by Leonard Wilson. He said your methods were unconventional, but they worked."

Leonard Wilson was my old yachting buddy. Cape Cod has a lot of rich people like Wilson who are always looking for a free deckhand. Last summer an acquaintance asked me to crew in a sailboat race. The forty-nine-foot sloop was owned by Leonard Wilson. We lost the race, but Wilson was grateful and bought drinks for us at the yacht club. Over gin and tonics Wilson told me he owned a large retail operation near Boston and that someone at his warehouse was stealing him blind. I offered my services as a private cop, went in undercover, studied the system, and recommended places where he could plug the leaks. Then I got lucky. The thief spotted my cop's flat feet and thought I needed a body to match. He tried to bury me under a pile of wooden crates. That was his first mistake. Missing me was his second one. I get excited when people try to make me short and wide. I came up swinging and he spent a few days in the hospital nursing a broken jaw and three cracked ribs. With him out of the picture, things just sort of fell into place and the pilferage stopped.

Walther was saying, "I took the liberty of doing some further checking. I'm very careful about whom I work with." A pile of manila folders sat on the table next to his brandy. He took the top folder and handed it to me. I opened it. Inside was a résumé I could have written myself. Born in Lowell, Massachusetts, studied Greek and Roman classics at Boston University, dropped out to join the Marines in Vietnam, did a stint with the Boston Police Department, now a fisherman and part-time private cop.

The most interesting item was an eight-by-ten color photograph. It showed a dark-haired guy with olive skin and a droopy mustache on the deck of Sam's boat pitch-forking cod into the dockside conveyor bucket. The picture of me was taken by someone standing on the fish-pier observation platform.

"Frankly, I don't think it does you justice," Walther said. He was watching for a reaction, so I gave him one.

"It's not my best side, but I wouldn't mind a dozen copies to spread around the family at Christmas."

Walther smiled. He didn't know I was serious. "I'll see what I can do. Now, down to business." He opened the next manila folder on the table, took out another photo, and handed it to me.

"This is my daughter Leslie."

The picture was of a young woman in her late twenties. She had strawberry-blond hair that was a color no amount of money could buy. She didn't resemble her father in the least. Even her blue eyes were different from his chill and distant ones. Hers sparkled with warm good humor. I memorized the soft features of her face without too much trouble and handed the photo back to Walther.

"She's lovely," I said, and I meant it.

"Yes." He studied the portrait dreamily as if he were seeing it for the first time. "Extremely so."

I waited.

Walther looked up. The dreamy look was gone, and in its place was the frozen stare. "Leslie has been missing for more than a month. I believe she is in the Cape Cod area. I would like you to find her. I could have hired a Boston detective agency, but I believe that as a local, you'd be more effective than a team of city detectives getting lost on back roads."

"Have you gone to the police?"

"Yes, of course. But they don't have the facilities to launch a proper search. They can only put the information on file. Unless they suspect foul play."

"Is there any evidence of that?"

"No, not in the strictest sense of the term."

Walther was beating around the bush. "In what sense of the term, then?"

He didn't flinch. "Let me explain," he said "Leslie is a lab technician. She lives in Falmouth and works for a man named Thomas Drake." He handed me another file. "This contains some background on Drake, as much as I have been able to cull from available sources. I believe this man has something to do with Leslie's disappearance."

"Why do you say that?"

Walther picked up the snifter. He swished the amber contents, studied their whirling patterns as if he were searching for auguries, then, without drinking from it, set the glass down. He ran a slender finger along one side of his pencil-line mustache, then the other, although every hair was exactly where it should be, and said, "She was involved with him, very much so." His voice had gained a carbon steel edge.

"Have the police talked to Drake?"

"Yes. But he told them Leslie simply didn't show up for work one day, and that he hasn't seen her or heard from her since."

"Did she leave any indication of where she might be going? A note maybe?"

"No. Nothing. Her apartment was checked several times."

"How about a paper trail? Did she pay for a hotel or plane ticket with a credit card?"

He shook his head. "We've kept in touch with her bank. Leslie made a large withdrawal just before she disappeared, but she hasn't written any checks since then."

"Did she mention anything to friends? Or was she acting unusual?"

"No again, I'm afraid."

"Has she ever just taken off like this before? Perhaps when she was a teenager?"

"Leslie has never left without saying where she was going."

A missing persons case always starts this way. A picture. A distraught relative. A story that may or may not hold the whole truth. Either you find them quickly or not at all. This case didn't seem too complicated. Rich daughter skeddadles. A few phone calls and interviews. I bet myself I could wrap it up in seventy-two hours, make some drachmas, and have a few days to play before Sam got back from Florida.

I said, "I would be glad to look into this for you, Mr. Walther."

"Thank you. It's been a strain, not knowing." I examined the frosty eyes and found it hard to believe anything could strain Walther.

He handed me the folder that held Leslie's picture. "This contains some background material on Leslie. I don't mean to tell you your business, but you might want to start with Drake. Perhaps you can be more persuasive than the police." He took an envelope from an inside jacket pocket. "This should more than cover your services for the first week, I believe. We can go on from there."

I rose and said, "I'll call you within a couple of days, whether I have something or not, Mr. Walther."

Winston Prayerly appeared. Quietly.

Walther got up and shook my hand. "Fine," he said. "I'm ever so grateful. And Mr. Socarides . . . I don't care what it costs or who you have to step on to find my daughter."

It wasn't the kind of comment that needed an answer and Walther wouldn't have liked the one I gave him. I picked a tin soldier off the battle table. The inch-high infantryman carried a shield and spear and wore a short pleated skirt.

Noting my interest, Walther said, "As you can see, I'm something of a military buff. This is the Battle of Chaeronea. Philip of Macedon crushing the Greeks with the phalanx." He bent over the table. "Several ranks of spearman in close array, so if one fell, a fresh soldier took his place. A technique perfected by Philip, father of Alexander the Great. Simple but effective. I have these tin soldiers custom-made, by the way. They're exact, down to the last detail."

Armchair generals turn me off even when I'm working for them. I felt the sharp point of the miniature spear with my thumb and put the soldier back on the table.

"Everything's real except for the shock, the bleeding, and the gangrene, Mr. Walther."

He chuckled. "Winston," he said without removing his gaze from the battle table, "please show Mr. Socarides to the door."

The interview was over. I was on the payroll. Dismissed.

Back in my truck, I tore open the envelope from Walther and looked at the check inside. It was drawn on a bank in Maryland. I wondered if Leonard Wilson had given Walther the wrong impression about my work. For a smart man, Walther hadn't the slightest idea of what he had just bought for his money. I'm not exactly a saint, but Walther didn't know me. I won't muscle anyone unless he tries to muscle me first, and even then I've got a lot of tolerance for stupidity, maybe more than I should have. I was tempted to tear up the check, tell him I was too busy, and go back and sit in the sun with Kojak until Sam got home. But I didn't. I folded the check and tucked it into my wallet. It would be unprofessional to refuse a case just because I didn't fall in love with the client. Besides, I was bored and broke. And there was always the chance Leslie Walther was in some trouble. Even if she weren't, I wanted to meet her in the flesh so I could see if her hair was really as beautiful as the photograph showed.

CHAPTER 2

•

The sun was starting to slide down the sky as I drove off
Merrill's Island. I debated heading to Falmouth immediately to chat with Tom Drake, but decided to cool the
Walther job and get a fresh start early the next morning.
It was just too nice an afternoon to waste in cross-Cape
traffic. I live on the outer forearm of the Cape Cod peninsula, which hooks into the ocean like a big arm swinging
in an uppercut toward the mainland south of Boston. Falmouth, where Drake had his lab, was near the shoulder.
The population of the Cape has zoomed since the Kennedy family focused the world's attention on their touch-
football games and sailboat races at Hyannis Port, but
most of the roads are no wider today than they were in
horsecart days. It's about an hour's drive to Falmouth with
the last few miles on Route 28, the main drag in and out
of town. Traffic would be bumper-to-bumper. I headed
back to the boathouse and went into the kitchen for a can
of Bud. Kojak was waiting by his empty dish, so I poured
him some dry cat food. He despises the stuff and was

giving me his pitiful how-could-you-feed-me-this-garbage look when the phone rang. It was my mother.

"*Tikanes*, Aristotle," she chirped. "How are you?"

I rolled my eyes toward the cobwebs on the ceiling and wondered if I could hang up and get away with the excuse of a bad connection. Ma was calling from Lowell, north of Boston, where the family lives and owns a highly profitable wholesale bakery operation called Parthenon Pizza. Don't get me wrong. I think my mother's a terrific lady. Intelligent, strong, compassionate. But she's run things for so long, she can't imagine her adult children coping with the world on their own. I've been a Marine and a cop and I still have the physical and mental scars from both jobs. I've killed men and have almost been killed by them. But I'm expected to report in to my mother regularly with updates on my health and my professional progress. What there is of it. I hadn't phoned home in weeks. I braced myself for a scolding.

"*Kalá*, Ma. I'm fine. How are you?"

"Fine, Aristotle. Everybody is good."

That was odd. No sermon. I took advantage of my good fortune and diverted the conversation from the well-being of the family to the health of the business. "How are the new Yuppie pizzas going?"

"Not Yuppie pizzas," she corrected. "*Gourmet* pizzas. Your brother George wants to call them the Olympus line so we can say food fit for the gods. I say okay to George so he doesn't get hurt. But we don't need fancy names. We put on the box All Natural. No chemicals. Light and lively. And we charge three times regular price. The artichoke, feta, and black olive pizza sells like . . ." She groped for the words. "How do you say it, Aristotle?"

"Like hotcakes?"

"*Neh*, yes, like hotcakes, Aristotle. Have you seen your sister Chloe?"

The leap from gourmet Olympic hotcakes to the whereabouts of my younger sister defied logic, but that was my mother. Chloe lives with my parents and helps out in the business. As the only daughter, she has to deal with the folks' ups and downs. She spends a lot of time away from home, and I can't say that I blame her. We talk occasionally, but probably not enough. She's a good kid and sometimes I wish I knew her better as a person. I hadn't seen her in months. The last I knew she was on a grand tour of Europe.

"Chloe sent me a postcard from France or Germany, Ma. But that was a while ago. Is she still traveling?"

"No, Aristotle, your sister is back. She came home last week."

"That's great. Hope she had a wonderful trip. How is she?"

Ma was silent for a few seconds. Then she said. "Good and not so good."

My mother is the original Cretan labyrinth. Her roots go back to the people who invented the maze. Crete is so mountainous it is virtually impossible to travel in a straight line from one village to another; you have to go up and down or around. She thinks in the same way. It's simple to communicate with her once you get the hang of it. She was trying to tell me something she didn't want to tell me. Or trying not to tell me something she wanted to tell me. Ma was obviously troubled by something, but I would have to dig with the patience of an archaeologist to find out what it was.

"What do you mean, Ma?"

She sighed. A mother's sigh. The kind that starts at the toes and travels up through heaving breasts before issuing from the mouth. In a single expulsion of air, it evoked the pain of childbirth, dozens of sleepless nights, thousands of meals prepared and laundry loads washed, and the unendurable burden of ungrateful children.

"Your sister is *very* angry at me."

This was going to be more complicated than I expected. I knew how Schliemann must have felt when he started to excavate the mountain of earth that covered the ruined city of Troy.

"I don't understand, Ma," I said patiently. "Why would Chloe be angry at you?"

"For *nothing*, Aristotle."

"Nothing, Ma?"

"Yes. Only one thing. I told her she should get married."

"So. She probably should. She's old enough. Why did she get angry over that?"

Another pause. "I told her *who* she should marry. She didn't like that. But he's a very nice boy," she added quickly. "Nestor Evangelos, a friend of your brother. He owns *two* restaurants."

"Ma, you know Chloe doesn't like to be told anything."

"I know. She's like your aunt Demeter who married that Polish butcher in Chicago. Strong in the head. She leaves the house with a suitcase. Slams the door. She doesn't tell me or Papa where she goes."

Chloe inherited her stubbornness from my mother not Aunt Demeter, but I didn't say that. "I'm sure she's all right, Ma. Probably cooling her temper at a friend's house."

"Yes, I think so too. But, Aristotle, you and your sister were always very close. I want you to find Chloe. And talk to her."

I paced back and forth with the phone. It was my own fault for blowing off the Walther case until the next day. If I'd gone right to work, I wouldn't have been home to pick up the call. "Ma, I don't have any idea where to look."

"Aristotle, you are a detective, no?"

"Yes, Ma. I'm a detective, but—"

"This is for the *family*, Aristotle."

My frail defenses crumbled in the face of Ma's on-slaught. She had trundled the ultimate weapon up to the front lines. The Family. It was the final nail in the coffin of whatever argument I tried to muster. Too busy. Going on vacation. Lying on my deathbed. There was always my obligation as the eldest son. I had broken away from the family to pursue my wayward ways, so my responsibility was a special one. This was implied, but never openly said. Whether my mother did it consciously or not, she knew how to strike the chord of guilt deep in my soul.

I caved in. Trying not to groan, I said, "Okay, Ma. I'll call some of her friends, check around. I'm sure everything's okay, so don't worry."

"*Kalá*, Aristotle. Good boy. One more thing. When you find Chloe, tell her . . ." She sighed again, perhaps impatient at herself for showing emotion.

"I know what to say, Ma."

"Yes, Aristotle. You tell Chloe that I love her. Bye-bye."

While I had the phone in my hand, I dialed the number of Beacon Research in Boston and gave my name. Norma Sheldon came on the line a few seconds later.

"Soc!" she said. "How are you, my dear?"

"I'm fine, Norma. How's the information business?"

"Couldn't be better, love. This is a wonderful time to be a professional snoop."

I said, "Are you telling me everybody wants to know everything about everybody else?"

"That's right, hon. Who do you want to know everything about?"

"A guy I just met. His name is Frederick Walther. All I know about him is that he's very rich, he has a house on Cape Cod and a car registered in Maryland." I gave her Walther's address, the number of his car license plate as I remembered it, and the bank's name from the check he gave me. "While you're looking into it, could you poke around and see what you can turn up on a Winston Prayerly. He works for Walther. He could be English or maybe South African."

"No problem, sweetie pie. I've got to be in New York for a couple of days, but I'll get my staff on it. Call you when I get back."

"Fine, Norma. I'll talk to you later."

Kojak was sniffing at his bowl as if the food I poured

him contained cyanide. I relented and opened a can of
9-Lives he knew I'd been rationing. I didn't want him
complaining to the Society for the Prevention of Cruelty
to Kitties. I finished my beer, popped another, and sat at
the kitchen table thinking about the ironies that abound
in my business. Walther hires me as a private investigator,
and the first thing I do is investigate him. Maybe it was
true as somebody once said that gentlemen don't read
other gentlemen's mail. But I'm no gentleman. Nor, I
sensed, was Walther, for all his money-green patina. And
Prayerly's cultivated accent didn't mask the smell of thug.
There was something else. Frederick Walther said he was
careful whom he worked with. But so was I.

CHAPTER 3

•

The next morning I kick-started my internal engine with breakfast at Elsie's. The home fries weren't as lethal as they usually are because Elsie had changed the grease in anticipation of the tourist season. Eating at Elsie's is proof Darwin was right. Only the fittest survive her cooking. The regular customers have built up an iron-stomach immunity to her food, but she doesn't want to poison any tourists. One of them might be a lawyer.

From Elsie's I drove to the Mid-Cape Highway and headed west, then picked up a series of back-road short-cuts that put me on Route 28 a few miles from Falmouth. Walther had included a map in the file he gave me. I appreciated his thoroughness. Drake's lab was hidden in a remote woodsy section of town where only a unicorn hunter would be likely to stumble over it. The turnoff leading from the main road was unmarked; anyone using it would have to know where he was going. The quarter-mile-long blacktop driveway passed through a quiet stand of tall evergreens that allowed only a few slivers of light to penetrate to the rusty carpet of pine needles below. At

the end of the drive was a blue-painted corrogated steel
building about 150 feet square and enclosed by a high
chain-link fence. Attached to the fence near the front gate
was a yard-wide white sign with NTI lettered neatly in
black.

The middle-aged rent-a-cop who sat in the phone-
booth-size gatehouse must have been bored to death from
watching chipmunks bury acorns. He eyed me as if he
were seeing the ghost of John Dillinger and asked if I had
an appointment. I said no. I showed him my private cop
license. He squinted at it and asked if I had any other
identification. I showed him my driver's license. He read
every word including the eyeglass restrictions on the back
that don't apply to me anyway. It didn't satisfy him. I
showed him my ID card from the videocassette store.
That impressed him. He called in on his phone and talked
to somebody, mispronouncing my name, so I sounded like
the luncheon special at the Acropolis II restaurant, then
passed me through the gate, directing me to the front
entrance of the building.

The glass door opened into a lobby painted in aquama-
rine and decorated with mural-size photographs taken at
the bottom of the ocean. Five minutes in this place and
I'd be reaching for the seasickness pills. The fish-eye decor
didn't seem to bother the receptionist, who sat at a con-
temporary metal desk. She had auburn hair with red highlights that went well with her pearl-gray business suit,
soft doe eyes, and a rosebud mouth. Her legs looked good
and her face would have been quite pretty, even with the
unflattering heavy-framed glasses, if she hadn't been trying to imitate a Doberman pinscher. The name on the
stylized desk plaque said Sharon Prescott.

"I happened to be in town and didn't have time to call
ahead," I said. "Is Mr. Drake in?"

"Yes, *Doctor* Drake is in. I'm sorry, Mr. Socarides, the
doctor is an extremely busy man and doesn't see people
without an appointment." She started to turn the pages
of a datebook on her desk. "If you'd like, I can make an

appointment for you. Dr. Drake has a time slot open in a few weeks. What company do you represent?"

She didn't know I planned to wrap the case up in three days. I pulled out my wallet and extracted one of my business cards. I borrowed a ballpoint pen from her desk without asking for it, and on the back of the card I printed two words in block letters a half inch high. I handed the card to the receptionist and gave her an Uncle Dudley wink.

"If it's not too much trouble, Miss Prescott, could you take this into Dr. Drake? Ask him to make sure he looks at the back of the card."

She held the card by the edges and with slow deliberation read both sides. Then, she appraised me, got up, taking her time, and disappeared through a door. A few minutes later she returned. Her severe expression had softened, and there was a curious glint in her brown eyes.

"Dr. Drake says he can spare a few minutes," she said. "Please follow me."

We passed into a pale green corridor lined with closed doors. One of the doors opened as we went by. A white-frocked man emerged from a lab that looked like Young Frankenstein's playroom. It was loaded with glass containers, wiring, electrical instruments, and hand tools. Miss Prescott ushered me into an anteroom at the end of the hall. She had me wait while she went through a portal. She came out smiling as if she had just heard something clever and pointed the way.

I gestured toward the doorway. "Dr. Drake?" I said.

She nodded and left me standing alone in a fragrant cloud of perfume.

I stepped into an office done in early nautical. There were old prints and paintings of ships in full sail on the walls. All originals, I guessed. Not like the Currier and Ives insurance-calendar art I use to cover holes in the plaster walls at the boathouse. A brass binnacle stood in one corner, its metal surface polished to a rippling eye-smarting shine. The office was full of antique sextants, barometers, spyglasses, and thermometers. Thomas Drake sat behind a massive oak desk that floated like a man-of-war on a thick sea-green wall-to-wall carpet. The doctor was turned away from me, making some computations on an IBM computer. I sat down in a contoured Naugahyde chair in front of the desk and waited.

He held up a forefinger and went back to his typing. Obviously he was in the middle of something important. Fair enough. I had busted in on him without an appointment. I relaxed in the comfortable chair with my hands locked across my stomach. If he wanted to take his time, that was okay with me. I was in no hurry. Seeing Drake was the only task I had assigned myself. The office was very pleasant. I could have stayed there all day.

Drake was in his late thirties. He had a classic profile, like the engravings of Caesar on old Roman coins. He had a noble brow, a straight nose, and a firm jutting chin that had a dimple in it. Cute. His dark brown hair looked as if it saw attention from a stylist's scissors at least once a week. There was a little-boy pout around his mouth that even women probably liked. The fingers dancing across the computer keyboard and throwing figures up on the screen were long and well manicured. He wore an expensive-looking blue shirt that showed off his bronze tan to its best, and a yellow tie with a small circular print that must have looked great across the table at a power lunch.

He stopped typing and gave me a grin that showed me his orthodontist earned his pay. There was a friendly twinkle in his hazel eyes. It wasn't the type of reaction you'd expect from somebody who had just had important work interrupted by a nosy private cop. He even apologized.

"Sorry to keep you waiting, Mr. Socarides. I had to finish these computations. Now, what can I do for you?"

Drake must have had a fair idea why I had come to call. My business card was on his desk blotter. The side with Leslie Walther's name lettered on it was faceup. I leaned forward, pushed the card a few inches closer to him, and tapped it a couple of times.

"I've been retained to find Miss Walther," I said. "I understand she worked for you."

"That's right," he said pleasantly. He picked the card up, examined it as if he were studying a mysterious blob found at the high-tide line, then put it down. "Leslie left about six weeks ago without giving notice." He pursed his lips, emphasizing the pout. "Damn sorry to lose her. She's a lovely lady and was a valuable part of the staff here at NTI."

"Do you have any idea where she might have gone?"

He gave his head an engaging little Shetland-pony shake I was willing to bet he practiced in front of a mirror. "No, I wish I did. One day she was here. The next she was gone."

I waited for him to keep going, but that was it. Drake had told me all he was going to except adieu, and he said that next. "Look, Mr. Socarides, I don't mean to be rude, but I've gone over this Leslie thing any number of times with the police. I'm sure if you talk to them they'd be more than happy to help you. Now if you'll excuse me . . ." He swiveled in his chair to face the IBM. It was a brush-off. Polite, but still a brush-off.

"I really appreciate your taking time to see me, and that's a good suggestion about the police, Dr. Drake, but I was hoping we could be more frank in our discussion."

Drake swung around in his chair. The grin was still in place, but the friendly little twinkle had vanished from his eye.

"What exactly are you getting at, Mr. Socarides?"

"Let me start over again. I'm trying to find Leslie Walther. Sometimes a missing person will say something to a friend purposely or otherwise about his or her plans. I understand that you and Leslie were very good friends."

"Please get to the point, Mr. Socarides."

"I'd be glad to, Dr. Drake. The point is, I believe, that you would have particularly good access to Leslie's thoughts because you and she were more than friends. You were lovers."

The grin went the way of the twinkle. Drake reacted as if I'd slapped him hard on the cheek.

"I do *not* believe this. Who the hell told you that?"

"That's not important, Dr. Drake. The question is whether it is true or not."

His face went red under the tan. He stood, leaned forward onto his desk, and glowered at me. He was at least six feet tall, with a good physique. I grinned, friendly-like. Drake lowered his head like a bull ready to charge. I wasn't too worried. Guys who wear hundred-dollar shirts don't like to wrinkle them. I'll never know if Drake was bluffing, because a side door opened and a balding bespectacled man with reddish-brown hair and beard entered the office. He saw the fierce anger in Drake's face, and stopped short.

"Oh, I didn't know you had somebody with you. Sorry to interrupt, Tom."

Drake kept his eyes on me. "You're not interrupting anything, Dan. Mr. Socarides was just about to leave."

I remained in the chair, doing a tolerably good imitation of a potted palm. The man looked at me, then at Drake. Tentatively, he held out a sheaf of papers. "I just wanted to give you the latest tensile-strength results."

Drake snatched the papers and scanned them. Then he exploded in anger.

"No, no, you idiot. These findings are all wrong, all wrong. Doesn't anyone know how to make a test anymore?" He stepped out from behind his desk. The knuckles of the hand that held the papers were white.

"Listen. You tell those stupid imbeciles to run those tests again. Tell them I don't give a shit if they have to stay here until midnight. And if they can't get it right this time, tell them I'll get some kids in here from the Falmouth High School science class to do their work for them."

"But Tom—"

"No buts about it, Dan. Get it done." Drake crumpled

the papers and threw them at a wastebasket. He missed, but he didn't seem to care.

Dan wasn't happy. He bit his lip. He brushed his beard. He looked at me, embarrassed at being dressed down in front of a stranger. I tried to interest myself in an oil painting of a four-masted sailing vessel. The test results had bounced off the wastebasket and under the desk. Dan had to get on his hands and knees to retrieve them. When he arose, his face was flushed. I couldn't tell if it was from the exertion, from embarrassment, or from anger. He left the office, and if he had a tail, it would have been tucked between his legs. The encounter was revealing. Our Dr. Drake was something of a bully.

Drake had expended his fury. He flopped back into his chair and we had a staring contest.

I glanced lazily over at a set of brass navigational dividers hanging on the wall. "That piece is a real old-timer. Seventeenth-century Spanish, isn't it? An antique like that is real museum quality. It must have cost you a bundle at auction."

Drake followed my gaze, then flicked his eyes back to me. There was a glimmer of a smile on his lips.

"Yes, you're right. It came off a Spanish ship. But I didn't buy it. I dived to a wreck off the Florida keys and found it myself."

I nodded and said nothing.

Drake picked up a pencil and tapped the edge of the desk. Thinking. After a minute he said, "So you want to know more about that little slut.

I was getting to dislike this guy real fast. "No," I said. "You've got it wrong. I'd like to know about Leslie Walther, a former employee of yours, who is missing."

He toyed with the pencil, then said decisively, "All right." He glanced at his Rolex. "But I don't have time now, Mr. Socarides. Tell you what. Drop by my house around seven-thirty tonight. We'll have a couple of drinks and I'll tell you everything about Leslie." He scribbled on a Cartier notepad and ripped the page off. "Here's my address. I'm out on the Point. That's my private telephone number in case you have any problems finding the house."

He got to his feet and punched a button on the phone. Miss Prescott appeared almost immediately. I turned to say goodbye to Drake, but the doctor had his nose buried in the computer. He was smiling. It wasn't a nice smile.

Leslie Walther's apartment was on the second floor of a gambrel-roofed condominium complex on the outskirts of Falmouth. I knocked on her door. Wouldn't it be nice, I thought, if she came to the door and that was that. No answer, I tried the units on either side of Leslie's. There was no one home at the first. The door to the second apartment was opened by an elderly man with a bushy thatch of white hair. He smiled when I said I was a friend of Leslie's who was trying to find her.

"I've been traveling out of the country and lost track of Leslie," I told him.

He shook his head. "I wish I could help you, but I haven't seen Leslie recently."

"Darn it." I sighed wistfully. "I've tried to reach her a couple of times by phone, but it's been disconnected. Do you have any idea how I might get in touch with her?"

He surveyed me sympathetically and then said, "Look, I'm just brewing up some coffee. I'd love the company, if you're interested in joining me, and I'll tell you what I can."

I glanced at my wristwatch as if I had an appointment and said, "Sure, thanks. I've got time."

Leslie's neighbor was named Evans. He said he was a widower who'd retired to Cape Cod from the insurance business in Framingham, a small city west of Boston.

"Always good to have somebody to chat with," he said, pouring me a cup. "My wife died a year after we retired here. Our kids live out of state and they're pretty much involved with their own lives anyhow. It gets lonely sometimes."

"Did you know Leslie pretty well?" The coffee was good, fragrant and strong. I leaned back in the kitchen chair.

"Miss Walther used to drop by occasionally. I always looked forward to her visits. I've got a bum leg and don't remember the last time I got out, it's been so long. So it was always a pleasure to see her." He chuckled. "When you're my age, I'm seventy-four, you get silly about young women. You kinda see them as a granddaughter, mine's out in California, but it's funny, the old male hormones never go, and there are times, lots of them, when you wish you were fifty years younger. So I was flattered that Leslie would pay any attention at all to an old guy like me."

I sympathized with Evans. I'm not seventy-four yet, and I get silly about pretty young women too.

"I don't mean to worry you," Evans said kindly, "but Miss Walther seems to have disappeared. I'm sure she's fine."

Time for some method acting. I said, "Disappeared! What do you mean?"

"I'm sure it's nothing to get alarmed about, but she simply left without telling anybody where she was going."

"That's incredible. Has anyone gone to the police?"

"Oh yes. Her family has reported her disappearance and the police have been by here several times asking questions. But I'm sure there's no reason to worry. Miss Walther is a pretty smart and capable young lady and I'm certain she'll pop up one of these days. I sort of wish she would. I miss her."

Evans removed a thin cigar with a plastic tip from a cellophane pack and offered me one.

"No thanks," I said. "I stopped smoking years ago when my lungs began to feel like the inside of an industrial smokestack."

"I know what you mean. I try to keep it down to a reasonable level, one cigar a day."

I picked a pack of matches off the kitchen table, leaned

over, and lit the tip of his cigar to show Evans I wasn't a
militant antismoker. He closed his eyes and drew back
happily on the stogie. We talked about the Red Sox for
ten minutes. I gave him my name and phone number and
asked him to call if he heard from Leslie. Evans said he
would and escorted me to the door.

My appointment with Drake was still a few hours off. I
drove home, puttered around on Sam's boat for most of
the afternoon, then headed back to Falmouth. The address
Drake had given me was outside the village of Woods
Hole, about four miles from Falmouth Center. The house
was part of a private enclave built on a long finger of land
that curled around the harbor. The only access road was
barred by a gatehouse. Drake had called the guard and
given him my name. He hadn't seen Drake come by yet,
but he said I could drive out to the house and walk around
the grounds until the doctor arrived. I took the guard up
on his suggestion and drove onto the Point. It was 7:30.

A house can tell you a lot about its owner, and Drake's
place was talking about deep yearnings. Massachusetts is
full of whiz kids who can turn a scientific degree into a
million dollars. They set up business in a low-rent office,
turn out computer hardware or software or high-tech
instrumentation, and before long they are buying expensive cars to drive to their big waterfront homes on the
Cape. But they are nouveau riche and they know it. Anyone with a brain doesn't give a damn about how new his
wealth is, as long as he can spend it on expensive toys,
but Drake had spent a bundle trying to buy himself the
look of old money.

The house was a rambling gray-brown Victorian estate.
It was probably once a summer place where overdressed
women in long cotton dresses sat in veranda rocking chairs
next to men in seersucker jackets and straw hats and tried
to pretend it wasn't ninety degrees in the July heat. A
wide lawn sloped down from the front of the house to a
private beach protected from erosion by a chest-high wall
of boulders. I parked in the white gravel driveway and

walked down to the edge of the lawn. It was getting dark. I listened to the lap-lap of the tide and looked across at Woods Hole. A quarter hour later I went back to my truck and waited until 8:00 P.M. Still no Drake.

A few minutes later I drove off the Point, first stopping to ask the guard to tell Drake I had come by. Around 9:00 P.M. I was back on my home turf, where I dropped by a bar called the 'Hole. I was there for two hours, long enough to hoist a few Buds and get into a loud argument with an obnoxious Yankees fan from New York. I was in a lousy mood. The Yankees had beaten the Red Sox. Normally the Sox don't take their suicide plunge until July. And I was still angry at Drake for making me drive to Woods Hole for nothing. I've been stood up by prettier dates than Tom Drake, but I've never gotten used to it. I guess I shouldn't have been so hard on him. As it turned out, he had the best excuse in the world.

CHAPTER 4

●

Hughie Miller showed up on my doorstep near midnight. I had conked out on the sofa watching the nightly news broadcast. A soft but insistent knock awakened me and I stared glassy-eyed at the black-and-white screen for a few seconds, thinking the noise had come from the TV. Johnny Carson was wrapping up his monologue with the swing of an invisible golf club. I got up, switched the set off, opened the front door, and stared into Hughie's tie knot. I lifted my eyes several inches to Hughie's mouth. It was set in a broad smile, as usual. Hughie is one of the nicest as well as one of the biggest cops I've ever met. Behind him was Petie Peters, a puerile rookie who acts like he's seen too many reruns of Broderick Crawford in *Highway Patrol*. As usual, Petie was frowning.

"Hey, Hughie, Petie, c'mon in." I yawned, stretching to work out the kink I always got in my back when I used the sofa as a bed. I shuffled into the living room and flopped into an overstuffed chair. "Can I offer you guys a Wild West sarsaparilla?"

The two cops remained standing. "Thanks, Soc," Hughie said. "Not tonight. We're here on business."

That woke me up. "Business? Oh, I get it. Did that Yankees yahoo down at the 'Hole complain about me? Okay, I probably threatened him, but he was running down the Cardiac Kids."

"Naw," Hughie said, "it wasn't the Yankees guy. You at the 'Hole all night?"

"Most of the time. Uh-oh. That sounds like a cop question, Hughie. What gives? Have a seat and tell me what's going on."

Hughie settled his huge body into my sofa. Petie stood nearby in case I made a break for the door.

"Falmouth cops called tonight," Hughie said. "They wanted to know all about you. We said you were okay. They still want to talk to you, though. I don't know the details, Soc. But I got the impression it's pretty serious."

I looked at the clock. The hands were almost straight up. I didn't feel like making another Falmouth run. "Okay, Hughie, I'll buzz them in the morning."

He looked pained. "Don't think you ought to wait, Soc. I'd advise you to give them a ring right away and go up tonight. I think if you don't get in touch with them real quick, they're going to come looking for you or maybe ask us to take you into custody."

"Yeah, I guess that is serious." I picked up the phone. "Got someone I can talk to?"

"Call Sergeant Gallagher, 555-6280."

I dialed the Falmouth police and asked for Gallagher. He came on the line seconds later. I said I just heard he was looking for me and asked him to fill me in. Gallagher said he couldn't go into specifics over the phone. He'd appreciate it if I could drive to Falmouth right away. I told him I'd come right by. The cops in my town had given me a good résumé, so he wasn't worried, he said, but it would probably be a good idea if I didn't waste any time. I said I was halfway out the door.

I washed the sleep off my face and rinsed the sour-beer taste out of my mouth. The night had turned cool, so I put on my Red Sox baseball cap and a light windbreaker. Hughie walked me to my truck and I thanked him for coming. He said he was glad to do it. Petie looked disappointed that he couldn't bring me into the jail in leg irons. I couldn't blame him, I guess. Small-town cops don't lead very exciting lives, but Petie Peters was going to shoot himself in the foot someday if he didn't lighten up.

Less than an hour later I was in Falmouth, cruising past an ugly and congested stretch of fast-food joints, gas stations, and big shopping malls with gland disorders. The police station was a one-story brick building amid the commercial schlock of Route 28 across from a 7-Eleven store. There were more cops on duty than I expected to see this time of night, this time of year, and the rustle, clack, and buzz of activity told me something was going on. I asked the dispatcher if I could see Gallagher.

The sergeant came out to the lobby a minute later. Gallagher was a pleasant round-faced guy pushing early retirement. He had a baby-pink complexion, blond hair going to white, and he combed what there was of it straight back. He shook my hand in a surprisingly gentle grip, thanked me for coming, then ushered me into an interrogation room haunted by the stale ghosts of old cigarette smoke and sweat. I sat down at a long beat-up plastic table. Gallagher took a seat to my right.

A guy in a blue blazer and gray slacks came in. He had crew-cut blond hair, frameless glasses, and sensible wingtip shoes with a high-gloss shine on them. He introduced himself as Detective Lieutenant Finch. No first name. Finch sat down across the table and looked me over. My hair is on the long side, my mustache never grew out of the 1960s, and I wear a gold ring in my earlobe. Finch was taking it all in, and I guessed from the frown on his face that he didn't like what he saw. I wasn't enamored with him, either. I figured him as one of the new college-educated breed of cops who learned their police work in a criminal investigation class at Northeastern University. If you pointed him in the right direction and gave him a shove, he might not trip over himself, but I wouldn't bet on it.

Finch cleared his throat officiously. "The boys up in your town said you were an ex-cop," he said in a Sergeant Joe Friday monotone.

"That's right, Lieutenant. Boston. I made detective before I quit the department."

"Well, I'm just a small-town police officer, but the drill's pretty much the same, so I'll get right to the point. Can you account for your movements tonight?"

The question had the word *suspect* written all over it. I glanced at the sergeant. "I guess this isn't about a parking ticket." Gallagher didn't reply; he was too busy inspecting the room's last paint job. They wouldn't tell me what was going on until they had a story from me, so I gave them one.

"Okay, gentlemen," I said. "Here's a blow-by-blow account of my exciting day."

Gallagher jotted notes in a steno pad while I told Finch how I had gone to see Drake at his lab and made arrangements to meet him that evening. How Drake hadn't arrived. How I went home via a detour at the 'Hole.

When I was through, Finch leaned forward and squinted at me. "Will the guys at the bar vouch for your being there?"

I squinted back. "No," I said.

Finch looked triumphant.

"Most of them weren't in any condition to vouch for anyone, including themselves, but the bartender was sober. I have an alibi, if that's what you're looking for. Now tell me why I need one. Guessing games just make me all giddy."

Finch stared at me for two minutes. Maybe it was a technique they're teaching now in cop school. If you look at a suspect long enough without saying a word, he'll be so intimidated he'll confess to the Brink's job *and* the

Plymouth mail robbery. The ploy didn't work on me, so Finch tried another tack. He reached into the breast pocket of his blazer and pulled out a small rectangle of paper. He put it down on the table. "Look familiar?"

I picked it up. It was a business card. Mine. Something was printed on the back. I turned the card over. The card was damp and Leslie Walther's name was smudged.

I put the card back on the table. "This looks like the card I gave Tom Drake when I saw him at his lab today. Where did you get it?"

"From Drake's wallet."

I was beginning to see which way the wind blew. "Has something happened to Drake?" I asked. "You can tell me, Lieutenant. I know how to keep a secret."

"A picture's worth a thousand words," Finch replied as if he were the first one who ever said it. "Let's go for a ride."

The three of us left the station and got into a police cruiser. Gallagher drove and Finch sat beside him. They put me in the backseat behind the heavy wire divider and headed west out of town. Falmouth has a schizoid personality. Once you leave the commercial sprawl and pass through the main-street business center, the town presents its more traditional side. We passed a picture-postcard green flanked by antique clapboard houses and a white-spired Congregational church, then turned onto the Woods Hole road. Five minutes later we were in Woods Hole, officially a village subdivision of Falmouth. Gobs of fog had drifted in from the harbor and the main drag was wet and shiny where the headlights touched the pavement. The cruiser bumped over the little drawbridge in the center of the village and carried us past darkened laboratory buildings.

Just beyond the Northeast Fisheries Center, a government-issue three-story box that houses the National Marine Fisheries Service, the street makes a ninety-degree right turn. On the immediate left is the aquarium run by Marine Fisheries. The aquarium's brick-and-wood facade was washed in the pulsating bluish-red dazzle cast by the blinding roof lights of two cruisers and a rescue squad truck. We parked and waded through murmuring knots of people, probably curious neighbors, and stepped onto a raised terraced area surrounding the aquarium's seal pool. The terrace was neatly cordoned off by a yellow strip of police tape. The pool was around twenty feet long, half as wide, and about ten feet deep. In the summertime kids line the waist-high fence that surrounds the pool to watch the antics of a couple of frisky little harbor seals named Skeezix and Cecil. The seals must have still been on vacation because the aquarium hadn't yet filled the pool with water. Its shiny green fiberglass surface reflected the unkind glare of floodlights.

About a dozen uniforms and rescue squad people stood around the pool. A photographer balanced on a ledge inside the seal tank and pointed his Nikon down past his toes. The camera shutter clunked and the motor drive whirred the film to its next exposure. I leaned over the cable fence for a better view, following the angle of his lens, and sucked in my breath. Even when you have seen it dozens of times, you can never completely prepare yourself for the sight of violent death. The crooked body of a man sprawled face-down at the bottom of the pool. His head and shoulders drooped into a rectangular drain about two feet across. The back of his blue shirt was stained scarlet and blood was trickling into the drain.

I looked at Finch, who'd been watching me, then back at the body. "That's no seal," I said.

"Nope. It's your pal, Dr. Drake."

I slipped my fingers under the baseball cap and scratched my head. "He was in a lot better shape the last time I saw him," I said. "What the hell happened?"

Finch obviously didn't care for my tone. Gallagher, ever the diplomat, cut in. "One of the neighbors was taking her poodle for a walk. The mutt went crazy when they passed the pool. The lady had a flashlight. She beamed it in and almost fainted."

"I don't blame her. The poodle may never be the same again. This wasn't an accident?"

Finch scowled. Gallagher shook his head.

"I didn't think so. Got any idea who did it?"

"Yeah," Finch said. "We were hoping to stick you with that honor."

I made a face. "C'mon, Lieutenant, you can do better than that."

"C'mon yourself," he snapped. "Drake's secretary told us you barged your way into his office and had an argument with him. You were seen sniffing around his house by a birdwatcher who was keeping an eye on a piping plover. He called the station with your license plate, and the guard on the road to Drake's place confirms you were there. Your card was in Drake's pocket. Unfortunately for us cops the time doesn't figure. Drake's car was seen in town around nine-thirty. The body was found around ten-thirty. The time you were allegedly getting juiced at your bar."

Finch's eagerness to hang a murder rap made me uncomfortable. "You've got a few things wrong," I said. "First of all, I didn't barge in. I dropped by in broad daylight, asked to see Drake, and gave him my card. Second, I was at his house because he asked me to meet him there. Third, there's nothing alleged about my alibi."

The lieutenant looked down at the body in the pool as if it were the police paymaster. The photographer took another photo. "Yeah." Finch sighed. "So what's your connection with Leslie Walther? Maybe we can pin her disappearance on you."

"No dice there, either. Her father hired me to find her. Seems the local fuzz either can't or won't do their job." It was a cheap shot, but Finch had asked for it.

He made a noise between a growl and a grunt. "We talked to Drake too at Walther's suggestion. Apparently Drake and the missing woman were seeing each other but broke up. We even tossed around the possibility that Drake had something to do with her disappearance. We dropped it.

"Why?" I said. "Boyfriends and husbands are always a good bet if there's foul play."

"You don't have to teach me police investigation basics, Mr. Socarides. There was nothing there as far as we could see. Drake was a charmer with the ladies. Rich, good-looking. He collected women the way some guys collect butterflies. The only thing he might hurt is their egos. We figure he dumped her and she went off somewhere to lick her wounds. Come to think of it, she might make a good suspect in his death. Nothing says a woman couldn't have done this."

"Nope, nothing at all. Maybe a couple of women. Or two men, or, . . ."

"Okay. Can it, wise guy." He gestured toward the pool. "How's this thing look to you? Smart city detective like you ought to come up with some answers in no time." He said *city detective* the way some people might say *child molester*.

I walked around the fence and Finch followed. Gallagher drifted off to talk to some other cops. I stopped under a small carved wooden seal's head that stuck out from over the aquarium's winter entrance to get another angle on the body, then went back to where I started, with Finch on my heels the whole way. I looked over the fence at the flecks of red on the fiberglass.

"Looks like Drake was standing here when he got nailed. What was it, gun, knife, club, or poison?"

Finch frowned. He was clearly hoping I would say Drake had been stabbed so he could say, 'How did you know it was a knife?' "

"Stabbed," he said.

I surveyed the pool again. "It looks as if Drake was knifed, then maybe he hung on to the edge of the pool here. It wouldn't have been too hard, even for a woman, to lift him up by the feet and push him over. Then he slid to the bottom. You got a murder weapon?"

"Not yet. The murderer might have tossed it into the

harbor or Eel Pond as he made his escape. We'll put some divers in."

"How did Drake get here?"

"His silver Jag's parked next door."

I pondered that. "So Drake comes here to meet someone. Maybe it's a man and maybe it's a woman. Maybe the guy owes Drake money or the woman is ticked off because Drake is playing around with somebody else. They have an argument. There's a struggle. The man or woman happens to be carrying a Swiss army knife. He or she pulls it out, opens the nail file or the miniature scissors. Then *bang!* Drake's a goner. Probably premeditated. They figure the pool is a great place to hide the body. Skeezix and Cecil aren't due back for months. But the murderer didn't count on one thing, the lady with the poodle. So it's easy, Lieutenant. All you have to do is find a man or a woman with a bloody jackknife. Should be simple. There's no charge for my advice, by the way."

"Thanks, pal."

"Hey," I said. "Maybe it was a man *and* a woman."

Gallagher came over and took Finch aside. They conferred for a few minutes then Finch came back. He was frowning as if he'd just been told his wife had triplets. "We checked your bartender friend," he said. "He wasn't too happy at being hauled out of bed but he backed up your alibi. He remembered your argument with the guy from New York."

"Does that mean I can go, Lieutenant?"

"Yeah," he said begrudgingly. "But don't go far. I can't stick you with Drake's death, but I think you're in this thing somewhere, so we're going to be talking again." Finch turned to the sergeant. "Sergeant Gallagher," he said, "take Mr. Socarides back to the cop house, get his statement, and give him some coffee so he doesn't fall asleep on the way home."

At the police station a cop who typed with one finger and half a brain took my statement. The coffee was as strong as paint remover, but Finch was right, it was the only thing keeping me awake, so I drank a gallon of it. Gallagher came over, shooed the speed typist away, and glanced over the stuff I had dictated.

"This is okay," he said. "Whaddaya going to do now on your missing person?"

"I dunno. Maybe I should try to follow up on Drake, dead or alive. He was my best lead in the Walther case. I've already stepped on your territory, so I might as well compound the felony, if you don't mind."

He shrugged and set down my statement. "Be my guest. The Walther woman's disappearance was bugging me too, but we don't have the personnel to follow through. Summer's coming and the department's got to get ready for really important stuff like noisy parties fulla Boston College kids who've had one too many. It's okay to go now, by the way, but don't take any trips to the Bahamas or you'll get the lieutenant upset."

As I stood to leave, an officer came in and gave Gallagher a slip of paper. The sergeant read what was on it and asked if I could wait just another minute. I slumped back into my chair. The minute stretched into ten. I dropped my head on my chest and dozed off. Then Gallagher was tapping me on the shoulder. "Hey, Soc. Someone here to see you."

I woke up and looked around. The tall bulky man standing beside Gallagher had black wavy hair worn long and combed back from a forehead broad enough to drive a truck on. His complexion was coffee and milk, heavy on the coffee. His eyes were dark, almond-shaped, and flat. He was wearing a conservative gray suit and a silver tie with a silver and turquoise Thunderbird clip on it. I couldn't believe what I was seeing. Rage followed surprise. Crazy thoughts raced through my mind. I saw myself springing up. Smashing his Adam's apple. Tearing his throat out. Kicking him in the crotch. I took a deep breath to still the adrenaline-triggered thumping of my heart. I slowly unfolded my arms and reached down and clutched the chair in a death grip. Sweet reason returned. My breathing became more measured. The violent pictures faded from my head.

"Hello, Flagg," I said. "What sewer grating did you crawl out from under?"

Flagg's heavy eyelids slammed halfway down like window shades. He smiled, showing his teeth like a mako shark. "That's not real original, Soc," he said tonelessly. "A comedian like you can do better."

Gallagher interjected: "Mr. Flagg asked to talk to you. He's with the government."

I rose from my chair. "I know the gentleman, Sergeant. We've met before, a long, long time ago. Tell me, Flagg, still dropping people out of choppers? I've always wondered if you gave them frequent-flier vouchers."

Flagg had put on about twenty pounds since I'd last seen him. Most of the weight had ended up in his chest, and he looked as if he had a barrel tucked under the front of his shirt. His shoulders strained against the seams of his suit. His top-heavy frame and short legs and narrow hips gave him the silhouette of a gravity-defying giant wedge. He would never make the fifty-yard dash or the Bolshoi Ballet, but his was the powerful bone-crushing body of a football lineman. He took a menacing step in my direction. I tensed. It was a phony move on his part; he chuckled and walked around to the other side of the table. The chair Finch had used creaked as Flagg settled his frame into it.

"Sergeant," he said, "would you be kind enough to leave us alone for a few minutes?"

Gallagher had caught the claustrophobic tension. He hesitated and nervously shifted his weight from foot to foot. He looked like a boxing referee who was wondering why someone hadn't rung the bell to end the round.

"It's okay," I said. "We won't break any of your nice furniture."

Gallagher screwed his mouth up doubtfully, nodded, and left. When the sergeant had shut the door behind him, Flagg leaned forward onto his elbows. I sat at the table and assumed the same position. We faced off like a couple of arm wrestlers.

"A few minutes of your time, Soc. That's all I want. Then we can go our separate ways and if we're lucky maybe never see each other again."

"Let's go our separate ways first, Flagg."

"Let's try it my way."

"Why should I do anything for you?"

"For old times' sake."

I sat back in my chair and folded my arms. "Okay, Flagg, go ahead. For old times' sake."

His thin lips twitched. "What are you planning on the Drake murder?"

The question caught me off guard. In truth, I hadn't planned a thing. Drake was a dead end. If I wanted to find Leslie Walther, I would have to turn over some new turf. Flagg's curiosity was intriguing, though. Patience isn't his strongest quality. It must be taking a lot for him to ask something of me; I wanted to know why. I decided to stall.

"What's your interest in Drake? This is just a small-town murder. Probably a *crime de passion*. The eternal triangle. Maybe a tetrahedral parallelogram."

He slowly shook his massive head. "You're wrong. It's more than just a small-town murder, Soc."

I watched his eyes for a clue and found none. "Tell me about it, Flagg."

"I can't. But I can tell you to lay off. This isn't a case for you. There's more here than you know. This is big, too big for you, believe me."

"Why the hell should I believe you?"

His mouth was curled in scorn. "Same old Soc. Everybody's telling lies except you. Knows all the answers before anyone asks the questions."

"I know all the answers as far as you're concerned, Flagg. I know I can't trust you further than I can spit."

He hammered his fist down, hard. The table bounced like a trampoline. The words tumbled from his mouth.

"You don't know diddly squat, Soc. You just think you do. Something sticks in your head, you don't let it go. You think the whole world's picking on you, so you just got to start swinging till something breaks and makes you feel better."

"I only break *things*, Flagg. I don't break people."

I could almost feel the heat blazing in his eyes. Then the anger faded and he shook his head.

"You still think that's the way it goes, don't you?" he said.

I didn't reply. I couldn't. My throat was dry. Nothing would have come out of my mouth. Not even a wisecrack.

Flagg nodded and said quietly, "Okay, Soc, you know who I work for. Stick your big nose in this and I'll see to it that your private cop's license gets yanked before you're out of town. Then you can spend as much time as you want to getting stinking drunk in gin mills."

The novelty of seeing Flagg was wearing off. I was tired and he was getting to be a bore. I wanted to go home. I stood and leaned toward him. It was his turn to tense. He rose. We faced each other across the table, our faces inches apart. I could smell his aftershave lotion. English Leather. I hadn't smelled that stuff since high school.

"Okay, Flagg," I said. I sat down.

Flagg studied my poker face for about fifteen seconds. He was running a mental computation, comparing my answer against past experience, not liking the tally at the bottom line. He nodded his head almost imperceptibly. "Huh," he said. That was all.

We unlocked stares and Flagg went to the door and called in Gallagher. The sergeant was just around the corner in the hallway. He stepped back inside.

Flagg shook Gallagher's hand. "Thanks for your cooperation, Sergeant. Lieutenant Finch said you would keep me posted on any developments in your investigation." Then he left.

Gallagher puffed his cheeks out. He looked beat. It had been a long day for a small-town homicide cop. "I thought for a minute I was going to have another murder on my hands. What the hell gives with you guys? And what was that stuff about dropping people out of helicopters?"

"It's a long story, Sergeant. I'll tell you about it sometime over a beer. How'd Flagg happen to be here?"

"He heard about Drake somewhere and went by the aquarium. Finch told him to come see me. When he found we'd been talking to you, he got really excited. Flashed his badge. Some federal agency I never heard of. I radioed Finch, that's what took so long, and Finch says to cooperate. What the hell did that guy want from you?"

"I guess he thinks I've been working too hard. He wants me to lay off the Drake case."

Gallagher whistled. "Jee-sus. What did you tell him?"

"I said I'd stay out of the murder investigation."

Gallagher was no slouch. He looked at me out of the corner of his eye. "You gonna stay out?"

I picked the baseball cap off the table and put it on my head. "See you around, Sergeant."

CHAPTER 5

●

Flagg and I first met in the non-commissioned officer's club at the MACV compound behind the walls of the Quang Tri City citadel. The club was kept as dark as the inside of a sneaker because the corrupt career sergeants who put their dirty deals together there liked it that way. From my seat at the long mahogany bar, I could see the red glow of cigarettes at the corner tables. Everyone knew what was going on. The sergeants had access to the best booze and the best brothels. They worked with CIA spooks, Green Berets, and marines to midwife the opium flow out of Laos only fifteen miles away.

It was Vietnam winter and a bone-chilling rain drummed against the windows hidden behind the drawn bamboo shades. Someone in a festive mood had strung colored Christmas lights around the walls. Get drunk enough, and you might think you were home for the holidays. For a buck, I could have picked up a pack of Salems laced with opium and got myself a real buzz quick and cheap, but I was destroying my brain the hard expensive way. I polished off another bottle of Ba Muoi Ba "33," the beer the guys called Tiger Piss. The formaldehyde they used to brew the stuff had given me a headache. I switched over to the primo and began tossing down San Miguels from the Philippines. I imagined I was waiting for my date. Blond and blue-eyed. Well scrubbed and virginal. Any minute now she'd walk in the door, tap me on the shoulder, say "Hi, honey," and we'd go out in the Ford convertible for a drive-in movie, pizza, and heavy petting.

A small hand touched my arm lightly. I turned and looked into the bottomless eyes of one of the club hostesses. She was a wearing a long flowing red *ao dai*, the Vietnam scapular, draped over black pants and high heels. Her gleaming hair fell down to the small of her back and she had a red rose in it. She was probably from Hue about forty-five miles to the south of Quang Tri where the most beautiful girls in Vietnam came from.

Her lips brushed my ear. "You want to dance?" she said. Iron Butterfly was playing on the jukebox, "In-A-Gadda-Da-Vida" pounding out the repetitive throbbing drumbeat and steel bass riffs that curdled your brain and curled your toes. Her teeth were white and even and she smelled good. I guessed she was about eighteen, although it was hard to tell. She could have been fifteen; some of them were. About my sister's age.

I shook my head. She nodded and snagged the guy on the stool next to me, another marine. I watched them until they disappeared into the mass of bodies writhing on the dance floor, let my gaze drift around the club to the statue of Buddha in one corner, then on to the dart board. It had a photo of Ho Chi Minh on one side and President Thieu on the other. The picture of the president was pockmarked with holes. Ho's photo was virtually unscathed. Nope, I told myself, this was definitely not Kansas, Toto. I ordered another San Miguel.

Someone took the seat beside me. "I'll have a Coke," a deep voice yelled over the noise of the music. "On the rocks."

I glanced at the big-shouldered man in the civilian

clothes. "That's the first time I've ever heard *anyone* order nonbooze in this place," I said.

"I've trained the bartender at the officers' club, but it's too civilized over there," he said. "Thought I might as well educate them here too." He looked around. "So this is where all the action is."

"Yep. This is where it is, all right," I said. "What part of New England you from?"

His eyes narrowed. "Martha's Vineyard. How'd you know?"

"The way you said bartender, with a broad *A* and no *R.* 'Bahtendah.' I do the same thing myself. The Vineyard's beautiful. I'm from Lowell. Not in the same league as the Vineyard. Big factory town north of Boston."

"I've been there. Yeah, you're right. It isn't in the same league." He extended his coffee-colored hand. "My name is Flagg, John Flagg."

"Socarides. My friends call me Soc."

"Nice to meet you, Soc," he said, and turned back to his Coke. Flagg obviously wasn't in the mood to talk, and that might have been the end of it if the marine who'd gone off to dance hadn't come back to claim his seat at the bar.

He tapped Flagg on the shoulder and said, "That's my stool."

Flagg barely acknowledged him and said, "I don't see your name on it, friend."

The marine glared at Flagg through drunken eyes and reached in his pocket. The Christmas lights glinted on something metal in his hand. He moved toward Flagg. I was half-turned on my stool, saw what was coming, and didn't like it. I lashed out with my boot, catching the marine in the elbow with my toe. He dropped the knife and turned to face me, which left him open for an ungentlemanly kick to the crotch that doubled him over. He'd hurt in the morning, but it was better than facing a court-martial on a murder charge. I slipped off the stool, picked up the switchblade, put the point against the floor and the weight of my boot against the blade until it snapped. Flagg had twisted around on his seat, still not sure what was going on. Just so he would get the point, literally, I put the two pieces of the switchblade on the bar and jerked a thumb at the marine, who was being dragged away by a couple of bouncers.

Flagg looked at the knife and said, "Thanks. Guess this seat did have his name on it."

The incident broke Flagg's reserve. He had another Coke, bought me a beer, and we began to talk. Flagg told me he was with a CORDS unit. The Civil Operations and Revolutionary Development Support cadre was a combined military and civilian command that was a special pacification service within the U.S. forces. Before that, Flagg had been with the 173d Airborne Division. When his tour was up, he got offered the CORDS work. Some of his buddies had been killed, he didn't have a job to go back home to, and it seemed like a way to balance the scales. I didn't ask him for details. Everyone in 'Nam knew CORDS was used as a CIA cover.

Flagg had the deceptive gentleness you sometimes see in big men, but he must have been tough to be with the 173d. It was the crack airborne unit that jumped in to help my gang, the marines when they broke out of Khe Sanh siege. Over our drinks we discovered we had something else in common. We were both struggling with a cultural identity.

I had abandoned a tight ethnic community and the obligations of a family business. The break hadn't been a clean one and the lines occasionally blurred. Flagg was a Wampanoag Indian from Gay Head. He had learned early that Native Americans were second-class citizens and that he'd better talk with his fists when white kids taunted him. He grew up half-ashamed and half-proud of his heritage. Then he put it aside because throwing in with the white man was the only way he'd ever get out of the poverty cycle

of his home. Like me, he had a younger sister. Her name
was Annie, and she was a pretty thing if you could believe
a high school snapshot.

The Military Assistance Command Vietnam at Quang
Tri was in a heavy North Vietnamese stronghold nearly
five hundred miles from Saigon to the south and fifteen
miles from the DMZ. Quang Tri was a picturesque old
city, a combination of tenth-century Vietnamese and
French provincial. It was where you went when you
weren't slogging through rice paddies and picking the
leeches off your skin. The main town was loaded with bars
and brothels, but most of the off-duty guys headed for the
MACV compound. The chow was good at the mess hall
and the vice available and cheap around the NCO club,
where you could order a Carling's Black Label or a Bud-
weiser when you got homesick.

After our first meeting Flagg and I saw each other fairly
often. I'd look him up whenever I blew into town and
he'd do the same. I had made it a point not to get too
close to the guys in my unit; too many of them ended up
in body bags. So it was nice to have Flagg to sound off
to. He was a good influence. He didn't drink. The white
man's firewater was poison, he said, and he was probably
right. I cut my own booze consumption down from a wide
river to a burbling stream.

We talked about the war, the corruption it spawned,
how everybody seemed to be in on the take. Quang Tri
was Fat City to a group of South Vietnamese generals.
While the soldiers under their command died and the war
ravaged their country, they could say they were at the
"front." But the only danger they were in was falling down
drunk on their way home from a brothel. They lived in
luxury, in contrast to the rest of the people in the province, which was dirt poor. The extremes disturbed us, but
by then the whole war disturbed us. Flagg said it was just
like the old west with the cavalry beating up on the Indi-
ans, and I had to agree with him. We talked about getting

together back in the States, me meeting his sister, going out to catch striped bass or bluefish.

Then all that changed.

My unit surprised a half-dozen North Vietnamese in an ambush near the DMZ, and they surrendered. We radioed ahead and a helicopter was waiting for us when we got back to the base camp. Flagg was there. He was wearing an army uniform.

I went over and shook his hand. "Small world, Flagg. You're in the wrong place, though. No peasants to organize around here. Just us, and the Marines are beyond organization."

Flagg's face was stiff as a mask. He said, "That's not all I do, Soc." He turned away without another word.

Then he and some hard-looking types in army uniforms hustled our prisoners on board the chopper. I figured the POWs would be brought back to the base, questioned, then offered work under the *Chieu Hoi*, the Open Arms program that was set up to encourage defectors. If they went for it, they got a good deal. The *Chieu Hoi* were dubbed Kit Carsons, given the same rank they held in the North Vietnamese army, and acted as scouts. Sooner or later, I might even be working with some of these guys.

My unit went back on patrol. It lasted six days, then a chopper came in to take us out. After we landed I chatted with the pilot, a kid from Oklahoma, and learned he was the same guy who picked up the prisoners. I was curious. I asked what happened to them.

"They got interrogated," he said. He looked embarrassed.

"They go into Chieu Hoi?" I asked.

He hesitated, then flapped his arms, and pointed to the ground.

"I don't get you," I said.

"Phoenix, man. Those guys who picked up the POWS were Operation Phoenix. They interrogated them all right." He started to walk away. I grabbed his arm.

"Tell me what happened."

Phoenix was a CIA operation whose job was to wipe out the secret government the North Vietnamese had established in the south. The CIA had assassination squads to do the dirty work. They killed or imprisoned tens of thousands of people. Sometimes they made mistakes. They liquidated guys on a rumor or a chance conversation in a bar. One of their jobs was murdering village chiefs who might be friendly to the communists. Phoenix operatives would wear black pajamas and boots with special soles that left barefoot prints. They would go into a village and kill people. They attacked at dawn usually, maybe go in with a few Kit Carsons who screamed, "communist, communist," in Vietnamese so the villagers would blame the Reds. I couldn't imagine the Flagg I knew as one of these guys.

The pilot took a deep breath and lowered his voice. "Look, I could get into deep shit for talking, but I've got to tell somebody. It was frigging *incredible*. They interrogated them at Quang Tri, then piled them back onto the chopper. They brought in one of their own pilots and had him fly over some jungle. I overheard one of the sons of bitches bragging about it when I went to check my ship later. Said how they'd grab a POW, say 'will you talk?' And when the guy didn't, they just threw him out. Then they did it with the others. They did it with four of them. Real quick like. The others started babbling. Probably gave them their girlfriends' telephone number, I would've. Then they threw them out anyhow. I puked when I found out what happened. It was my chopper they used, for Chrissakes."

"What about the big guy, an Indian? Was he part of it?"

"I guess so. I mean I don't know who was on the chopper for sure, though, except for the POWs. I saw him talking to the others back at the base before they took off."

I felt betrayed. All Flagg's misgivings about the war, all

the nights we'd sit around grousing about the morality of
what we were doing were a load of crap. He was in it up
to his neck. That was his business, I guess, but it was my
unit that captured the North Vietnamese and turned them
over to Phoenix. I wasn't proud of some of the things I
did, but somehow through those years I had convinced
myself that I hadn't lost my basic humanity. Now Flagg
and his buddies had taken that away too.

Two weeks later I was coming out of the men's room
at the NCO club. I was drunk, but not drunk enough to
miss Flagg. He was sitting at the bar with his back to me.

"Flagg!"

He turned and started to smile.

A switch clicked in my head. "You bastard!" I screamed.
Then I hit him. It was a good, solid punch even for a
drunk. The roundhouse right to the jaw knocked him off
his perch. They say I grabbed the stool and picked it up
over my head and was about to mash his brains into the
floor when half the Green Berets in the province pounced
on me. I don't recall that. But I do remember Flagg's
eyes. I thought about that a lot later. I should have seen
fear or anger in them. But there was only resignation. I
spent the night in the brig. The next day I was released.
I was told Flagg had got me out, explaining I was under
stress. They sent me back to the front lines, where I could
work the stress off trying to kill the enemy instead of my
own people. When I returned I was transferred south near
Saigon, and not long after that I mustered out. I heard
Flagg had gone to work as a spook. But until our meeting
in the police station, he and I hadn't set eyes on each
other since Vietnam.

The knees of the gods again.

It was about 4:00 A.M. when I got home from Falmouth.
I flopped into bed, listened to the shush-shush of the
incoming tide, got up and brewed a cup of Sleepytime
tea, then stared at the blackness of the bay. I was too
wired from the Falmouth police coffee and the bizarre

events of the night to sleep. I thought about Flagg. Hard, solid thoughts. He had been unnerved at our encounter. He was off his stride. That wasn't like him. Something to do with Tom Drake worried him a great deal. And I wanted to know what it was. I went back to bed and drifted off into a jittery sleep. Around 8 I was awakened by the noise of seagulls squabbling over a fish head outside my window.

An hour later I called Frederick Walther's number and told Winston Prayerly that Drake was dead. He said he'd heard the news on the radio. Not even a gosh or gee-whiz. Only that he would inform Mr. Walther of my call immediately.

Over a cup of coffee I opened the Leslie Walther folder and looked at her photo again. She was smiling, but it was a sad smile somehow. Her trail ended in Woods Hole, and that's where I would have to pick it up. Commuting back and forth was getting to be a pain. I decided to stay in Woods Hole for a few days. I phoned a neighbor friend and asked her to feed Kojak. Then I removed the gold ring from my ear, put on a conservative navy crewneck sweater and chinos, and threw some clothes into a duffel bag. I locked up the boathouse, kissed Kojak on his furry head, put the key under the welcome mat, and by late morning I was back in Woods Hole.

A real-estate office near the ferry terminal suggested a guest house called the Seaside, a five-minute walk from the village center. The clapboards on the two-story house sported a new coat of white paint. There was a No Vacancy sign out front but I rang the doorbell anyway. A plumply attractive blond came to the door. I told her I would be doing some scientific research in Woods Hole and needed a room. She tapped her chin. Normally she wouldn't open this early, she said with a slight accent, but she just had the house painted and needed to pay for it. She introduced herself as Mrs. Stapleton.

She showed me a simple, but pleasant second floor room reached by a separate entrance. The room had a wrought-iron bed painted glossy white, a mattress that didn't sag too much, an antique dresser, a stiff chair, and a small couch covered in some flowered material. I pushed aside the lace curtains and looked out the window at Eel Pond and the surrounding scientific buildings. I told Mrs. Stapleton the room was perfect.

I paid my new landlady for three days. From the pay phone in the first-floor hallway I called the friend cat-sitting Kojak to let her know where I was. Then I strolled down the street to a stone bell tower in a quiet garden overlooking the pond. The garden was maintained by the Catholic church across the road. At the base of the campa-nile was a bronze plaque that said the bells in the tower were named after a couple of eminent Catholic scientists, Mendel and Pasteur. Funny place, Woods Hole, where science and God not only coexist, but are joined to ring out the Angelus.

From the garden I circled the pond, now crowded with sail and motor boats, passed the dormitories for the Marine Biological Lab, then cut through the deserted ten-nis courts to Albatross Street and the aquarium. The seal pool was empty. No one had cleaned off the bloodstains yet. From the aquarium it was only a few steps to Water Street. Woods Hole's main drag is aptly named. It's basi-cally built on a strip of land that runs between Eel Pond and Great Harbor. I tarried for a minute at a pretty little park overlooking the harbor and the Woods Hole Oceano-graphic Institution pier. The Cape Cod spring is a quick-change artist. The sun had disappeared behind an overcast of heartbreak gray. The temperature was down at least ten degrees since early morning. Thick fingers of fog reached in from Great Harbor and curled around the research vessel *Atlantis II* moored at the Oceanographic dock.

Woods Hole was starting to wake up after a long win-ter's sleep. The first pale-faced tourists, mostly older peo-ple who didn't have kids in school, congregated around the gift shops and waterfront restaurants and took pictures

of the solid stone "candle house," built in the 1800s to
process the sperm oil brought in by the village's whaling
fleet. Students taking courses at the Marine Biological Lab
strolled along Water Street books in hand, with the care-
free pace that goes with being young and immortal. I
crossed the drawbridge and headed toward the cinder-
block ferry terminal where cars were lining up to go onto
the next boat to Martha's Vineyard. From there I walked
along the other side of Eel Pond and back to the guest
house.

Fifteen minutes later I was in the Falmouth police station asking for Gallagher. He smiled when he came out
into the lobby and saw me. He ushered me into an office
slightly bigger than a phone booth, shut the door against
the clatter of typewriters and buzzing of telephones, and
eased behind his desk. "Guess you're staying in for the
long haul," he said.

I took a chair. "You've probably solved the Drake case
by now, but in the event you haven't, I wondered if you
might be persuaded to share anything you've turned up
as it applies to Leslie Walther."

Gallagher smirked. "Lieutenant Finch is in charge.
Which means the perpertrator is as good as doing time in
the can."

"Do I detect a bit of sarcasm, Sergeant?"

"Finch isn't a bad guy, but you know how it is. I was
here for years, working up to sergeant the hard way.
Finch comes down from the city with a college degree,
and all of a sudden he's my boss. I got a kid not much
older than him." He snorted. "Just as pigheaded too."

"It happens everywhere, Sergeant, even in the big city.
It's called politics." And it was the reason I left the Boston
Police Department.

"Yeah, I guess so, but it sort of sours a guy. Hold on."
Gallagher opened a folder on his desk. He put on a pair
of wire-rim reading glasses. "Okay, Mr. Private Detective,
let's see what we got. The deceased's secretary, Miss

Sharon Prescott, left the lab at five P.M. The rest of the staff quit between five and six, leaving Drake alone in the building. The guy at the gate logged him out at six-thirty. The guard remembered you, by the way. He says you were a highly suspicious character."

"He's right about that. Any idea of Drake's movements after he left the building?"

"Not a lot. One of the guys from the lab was on the shore road out toward the lighthouse and saw Drake's car drive by."

"Did he actually see Drake driving?"

"We asked him the same thing. It was dark. He can't be sure."

"Was there anything in Drake's appointment book?"

"Funny you should mention that. He had an S beside seven-thirty. Nothing scheduled after that. I'd guess the S was you. I'd also guess that he got detoured."

"It's not the first time I've been stood up, and it won't be the last. Time of death?"

"I don't have to wait for the medical examiner. Drake's car was seen at nine-thirty. The call from the lady with the poodle was logged in at ten thirty-two P.M. Drake was killed between those two times."

"You got a preliminary on the cause?"

"Yeah. He was stabbed from behind with a long thin knife. Only once. It punctured his heart. He was probably standing right next to the seal pool, 'cause he wouldn't have gone far on his own. Still looking for the murder weapon. Probably got tossed in the harbor. The divers are going start searching for it in about an hour."

"Got any suspects?"

"Finch was pinning the whole case on you, so we got to start fresh. If we concentrate on angry ex-husbands, ex-girlfriends, and ex-wives, we should start to narrow the list down to a hundred suspects in about ten years."

"Dr. Drake was that kind of guy?"

Gallagher looked up over his glasses. "Yeah, he was that kind of guy."

"What about a funeral?"

"You won't get Drake's mourners celebrating all in one place, not for a while. His body's going to be cremated after the autopsy, ashes spread at sea, and his wife is planning a memorial service for later."

"I didn't know Drake was married. Does she figure as a suspect?"

"Spouse is usually the best bet, as you know. But the lady claims she hadn't seen him in months. They were estranged. She's got an alibi, anyhow. She was at a local art gallery about the time her ex got it. I'm just as happy. She's a real looker. I'd hate to be the one who had to nail her. But unless the gallery guy is lying, she's clean."

"Too bad. Anything else?"

"That's about all I got for now. Bulldog Finch is hot on the trail. He's heavily into computers. Like I say, Drake pissed a lot of people off. We're compiling a list of who they are and where they were when he was killed. You know, feed the data into an electric box and a picture of the murderer pops out with a signed confession. I'll pass you info in case he turns something up by accident, but don't count on it."

"I'd appreciate that, Sergeant." I got out of my chair and shook Gallagher's hand. "I'll be staying in Woods Hole for a few days. I've got a room in a guest house run by a Mrs. Stapleton. It's called Seaside. Behind the pond."

"I know the place." He raised an eyebrow. "You *are* serious about this."

"Let's just say I'm enjoying the scenery."

"Have it your way, pal. Say, what do I tell your friend Flagg if I run into him?"

"Sergeant, you can tell him anything you want."

Back at the guest house I lay on the bedspread and opened the folder on Leslie again.

The material told me that Leslie was thirty-one. She was born in New York City, attended private school, and graduated from Skidmore College with a degree in chemistry. She worked for a corporation whose name I had read in connection with the defense industry. Less than a year ago she joined Neptune Technologies Inc., Drake's company. She had never been married. I wondered how and why she had moved from an international megacorporation to Drake's small operation, but there was no one to give me an answer, so I picked up Drake's folder and opened it.

Drake was thirty-seven. He was born in California and attended UCal undergrad, graduating summa with a degree in mechanical engineering. He did his graduate work in optics and computers at MIT, and a stint at the Marine Systems Engineering Laboratory University of New Hampshire in Durham, where he worked in undersea robotics. The file held a batch of clips from newspapers and technical magazines, in which he was described by colleagues as brilliant. Drake worked for a couple of corporate giants on the West Coast and moved to Woods Hole around three years ago. He had been a tenured associate at the Woods Hole Oceanographic Institution, but that tie was apparently severed.

I reread the folders, then went in the bathroom and splashed cold water on my face to wake my brain up. Twenty minutes later I was pulling up outside the Neptune lab. The gateman scowled when he recognized me. Probably hoped I had been thrown into jail for good. I was happy to disappoint him. I told him I wanted to see Dan, Dr. Drake's associate.

"That would be Mr. Whipple," the guard said. "He's not in."

I suggested he call someone to see when Whipple was arriving. Still scowling, he picked up the phone. He kept his eyes on me and his hand on an invisible holster. He talked for a minute, then opened the gate and told me to go directly to the reception room. Sharon Prescott was behind her desk, as yesterday, but she did not look like the same woman. Her eyes were red-rimmed. Strands of hair fell into her face. She was blowing her nose with a wrinkled clump of blue Kleenex.

I took a seat near her desk and said, "I'm very sorry to hear about Dr. Drake."

That really set her off. She looked at me through watering eyes. "How could you be sorry?" she choked. "You didn't even know him."

"You're right. I'm not sorry about Dr. Drake."

She gave me a drop-dead look.

"But I can see that you're very distressed by his death and I am sorry, truly sorry, about that."

The glare softened. "At least you're honest."

"I try to be." I dragged a handful of tissues out of the box on her desk and handed them to her. "Will you be okay?"

"Yes." She blew her nose daintily. "Thank you."

"You obviously cared a great deal about Dr. Drake."

"We were good friends."

I left it at that. I sensed that Drake didn't make friends of women. Only conquests. "I came by to talk to Dan Whipple, but I understand he isn't here."

"He took the day off. Nobody's here, really. Tom, Dr. Drake, pretty much held this place together. No one's exactly sure what to do."

I looked around the reception room at the undersea photographs. "What exactly do you do here?"

"We conduct research and development in submersible engineering."

"Underwater stuff?"

She smiled slightly, maybe glad to get off the subject of the late Dr. Drake. "That's right. Underwater stuff. We design machines that go deep into the ocean and do inspection and other tasks. Or take photographs like this." She gestured toward the wall posters.

"I understand. May I ask you another question?"

"Of course."

"Why did you see me today? You could have told the guard to send me away."

It was time for a fresh tissue, but she was pulling herself together. "Yesterday, when you were here, I couldn't help overhearing . . ."

"About Leslie Walther?"

"Yes. Leslie. You're trying to find her."

"That's right. Do you have any idea where she might be?"

"No. She and Tom were friends as well as colleagues. Before me. I mean . . . Anyway, they had a falling-out. She left. That's all I know. I'm sure she's all right."

"Miss Prescott, I don't mean to be presumptuous, but if you just want someone to talk to, someone who's neutral, I'll be in Woods Hole for a few days. I'm staying at the Seaside guest house."

She shook her head. "You're not being presumptuous. Thanks. I might take you up on it."

"If you run into Dan Whipple, please tell him I'd like to talk to him. I don't have an office as such, but I'll probably have a sandwich early this afternoon at that bar in the center of town. He can find me there."

She crumpled the tissue in her hand and searched for a new one. "Dan will call in shortly. I'll tell him you're looking for him."

The gateman eyed me as I swung behind the wheel of my truck. I didn't care. I was busy tallying up what I had learned so far. That Tom Drake got around. That his company did underwater engineering work. And that Sharon Prescott, even in her grief, was a remarkably lovely woman.

CHAPTER 6

●

It was around one o'clock when I stepped into the dim interior of the taproom on Water Street. Two men were having a lively debate at the far end of the bar. I figured them for Woods Hole scientists talking about some esoteric subject like ocean thermal strata. I was wrong. They were arguing over the name of the John Wayne movie on the TV set over the bar. I could have told them it was *Red River*, but I didn't want to spoil their fun. Instead, I ordered a beer and the luncheon special and carried the mug and a barbecue beef sandwich that had been cooked with a blowtorch to a circular table next to the fireplace, hoping somebody might put a match together with a couple of logs. The barroom was built on pilings over Eel Pond, and a chill dampness had seeped up through the floorboards into the unheated interior. I changed my mind about the fire after one bite of the sandwich. The barbecue sauce was heavy on the Tabasco and I was ready to ask the management to turn on the air-conditioning as soon as I could talk again.

I was fanning my mouth with a napkin and cooling it

down with gulps of beer when the front door opened and Whipple made an entrance. He spotted me and walked over, weaving like a commercial for the Ladies Christian Temperance Union. He pulled out a keg stool and managed to get it under his butt. His features were puffy and flushed. He had gin on his breath, so naturally I bought him a drink to loosen his tongue. He was a martini man. Very dry. Which told me that he was a serious drinker.

"Sharon Prescott says you're a private detective and that you want to talk to me," he said. His voice was thick from too much booze.

"That's right," I said. "I'm trying to locate Leslie Walther. That's why I was in Drake's office yesterday, to see if he knew where she might be."

He raised his martini. "To that dear late and recently departed son of a bitch, Dr. Tom Drake. May he burn in hell."

Whipple's poignant eulogy to his dead boss was touching. "Sorry to intrude at this obvious time of great sadness," I said.

He blinked behind his thick glasses as if he had just swallowed a bowl of feathers. His body vibrated. His face turned the color of a fresh beet. He exploded in a moist guffaw. He wiped the tears from his eyes and gulped down half his drink faster than even a martini deserves.

"As a wise man said, you should only speak good of the dead." He took a sip. "So, *good*, he's dead."

"I think I'm getting the point. You and Dr. Drake didn't exchange cards on Valentine's Day. How come?"

His eyes were so glassy you could comb your hair in their reflection, but there was no mistaking the hate that burned in their drunken depths.

"You were in the office yesterday when Drake did his very best to humiliate me. You saw what a sadistic son of a bitch he could be. No, Drake was not one of my favorite people. My hat is off to whoever did him in." He downed the rest of his drink. "I have an alibi, by the way. I've already talked to the cops. They've checked me out."

"I'm happy to hear you haven't murdered anyone lately. But in fact, I'm more interested in Leslie Walther. I want to find her. So let's carry your premise further. Would Drake have been son of a bitch enough to hurt her?"

Whipple shook his head, "No, not physically. Drake didn't have to. He was capable of inflicting a great deal of emotional destruction. The bastard would zero in on your weaknesses, real or supposed. He'd cast doubt on your ancestry, your parentage, your intelligence, your sexual prowess, usually in front of an audience. Poor Leslie. Drake simply tired of her. He was carrying on with Sharon right in front of her. Leslie should have known better than to get involved with Drake. He did the same thing to his wife when Leslie was the rising star."

The John Wayne movie ended and another began. Whipple started on his second martini. "Have you given any thought to who might have killed him?"

"That's a tall order. The good doctor had many enemies."

I shook my head. "Drake was abrasive, he was cruel, he was a philanderer, and he was a bastard. Lots of people with people with those credentials go through their entire lives acting like human threshing machines and nobody ever sticks a knife in them. So what was different about Drake? What pushed somebody over the edge?"

Whipple drunkenly considered my questions. "C'mon," he said suddenly. "I'll show you the difference."

He drained the last drops from his drink and we left the dark bar, blinking like moles in the daylight. Whipple pointed to a squarish building on the other side of the drawbridge. "That's the Redfield Lab. It's run by WHOI." He pronounced it "Whoee." "That's what everyone around here calls the Woods Hole Oceanographic Institution for short. You should catch a lecture there sometime. Fascinating stuff like isotope studies of phytoplankton or magnetic segmentation of the midocean ridge."

"I'll see if I can line up a date for one on a slow night."

"Make sure she's got a Ph.D. She'll have lots of company."

He continued along Water Street. I ambled a step behind. He pointed to an unembellished brick-and-glass structure and an ivy-covered four-story Georgian building with a turquoise-topped cupola. "That's Smith Lab across the street, another WHOI building. And the Bigelow Lab. There are more labs on the outskirts of the village. The Institution has some eight hundred staff people. Nearly fifty million dollars in funding, about a third of that from the Navy, gets channeled through this little village."

Just beyond the candle house we drew abreast of another building. "This is also one of our hallowed local institutions. The Marine Biological Laboratory is internationally known. More than forty Nobel laureates have been associated with it. Their library is one of the biggest and best biological and marine science collections in the world. It has more than a hundred and eighty-five thousand books. It stays open twenty-four hours a day, three hundred and sixty-five days a year, for research. But it's what you *can't* see that's important."

"Pretend I don't know what you're talking about."

He stopped and jammed his hands in his pockets, scanning the short main street like a gunfighter waiting for Mingo, then he turned and unleashed a ninety-proof breath in my face.

"I'm telling you that there's no place like this, anywhere on earth. The amount of sheer intellectual brainpower in this tiny community, all focused on one goal, trying to learn something about the sea, is absolutely staggering. You've got other places doing serious ocean work, like the Scripps Institute of Oceanography in California, but nothing like Woods Hole."

"What makes Woods Hole so different?"

His gesture encompassed the whole town. "The system. Competition here is unbelievably fierce. Say you're a tenured scientist at the Institution. You get the prestige and credibility that goes with it, but you've got to go out and find the money to pay yourself and any staff. You set up a company, pull some other scientists around you, then the scramble for funding is on. The Institution is sort of a weak government. Each company has its own ruler, a scientist. What you end up with are highly intelligent and driven people engaged in the most basic forms of entrepreneurship."

He led me to the small park at the edge of the harbor. We sat on a bench and Whipple gestured toward the water, invisible now behind its cloak of fog.

"It's like the sea out there. The surface is calm, but there are hundreds of life-and-death struggles going on underneath."

"That sounds a little overly dramatic, if you don't mind my saying."

He laughed and shoved his glasses up on his nose. Our walk had sobered him a little. "You're right. Actually the competition here, for all its intensity, is generally civilized. But Drake was a shark."

"Let's see if I understand. You're saying Drake might have been killed by a competitor?"

"Put it this way. Even if you didn't count the broken hearts, Drake left a long and bloody trail behind him. Bruised egos, damaged careers, people he cheated, insulted, destroyed in his ego-maniacal need to reach his goal."

"Exactly what was his goal?"

"To amass as much money as he could in the shortest possible time."

"No, I mean, what was he working on at Neptune?"

"Neptune I or Neptune II?"

"I didn't realize there were two Neptunes."

"Aha. Many people don't. There are actually two divisions at NTI. I worked for Neptune I. I didn't go to MIT, you see." There was bitterness in his voice. "We handle the commercial end. We build ROVs."

"ROV?"

"Remote Operated Vehicle. An ROV is basically an underwater robot. A submersible. It can go down where divers can't or shouldn't. The Woods Hole team that found the *Titanic* used an ROV. The submersibles are used to conduct underwater tasks on oil rigs, bridges, things like that. Neptune II, on the other hand, was a small cadre of people who worked on defense projects."

"What kind of projects?"

Whipple shrugged. "Even I didn't know all the details. Drake was no fool. He set it up so all the information was coordinated through him. If you talked to other NTI people, you might put something together."

"And did you?"

Whipple shook his head. "He had salted the staff with paid spies, and if he found out you'd been snooping, you'd be out on your ass."

"From what you said about Drake, and from the way I saw him treating you in his office, getting fired might have been a blessing."

"You might think so, but he did have one endearing quality. He paid extremely well. And we were on the cutting edge of submersible research, so there was always the lure of big money with a scientific breakthrough."

"Did Drake have any close confidants within the lab? How about those spies you mentioned?"

Whipple chuckled sourly. "Oh no, he didn't even trust them."

"There must have been somebody," I pushed. "A guy with an ego as big as Drake's has to have an audience he can impress with his accomplishments. Did he have any friends?"

"There was one person. His name was Skip Mallowes. *Marsh* Mallowes the fishermen call him, because he's soft in the head. Skip is no fool, though. Eccentric maybe, but bright in his own way. A local who went to college and dropped out to become a sometime fisherman. He's got a boat over at the fish pier and runs dive trips too. He and Drake used to go diving together. They were sort of an odd couple, the brilliant young scientist and the crazy townie."

Whipple was restless. He got up and started walking again. I caught up with him.

"Where does Drake's wife figure in all this?" I asked.

"Jane is an angel. Beautiful, patient, talented, and beautiful."

"You sound fond of her."

"I was fond of all Drake's women. I couldn't understand why they put up with him and why he'd drop them. I'm not too proud to say I would have been happy to dine on any of his leftovers. Jane is an artist. Not bad, either, if you like semi-abstract. She's got a studio on the beach near Nobska Light. She moved in there when she and Drake split up. Their house was in his name. He was careful about things like that." Whipple stopped in front of the aquarium. "Well, here we are at the scene of the crime. The murderer had a sense of humor, don't you think? All sorts of punny possibilities. Drake's fate was *sealed*, and so on."

"I don't think murder is ever funny," I said.

He stared out at the misty harbor. "It's getting damned cold with all this fog. I'm sick of it. When the hell is summer going to come?" The martinis were wearing off. Whipple was getting cranky. "Well, I'm going home to have a hot toddy." He walked off without saying good-bye. I watched his solitary figure head toward Water Street, his thin shoulders hunched against the raw air, until the murk swallowed him up. Then I went around behind the aquarium to the fish pier, pausing first at the seal pool. I remembered Homer's words: "Men flourish only for a moment."

A couple of grizzled fishermen were hanging out at the pier. I asked them where I could find Skip Mallowes. They waved toward the harbor and said Skip was out on his boat.

The visibility was down to the end of my nose. "Pretty tough finding your way home in this soup," I said.

The fishermen laughed. One of them said, "Some of the guys say Skip is a little crazy, but they're just jealous. He knows these waters like the back of his hand. He could make it in blindfolded."

I thanked them and went back to my truck. There was a parking ticket on the windshield. I took it off and threw it in the glove compartment, then drove to the guest house and looked up Jane Drake's address in the directory next to the hall pay phone. As I was searching for a scrap of paper to jot down the information Mrs. Stapleton opened the door to her living quarters and peeked out of her kitchen.

"Oh, Mr. Socarides. Thought I heard you come in. I'm glad to see you. A woman called earlier and asked for you."

"Did she give her name?"

"No," Mrs. Stapleton said. "She sounded excited and hung up without leaving a message."

Maybe it was Sharon Prescott. I tried to reach her at the lab, but she had left for the day.

Nobska Road was a winding and bumpy blacktopped horse track that skirted the edge of Vineyard Sound between Woods Hole and Falmouth center. I turned off at a drift-yard sign with the name Drake painted on it. Beach-plum bushes hemming the sand driveway on both sides were bursting into snowy blossom. The driveway ended at a tired old two-story gray shingled box that was defying the laws of gravity by not collapsing into a pile of kindling. The flat-roofed cottage was perched on a low grassy rise overlooking the beach. I parked behind the cottage next to a red Jeep Cherokee and went around to the front door. My knock attracted a dog, who barked in a friendly sort of way and pawed the screen. A female voice yelled over the noise. I stepped back and looked up. A woman's face was framed in the second-floor picture window.

"Can I help you?"

"Are you Jane Drake?"

She nodded and pointed to herself.

"My name is Socarides. I need some information and I think you can help me."

She hesitated a moment, then shouted, "The house is unlocked. Come on up."

I started toward the door. The face reappeared in the window and she called down again.

"Please don't let the dog out, Mr. Socarides."

The mutt was a breed the locals call a Cape Cod black dog, part Labrador retriever and part everything else. They're smaller and slighter than the heavier-built Labs, they've got a splash of white on their chests, and their nose is more pointed than the purebred retriever. A lot of people have them because they're good-natured pets. Thanks to the libidinous and wandering ways of their progenitors, there's always a litter to pick from at the dog pound. This one was all waggles and wiggles. He wanted to sniff my shoes and lick my face at the same time.

The doll-sized combination dining area and living room was cluttered with paintings. They were on the walls, on the floors, and propped against chairs. The canvases were glowing gobs of color that floated against monotone backgrounds like exploding stars. You could see things happening on the canvas even if you weren't sure what it was. A steep set of stairs led off the kitchenette. I brushed the mutt from my ankles and climbed to the second floor. The dog stayed below. Upstairs was apparently off limits. The stairway ended in a studio that smelled of oil paint and varnish. Piles of *American Artist* magazine lay on the braided rug, in the chair, on the table. The studio was bathed in the pure sea light pouring in from the window and from two large skylights. A gentle breeze tossed the white cotton curtains. At one end of the room was a couch made up for sleeping. At the other end was a heavy-duty wooden easel holding a giant canvas.

Standing in front of the easel, her back to me, was a woman wearing jeans and an untucked blue work shirt. She turned. She had a brush clenched in her teeth like a bone and another brush in her hand, which she used to point toward the couch. I sat down on the orange and black India-print slipcover, sinking into the soft mattress. She went back to her painting, mixing colors on a huge wooden palette, carefully daubing it on the canvas. She kept a brush in her mouth at all times, sometimes exchanging it for another.

After several minutes she laid her brushes and palette down and stepped back so I could see the painting. She looked at me and said, "What do you think?"

"I think you should keep your front door locked. That's not much of a watchdog down there."

She regarded me frankly, must have decided she had nothing to fear, and said, Rembrandt would lick the hand of the first burglar to give him a doggy bone, but I haven't locked a door since I moved to the Cape from the city, and I've never felt afraid. Now, tell me what you think about the painting."

"I like it." I was looking at Jane Drake, not her painting. She had the kind of hair that made you wonder what it would look like against the white linen of a pillow. It was Spanish black and fell in soft curls down to her shoulders.

"What do you see in it?"

A mine-field question. Maybe if I kept my answer vague, I'd be safe. I squinted at the great splotches of color and said, "I see a great deal of passion."

She kept her gray eyes fixed intently on my face. General answers weren't going to save me here.

"Good," she said.

"And energy. Lots of energy." I gave her a questioning look, searching for help.

"Yes." Impatient. "That's what you *feel*. What do you *see*?"

I took a stab. "I think I have it. Red sails in the sunset?"

She rolled her eyes. "It's a picture of Nobska Light."

"Where's the lighthouse?"

She pointed to a yellow blob in the upper left-hand corner. "Here."

"Ah," I said. "Of course."

She wiped her hands on an oily rag. "I apologize for putting you through that. But sometimes you get so close to a painting you can't tell whether it's good or not. I just hate it when people ask what I see in a painting. I must have been in a sadistic mood."

"That's okay. I'm in a masochistic business."

"Are you from the police? They said they were sending someone out to see me today."

I handed her my business card.

She looked at the card and furrowed her brow. She didn't look like a bereaved widow. "Why does a private detective want to see me? Is this about Tom?"

"Not directly," I said. "I've been hired by Leslie Walther's father to find her. As you may know, she is missing. I don't know if you can be of help. I'm just talking to everyone who knew her."

She sat down on a paint-splattered wooden box and shook her head. "It never seems to end."

Jane Drake was quite beautiful even with the excess makeup she had used to try to cover the dark circles under her eyes. Her skin was as creamy white as a cameo. Her lashes were long and full. She had a mouth that liked to smile but was having a hard time doing so. I couldn't blame her. Tom Drake had only been dead a matter of hours. It wasn't the best time to talk about her estranged dead husband's ex-girlfriend.

I said, "Maybe I should come back later."

She gave me a bleak look. "It's not you. It's Tom. I can't shake him out of my life, even now."

Dead or alive, Tom Drake produced strong reactions. Sharon Prescott was putting the Kleenex factory on overtime. Whipple acted as if he were ready for the giggle farm. Jane's response was swift and strong. She stood abruptly, picking up her palette knife, and began to apply thick layers of color to her painting. She grabbed tubes of paint indiscriminately, squeezed out half their contents, and smeared them onto the canvas. Blue. Yellow. Orange.

Cadmium red. It didn't seem to matter. Green. Umber. She was ruining the painting, turning the canvas into a mad mass of mud. Magenta. Ocher. She worked in awful silence, slapping the paint on with such force that it seemed as if she would rip a hole in the fabric. It was a terrible expunging of sorrow, worse than any physical crying could have been.

Then, just as suddenly as she had begun, she stopped. She looked at the mess she had created. She put the palette knife down and sat on the box again, her hands on her knees. Then she began to sob, quietly, terribly. When she finally looked up, she wiped her eyes with the back of her paint-stained hand, leaving a streak of red on her cheek.

It wasn't the first time I had intruded on a surviving spouse. I had to do it all too often as a city cop. I always tried not to be heavy-handed, just ask my dumb questions and get the hell out of their lives. My hardened detachment deserted me as I watched Jane Drake's ravaged face. I decided to leave. I stood and said, "I'll come back another time."

I must have worn my discomfiture like a neon sign. Jane put her hand on my arm, as if she were looking for support. "I'm sorry, it was terribly rude of me to let go like that in front of a total stranger." Her voice was husky with tears. I cupped my hand over hers, just for a second, and gave it a quick squeeze. It seemed like the thing to do. She looked surprised and pleased at the same time. Our eyes met.

"Please stay," she said.

I shrugged and sat down again.

She turned to look at her painting and laughed nervously. "Maybe it was time to change my style," she said philosophically. "It certainly has that passion and energy you were talking about."

"You still cared for him."

She nodded sadly. "Absolutely incredible, isn't it? Tom and I have been separated for months. Our divorce was only a question of how soon the lawyers could prepare the paperwork. Yet here I am, the grieving widow. Falling apart at the seams when I should be dancing with joy."

"One word frees us all the weight and pain of life," I said. "That word is love."

"That's very beautiful."

"Thanks, but it's not mine. Sophocles said it a couple of thousand years ago."

Jane looked at me curiously.

"Well, that's not what you came for, is it, Mr. Socarides? In answer to your question, yes, I'm aware Leslie has disappeared, but didn't really think much of it. I have no idea where she is. I haven't seen her for months. I never knew Leslie very well. Just that she worked in the lab, and that she became . . . well, let's say she became my replacement."

"Well, then, I won't bother you with any more questions," I said. I got off the couch and shook her hand. It was warm and nice to hold. When I tried to let go, Jane held on.

"Where do you live, Mr. Socarides?"

"I'm staying in town for a few days."

She pondered that for a moment.

"Mr. Socarides, would you," she stumbled, "that is . . ." She took a deep breath. "Are you free tonight?"

"As far as I know. Why?"

She made up her mind "There's an opening of my work," she blurted. "I could use an escort."

I hesitated. "Are you sure?"

"If you're wondering whether I'm a crass person who can turn the waterworks on and off at will, the answer is no. When I left Tom my career became even more important, because it's all I had. This opening has been in the planning stages for a long time. Being the black widow will add some cachet, I know, but I'm feeling a bit weak and really could use a strong arm to hang on to. There will be a lot of the local intelligentsia there. You might learn something about Leslie."

I had pretty much resigned myself to a lonely night watching TV reruns with the guys at the bar, so an unexpected offer from a beautiful woman was easy to accept. "I'd be flattered and pleased to be your escort. Even without the intelligentsia."

She sighed with relief. "Fine. I really appreciate this. I can meet you at the gallery around six thirty P.M."

"It would be no problem to pick you up here, Mrs. Drake."

"I'd appreciate that," she said. "And please, call me Jane."

"People who don't like to wrap their tongues around my name call me Soc."

"I'll be one of them, although I think Aristotle is much nicer and fits you better." She shook my hand once more, then turned back to the canvas and stared at her ruined painting. It was time for me to leave.

CHAPTER 7

•

The Travers Art Gallery in North Falmouth was in a graceful yellow and white captain's house that looked like a
giant three-layer lemon wedding cake with a white frosting
widow's walk on its roof. Both sides of the narrow street
in front of the gallery were lined with cars, and we had
to hunt around to find a space for Jane's Jeep. Jane had
taken a look at my truck and politely suggested we drive
her Cherokee to the gallery. I wasn't insulted. I wanted
to get to the opening too.

As we went up the front walk Jane surveyed the cars
parked bumper to bumper, and the milling crowd visible
through the gallery's windows. "I guess it pays to be the
object of pity or curiosity," she said. She was right about
attracting attention. The stares were bound to come her
way, but not just because people felt sorry for her. The
black dress she was wearing set off her ivory skin and
showed respect for her curves and her dead husband at
the same time.

A clean-cut ascoted man lay in ambush just inside the
front door. He grabbed Jane in a gushy embrace and said,

"It's so *wonderful* to see you, darling. You're *so* brave to come."

"Thank you, Geoff. This has been a long time coming. Besides, I couldn't let you down." She gave him a buss on the cheek and introduced us.

The man was Geoffrey Travers, the owner of the gallery. He shook my hand without much interest, then took Jane's arm and plowed into the waiting art lovers, who parted and closed like the Red Sea. Left to my own devices, I wandered aimlessly through the gallery. Jane's paintings were spread under track lighting on the white-washed walls of three rooms. Two canvases had red-dot "sold" tags on the frames. The prices listed in the brochure were not unsubstantial.

With Jane attracting all the attention, I had the food table to myself. I poured Chablis into a plastic glass and inspected a platter of little crustless sandwiches. One smelled like cat food, the other like dog food. I attacked the wheel of Brie and smeared half a pound of the mushy cheese and a slice of boiled ham between two stoned-wheat crackers, cleansing my palate with another glass of wine.

Apparently satisfied with their glimpse of Jane, the art lovers were trickling back to the important stuff, the free food. I stood in a corner munching my cracker sandwich and watched the crowd. It was the usual Cape Cod art-gallery mix. Large women in muumuu dresses who cruised in search of familiar faces like battleships on patrol. Sad-eyed little men wearing goatees and sandals who looked as if the only square meals they ate were at gallery openings. Town officials running for reelection who squinted at the price tags and muttered how their four-year-old kid could paint a picture better than that. Handsome young art students in *Tess of the D'Urbervilles* frocks or Lord Byron wide-collared shirts open to the navel. There was a healthy contingent of tweedy bearded men in crewnecks who looked as if they might be from the Woods Hole scientific community.

I circulated and talked to three people, all connected with Woods Hole. Two of them, an engineer and an oceanographer, only knew Tom Drake by name and reputation. The oceanographer told me that if I really wanted to hear the inside dope on Drake, I should talk to Dr. Bertram Ivers. He pointed out a powerfully built man with stooped shoulders who was pinned in a corner by a mousy redheaded woman. Ivers was listening to her with a pained expression on his florid face. I went over and introduced myself. The redhead didn't like being upstaged. She went off to find another victim. Ivers was about fifty-five, with curly sheep-fur hair, a prominent nose, and buckteeth you could open a bottle on.

He took a deep gulp from the glass of wine in his hand. "Thanks for rescuing me from that creature. Every time I tried to get away, she stepped in front of me. I was getting desperate."

"Don't mention it," I said. I looked around. "I think Jane's pretty brave to come face all these people here tonight, so soon after her husband's death, don't you?"

The color deepened in Ivers's ruddy cheeks. "Jane should be celebrating that bastard's demise," he growled.

Another grief-stricken mourner praying for Tom Drake's soul. "I didn't know Drake very well," I said. "I only met him once, but I'm beginning to think he wasn't the most popular guy in town."

"Hah," Ivers crowed. "That's an understatement. Good thing they're cremating him. Drake was so crooked that if they tried to bury him, they'd have to screw him into the ground." The joke was prehistoric when Ogg the Caveman wowed them with it at the Neanderthal Comedy Club, but Ivers chortled at the thought of Drake being corkscrewed to his great reward.

"I've heard he was a brilliant scientist," I said. "Is that true?"

"Oh yes, he was intelligent. Which is all the bigger shame. He was so smart he could have accomplished anything he wanted without resorting to unethical tactics."

"Wow," I said, "that sounds like a pretty hefty indictment."

"It's based on personal experience, I regret to say."

"How so, Dr. Ivers? If you don't mind my asking."

He blinked at me through thick glasses. "No, not at all. It's no secret in town how I feel about Drake." He fortified himself with more wine and told me his story. "A few years ago Drake and I were competitors for project funding. A substantial amount of government money was involved, so both our project teams were working straight out. We had the edge, or at least I thought we did. Then things started to go wrong. There would be a mistake in the calculations, or an erroneous reading. Maybe a delicate instrument would go on the fritz. Little glitches, mostly, but they wasted precious time."

"Sounds like accidents from working under pressure."

"We thought so at first. But when we analyzed these mishaps, we detected a pattern. The epicenter was one of our staff people. We were naive. We didn't realize that Drake was involved in all-out war, and that he used some of the standard tools of warfare: espionage and sabotage. We confronted the man we believed was working for Drake. He denied it, of course. We fired him anyway, and there was no doubt, as it turned out later."

"What happened to the project?"

"Oh, we lost out on the funding."

"I'm sorry to hear that."

He shrugged, "Thank you. It hurt like hell at the time and we never recovered financially, but I did get back at Drake."

"How so, Dr. Ivers?"

"I lodged a formal complaint with the WHOI board. Interestingly, you see, some of our better design features showed up in Drake's proposal. The man had no hesitancy about using the work of others to advance his own ends. I was able to prove it. They terminated his association with the Institution. That doesn't happen very often. Usu-

ally you're left pretty much alone as long as you don't
tarnish WHOI's image."

"What sort of work were you doing?"

"We were designing Remote Operated Vehicles for spe-
cialized tasks. ROVs."

Another mention of ROVs. First Whipple, now Ivers.
Probably not unusual in a scientific community like Woods
Hole, where people must talk about undersea hardware
over their bacon and eggs, but novel enough to me, an
outsider, to tuck into a memory niche for further
reference.

"I do some underwater work occasionally," I said.
"Where could I learn more about ROVs?"

"Oh, there's lots of literature in the technical journals,
but tell you what. Drop by my office sometime. I'm at
the Bigelow building. I'd be glad to answer your questions
as best I can. It's the least I can do for saving me from
that redhead."

Jane was walking by. She smiled at me. I thanked Dr.
Ivers for his fascinating story, excused myself, and caught
up with her. She grabbed my arm and held on. "Sorry to
abandon you like that. It's part of the thing."

"How are you holding up?"

"I'm doing fine. Adulation does have its therapeutic
side." She squeezed my arm and moved close so her
shoulder brushed against mine. "I really appreciate your
being here with me tonight. I don't think I would have
had the courage to face this on my own."

"My pleasure. I'm glad you asked me."

"Have you learned anything about Leslie?"

"No, but the Brie isn't bad."

"I saw you talking to Bert Ivers. Did he help you at
all? He may not be the most objective person. He and
Tom were not on very good terms."

"I gathered that. But every little bit is useful."

She looked across the sea of heads and started to say
something, but stopped when the front door opened and
a man walked in. He was about six feet tall and built like

a bear, with heavy arms and legs. He looked about forty-five, but the sun could have added ten years to his wide features. He had a thick thatch of unruly straw hair, and a fringe of beard rimmed his weathered face and framed his blue eyes. He was dressed in jeans and, because the night was cool, wore a green flannel shirt and a black woolen jacket. Jane went over and gave him an affectionate hug.

"Hello, Skip," she said. "I'm so happy you could make it."

A glow came into the man's plump cheeks. "I had to come," he said softly. "This is a night when you need your friends, Jane."

"Skip, you're so sweet. Come here, I'd like you to meet another friend of mine. Mr. Socarides, this is Skip Mallowes."

We shook hands. "This is really a coincidence," I said. "I was looking for you today."

The round face lit up. "No kidding. What for?"

"I'm staying in Woods Hole for a few days and might like to do some diving. I heard you take people out."

"Sure, anytime. I'm not exactly booked full this time of year. There are a couple of interesting wrecks not far offshore."

"I'm not doing anything tomorrow."

"Me neither. Weather's supposed to break. Give me a call in the morning if you want to go." He pulled his wallet out and handed me a business card just as Jane corraled him and they went off on a tour of her work. I wandered about some more. I was tired of talking to people about Tom Drake. I had the feeling I'd just hear more variations of the same old story. I was studying a metal sculpture made of old auto parts, wondering whether my truck would qualify as a piece of art if I built a pedestal for it, when Geoff Travers, the owner of the gallery, came over and insisted on showing me around.

As we strolled through the rooms, he said: "Tell me, Mr. Socarides, can you define art?"

I thought about it. "I'm afraid you've got me on that one."

"Then let me give you a hint. At one time van Gogh couldn't give his work away. It was not considered art. Today, a single van Gogh is worth millions. And today everybody agrees van Gogh was a great artist."

"I think you're saying that if it sells, it's art."

His face lit up. "Precisely." He paused before a chest-high fluted pedestal. There was a white plastic gob on top that looked as if it had been squeezed from a giant toothpaste tube.

"Art?" I asked.

Travers pointed to the $5,000 price tag. "Only if the artist comes down thirty-five hundred dollars in price. Then some Manhattan psychiatrist will scoop this thing up and install it in his waiting room, where it can make his patients even crazier than they already are."

He led the way into another room and gestured toward an oil painting. "Do you know what really sells, Mr. Socarides? This, er, stuff. The artist reached his maximum potential five years ago and decided, wisely I think, to go no further. This is all he does. Snow fences and sand dunes. He cranks them out like sausages. I practically scream each time he brings in another batch, but I can't refuse him. He's extremely successful. He just built himself a new home on the water and spends the winters in Palm Beach. His work graces the walls of dozens of houses from here to Paduka."

We went into the space where Jane's work was displayed.

"Art?" I tried again.

"True art. Here, let me show you." He walked over to a large oil. "The colors are beautiful, the shapes subtle, yet you can almost taste the sea in each brush stroke. This is a lovely painting. And do you know what makes it lovelier still?" He touched the red "sold" dot on the frame.

"Jane's art sells?"

"Correct. Hope I haven't shocked you with my mercenary theories."

"No, not at all." I looked around at the milling crowd. "I may be in the market for something myself, but I'd like to come back when there aren't so many people."

Travers walked over to adjust a frame that didn't need adjusting and stepped back to look at it, cupping his chin in his hand.

"I know exactly what you mean. Openings are so dreary. All these impossible people posturing as if they really knew what they were talking about or had the money to buy. Openings should be banned. You never sell anything because most of the people who attend are freeloaders who come merely to feast on the wine and cheese and be seen by other moochers. Present company excepted, of course. Openings are mostly to boost the ego of the artist and the gallery management."

"Jane certainly needed some positive reinforcement."

"I agree. It must have been a terrible shock. I can't believe she was right here the night that awful thing happened."

"Here? At the gallery?"

"Yes, the poor dear. She was helping me hang her paintings. It was all very odd."

"Odd?"

"First she got that phone call and went rushing off, all excited. Said it was important. We had to cancel our dinner engagement. Then she came back to the gallery a couple of hours later and we finished hanging the show."

"Maybe the call was from the police to tell her about Tom," I said.

"Oh no, it was too early. His body wasn't found until much later, if what I heard on the radio is true. Jane left around seven. She came back a little after nine and stayed until nearly midnight." Travers spied a bearded man across the room. "Would you excuse me for just a moment, Mr. Socarides? I may have a buyer for the five-thousand-dollar lump of Elmer's Glue in the other room. That chap looks like Sigmund Freud."

As he walked off, practically rubbing his hands in anticipation, Jane peeked into the room, then came over. "I saw Geoff giving you the grand tour. Hope he didn't bore you."

"Oh no," I said. "I learned a lot about art."

"That's good." She looked around. "This has been exhausting, but the crowd is thinning out and I think we can go now."

She said her good-byes three times over and soon we were breathing the cool night air. On the drive home, Jane appeared deep in thought and I was thinking about my conversation with Ivers. Neither one of us talked. I didn't know what was on Jane's mind until we pulled up behind her studio. I turned off the ignition, and she touched my fingers, purposely I think, when I handed her the keys.

"Thanks again, Soc." She sat there for a moment, then asked, "Would you like to come inside for a drink?"

I pondered that one, looking out into the gray fogginess, listening to the chuckle of the incoming tide. Jane was beautiful. She smelled incredibly good. She was also incredibly vulnerable. Any other time I would have accepted her offer in a minute. But not this minute. I remembered the mad painting she had done in her studio that morning.

"I would like to, very much," I said. "But maybe not tonight."

She was silent a moment. "It always gets like this, the fog, I mean, when the breeze comes in off the sound."

"It's the moist air condensing as it hits the cooler water," I said.

"I suppose you're right. Not about the fog." She laughed softly. "I'm *sure* you're right about that. About coming in, I mean." She put her hand on the door handle.

"I'll call you tomorrow to see how you are."

"I'd like that," she said.

We got out of the Jeep and she pecked me warmly on the mouth. I watched until she was safely in the house with the lights on. She waved out a window. I ran my tongue over my lips, trying to taste her, then got into my truck, not entirely happy at the prospect of my empty room. She was alone. I was alone. Maybe I should have accepted the invitation. I had a good idea that we'd be eating English muffins together the next morning if I did. The amateur shrink in me was saying I was making excuses for her, acting like a Victorian gentleman, because I didn't want to get involved. No no, I said from my imaginary analyst's couch. It was for *her* good, not mine. Besides, spending the night with somebody doesn't mean you're engaged, or does it? I headed out her sand drive to the road, and I was still arguing with myself when I pulled up behind a dark blue LTD parked in front of Mrs. Stapleton's guest house. All was quiet. Fog nibbled the light away from streetlamps. As I walked by the Ford the door on the passenger side swung open. A man stepped out and blocked the narrow sidewalk like the Grand Coulee dam.

"Evening, Soc," Flagg said.

Flagg's visit wasn't a big surprise. It was a small town. I knew he would hear I was poking around.

"Oh, it's you, Flagg. For a minute I thought you were something respectable, like a mugger."

"You're a piece of work, Soc."

"You're a piece of . . . never mind."

I was tired. I was in no mood to deal with Flagg. And I was mentally lashing myself for not taking Jane up on her offer. I attempted to step around him when he put his hand out to stop me. Anger boiled up in my chest. My mother says I've got a dark side and that's why she sent me to college to study the classics, hoping I'd become a professor. It isn't my fault, she says. Just the genes inherited from her gentle grandfather Nikos who became the terror of the Turks when the Cretans were fighting for independence. She may be right. Mostly I'm about as violent as a stuffed mushroom. Guns turn me off and I still bite my fingernails watching Cary Grant dodge the crop-dusting plane in *North by Northwest*. But there are times, like now, when the white lights explode behind my eyes and I want to demolish the nearest object.

I said, "That's not a friendly move, Flagg."

Flagg caught the quiet threat in my voice. He was bigger than me and could crush my head like a melon, but he was slower and out of shape and he knew it. He stepped aside.

"I need a few minutes of your time." He nodded at the LTD. I glanced into the backseat to make sure nobody was waiting to garrote me, then got in the passenger side and slouched down.

"What gives, Flagg? Make it short. I've had a long day."

He didn't answer right away. And when he did speak, his voice was as tight with tension as the E string on a guitar.

"You were lying, Soc. You said you were off the Drake case. I didn't think Eagle Scouts like you told fibs."

I put my foot up on the dashboard. "Flagg, your lack of faith in human nature disappoints me. I wasn't lying. I'm not trying to solve the Drake thing. I'm trying to find an old girlfriend of Drake's, name of Leslie Walther. I'm hoping Drake can lead the way to her, dead or alive."

"Who hired you?"

"The woman's father. Rich guy named Frederick Walther."

He looked hard at me. "What if I told you it was important to let this one go? That you'd be doing it for the good of your country."

"You make me want to vomit, Flagg. Is that what you did in Operation Phoenix? Doing it for the good of your country?" I put as much contempt as I could into the questions. Flagg must have taken a Dale Carnegie course, because he didn't rise to the bait.

"Yeah, Soc. Something like that."

"I'm not buying what you've got for sale today, Flagg." I sat up and reached for the door handle.

"What the hell do you want, Soc?"

Now we were getting somewhere. "For starters, I want to know more about Neptune II."

Flagg made a noise that sounded like a laugh but wasn't. "Guess you *have* been nosing around. How much do you know?"

"A little bit. Hush-hush stuff. ROVs. Things that go underwater."

He knew I was fishing with an empty hook. "As usual, you're a little right and a little wrong."

"So enlighten me. For old times' sake."

"I can't. Not even for that. It's a question of security."

I got out of the car and walked around to the driver's side. Flagg rolled the window down.

"You know," I said. "You're really much too obsessed with security. You should go out and have a good time. Get loaded. Find some flashy women." I headed for the guest house. " 'Night, Flagg."

The engine started and the LTD pulled away from the curb. Damn spooks. They're like vampires. They don't know how to function in daylight. I went up to my room and flopped on the bed. I was getting nowhere. Maybe my brain would be sharper in the morning. There was a soft knock. Flagg coming to make another try? I rolled wearily off the bed and opened the door. And gaped.

One of my missing women had just found me.

CHAPTER 8

•

With her soulful brown eyes and high cheekbones, my sister Chloe could pass for a younger and slightly fuller-bodied version of the Greek film actress Irene Pappas. But the woman at my door with a suitcase clutched in her hand was not what I would have called a trip to Hollywood. Her red dress was wrinkled and creased. Her dark shoulder-length hair was as damp and attractive as seaweed. Two limp strands fell like soggy pieces of eelgrass over her forehead. A glistening tear trickled down one round cheek, leaving a thin trail of eyeliner. She dropped her bag, lunged forward, wrapped her arms around me, and broke into a series of convulsive sobs.

"Oh, Soc," she wailed. "I've been looking all over for you."

A pang of guilt hit me. I gritted my teeth. God, I'd been so wrapped up in the Walther case and Drake's death that I had forgotten my mother's request to look for my sister. Chloe's sobbing was breaking my heart. I gave her a big hug, grabbed her suitcase, led her into my room, and shut the door.

"Chloe, are you okay? You look—"

"I know," she interrupted. "I look terrible. You don't have to say it."

"Shhh, sweetheart. Come, sit down." I stuffed her into a chair and poured a glass of water from the bathroom sink. "Here. I'm sorry I don't have anything stronger."

She slurped the water and sighed pathetically. "That's okay, I feel better now."

I sat on the sofa. "Where have you been, for god sake? Ma called me yesterday trying to find out where you were. She and Pop are worried to death about you."

Chloe set her pretty mouth in a grim line. "Ma and I are no longer on speaking terms. She has absolutely no concern for my welfare."

"Ah c'mon, sis. What's this all about? So she said you should get married. She says that to me all the time. Big deal."

"Big deal is right. His name is Nestor Evangelos. And he looks like a giant eggplant. *That's* who she thinks my husband should be. A good match, she says. My own mother wants me to marry an *eggplant*."

"Nestor? I remember him. He was a fat little kid with a snotty nose. Had the biggest paper route and the widest butt in town. But he's a restaurateur now with a lot of dough. You could do worse, sis."

Her eyes raked me. "And you could do better minding your own business. Is *that* what you want for me? Making moussaka every night for a fat husband who thinks he's Zeus, chasing around a bunch of kids named after Olympian gods?"

Time to back off. "No, sis. I was only joking. Just take it easy."

"Take it easy?" She addressed an invisible third party. "*He* wants me to take it easy. Where does Ma get off picking a mate for me? She even wanted to bring him over to the house so we could get to know each other better. You know what her trouble is, Soc? She still thinks she's in the Old Country. She still thinks you can trade women around like goats."

"Aw, she's not like that." I thought about it a second. "Okay, she's a little bit like that. But nobody's forcing you into marriage."

"Sure, Soc. Nobody's forcing me. But she says maybe the family has done enough to keep me amused. If I'm not planning to get married, she says, maybe I should come and work in the business full-time. If that's not a threat, I don't know what is."

"In all fairness, sis, the family business has done a lot for you."

Her tone softened. "Oh, I know that. All those Parthenon frozen pizzas sent me to school in France and paid for my trips through Europe. Ma and Pop bought me that nice little Toyota Supra I drive. But they've never threatened to cut me off."

"What does Pop say?"

"What does he always say? He says, 'I don' wanna hear about it.'" She mimicked my father's thick accent. She looked at me and let out an anguished plea. "What do I *dooo*, Soc?"

I hadn't the slightest idea. But I said, "We'll figure something out. Anyhow, Ma had a message for you."

She crossed her arms. "I don' wanna hear about it."

"She said to tell you she loved you."

Chloe's eyes widened. "Ma said *that*? She *never* says that. Are you sure you weren't talking to somebody else's mother?"

I nodded. "I'm sure. Now, when did all this happen?"

Chloe groaned. "Last week. I'd just gotten back from Europe when both of them laid into me. I don't know what started it. Maybe they've just been working too hard and my trip set them off. They didn't like my being away so often, they said. I said maybe I should move out of the house into a place of my own so they wouldn't have to worry."

"That's probably not the kind of assurance they wanted to hear, Chloe."

"Oh, I know that. I didn't really mean it, but that really got them going. You know how they think. Good Greek girls don't go off on their own, because it makes the family look bad. Good Greek girls are supposed to live at home until they get married. They were becoming positively unbearable, one feeding off the other, until I couldn't take it anymore. I picked up my suitcase and spent a few days with an old school friend in Cambridge, but she's got a husband, so I couldn't impose on them. Then I thought of you, my sweet older brother, who's the only person in the whole world who has ever understood me." She pinched my cheek.

"Hold on a minute, little sister, the only thing I understand is that you were spoiled rotten from the start because you were the only girl in the family."

"Oh Soc, you were always such a great big brother."

"See, I helped spoil you. But enough of that. How did you find me?"

"After I left Cambridge, I drove down to your boathouse. There was a lady there feeding your cat. I told her who I was and said I was looking for you. She gave me your number. I tried calling you today. The landlady said you were out. So I came here. It was awful. I kept getting lost in the fog. What are you doing in this place anyhow?"

"I'm working on a case. Look, why don't you spend the night. We'll try to sort things out in the morning. Take a shower, get into some PJs, and crawl into bed. I'll sack out on the couch."

She wrapped her arms around me and gave me a moist kiss. Then she disappeared into the bathroom and a minute later the water was running. While she was in the shower I found some spare pillows and blankets in the closet and made up the sofa. I stretched out with my feet hanging over the sofa's arm. Chloe came out in her bathrobe with a towel wrapped around her head. She looked a lot happier. She also looked sixteen years old. She crawled into bed, plumped the pillows, lay back, and sighed. "Thanks. This is sheer heaven." After a minute she said, "Tell me, big brother. Did you ever wish you were born an Anglo-Saxon Protestant?"

"Naw. Pot roast and boiled potatoes would have stunted my growth. Besides, ASPs never have any fun. Do you remember the time I brought my friend Dillingham Bradford to the church picnic? Sahara the belly dancer was there to help raise money for the new rec hall. Dilly went home and told his parents they had a stripteaser at the church. I tried to explain that it was simply an innocent Mid-Eastern ethnic folk dance, and that it wasn't inside the church, but they wouldn't hear of it. He was barred from hanging out with me. He came to a few more picnics, but he didn't tell his parents."

Chloe sat up in bed. "I remember that picnic! Uncle George was leading everyone in a dance. He slipped and crashed into a table and Father Spyridon's baked lamb and pilaf ended up on his lap."

"My God," I said. "I haven't thought about Father Spyridon for years. He went around blessing all the new pizza parlors and restaurants."

"Yes. And he always managed to show up conveniently at dinner time. He must have weighed three hundred pounds."

"Four hundred easy, give or take a couple of ounces. The diocese made him stop blessing for his health. Now sis, tell me, could you ever picture Dilly Bradford's Episcopal priest saying 'Bless this pizza house,' then sitting down for the four-way combo with extra cheese?"

Chloe almost fell out of bed with laughter. We swapped a few more family stories. Before long her answers trailed off to drowsy mumbles and she went to sleep. I got up and tucked her in, the way I used to when she was little, flicked off the lights, and curled up, as best I could, on the flowered sofa.

I awoke at dawn the next day and worked the aches and pains out of my contorted joints. Chloe was still sleeping serenely. I sat on the couch and debated what to do with her. I could simply call my mother and tell her Chloe was here. I pictured my sister's fury clashing with my mother's iron will and discarded that option. Maybe I could talk Chloe into a reconcilation. I looked at her again, remembered her tirade of the night before, and decided to procrastinate.

Around eight I went downstairs to the hall phone and called Jane.

"Have you recovered from last night's opening?" I asked.

"Yes, thanks. I was exhausted from all the excitement, but I got up early and got right to work. I threw out that canvas you saw yesterday and I've been working on a new one. Come by some time and see what I'm doing."

"I'd like to do that. I may go diving with Skip Mallowes today."

"Oh, wonderful. You'll like Skip. He's incredibly intelligent, but so down to earth."

"I'll call you either tonight or tomorrow."

"I'll look forward to hearing from you."

That conversation ended on a promising note. I dialed the number on Skip's business card, reintroduced myself, and asked if he were still interested in a dive.

"I'm laying out my gear right now," he said in his deliberate, slow-talking manner. "It's going to be a beautiful day. I was going diving whether you called or not, but I'm glad you did. How about an hour or so from now? I'm at the fish pier behind the aquarium. My boat is named the *Gannet*."

"I'll find it. See you in about an hour."

Chloe was still sleeping soundly when I went back to my room. I left her a note saying I'd be back later. I suggested she make herself at home and let me know if she decided to leave. It was a subtle hint on my part.

Ten minutes later I was in a Falmouth dive shop renting a wet suit and scuba gear. Then I drove back to Woods Hole and parked next to the aquarium. The white-hulled *Gannet* was moored up tight to the concrete pier, engine idling. Skip, who was on the deck coiling line, saw me trundling toward him with an armful of diving equipment and waved me aboard.

"Glad you could make it," he said. "Drop your gear anywhere." He glanced at the hazy sun. "Looks like the weatherman was right for a change. It's going to be a great day once the fog burns off. All set to head out?"

"I'm ready to go if you are."

The *Gannet* was a sleek work boat about forty-five feet long with a high flaring bow. There was a big fish-holding box on the deck and an all-purpose boom that could have been used for lobstering, net setting, or hauling salvage off the ocean bottom. You would have been hard put to find a spot anywhere on the paint or brightwork. I set my diving equipment in a corner next to a rack holding several air tanks. While Skip took the helm, I cast off the lines holding us to the dock, then joined him in the pilothouse.

"Glad to have an excuse to go diving," he said as he eased the boat out of its slip. A few minutes later we were clear of the harbor, burrowing like a mole into the gauzy mists lying just offshore. Skip kicked up the throttle a notch and we skimmed over the waves. We were going faster than I would have traveled with visibility down to a matter of yards, but Skip seemed to navigate by pure instinct, picking up channel buoys with a built-in radar.

He pointed ahead. "Wreck we're going to is only a few miles from here in Buzzards Bay. She's called the *Betsey*, a nineteenth-century coastal schooner in about thirty feet of water. Not a lot of her left, but the timbers are in a pretty interesting configuration." He opened a drawer, pulled out a sketchbook, and handed it over. I opened the book to page after page of pencil drawings. They showed ship timbers in fine detail.

"Did you do these?"

"Uh-huh," Skip replied.

"They're very good."

"Thanks. Kinda have to do it by memory. Dive, make a few lines on your slate, come up, and get them down on paper. There's a new system out I'd like to get my hands on. Draws the wreck on a computer using transponders and sonar. But this'll do until I go space age."

"You sound like you're familiar with electronics."

"I should be. I studied engineering at Rensselaer Polytech. Dropped out after a bit, but a little of what I learned sunk in."

"How'd you end up in Woods Hole?"

"I was born here. Go up to the cemetery and you'll find the name Mallowes on a whole slew of old gravestones. My ancestors were in the whaling business. Not the guys who owned the ships, but the hands who ran them on those voyages that went a couple of years. Lot of those graves up there are empty because the body went into the sea off Fiji or some godforsaken place. My father worked for the summer people as a caretaker for some of the big old houses you see around here. Never made any money, but he wanted me to go to college, so maybe someday I could live in a big house too. Didn't happen that way, though. I had other ideas."

"You said you went to Rensselaer."

"Yeah, but I dropped out. I had the wanderlust. It was a big disappointment to my dad when I left college. He had done a lot of scrimping to send me there. But a classroom was just too damn small to hold me."

"Maybe those whaling ancestors of yours passed the wanderlust along in the genes."

"I've often thought the same thing. Anyway, I saw the world, had some good times, then came back to the Cape when my parents died, and moved into the family homestead. I fished with a buddy back when you could make a buck and keep it, saved my money from a couple of good seasons, and invested it in the *Gannet*. I do some lobstering and take out dive parties and manage okay."

"Nice-looking boat," I said. "You keep it shipshape and Bristol fashion."

Skip smiled and said, "Some people say it's too neat; sign of a deranged mind. But the Malloweses have always had a reputation for eccentricity, and it doesn't bother me. So tell me, what do you do for a living?"

"I'm a college dropout too. I studied the classics at Boston University. Banged around for a bit, like you, then settled down here. I do some fishing to pay the rent. Then in my spare time I'm a private cop."

He raised his eyebrows. "That's an interesting combination. So what are you doing in Woods Hole, fishing, copping, or just plain vacationing?"

"I'm working on a missing person case. That's the reason I went to see Jane. I'm trying to locate a woman named Leslie Walther. You probably knew her through Dr. Drake."

Skip grunted. "Yeah, I knew her."

There was a disapproving note in his voice. "You don't sound very enthusiastic about Leslie."

Skip didn't answer right away. He pointed off our starboard side where a flock of large black and white birds were dropping out of the sky into the sea. The smell of schooling fish was in the air.

"Real pretty birds, aren't they?" he said after a moment. "I remember as a kid being fascinated by the way gannets can swim in the air and underwater. I wondered how they could be two things, a flier *and* a swimmer. It seemed they had to be one or the other. That's the way I think; everything's got to be in its place, in its own category. Maybe that's why I didn't like Leslie. Pretty woman and smart. But she turned out to be on the make. She was after Dr. Drake. She got him, at least for a while. Broke up the marriage. That made Jane unhappy. I like Jane, so it made me unhappy."

"Maybe it was Drake who made her unhappy. From what I hear, he was a real ladies' man. If it wasn't Leslie, it would have been somebody else."

"Yeah, I guesso." He paused. "What do you think of Jane?"

"I just met her yesterday. She's a nice lady. Talented too."

"You said it."

"How did you like the doctor?"

"We got along okay. Tom and I both like to dive." It occurred to me that this was the first time I heard anyone say Drake's name without spitting or going into hysterics.

"When was the last time you saw Leslie?"

He thought about it a moment. "Just before she disappeared. The doctor and I had come in from a dive trip. She was on the pier, waiting, which was kind of unusual. In fact it was the first time I had seen her there. The doc went over to talk with her."

"Could you hear what they were saying?"

He shook his head. "They were too far away, but he looked like he was angry. He was waving his arms and Leslie was crying. Then she got into her car and squealed rubber up the street. I think they broke up and she's probably staying with friends somewhere, trying to get over it."

"Could be," I said, although I wasn't entirely convinced Leslie had run off to lick her wounds. She and Drake may have had a falling-out and busted up, but most people whose love hits a wall will dust themselves off, swallow their pride, try their best to soothe their hurts, then get on with their lives. If people dropped out of sight every time a heart was broken, half the world would be in hiding.

The fog had burned off and there was a sparkle of sunlight on the green water. We cruised for another half hour, chatting mostly about fishing. As we talked Mallowes kept an eye on his compass and the bearings on his Loran, the electronic navigational system that tells you where you are. We were off the Elizabeth Islands, heading through a passage around a half mile wide between two low-lying points of land, when Skip slowed the boat to a stop and let it drift.

"We're here," he said, glancing at a depth finder. "Water's about five fathoms and the current's not much, right now anyhow. Let's check her out."

We threw the anchor over the side and helped each other on with our wet suits and air tanks. Skip went into the water first, working down the anchor line, and I followed. The first flush of cold water next to my skin was like diving into an ice bucket. The current on the sandy bottom was about a couple of miles per hour. Skip circled a few times to get his bearings in the murky sea. It was obvious he was well acquainted with the spot, because we were on the wreck within minutes. The grayish-brown remains of the hull were about thirty feet long and covered with seaweed and barnacles. We prowled over the timbers for fifteen minutes, with Skip pointing out the keel and several dark patches between the worm-eaten ribs. Then we explored the surrounding bottom, chased a few fish and lobsters, and surfaced. We stripped off our gear and munched on ham and cheese sandwiches Skip had thoughtfully prepared.

"There's something about an old wreck," he said. "This one isn't especially dramatic, but I've been down there a dozen times, and I always see something different. She sank in a storm and all the crew got off her okay. Cargo was coal. That's the black stuff in the muck I was pointing out."

"No treasure?"

He gave me a thoughtful look. "Naw. Not yet. Maybe tomorrow. Maybe never. One more dive?"

We changed tanks and went down for another look. The current was stronger now. We had been diving in a slack tide between the ebb and the flood. Now the tide was changing, and with the shift its pull became stronger. It's called the Venturi effect, the extremes of current that come when the tide squeezes in from the open sea into a narrow passage. I had to hang on to the wrecked timbers to keep from being moved off the site. Skip had solved the problem by wedging his body between timbers. He was sketching on an underwater writing pad and measuring the timbers. This wasn't fun anymore. I thought we should go up before the current became more unmanageable. I tapped his arm and pointed toward the surface. He nodded, touched his watch, held up five fingers, and resumed sketching.

Five minutes passed and I was getting tired. I touched his arm again. Only his eyes were visible through the face mask, but he looked annoyed. He stopped drawing and pointed off into the murk toward the anchor line about twenty feet away. Then he let go of the wreck timbers and kicked. I followed. the current was moving us back. We kicked, harder. After a few minutes of going nowhere, I headed off at a diagonal to the current and gained a few inches. I built on that and covered several feet, with Skip swimming beside me.

My muscles were ready to call it quits when I spotted the anchor line just a few yards away. I made one last surge, reached out, grabbed the line, and held on. Skip started to slip backward, but he got a grip on my swim fin, then worked his way up by the weight belt and harness until he too clutched the anchor line. We inflated our buoyancy compensators and rose to the surface. Seconds later we were on the *Gannet*'s deck. Both of us were panting.

Skip got his breath back first. "I'm sorry about that," he said. "I knew the current gets bad here on a tide change, but I wanted to get that sketch done and figured we had more time."

I spit out a mouthful of seawater. "No problem, I needed the exercise." Like a hole in the head.

We got into dry clothes and pointed the boat toward Woods Hole. It was late afternoon when the *Gannet* pulled into the harbor. We didn't talk much on the way back. I wasn't angry at Skip. He was like a lot of wreck divers I had come across. Good sailors and captains when they're navigating a boat, but get them underwater, near a wreck, even one of no value, they start drooling at the mouth, and their judgment just goes out the window.

The *Gannet* was passing Drake's sprawling house on its well-groomed lawn. I studied the house's location and retraced the route I had taken the night I went out on my appointment with Drake. The only land access to the houses on the Point was the narrow causeway where a guard was on duty twenty-four hours a day. But driving wasn't the only way to get to Drake's house. I noticed a pair of divers working close to shore. Probably looking for Drake's murder weapon. I pointed them out to Skip and said casually, "What's the current like in the harbor?"

"Not bad," Skip said, keeping his eyes on the channel. "Depends on the time of year. You get some during tide change, but not like back where we were today."

The *Gannet* sidled up to the dock. I jumped off and cleated the lines.

"You go on ahead," Skip said. "I want to stay on board and clean up."

"What do I owe you?" I said.

He shook his head. "Nothing. It was a pleasure having your company. We'll do it on a professional basis next time. Give me a call if you want to make a dive on something special."

"Thanks. I'll do that."

On the way back to the guest house I thought about Leslie Walther. She must have spent some time at Drake's house. Maybe she had left a trace, a letter or a note there, something that might tell me where she was. It was a long shot, I conceded, but better than nothing. And right now, nothing was all I had.

Familiar voices were chattering in the downstairs sitting room of the guest house. I poked my head in the doorway. New clothes were draped over every stick of furniture. Mrs. Stapleton was talking to my sister and smiling broadly. When she saw me, the smile got even wider. She put her arm around Chloe, who was also very happy, apparently having been on a successful shopping expedition.

"Mr. Socarides. I've just been talking to your delightful sister. She was showing me the clothes she bought in town. She told me she was planning to stay at some drab motel in Falmouth while she visited you, but I've offered her a room next to yours so she can see you more often."

"Well, that's just wonderful, Mrs. Stapleton. Chloe, my love, when you're through showing Mrs. Stapleton your booty, would you please drop by my room?"

Chloe came upstairs a few minutes later. I laced into her, angrily.

"For god sakes, Chlo', I can't have you hanging around here. I've got work to do."

She looked crushed. "I won't get in your way, I promise. Maybe I can even help."

"Can't you get it through your head? I don't need your help. Have you called Ma?"

"No."

"Do you intend to?"

"I don't know." She stuck her chin out. Stubbornness had crept into her voice.

"She's worried about you. Doesn't that mean anything?"

"Oh, and I suppose she never worried about *you*."

"Yes, plenty of times. And I've regretted every minute."

"That's really big of you. I don't see where you're in any position to lecture me on familial obligations, Aristotle Socarides. I wasn't very old, but I remember Ma and Pop's reaction when you dropped out of college and joined the marines in your early macho phase and went off to Vietnam. Talk about worried! They were absolutely tortured. Anything I've done is totally anticlimactic. I've been a royal pain, and I still am. But you hurt them, Soc, you really hurt them."

She clamped her mouth shut. There was rock-hard silence between us.

"You're right," I said after a few moments. "I am truly a despicable person. I've abandoned the family, left poor George to tend the business, and you to wet-nurse the folks."

"Stop talking like that." Furious now. "I hate it when you whip yourself with guilt so people will feel sorry for you."

"Yeah, but Chloe, it's true."

"It's not. You're a wonderful person. You're unselfish, you're kind, you're always helping people."

"And you're a great sister. I've seen the way you've babied the folks when they've come home from the bakery so tired they could hardly walk."

She shook her head and put her arms around me. "Ugh, I don't think I can stand this mutual admiration. I'm sorry about what I said. This is all so childish. We're squabbling like when we were little kids."

I held her at arm's length. "I really am happy to see you," I said. "But I get testy when Ma starts bugging me in the middle of a case that's driving me crazy. So do me a favor. Please call her."

She frowned. "I don't think we're ready to talk yet. I know I'm not."

Chloe's stubbornness again. There was no fighting it.

"Okay," I said. "But promise me you'll think about it."

The frown changed to a grin. "I will, big brother, I really will. In the meantime, would you like to have dinner with Trudie and me tonight?"

"Trudie?"

"Sure, Mrs. Stapleton, your landlady. I'm taking her out. You're welcome to join us."

The image of Drake's house on its point of land was going through my mind. "Thanks, sis," I said, "I'd really like to come along. But I've already made plans for tonight."

CHAPTER 9

•

A cool dry northerly breeze was nudging the fog offshore with little cat's-paw puffs as I parked the pickup in a scrubby stand of pitch pine near the private road to Drake's point. It was around ten o'clock and the harbor gleamed with a leaden sheen cast by the cold light of a gibbous moon. I stripped down to my bathing trunks and got into my rented wet suit. Then I hauled the dive bag with the rest of my gear to the beach, a walk of around a hundred feet from the truck. I paused at the crest of the beach and listened to the soft gurgle of the waves washing the shore. A shiver went up my spine. Swimming at night never fails to evoke primordial fears. I just knew something big and mean was waiting for me out there in the inky-black water. It would swim silently below my dangling legs, then move in, its fang-lined maw yawning hungrily. . . .

A mental stop sign went in place. At this rate I would talk myself into a dash for the nearest and warmest bar. Moving quickly, I pulled on a small waterproof backpack, then my fins, hood, and mask with the snorkel attached.

I backed into the water, turned, and breaststroked around fifty feet, then swam parallel to the shore toward Drake's house, rapidly covering the yards with strong rhythmical strokes and kicks. Within minutes I was passing the guardhouse. Through the lighted window I could see the guard watching television.

Skip was right about the weak current. I made good time, even with the pack hanging between my shoulders. About twenty minutes later I angled my course closer to shore. Soon my fins touched a gravelly bottom. I paddled into shore and crawled onto the wet sand like a basking crocodile. Stopping only a moment to catch my breath, I yanked my fins and mask off and walked up to the massive boulders of riprap that edged Drake's property and protected the embankment from wave erosion. Leaving my gear under a stairway where I could find it again, I climbed off the beach and set a course for the house.

I strolled across the wide lawn nonchalantly, as if I were walking in the park. My neoprene wet suit was black, like a commando's uniform. Even in the light of the moon, I would just be a shadow to anyone who might be watching. Minutes later I stood at the foot of the veranda steps. The house had a broad sloping roof, broken by a dormer that went most of its width. The edge of the roof hung over the wide porch. A garage wing was attached to one side of the main house.

I went up the stairs onto the porch. The front door was locked, naturally. I checked the windows, looking for wires or motion sensors, but there was no sign of an alarm system. Kneeling on the porch, I slid the pack off and opened it. Inside was a small flashlight, files, pliers, picks, and a short crowbar, the kind of goodies that could land me in jail for possession of burglar tools. Straightening, I selected a window where my handiwork wouldn't be immediately obvious to the casual eye, cut a hole in a pane with my glass cutter, and turned the lock. The window was stuck tight and I had to pry it open with the crowbar. After one last look around, I crawled into the house and shut the window behind me. Hooding the flashlight beam with my fingers, I crossed the large sitting room, opened a door, and stepped into a hallway.

A few minutes later I was going through the desk in Drake's study. The drawers were unlocked. A fast search turned up some ComElectric bills and letters to plumbers and electricians. I looked halfheartedly through the rest of the study. Flagg and his minions undoubtedly had combed the house before me, but I was banking on the fact that they wanted information on Drake and his scientific work, not on Leslie Walther.

From the study I crossed the hallway and climbed the stairs to the huge master bedroom on the second floor. The centerpiece was a king-size water bed, placed so you could lie in it and enjoy the view through a set of wide patio doors that opened onto a deck. I pictured Jane lying there. Then Leslie. I pushed the thoughts out of my head. They were either prurient or jealous and I didn't like the fit of either one. I rummaged through dressers, checked the pockets of the suits hanging in the closets, and learned one thing: Drake had good and expensive taste in clothing. I looked behind pictures, under chairs, and in wastebaskets. Nothing.

Drake had a smaller desk in his bedroom. It took about five minutes to go through that and to find more nothing. On top of the desk was a tin box. I flipped back the cover. It was filled with stationery from Neptune Technologies Inc. The logo was black NTI letters imposed over a seagreen picture of the seagod. Letterhead is the private cop's friend. You can use it to break through all sorts of corporate or governmental barriers. I don't know how many times I've sent off a letter on official-looking correspondence and followed it up with a phone call. I've collected reams of the stuff. I've signed my name as president, veep, treasurer, or personnel manager of everything from Amalgamated Buttonhooks to Zany Partifavors Limited. Resistance fades and people become putty in your hands when they see a corporate logo.

Drake's stationery might come in handy in the hunt for
Leslie Walther. Besides, after all the trouble I had gone
through to get here, I didn't want to go home empty-
handed. I peeled about a half inch of letterhead off the
top of the pile. It didn't feel right. Too crinkly. I fanned
the stationery on the desk and saw a layer of onionskin
papers, some typed, some handwritten, sandwiched in between. I held the flashlight close and tried to read them,
but couldn't, for a very good reason. They weren't in
English. I grunted. The papers had no apparent bearing
on Leslie Walther, but Drake had wanted them out of
plain sight, so he must have attached some importance to
the stuff. I put the onionskin with the rest of the letterhead in my pack.

Time to go. I glanced once more around the room, saw
nothing of interest, and started out into the hallway. At
the top of the stairs I froze. A light thump had come
from below. The sound an ashtray might make if someone
knocked it off a table onto wall-to-wall carpeting. But in
the cryptlike silence of the empty house it was like crashing china. I held my breath and waited. My ears were
cocked for the slightest noise. All was quiet. I strained my
eyes, vainly peering down the stairway into the shadows of
the darkened foyer. Then I saw an eddy of gray—a face
or hand maybe—disturbing the blackness at the foot of
the stairs.

Somebody was moving up the stairway in my direction.

I ticked off the possibilities. Cops. Feds. A second-story
man working my turf. Vowing to file a grievance with the
Burglars' Union, I backed into Drake's bedroom, shut the
door with a barely audible click, then stepped out through
the patio doors onto the broad second-story deck and
looked over the railing. It was a long way to the ground.
No problem. If I couldn't go down, I would go up. I
climbed onto the railing, grabbed the wooden rain gutter,
and hoisted myself onto the main roof, whose broad sweep
was silvery in the moonlight. I scrambled across the shingles, then dropped down a couple of yards onto the garage

wing. I estimated from my daytime visit that the garage roof was about ten feet off the ground. At my height, that made a drop of four feet. Easy.

I lowered myself feet first, moving down the slope like a spider. Within seconds I was at the edge of the roof. I took the flashlight from my pack. I wanted to make sure a spiked fence wasn't waiting for me. I switched the light on for just a second, and pointed it at the ground. There was only a tangle of rosebushes below. I held on to the gutter and let my body slide off the roof. The rubber wet suit refused to glide easily over the shingles and I had to use a little body English. I dangled from the gutter, gathering the courage to drop into the darkness.

Thut!

The roof shingles exploded a foot away from my right hand. Splinters showered my head.

It was the cough of a silenced pistol. I looked over my shoulder toward Drake's bedroom. A red tongue of flame licked the blackness. Splinters flew again.

I closed my eyes and let go.

I seem to hang in midair forever before I crashed into the rosebushes, my legs folded like an accordian to cushion the impact. The thorns clawed at me. I untangled myself from their sharp embrace and stumbled through the dense shrubbery alongside the house. At a corner of the house I paused, looked quickly around, then stepped out onto the grass and raced toward the beach across a lawn as big as a football field.

Within seconds, my brain began began to boil. The wet suit was designed to hold heat and it was doing its job all too well. There was another problem. The ankle-high dive boots on my feet were made to keep my toes warm and to go easily into a swim fin, not for broken field running. The rubber soles are smooth. With no tread to provide traction, the boots had a tendency to slip in the grass and I had to run in a ridiculous, jerky little trot so I wouldn't fall.

A powerful flashlight beam strafed the lawn, catching

me in its beam. Seconds later a divot of grass flew into the air about ten feet to my left. I veered sharply to the right and glanced over my shoulder. The light on the porch moved down the front steps and bobbed across the lawn, moving fast on an angle that could cut me off from the beach.

A second shot kicked up a another piece of lawn.

I tried to zigzag.

Each attempt to change direction was a near disaster. It was like running on a field of banana peels. I would have paid anything for a pair of cleats. As I made a sharp left turn, my foot skidded out from under me. I did a split, half gainer, and swan dive, all rolled into one, landing on my chin. I ignored the pain and sucked in a deep breath to retrieve some of the air knocked out of me. I pushed myself off the ground and started running again. The light was getting closer.

I swung away from the beach and headed toward the causeway. If I could make it to the marsh at the edge of the road I might be able to lose my pursuer in the thick grass and crawl into the tidal creek that would take me back to the harbor. The mind does strange things under stress. As the flashlight beam got closer, one side of my brain was lashing my legs on, urging them to move faster. The other side worried about getting bullet holes in my rented wet suit.

The marsh was a hundred yards away. I put my energy into one humonguous sprint.

The light was closing on me.

Fifty yards.

Damn! It was my luck to be chased by a marathon runner.

Twenty-five yards.

The spot of light dancing around my feet disappeared. He had stopped to take aim. I clenched my teeth, feeling the bull's-eye of the beam on my back, waiting for the shock of the bullet smashing into my spine. I put my head down, gulped a swallow of air and made one last frantic dash for the marsh, my lungs burning. The edge of the lawn was less than thirty feet away. Almost there. Maybe I would make it after all.

A few yards from the marsh a wall of flesh sprang from the ground and blocked my way. I had been cut off at the pass.

CHAPTER 10

●

I yelled "yahh!" and dug my heels into the slippery grass in a doomed attempt to stop. My boots skidded, my legs shot out ahead of my body, and I went flying onto my back. The impact knocked the wind out of me and I was seeing more stars than there are in the sky. Someone loomed over me. I struggled to get to my feet. A big hand grabbed my face and pushed me down. A voice hissed in my ear.

"Stay down, for Chrissakes! You'll get us both killed."

The smell of English Leather. Flagg.

The hand came off my face and I rolled over onto my belly to catch my breath. Out on the lawn a crimson sunburst flowered. Turf exploded a few feet in front of me, sending up a shower of flying dirt that stung my eyes. I drilled a hole in the ground with my nose and locked my hands over my head as if the flesh and bone in my knuckles could stop a slug.

Blam!

A cannon went off over my head. Then roared again. Flagg was shooting back.

My ears were ringing from the gunshots but I could hear Flagg yell, "Move your ass! They'll aim for the muzzle blasts."

Flagg scrambled. I followed him, and did the twenty-foot Olympic rolling competition in three seconds. I slammed into Flagg again. It was like hitting a stone wall. He was lying flat on his stomach. He had a pistol in his right hand and was peering through what looked like a telescope. I recognized it as an infrared night-vision scope. The pistol barked again.

The cowboy who had been popping at us didn't like the competition. The firing from the lawn stopped. A couple of minutes later an outboard motor sputtered and caught and its muted buzz soon faded into the distance.

Flagg got up on one knee. He panned the nightscope across the lawn and house, then grunted.

"It's okay," he said. "Your friend's gone for a little boat ride."

He stood, grabbed me under the armpit, and helped me up. He produced a flashlight from his jacket and played the beam over the mud and blades of grass caked onto my wet suit and chin.

"Funny place for you to go diving, Soc."

I spit out a mouthful of turf and wiped the dirt from my eyes. I was half-deaf from the gunfire and in no mood to exchange pleasant banter. "Who the hell was that?

Flagg looked off into the night. "Don't know. Wish I had gotten a better look at him. One thing I do know. He sure wanted your ass."

"Shit," I said.

"Yeah, Soc. You were up to your neck in that all right." He hefted the scope. "I was keeping an eye on you through this baby."

"You watched the whole thing?"

"Just about. I saw you come out of the water and go in the house. Couldn't tell it was you, but it looked interesting, so I waited. Then that other fella comes loping from the beach. He goes into the house. Figured the two of you would introduce yourself to each other before long and things would start to happen. I was right. Next thing I know you're climbing down the roof like you'd been caught with someone's wife, and all hell is breaking loose. I got a better look at you when you started running in my direction. When it seemed like that guy was going to cut you off, but good, I thought I should lend a hand."

"What the hell took you so long?"

"Didn't want to hit you, man." Flagg's mouth opened in a toothy grin. "You sure looked funny, though, skidding across that lawn like a big ol' black frog, with that fella on your tail trying to rip you a new asshole."

"I'm glad I could provide amusement," I said, brushing the gunk off my wet suit. "Why were you watching the house?"

"Didn't seem to be anything better to do. How about you?"

I tenderly messaged my rear end, bruised from my fall. "I was pursuing an investigation in my usual unorthodox fashion. Didn't seem to be anything better to do."

"Looked more like the investigation was pursuing you. Did you expect to find Leslie Walther in Drake's place?"

"In a way. A woman sometimes leaves traces."

"You find any?"

The German papers I had taken from Drake's desk were burning a hole in my pack. "No," I said. It wasn't really a lie. I hadn't found any sign of Leslie. "Your guys must have scooped up all the good stuff."

"Yeah, we were all over the place a few hours after they found Drake's body. Nothing real interesting."

"Well, thanks again. Can I hook a ride out? I've had enough swimming for one night."

"Sure. I don't blame you. With your luck there are probably sharks in the water."

Flagg's sardonic humor again. I remembered that it was one of the things I liked about him. That and his fierce Native American pride. I laughed in spite of myself. A quote was going through my mind. Something Euripides had said about fate being stranger than anything he had known. Flagg and I had been friends who became enemies. Now, because of a bizarre coincidence, he happened to be in a spot where he probably saved my life. Euripides was right about fate.

I retrieved my gear from the beach stairway and got into Flagg's car. The guard had slept through all the shooting, which is just as well, because the point would have been swarming with cops. He woke up when we drove by and waved at Flagg as if they were old friends. We stopped near my truck. I got out of the LTD and came around to the driver's window. "I guess I owe you one," I said reluctantly.

"Don't mention it. You did me a favor tonight too."

"How so?"

"I know someone is very interested in Drake, interested enough to try killing you. Why would anyone want to do that? You tell him one of your jokes?"

"You're becoming quite a funny man yourself, Flagg. Anytime you want to use me as a human decoy, give me a call. I'll make sure I'm not home."

He ignored my repartee. A hand holding a piece of paper came out the window. "If you're going to stay in this case, I really can't stop you. Maybe we can put our heads together. Here's my number if you want to talk. I'm staying in Falmouth."

I took the paper from his fingers. "I said I owe you one, Flagg, but that's as far as it goes."

"You don't owe me a thing. I haven't forgotten that marine who tried to ventilate me with his switchblade back in Quang Tri."

"Okay, Flagg," I said. "I'll consider us even."

He nodded. "Just kick around what I said about talking. I'm not jumping for joy at the thought of working with you, but maybe we can call a truce."

"I'll think about it. That's all I can promise."

"Fair enough." He started the car engine. "Just remember, Soc, back in 'Nam, things weren't always what they seemed to be."

Flagg rolled up his window, put his car into gear, and drove off. I watched his taillights until they were out of sight, then stripped out of my wet suit and got in my truck. Flagg's parting words echoed in my ears.

CHAPTER 11

●

A jolly sun woke me up the next day. The room was bathed in a jolly yellow light. Jolly robins and chickadees chirped in a tree outside my window. I slowly swung my legs out of bed, planted my feet on the braided rug, wiggled my toes, and stared vacantly at them, thinking about last night. I was *not* in a jolly mood. I didn't like being shot at. I didn't like being obligated to Flagg even for a minute. I didn't like getting nowhere in my search for Leslie Walther.

I reached over to the side table and slid Leslie's photograph out of the file her father had given me. Sometimes a photo of a missing person sends out telling vibrations. The eyes will have the haunted look of a victim and you just know there's a body in a shallow grave somewhere. I studied Leslie's face for a message. Her eyes sparkled with life. She was telling me that she was alive. But where? Leslie had an affair with Drake, whose untimely death evoked more cheers than tears. Drake blew her off, and she disappeared. Did he kill her? Did she kill him?

I tried another tack. Drake was working on a hush-hush

project. Was that linked to his murder? And back to last night. There was a lot of action at Drake's place, more than you'd expect at a big empty house owned by a dead man. Who tried to plug me? And why? My head ached. I took a shower and dressed, then went downstairs to the pay phone with my credit card in hand.

Always deal with the worst task first. What could be worse than a family matter? Not any family. My family. I dialed a number in Lowell.

Athena Kostas, who runs the front office at my parents' bakery, answered the phone. "Good morning," she said. "Parthenon Pizza Company."

" 'Thena, it's Soc. How are things?"

"*Soc*," Athena said. "Thank goodness you called! I'm fine, but the bakery's in an uproar. *Please* say you've found Chloe."

I glanced up the stairs at the closed door to my sister's room. Chloe was a late sleeper. "I've found her, 'Thena, but I don't know what to do with her. May I speak to my mother?"

"What a relief. That's good news about Chloe. But your mom's not in. I'll connect you with the bakery. Hold on."

A voice came on the phone. "Allo."

"Pop, is that you?"

"Aristotle. S'Poppa. Where's Chloe?" My father went on before I could answer, his words poured out nonstop. "Aristotle, you gotta find your sister. Your mother's making us all crazy. Night and day. Day and night. The same thing. No sleep. No work. No eat. The business . . ." I lost him as his speech degenerated into an incomprehensible jumble that was neither Greek nor English but a little of both.

My younger brother George came on the extension.

"Christ, Soc, where the hell you been? Ma's been going out of her mind not hearing from you. She's driving Pop and me and everyone in the bakery bananas. We're all ready to quit."

"Day and night, night and day."

"Dad," George growled, "get off the extension, I'll handle this."

My father mumbled something that could have been a curse or a prayer and hung up.

"I'm sorry I didn't call sooner, George. Just tell Ma that Chloe is fine. I've talked to her."

"Man, I *told* Ma she was okay. But she had a cousin back in the Old Country who jumped off a cliff into the ocean 'cause the family picked a husband for her, and that's all she's been talking about. I think she's out buying another black mourning dress. When's Clo' coming home?"

"That's the problem, George. I don't know when she'll be back."

"Jeez, Soc." He was almost pleading. "We're all ready to walk out and close the place. Even Pop. You heard him. You know it's gotta be something when he starts squawking."

"Tell Ma that I'm working on it. Say I'll keep an eye on Chloe. Just tell her."

"Can't you do better than that, for godsakes?"

"Bye, George." I cut the call short. I was afraid George would ask for my telephone number and I didn't want to give it to him.

I sat down on a deacon's bench in the hall. My first phone call and I was nearly drained. I quickly dialed another number before I lost strength completely. One of the assistants at Norma's research firm said Norma was out of the office and would return soon. But she had left a message for me: "Important. Get back to me soonest." I said I would call back in an hour.

Next I called Frederick Walther's number. Winston Prayerly answered. I told him I wanted to talk to Walther.

"He's busy right now," Prayerly said. "May I give him a message?"

"No. I'd like to give it to him directly."

Walther's voice came on phone instantly, like somebody who had been busy listening on another line.

"Good to hear from you, Mr. Socarides. Have you turned up anything on my daughter?"

"I'm following up several leads, but I have nothing solid to report at this time."

"I'm disappointed, of course, but I have confidence in you. Too bad you didn't get to talk to Tom Drake."

"I did talk to him."

"Oh? Winston didn't tell me that."

"He didn't tell you because I didn't tell him."

Walther chuckled. "Did you get anything out of Drake?"

"Nothing substantial. We had arranged to talk again, but he was found dead a few hours later."

"That is unfortunate." His soft voice didn't sound grieved. "How do you plan to proceed?"

"As I said, I've got a couple of leads. Please let me know if you think of anything, even if it's minor, that might help."

"I will, Mr. Socarides. And what I said before, about stepping on people if you have to, still holds. I don't mind breaking heads if it means finding Leslie."

"I think we can track her down without having to give anyone a headache, Mr. Walther."

"Very well. Use your best judgment. Leslie was my only child. You can understand my feelings. Please keep in touch."

He hung up. I looked at my watch. Maybe I could squeeze in a quick breakfast. I drove to Water Street and parked outside the restaurant near the drawbridge, buying a *Boston Globe* on the way. I sat next to a window overlooking the harbor and devoured bacon and eggs, wholewheat toast and home fries, and drank a gallon of coffee while I read the sports section. The Sox were doing lousy. That made two of us. I was checking the box scores when a voice intruded.

"May I join you?"

I looked up from my paper. Sharon Prescott, Drake's

secretary and latest and last paramour, was standing next to my table. Her hair was neatly combed, her makeup was in place, and best of all, she was smiling a lovely smile. I motioned to a chair and set the paper aside.

"I was passing by and saw you in here. I'm on my way to work, but I just wanted to thank you for being so kind the other day. I really appreciated it."

"You're welcome," I said. "Sometimes it's helpful to talk."

"There was something else." She paused. "Did you see Dan Whipple after you talked to me at the lab?"

"Yes. He caught up with me. We had an informative chat."

She was quiet for a moment and then, as though coming to a decision, looked at me and said, "I'll bet he didn't tell you about the argument."

My ears perked up. "No, he didn't. What argument?"

"It was the day you came in to see Tom. Later that afternoon, after everybody else was gone, they had a terrible fight."

"What did they fight about?"

"It started with Dan saying he was sick and tired of being humiliated. Tom just laughed at him, taunting Dan. Telling him to quit if he didn't like it. Dan said Tom knew damn well he couldn't quit. That Tom would ruin him in a second if he walked out on the job."

"What do you suppose he meant by that?"

She shook her head. "I don't know. Anyhow, Tom said Dan was right. That he'd be washed up in Woods Hole or anywhere else. He'd do such a job on his reputation Dan couldn't get a job feeding fish to the seals at the aquarium."

The seal pool. That was interesting.

"Go on."

"Dan said if Tom did that, he'd kill him."

"What happened next?"

"Nothing, really. Tom was still laughing when Dan

stormed out of his office. I saw him as he went down the hall. He was furious." She paused, then said, "You don't suppose Dan could have . . . ?"

"Anything is possible. But I wouldn't read too much into it."

"Should I tell the police?"

"If it makes you feel better. Angry people say things they don't mean. It could be just a coincidence. Is Whipple back at work?"

"Yes, he's trying not to act happy about Tom, but you can see that he is. A number of Navy people have come in and he's been meeting with them." She looked at her watch and said she had to go. I thanked her and went back to my sports pages. I was feeling pretty good after breakfast until I saw I had forgotten to feed the parking meter. I took the red parking ticket from under the windshield wiper and tossed it in the glove compartment.

A police cruiser was coming down Water Street toward me. Probably wanted to give me another ticket. The cruiser pulled up to the curb and beeped its horn. Gallagher was behind the wheel. He motioned at me. I opened the door and got in the cruiser.

Gallagher was grinning, "How's it going, Mr. Private Eye?"

"Great. I think I just broke the record for parking tickets. Are you guys on a fund-raiser?"

The sergeant laughed and said, "Wish I could do something for you, but we can't fix tickets like in the old days. You got any leads on your case?"

I thought of what Sharon Prescott had told me. "Nothing big. I've got a question for you, though. How does Dan Whipple's alibi hold up?"

Gallagher gave me a cop look. "On paper, it seems pretty good. Whipple left the lab a little after five. He went out for dinner. The waitress remembers him because he left her a good tip. He went to the liquor store. The salesman remembers him because he buys a lot of booze there. He went to the movies, alone. The cashier remembers him because he dropped his change, gave her a big bill and apologized, and said how he had wanted to see this flick for a long time."

"Sounds like he wanted people to remember him. Anyone see him come out?"

"No, but that's not surprising."

"Could he have left early without being seen?"

"Possible. The ticket office closed up. There are no ushers. He coulda gone to the john and when the popcorn girl's back was turned, slipped out, I suppose."

"Still no murder weapon?"

"Nope. Divers have been working the harbor. We'll take a look at Eel Pond too. Maybe the murderer threw it out further or dumped it by the side of the road."

"There's another possibility."

"What's that?"

"Maybe the murderer isn't through using it."

"You're a bundle of joy, Socarides."

I opened the door. "Nope. I'm a realist." I got out and came around to the driver's side. "Keep in touch, Sergeant. Sorry to rush off, I have to move my truck before I get hit with another ticket."

After leaving Gallagher, I drove out onto the Nobska Road and dropped by to see Jane. She had put a new canvas on the easel and was fiddling around with pastels and a sketch pad when I got past Rembrandt the friendly watchdog and climbed the stairs into the studio. She smiled when she saw me.

"I'm glad you came by," she said. "Thanks again for your escort services at the opening."

"Thank you for asking me."

"Did you go out diving with Skip yesterday?"

"Yes, I enjoyed it. Just as you said, Skip is an interesting guy."

"He's nice too. He's called a couple of times to see how I'm doing." Jane stifled a yawn and said, "Excuse me, it's not the company."

"Didn't you sleep well?"

"Like a baby. Except . . ."

"Except what?"

"Probably nothing. But I think somebody was outside the cottage last night. I sleep with the windows open, and around one. I woke up. You know how sometimes a very quiet noise will awaken you out of a sound sleep? That's how it was with me. I thought I heard a snap, like wood breaking, so I got up and flicked on the outside light, but the fog had come back in and I couldn't see anything. After a while I went back to sleep, but I left the light on."

I pointed to the dog. "Did the pooch bark?"

Jane laughed and shook her head. "He was snoozing. Rembrandt wouldn't hear a robber stealing his food bowl."

I got up and said, "I'll check it out." With Rembrandt dancing at my heels, I headed toward the beach. Near where the path breaks out of the dunes, the dog stopped to sniff a horseshoe-crab shell about ten inches across. A horseshoe crab is a roundish, prehistoric creature that looks like a Leonardo da Vinci model for an army tank. They shed their covering as they grow and you can find the empty shells all over Cape Cod beaches. I picked the shell up by the spiked tail. The brittle armorlike covering was crushed. I dropped the damaged shell and walked a few yards until I found another, this one undamaged, about the same size as the first. I stepped on the top and put my full weight on it. The shell cracked with a hollow snap. Jane could have been awakened by a similar encounter of somebody's foot with a crab shell.

Continuing along the beach, I followed a grass banking about four feet high. Sea and wind had chopped away at the sand and exposed long roots of the beach grass reaching down to the base of the dune. *Ammophila*, the grass is called. Sand lover. And it lives up to its name, sending out a network of roots that connect with other bunches of grass to hold the dune together. I stopped at a point where the roots were torn, allowing a delta-shaped rivulet of sand to cascade down to the beach.

I climbed up the side of the banking and walked a few steps back from the edge, keeping my eyes on the ground. Something white caught my eye. Lying in the sand were three freshly smoked cigarette butts. I picked one up and checked the name on the filter. It was a French Gauloise. I looked back toward the silver-shingled cottage on its low rise. From where I was standing I would have a clear view of the front door and windows. Somebody with an interest in Jane Drake had stood here last night.

I put the cigarette butts in my pocket and went back to the house. Jane was stretching canvas on a frame. "Did you find anything?" she said.

"It was probably a couple of high-school kids doing some heavy petting. Maybe you just heard the popping of teenage libidos."

Doubt flickered across her gray eyes. "I guess so. Kids have come down here in the past to drink beer."

"There you go. Speaking of drinking, how would you like to have a little wine over dinner tonight?"

The tenseness left her face and she brightened. "I'd like that."

"Would seven be okay?"

"Fine."

I gave her a light squeeze around the shoulders and said, "See you then." On the way to my truck I stopped and surveyed the knoll where the Gauloise smoker had stood. I didn't like the look of things. Whoever was outside last night was moving toward the cottage when Jane heard him and turned on the lights. I didn't have an idea why anyone would want to stalk Jane, but I was pretty sure of one thing. He'd be back.

Norma was in her office when I called her from the guest house.

"Soc," she blurted. "For a man who's done his best to escape from the outside world, you work for the most worldly people."

"Walther?"

"Yes, my love, Walther. I've sent you some material, but in a nutshell, your current employer is what they used to call a merchant of death."

"I think you're saying he's an arms dealer."

"One of the biggest, my friend. But more of what I'd call a facilitator. He puts deals together, sees that they go through, brokers a fee. Say Iran needs spare parts for its worn-out American tanks. Walther arranges the deal. Surplus Stingers for Libya from Afghanistan? Pieceacake. Wanna hear more?"

"I'm all ears."

"Okay, my love. He's well connected in Washington, where his main base of operations is. He's got branches in London, Paris, you name it. He handles everything from zip guns to Phantom fighters, although lately he's been specializing in Navy hardware. You'd be surprised at what a chummy club the military-industrial complex is worldwide. These guys even hold conventions where they set up booths. They give away ballpoint pens and plastic bags to hold your brochures in while they sell you the latest tank killer. Walther keeps a low profile, but he is right in the middle of all this."

"At least I won't have to worry about the money running out."

"There's another thing, Soc. I'm not the first one interested in him. I've been following in somebody's tracks. Feelers on Walther went out in the last year. I don't know who was looking into his background, but now I'm curious about the competition."

"I am too. Did you dig out anything on Winston Prayerly, the trusty valet?"

"Ah, there's another whole story, my love. Interpol was very helpful. Prayerly is forty-three, born in Liverpool, England. Soldier of fortune, mercenary in Africa. He's not wanted by the law right now, but give him a few minutes. A very tough hombre. Be most careful around him."

"No problem. I'm working for his boss, right?"

"Just be careful, Soc."

"I will, Norma. Thanks loads."

"I'll let you know when I have more. Bye, dear."

I hung up and wondered what I had stepped into. This was getting to look less and less like a simple missing persons case. Walther was an arms merchant and Winston was an international hood. I shook my head. That's the great thing about my line of work; the hours are lousy and so is the pay, but you get to meet such fascinating people.

CHAPTER 12

●

The lunch they served at the second-floor restaurant with a view of the island ferry terminal wasn't half-bad. Over a fried scrod sandwich on a soft bulky roll I thought about the information Norma had dug up on Walther and his aide-de-camp Mr. Prayerly. Several facts stood out like signposts. Frederick Walther was in the arms business, specializing these days in navy hardware. Drake was involved in a secret navy project. Walther's daughter Leslie was working for Drake and had an affair with him. The connections between the major figures in this case, missing and murdered included, were just too cute to be coincidental.

Using a ballpoint pen, I drew a triangle on a napkin. At the apex I printed the name Frederick Walther. At the lower points I wrote Drake and Leslie. The diagram established a connection between the three. Next I drew the letters *ROV* in the center of the triangle. I took a crunchy bite of sandwich and a dab of mayonnaise fell onto the napkin. I mopped up the glob and drew lines across the triangle from each corner. The lines intersected over ROV. Off to the side of the triangle I wrote:

ROV = Common Denominator.

I inspected my handiwork. It was pretty good for some-one who flunked plane geometry.

I found a pay phone in the restaurant bar and looked up the number for the Woods Hole Oceanographic Insti-tution. Dr. Bertram Ivers was in when I called him. Even better, he remembered me from the art-gallery opening. "Hello, Mr. Socarides," he said heartily. "Nice to hear from you. I enjoyed talking to you at Jane's show the other night."

"Thanks, Dr. Ivers," I said. "In fact, that's what I called about. I'd like to take you up on your offer to talk about ROVs."

"Let me check my schedule." Seconds later he said, "We're in luck. The appointment I had this afternoon has been canceled. How flexible are you?"

"Very flexible, I'm afraid."

He chuckled and said, "Why don't you drop by after lunch, then. I'm in the Bigelow lab building on Walter Street. Just ask the receptionist in the lobby to let me know when you arrive."

I finished my sandwich, then tarried for another fifteen minutes over a Bud and stared at the napkin, but the diagram had revealed all the secrets it was going to. It was only a few minutes' walk to the Bigelow Lab. The receptionist called up for me and Ivers came to the lobby. He was wearing baggy chinos and a brown crewneck sweater. He led me to his third-floor office. It was a spar-tan space. Metal desk, bookshelves, charts, and maps crammed into a room that Huckleberry Finn would have described as hardly big enough to swing a cat in. There was a superb view of the harbor out the window. The in-again, out-again fog was moving in again.

Ivers filled a couple of mugs from a Mr. Coffee machine

and said, "I'm glad I got to see you again. I wanted to apologize for going on about Tom Drake the other night."

"I guess you had good reason, with Drake sabotaging your project and all."

"Yes, of course," he said absently. "Drake went on to become rich." He looked around at his office. "I have this highly prestigious sinecure and my own coffeepot. But that's all water under the bridge. Now, tell me, how did you come to be interested in ROVs?"

"Did you know Leslie Walther?"

"Only by name. She worked for our friend Drake, didn't she?"

I nodded. "She disappeared about a month ago."

"Sorry to hear that."

"Her family is quite anxious to locate her. They hired me to track Leslie down. I'm a private detective."

Ivers's eyebrows did a little fox-trot. "A *detective*. Well, that is a surprise." He lowered his voice conspiratorially and glanced around like someone who thinks there's a microphone hidden in the flowerpot. "You don't suppose Drake had anything to do with the girl's disappearance, do you?"

"I can't be sure yet. It's just like one of your experiments. You can't come to a conclusion until all the data are in."

He nodded. "That's very wise. But I'm not sure where ROVs come into the picture."

"I'm not sure either, Dr. Ivers. But here's what I've got. Leslie was a technician at Drake's lab. Drake was working on ROVs. The connection may have had nothing at all to do with her disappearance. On the other hand . . ."

"I wouldn't put it past Drake to be involved. Hell, there I go again. Sorry. So you think ROVs played a role in this?"

"I was hoping you could help me decide that."

He spread his hands. "I'm afraid I can't aid you with your missing lady, so let's talk ROVs." He pulled a copy of *Sea Technology* magazine off his desk and handed it over. "You can keep that," he said. "I've marked a couple of ads for commercial off-the-shelf ROVs, including one made by NTI."

I leafed through the magazine pages. The ROVs shown in the glossy color ad photos differed from each other in shape and size, but the basic design appeared essentially the same. All models had a more or less streamlined housing. Some were cylindrical, others were cubical. One ROV looked like a miniature jet-fighter plane. The machines shared certain characteristics. There were small propellers at one end, lights and a Plexiglas dome that resembled a big glassy eye at the other. The entire setup rested on sled runners like the old Flexible Flyers.

"They look like one-eyed water bugs," I said. "How long have these things been around?"

Ivers leaned back in his chair. "Remotely controlled submersibles were developed in the seventies," he said. "The military started fooling around with ROVs for mine-detection work, but the real driver behind the technology was the offshore oil industry. The oil companies used them to inspect oil platforms. When the oil boom fizzled, people began seeking a newer and wider range of applications."

"What kind of applications, Dr. Ivers?"

"Virtually any underwater task that's not too complicated," he replied. "You can send an ROV to check out bridge supports, ship hulls, dams, underwater pipelines. Some people have used them in salvage or treasure hunting. You just stay on your boat and control the machine. You never have to get your feet wet. You don't have to pay a diver or give him a lunch break. You don't have to worry about decompression sickness."

"Maybe I should sell my scuba equipment."

"Hold on to it for a while. There will always be a need for human divers, at least until the science of robotics advances to a point where mechanical hands can do the same tasks underwater as human hands."

"How close are we to that point?"

Ivers examined his palm, flexing his fingers. "*Very*

close. But you're quite right. The ROV is usually cheaper than a diver or a team of divers. Commercial diving can be extremely dangerous. There are places where a diver simply should not go. The nuclear power industry is a big user. You can put an ROV into a nuclear reactor's pipes where a diver would be exposed to radioactivity."

"Could you send an ROV to depths where the water pressure is too great for a diver?" I asked.

"Oh, absolutely," he said. "You can build an ROV to go to *any* depth. The same can't be said for a human. The *Titanic* project was a good example. The ship lay two miles beneath the surface of the North Atlantic."

"A diver would have been compressed to the size of a basketball at that depth," I said, pointing out the obvious.

"That's right. Once they had used remote sensing to locate the ship, they sent down the Argus to confirm the find. It was a primitive sort of ROV, basically a sled carrying still cameras, and attached by a power tether to the surface. Some people called it a 'dope on a rope,' which was rather unkind, because it did the job."

"But human observers eventually did visit the wreck."

"True," Ivers said. "Dr. Ballard and his crew dived in the deep-sea sub *Alvin* to take a firsthand look. It was a dramatic excursion, as you can imagine. Human eyes seeing this legend after so many years. Even so, the *Alvin* crew was limited. They couldn't leave the sub and poke around the wreck, so they used a more sophisticated ROV, the Jason Junior, to do what humans couldn't do. They called it the swimming eyeball."

"I've seen some of the pictures Jason Junior took. They were spectacular."

"Damned right they were," Ivers said, his eyes lighting up. "The *Titanic* project was the first time a remotely operated vehicle was crucial to the success of an undersea mission. But *think* of the possibilities." He spread his arms like a country preacher describing the promised land. "With the right ROV there would be no need for humans to go down on that long and dangerous dive. You could sit on the deck of your vessel and run the ROV while you have a cocktail. The possibilities inherent in the new technology gave some people in this town another reason to dislike Drake."

"What was that, Dr. Ivers?"

"Drake used to go around saying that with the remotes he was designing, manned submersibles like the *Alvin* would become as obsolete as the horse and buggy. That didn't make him any friends with those who insist manned submarines are the way to go. There's a lot of competition for a limited amount of underwater research funding."

"What do you think about Drake's position?"

Ivers leaned forward and rapped the desk lightly with his fist. "I think Drake was right. I believe remote-operated submersibles are the future of deep-sea exploration. Damn, it sticks in my craw that I wasn't able to stay in the field—thanks to Drake," he added bitterly.

I tapped a picture in the magazine. "What's inside one of these things?"

Ivers got out of his chair. "Follow me," he said. "I'll show you."

We walked down to the first floor then out the back of the building to a workshop on the dock. Sitting inside on a table was an ROV about three feet long. Ivers patted the shiny orange plastic housing.

"Cute," I said.

"Damn useful too. This is a commercial model we use for routine tasks. Anybody with thirty thousand dollars or so can buy one off the shelf. The basic components are pretty much the same in all ROVs. Behind this Plexiglas hemisphere in front is a high-resolution video camera designed for low light situations. You can manipulate the lens a hundred and eighty degrees in any direction. These quartz halogen lamps provide the light."

I touched a metal arm with a claw at the end of it. "This looks like a fancy beer-bottle opener."

"You're not far off. That's what we call an articulator. This one happens to be two-function. It can open and close and has wrist movement. At the back end we have these little propellers, which provide the forward thrust. You've got other propulsion units on the sides and top and bottom so you can make turns."

"How fast does this thing travel?"

"This model is good for about five knots." That translated into seven or eight miles an hour, about the same speed a sailboat makes with a good wind in its sails.

A thick black rubber cable ran from the ROV to a spindle about a yard in diameter where some hundred feet was coiled. I picked up a section of it. "This is for your power, I'd guess."

"That's right. The coaxial carries the power for the thrusters and the line for the telemetry and video camera."

I squatted down and looked through the Plexiglas. A camera lens stared back. "What does the camera show the person who's operating the ROV?"

"Basically what the ROV sees. Here, back up a few yards and stand in front of the machine."

I did as I was told while Ivers walked over to another table. He turned on a video screen and manipulated some switches on a black box not much bigger than a portable radio. The screen lit up and I was looking at myself. I waved at me. The picture on the screen waved back.

Ivers said: "The screen will also project a graphic overlay that gives you information on depth and direction."

He fiddled with the black box. The camera motor whirred and the Cyclops lens did a circular pan. He worked some other switches. The metal arm rotated and the claw opened and shut.

"Now it's acting like a lobster," I said.

Ivers laughed and said, "This is one lobster you wouldn't want to get a hold of you." He flicked a few switches. The arm stopped moving and the video picture died. I went over and looked at the control box. Two stubby joysticks you could work with your thumbs stuck out of the top.

"How hard is it to run one of these things?"

"You could learn to manipulate an ROV like this in a few hours. You'd have to be an experienced underwater pilot if the vehicle were in tight situations where the tether could get tangled. It depends on the size of the ROV. They run from a couple of feet long to a submersible as big as a car."

"You mentioned military applications."

"They've been used to identify mines in the Persian Gulf. There's nothing hush-hush about that. You can use a modified commercial model. You'd have to make parts out of material that wouldn't trigger a mine. You'd send it down to take a look at a suspicious object. Then you'd dispose of the mine. The Navy is putting some money into new systems. The goal, I believe, would be to develop something that could go down, find the mine, then neutralize it in some way."

"Is that what Drake was working on?"

"More than likely. But knowing Drake, I suspect he had something more advanced than any of the vehicles we've talked about."

"What would an advanced ROV be like?"

Ivers led the way back into the building, talking as he walked. "It could have improved optics, a laser sensor system maybe, and more functional mechanical arms. But the logical and most exciting evolution for ROV science is the AUV."

I shook my head. "Now you've really got me confused. What's an AUV?"

"Sorry. Autonomous Untethered Vehicle. Simply put, it's an ROV without a tether. But it's much more than that."

"In what way?"

"In an ROV all decisions are made by a human. The orders go along the power tether. But a tether can get tangled in a propeller or underwater object. In an AUV, sonar is used to communicate with the machine. Sonar carries a limited amount of information, so the untethered vehicle has to operate on its own. This means that it must be able to go down and perform a mission, secure information, make judgments, and modify plans in the face of changing circumstances."

"That's quite a lot to expect of a machine," I said. "Hell, it's a lot to ask of a human."

"You're very right. We're talking about a machine with its own power and navigational systems. The heart of a vehicle like that would be its computer software and sensors. The sensors would be a key component. Sonar, laser, optics, or a combination of all three. They'd feed the information to the computer brain so it could react. Ideally, as one researcher pointed out, you'd have a bionic-type system that works the way a barn owl goes after its prey."

"An owl? How about a shark or a killer whale?"

"Sharks and killer whales are quite sophisticated killing systems, but the owl has them beat by a mile. It can detect a wider spectrum of sound. Even in flight it triangulates its prey and adjusts as the situation changes. The mouse makes a run for it; the owl recalculates automatically in a continuing series of yes-no decisions. All in a split second. It swoops down, the talons extend, mouth opens, and *poof*, no more mouse."

"Is there anything like that around?"

"Not that I know of. But it wouldn't be hard to duplicate. Here, I'll give you a demonstration. Turn your head away from me."

I did as I was told. A second later he clapped his hands a few inches from my ear. My head jerked around.

Ivers was beaming. "There you go. When I clapped, your head turned and your eye focused on the sound. All without using that vast amount of information stored in your brain. You didn't need intelligence to respond. You could build an AUV the same way so the decision-making is quite as simple. The technology has expanded at an incredible rate. A practical application of AUV technology would be scientific, but as in many things, the primary driver behind the research is military."

"For instance?"

"The Swedish navy has been heavily involved with ROVs for inspection and recovery of lost torpedoes at depths where divers can't go. They've also used ROVs in mine hunting. They've seen the limitations of the tethered vehicle at first hand, so they're heavily invested in developing an untethered machine for military use. There's been a great push on the technology of AUVs. A number of private companies have been working on research in this and other countries, and right here in Woods Hole, of course."

"Would Neptune Technologies be one of them?"

"Oh sure. That was pretty much of an open secret. Drake was heavily funded by DARPA. That stands for the Defense Advanced Research Projects Agency. An improved AUV would be quite a prize for the navy, I would think."

"For use in the mine warfare we were talking about."

"Precisely. You could program the vehicle to neutralize mines. It could cut them loose so they floated to the surface for destruction. Or it could plant an explosive charge and blow up a mine or anything else, for that matter. By eliminating the tether, and the surface craft at the other end, the military possibilities are endless."

"Could you give me an example, Dr. Ivers?"

"Sure. You could use an AUV in submarine warfare. Perhaps packs of them, with each submersible performing a different function. The submarine could send out AUVs to scout for other subs and report back on their location. Theoretically, we're talking about a range of hundreds or thousands of miles. You could send a vehicle across an entire ocean on a mission. Yes, it's very doable."

"By Drake?"

"If anyone could do it, it would have been Drake. Sad in a way, that loss of brainpower. Well, here we are."

We shook hands in the lobby. "Thanks very much for your time, Dr. Ivers."

"My pleasure. I'm not sure anything I told you this afternoon will help you find a missing person, but good luck with your case."

Somebody hailed me as I came out the front door onto Water Street. "Hey, Mr. Detective. How are you doing?"

Dan Whipple was crossing the street in my direction. He walked with a jaunty step and he had a wide grin on his face. His car, a black turbo Saab, was parked outside the bar.

We shook hands like the old drinking buddies we were. "I'm doing just fine, Mr. Scientist. How about you?"

"Just great. Things are perking along at the lab."

"Glad to hear that," I said.

Whipple glanced over my shoulder at the Bigelow building. "Looking for a job in oceanography?"

"No. I just had an informative chat with a guy named Ivers. You must know him."

Whipple hesitated, then said, "Oh, Ivers. Sure, he's a big gun with WHOI. Did he tell you what a great guy Tom Drake was?"

"Not exactly."

"I'd be surprised if he did. He hated Drake. Once threatened to destroy him. Ivers had him thrown out of WHOI, but it pissed him off that Drake went on to become successful without the Oceanographic's backing."

"We were talking about ROVs."

Whipple looked nervous. "I don't get it. I thought you were trying to track down Leslie."

"That's right, I am. But in this business you spend a lot of time plucking at threads. Sometimes they break off or lead you down blind alleys. Sometimes things unravel. It's probably like your scientific research in a way."

"I suppose so. Look," he said, "it was great seeing you. I've got to run. Busy at the lab and all that."

He strode across the street, got into his car, and drove off. It was a strangely truncated conversation, and an even stranger parting. But Whipple was a very strange man. I walked across the street and stepped into the bar for a beer. Someone waved at me from a table. It was one of the fishermen I had talked to on the pier the first time I tried to find Skip Mallowes. I went over to say hello and he offered me a chair. I got a beer from the bar and sat down.

"Ever catch up with Skip?" the fisherman asked.

"Yeah. Thanks. I went out diving with him, in fact. I guess that's what he mostly does, huh? He can't do much fishing. His boat was clean as a whistle."

"I know what you mean. My tub looks like a rustbucket and smells like a sardine canning factory. Skip had other things going besides fishing, though."

I sat down. "You mean the diving?"

"That too. But I think he was working with that scientist fellow, the who who got killed this week."

"Dr. Drake?"

"Yep. That's the one."

"What sort of work?"

"Dunno. I know they did a lot of diving together. Coupla times while I was at the pier I saw them hoisting around some heavy equipment. Figured they were doing some scientific stuff."

"Any idea what it was?"

"Nope. When you live around here awhile, you get used to boats going in and out all the time to do jobs like test water temperature or count codfish eggs. Whadja think of Mallowes?"

"I think he's a lot brighter than people give him credit to be."

"Ha. Me too. I've known Skip since he was a kid. The Mallowes family goes back a long way, and some people say the brains started to run out by the time Skip was born. But he's not simple. He's got more smarts than most of the people in this bar. 'Cept you and me, of course." He looked at his watch and said, "Got to go. Promised the wife I'd get home early."

I stayed and sipped my beer. I was getting to like the

bar. For all its gloominess, it was a friendly oasis where I could escape the passions that seemed to stick like the fog to everyone who knew Tom Drake. I would have loved to have another beer, but there was work to do. I downed the contents of my mug and went outside. There was a parking ticket on my truck windshield.

Chloe was getting out of her red Supra as I pulled up in front of the Seaside guest house. She waved and came over to give me a hug.

"Guess where I've been," she said excitedly.

"You don't have an armful of bags, so I guess you weren't shopping."

"I *started* to go shopping, but you can't imagine who I ran into in Falmouth."

"I give up. Jackie Kennedy?"

"No. Better than that. I saw Cousin Maria. She and her family are down at their summer house in Mashpee. They want us to come over to dinner."

"God, Chloe, I hate to refuse the second night in a row. But I'm going to be working on my case."

Chloe squeezed my elbow. "Hmm," she said. "Are you sure you won't be working on a blonde?"

I thought of Jane's long raven hair. "Yes, Chloe," I told her. "I'm very sure."

CHAPTER 13

•

Jane was wearing another black dress. She had tied a red belt around her slim waist and a red scarf in her dark curly tresses. She looked smashing. We drove the Cherokee to a seafood restaurant overlooking the habor in Falmouth. She ordered sole. It was tender and not overcooked. My mussels were fresh and came in a bowl the size of a washtub. I splurged on a bottle of Chardonnay wine that was worth the week's pay I spent on it.

"Tom and I came here last year," she said, looking around the uncrowded dining room. "It's changed. The food is much better tonight."

"Did you and Tom meet on Cape Cod?"

Jane picked up her wineglass, then put it back on the table without drinking from it.

"Perhaps I shouldn't have asked," I said. "I'd understand if you'd rather not talk about it."

"I don't mind, really. It helps in a way, rehashing aspects of my life." She collected her thoughts, then continued. "We met at an art-gallery opening. It was for another artist, a woman Tom was seeing. I was attracted

139

to him from the start. He was a very handsome and charming man. He broke off with the other woman and courted me in a most respectable fashion."

"That courtliness would seem to go against his popular image."

Her finger touched the rim of her glass. I noticed she still wore her wedding band. "Oh, I know, Tom's behavior antagonized many people. He had a terrible temper and he could be ruthless in his business dealings. But he knew his women, knew I wanted to go slow because I was on the bounce from another relationship. For all his bluster, Tom was unusually sensitive. He seemed to have an intuitive sense of your innermost fears and desires."

"That's a side of him I hadn't heard," I said.

"It's true, though." There was an acolyte's wonderment in her voice. "He could reach down deep inside you, to know what your thoughts were before you did, to anticipate them, to be ready with the right response. At the same time . . ." She paused, a distant look in her eyes. She was leaving me.

"More wine?" I said, picking up the bottle.

The faraway expression disappeared. "No thanks, I've had enough."

"You were saying about Tom. . . ."

"Only that he had a childlike insecurity. I think he was afraid of becoming too close to people. Afraid he'd lose them. So he would change partners before that happened."

"Skip Mallowes seemed to think that Leslie Walther set her cap for Tom."

"It's possible, I suppose, although Skip would say that. He's been like a big brother to me when I needed him. I don't know if he is right about Leslie. She was a beautiful girl, and Tom worked many late hours with her at the lab, probably more time than he spent with me. One thing simply led to another. When I learned of their affair, I gave Tom an ultimatum. He said he cared for me, that he would stop seeing Leslie." She gave a bittersweet laugh. "He didn't, of course. I left the big house on the

Point and rented the studio on the beach. I've been there ever since." A tear glistened in her eye.

"I'm sorry things worked out the way they did."

Our dessert came. Jane played with the chocolate mousse, drawing whirly lines with her spoon. "It's much neater this way, when you think of it. Much more so than if he had remarried and I had to see my replacement in the supermarket. Maybe even kids by that time. Tom's gone. Period. End of story."

"Not quite the end. The person who murdered him is still out there."

She dropped her spoon as if the metal had become red-hot. "Murder. It's such an ugly word, something you read about in the papers that always happens to other people. It still seems so unbelievable to me. Do the police have any ideas yet on who may have done it?"

"No, I'm afraid not. It could be a complex case." I was thinking of Flagg's warnings and the shots fired in my direction at Drake's house.

"I'm not surprised to hear that. Many people are probably happy to see him dead. I could have been one of them. I hated Tom that much for a while." She gazed out the window at the lights reflecting on the water, then reached across the table and touched my hand. "Can we go?" she said.

I signaled for the bill, and minutes later we were driving along the shore road. "Where to?" I said.

"Back to the studio. Come in for a drink." She tugged playfully at my sleeve. "This time I won't take no for an answer."

I parked the Jeep behind the cottage and we went inside. Rembrandt was asleep in a corner. He looked up and, when he saw we weren't burglars, put his head between his paws again. Some watchdog. Jane made two tall gin and tonics. She lit an old kerosene lantern and a couple of fragrant bayberry candles. She turned the lights off and we sat at the kitchen table, almost side by side. There was a large painting, about six by four feet, hanging on one of the walls. Shadows cast by the flickering flames danced on the canvas and the colors and shapes seemed to move with life.

Jane saw me looking at the painting. "What do you think?" she said.

"It reminds me of a Turner."

"You know Turner. Are you interested in art?"

"I guess I'm like a lot of people. I like the Impressionists, Cézanne and Monet. Renoir gives me a lift because his paintings are so full of his love of life. The Cubists have always intrigued me. I can take or leave Picasso. Pollock and Motherwell are okay, I guess, but to be honest, the throw-paint-at-the-canvas school of art just makes me dizzy."

"You constantly surprise me. A private detective who quotes Sophocles in one breath, discourses on impressionism and cubism in the next."

"Just be glad I didn't launch into a diatribe on the minimalist movement."

She smiled and slowly undid the red scarf, tossing her head back so her black curls tumbled carelessly onto her shoulders. I caught myself dwelling on the alabaster whiteness of her skin, wondering how in God's name Drake could have thrown her over, even for a woman as lovely as Leslie Walther.

"How do you feel about Gauguin or van Gogh?" she said.

"Both in a class by themselves," I said. "There's a painting at the Museum of Fine Arts in Boston I've always liked. It's painted on—" Jane pressed her knee against mine. An electrical tingle momentarily shortcircuited the connection between my brain and my tongue. "I think it's painted on burlap."

She was looking at me, expectantly, her features soft in the candlelight, that almost smile playing around her lips.

"I know the one," she said, her voice velvety now. "You're right, it is on burlap. Gauguin didn't have the money to buy canvas."

She was leaning forward with both arms resting on the table. I put my hand on her forearm and brushed her warm skin lightly with my fingertips. Her half smile broke into a full one. I moved my hand up her arm and around her shoulder and played with the loose strands of hair. She closed her eyes and lifted her chin slightly. I brushed her hair with my hand. Her lips parted. I moved closer and kissed her neck, inhaling the delicate scent of her perfume. She trembled. I kissed her ear. She shivered. I kissed her mouth. She pressed back, harder. I stood, pulling her up to me, and kissed her again, a long lingering kiss. She ran her hand down my back as far as it would go.

Gently, I took her by the arm and we climbed the stairs to the studio.

Through the open windows came the mournful moan of the Nobska Point foghorn. Jane pulled back the India-print cover on the sofa bed and stood beside it. I undressed her, slowly, deliberately, with no sense of urgency, then she helped me out of my clothes. We clung to one another a moment, reveling in the mutual warmth of our bodies, before we slipped between the cool sheets. We made love in the little room, with its smell of oil paint and varnish and old wood, and the damp sea breeze rustling the white muslin curtains. We made love tenderly, with a growing surety, as if we had known each other a lifetime. And after a while we made love again.

It was just after 3:00 A.M. when something awakened me. I lay on my back, listening intently. The night was still. Only the lonely lament of the foghorn and the faint whisper of waves washing against the shore. I looked over at Jane. She lay close beside me, her nudity emphasized by the sheet carelessly draped across well-formed breasts that rose and fell with each peaceful breath. One bare thigh was exposed. I covered it with a corner of the sheet, then eased out of bed, reluctant to forsake the heat of her body. Jane stirred in her slumber and reached around a pillow, clinging to it desperately as if she were sinking. She sobbed and called out a name that I didn't recognize but somehow knew wasn't mine, then went back to sleep.

I moved quietly to the window and peered out at the gray wall of fog. After a few seconds my olfactory nerves twitched and I knew what had awakened me. The scent of tobacco, mingling with the salty fragrances of the sea.

Pulling on my slacks and shirt, I padded down the stairs. Rembrandt was curled up on an old braided rug. He lifted his head, gave me a bored yawn, and closed his eyes again. The candles had burned themselves out. The kerosene lantern was still alive, so I ducked down and crawled across the floor, trying to recall the topography of the land around the cottage as I had seen it in daylight.

One path ran from the front door through the tall compass grass, gradually descending to the beach where I found the crushed horseshoe crab. Another led from the back of the studio, where the pickup and Jeep were parked, and followed the contours of the sand dunes for about a hundred feet, curving behind the low hillock where I had found the Gauloise butts. I took the back way, opening the door just wide enough to slip through. The hinges squeaked, not too loudly I hoped, and I stepped out into the night.

The sand was freezing under my bare feet. Even the most careful step made a grainy scrunch that sounded in my wired imagination as if I were walking on strawberry boxes. I took my time, crouching low, feeling the path with my toes more than seeing it, hoping the onshore breeze would muffle my steps.

Under the combined cloak of fog and darkness, visibility could be counted in inches. I circled behind the smoker's hillock, relying almost purely on instinct to compute distance and direction. When I thought I was nearing my target, I dropped to my hands and knees and crawled, following the bare patches, trying to avoid clumps of brittle beach grass and ground-hugging clusters of poison ivy.

The grass rustled with the faint scurrying sounds made by field mice, rabbits, and snakes.

My strategy was simple. Creep to the hillock like a python. Spring on the watcher like a panther. And pummel him to the ground like a bear. If there was more than one watcher, I would simply conjure up a new menagerie. It wasn't a great plan and rested on a shaky foundation of assumptions and probabilities, but it was all I had and would have to do.

The ground began to slope upward. I calculated I was within a few yards of the hillock. I half stood, coiling my body in readiness for a catapulting leap. I was fixated directly ahead. But that's not where the action was. From behind me came the crumpling snap of grass. This was no bunny rabbit. I turned. A shadow detached itself from the pale outline of a beach-plum bush. Something fanned the air like the spring in a trap. My left arm jerked up in a protective reflex. The bony edge of my wrist blocked the soft flesh of a moving arm. There was a grunt of pain. Metal glanced off my head. The blow hurt, but didn't knock me out as intended. I didn't like knowing my assailant was armed, but at least I knew whatever he had, it wasn't a gun, or he would have shot at me instead. It was a small comfort. If he did connect, he'd spill my brains out onto the beach.

A hand grabbed at my shirt, trying to line me up for another shot. I twisted away, crouched and spun to the right like a cossack dancer, slicing the air with my right hand in a low flat karate chop. The edge of my hand knifed into a muscular gut. It must have hurt him because his advance stopped, but only for a second. His hand groped for me again. I tried to scramble out of reach. My feet were mired in the soft yielding sand and I only took a few steps before I stumbled and fell onto my knees.

There was scuttling movement in the foggy darkness. Hard breathing. He was coming for me again. The skin prickled on the back of my unprotected scalp. Leaning forward onto my knuckles, I lowered my head bronco style, and put the full force of my body into a hard thrusting kick with my right leg. He dodged the full force of the kick, but it knocked him off balance and he fell. I dug my toes in, trying to get some space between us so I could turn and face him head-on before he recovered and came for me again. It was a forlorn hope. This guy moved like a cat! He was up in an instant and on my heels, coming for me again.

I scrambled and fell again, clawing frantically at the clumps of grass, trying desperately to pull myself out of the way of the down-swinging blackjack that could crush my skull like tissue paper. Hoarse panting behind me again. I waited for my head to explode.

"Soc!" Someone was calling my name.

The outside light had just flicked on at the cottage. Jane stood on the front step. She was wrapped in her sheet and was looking into the night.

"Soc," she called again, "where are you?"

Something hard cracked me behind the knee. Burning pain shot up to my thigh and down to my toes. I went crashing down onto my hands and knees. I rolled over and glimpsed a dark figure disappear over the crest of the dunes. I tried to get up. My leg was on fire and wouldn't take the weight. Wincing with pain, I sank onto one knee like an anxious suitor proposing marriage.

"Over here," I yelled. I tried to stand. Again I sank down.

Jane was by my side in seconds. "What happened? What are you doing out here?" She was frantic.

I was in no shape to answer questions. "I'll explain in a bit," I said when I had caught my breath. "Just give me a hand."

Using Jane's shoulder as a crutch, I hobbled back to the cottage and sat in a kitchen chair. Jane wrapped some ice cubes in a towel. I draped the wet dripping ice pack on my head, then moved it to my leg. While the cold numbed my knee I swallowed a shot of gin, neat, to numb

my brain. After a few minutes the improvised ice pack
began to work.

Jane poured me another shot of gin.

"Someone was watching the house," I said, nursing my
drink. "I went to check him out. He didn't want to be
checked. We had an argument. He clubbed me on the
leg and then took off so I couldn't get in the last word."

Jane wore a mask of worry. "Did you see who it was?"

I shook my head. "We didn't introduce ourselves and I
didn't get a look at his face in the dark. I think he had a
cap pulled down over his head."

She sat into a chair next to mine and put her arm
around me. "This is awful. You could have been killed."

"Thanks for coming out when you did. Tell me, do you
have any jealous boyfriends? Secret admirers? Real-estate
agents who like to look at beachfront property in the dead
of the night?"

"No, nothing like that. I just don't know. . . ."

Jane's reply had trailed off; there wasn't the kind of
emphasis you might expect on the last word. It was only
a little thing, but it was a thing. I scanned her face for
some clue and saw only the nervous fear in her eyes.

I tugged at a corner of her sheet. "You look like you're
going to a toga party," I said.

She pulled the folds closer around her body. "I woke
up and you weren't there. I panicked. I just grabbed the
sheet and went downstairs. I couldn't imagine—"

"C'mon," I said. "Help me up those stairs so I can get
off this leg. And bring the gin."

It was a slow climb to the studio and I was glad when
we reached the top. We undressed and slipped back into
bed. I lay on my back with a pillow under my aching leg.
Jane's skin gave off heat like a radiator. I dozed off a few
times. In between, I looked over at Jane. Her breathing
was steady and deep, but I sensed that she too was awake.
Before long, the dusty yellow-gray light of dawn filtered
in through the window. The gulls on the beach got into
one of their eternal squawling food brawls. Any attempt

to sleep was futile. We got sleepily out of bed and went downstairs.

Over a cup of coffee, I said, "I may have scared the prowler off last night but it might only be temporary. If you have someplace to move to, maybe you should consider it."

Jane was adamant. "That's out of the question. This is my home. This is where my work is."

"Okay," I said. "But keep your door locked, even in the daytime, and call me or the police if you see or hear *anything* out of the ordinary."

Jane wrapped her arms around me and kissed me lightly on the neck. "I promise," she said.

After finishing my coffee I limped out of the house and retraced my course of the night before, following the path to the hillock. The fog had retreated offshore and the sun was burning a hole in the overcast. Two more Gauloise butts gleamed in the sand. Around the rise were mute signs of struggle. Clumps of beach grass had been torn up. The vegetation was matted down where my bronco kick had sent the watcher flying into a big patch of ground cover. I moved closer and examined the broken stems of the shiny, three-leaved poison-ivy plants, and despite the throbbing pain in my leg, I began to laugh. I wondered if the Gauloise-smoking watcher had any calamine lotion, because he was going to need it.

From Jane's cottage I drove back to the guest house. My leg was as stiff as an overstarched shirt. I filled the claw-footed bathtub with steaming-hot water and soaked my body until the skin puckered. The bath helped soothe the pain in my knee. The leg still hurt, but it was workable as long as I didn't try running the Boston Marathon. As the heat seeped into my body I brooded. Who was the watcher who smoked French cigarettes and carried a cosh? Drake's killer? The same guy who shot at me? The incidents had one thing in common. Both times I had surprised somebody and in each instance the reaction was violent and nearly deadly.

Jane should not be living on the beach alone. It was impossible for me to protect her every minute, but I knew somebody who could. I got out of the tub, toweled myself dry, and dressed. I went downstairs to the pay phone and fished a piece of paper with a number on it from my wallet. Then I called Flagg.

CHAPTER 14

•

The blue Ford LTD crawled slowly along the shore road and up the hill toward Nobska Light. It was the first car I had seen in ten minutes. Flagg had suggested meeting at the lighthouse on Nobska Point. Security again. I was sitting on the concrete apron that encircles the base of the white-painted lighthouse, my back against the cold cast iron. The car turned into the small parking lot bordering the road and parked next to my pickup truck. Flagg got out and climbed the grassy slope to the lighthouse. He had taken his suit jacket off and replaced it with a navy-blue windbreaker, trying to be informal. It didn't work. His tie looked as if it had been knotted by a midshipman and the high-gloss spit shine on his plain black shoes reflected the sun like Chinese lacquer.

"Nice day," I said cheerfully. "Great view of the Vineyard from here."

Flagg squinted beatifically across the sound. A thick tentacle of fog was snaking its way in between Martha's Vineyard and the tip of Penzance Point off Woods Hole, but otherwise visibility was exceptionally good. He nodded. "Uh-huh. Island looks close enough to touch."

We gazed out at the low brown-green bluffs. After a moment I said: "How's Annie? She still living in Gay Head?"

The sleepy expression vanished from Flagg's face.

"Yeah," he said. "She's still in the house on the Lobsterville Beach road. Doing okay, no thanks to you."

"Look, Flagg—"

"No, you look," he interrupted. "Whatever went down between you and me is our business. We'll settle it one way or the other or maybe not at all. But I still can't believe that you involved her in our little mess."

"Justaminute, Flagg. You know how I feel about Annie."

"Yeah, and I know how she felt about you. Annie fell for you in a big way, then you dropped her. That wasn't nice."

"I did it for Annie's benefit."

"Right, Soc. Your altruism is just awesome."

I lashed back. "I thought you and I were going to talk about working together," I said. "You know, like the Lone Ranger and Tonto."

He swept aside my insult. "I'll get to that."

I stood slowly, planting my feet in a John Wayne spread, and jabbed a finger at his broad chest. "You're being the protective big brother and it doesn't fit. You're not around enough to play that role. What went on between Annie and me is none of your business, Flagg."

"Hold on, Soc."

"No, *you* hold on. It's been a long time since I wrote 'Kill John Flagg' on my daily list of things to do, but I don't think either one of us wants to be brothers-in-law. So screw off."

Flagg opened his mouth to respond, and I braced myself for a barrage, but all he said was, "Huh." He broke off the confrontation and paced slowly around the base of the tapering forty-foot-tall tower, glancing up at the black lens housing. But he wasn't through with me yet.

"You make me sick, Socarides. You know why?"

"No, Flagg. You tell me why." What the hell. He was going to tell me in any case.

He poked at my chest so hard it hurt, but I didn't budge an inch. "You had it all. Money. Family. Education. Best of all, you were born with white skin. And you pissed everything down the drain so you can play private dick and fry your brain in gin mills."

I gave him a head-to-toe inspection. "Tell me, Flagg. When did you turn into an Anglo-Saxon?"

"What the hell are you talking about?"

"I remember when you used to be a Wampanoag."

"I'm *still* a Wampanoag, and don't you forget it."

I zeroed in on Flagg's pride. "Naw. You're just an apple. Red on the outside, white on the inside. Hell, you even *smell* like a white man. What is that stuff, English Leather?"

"Some kind of detective you are. It's Calvin Klein and it costs a lot of money."

"Christ, Flagg."

His dark eyes glittered with anger. "You don't know shit, Soc. Look at me. I'm part-Indian, part-black, and part-white. All mixed in. You know what that makes me. That makes me *nothing*. That makes me something you don't know anything about."

"Don't try to lay the poor downtrodden Indian crap on me, Flagg. I know all about being nothing. But that's not what I came here for. So let's talk or break out a picnic lunch."

We stopped arguing. Our voices had risen to shouts, and we were both embarrassed by it.

Flagg glared toward the Vineyard for a few seconds, clenching his teeth. The muscles were working in his jaw. When he had his temper under control, he said, "You're trying to locate Leslie Walther. There may be some overlap with my case. I'm not asking you to hold hands with me. Only that we call a truce, maybe share anything we come up with. Are you in?"

I stuck my hands in my pockets and perambulated around the lighthouse the way Flagg had done a few minutes earlier. The stiffness in my knee was a painful reminder of the scuffle outside Jane's cottage.

"I'm interested," I said, rejoining Flagg. "But it depends on whether you can do me a favor."

Flagg eyed me with suspicion. "What kind of favor?"

"No big deal. I'd like you to arrange to keep an eye on Jane Drake. I think she's in danger."

"Drake's wife? I don't get it. Who would want to hurt her?"

"Somebody has been watching her place on the beach. I went out to introduce myself to him last night and he tried to put a dent in my skull."

"You're not very popular, Soc. First the shooter, now this."

"It wasn't one of your guys, was it?"

"C'mon, Soc. Use your bean. We've got no reason to do anything like that." He pondered, then shrugged his fullback's shoulders. "Okay, I'll have someone start watching her house tonight. Is that all you want?"

I reclaimed my seat on the base of Nobska Light. "That's it. Now tell me what this is all about."

Flagg sat down next to me and said, "You read the papers, Soc?"

"Sure. The sports page. Sox are doing lousy."

"Figures with the pitching they've got. But the stuff I'm going to tell you about wasn't on the sports pages. You remember what a mess things got to with some mines in the Persian Gulf a while ago?"

"Yeah. The Iranians planted mines and we found to our amazement that a little guy can go up against a big guy and score hard points without too much trouble. That's nothing new. We learned the same thing in Vietnam, but the lesson didn't sink in. It never does."

"You got it. Some of those mines were designed in 1908, but they still caused us big headaches. We found out that this country was still back in Civil War days when it came to mine warfare. Old ships, not enough of them, outmoded equipment that would never be able to deal with some of the new mine designs. We got maybe sixty oceangoing minesweepers. They were built about 1950 after the North Koreans mined Wŏnson Harbor. The navy brought a half dozen of these old Korean War ships into the Persian Gulf. They had to be towed to the gulf because the navy was afraid they'd blow their diesel engines if they traveled on their own power. The Pentagon got worried. The navy decided to spend some bucks."

"I'll really sleep a lot better knowing that my tax dollars will prevent Iran from invading Cape Cod."

"You ought to. The new mines can sense the pressure wave a hull makes going through water, so you've got to go after them one at a time. Iran is a raggedy-ass little country. Say somebody with real mines disrupts our shipping. Things escalate. No one wants that, so there's going to be a new fleet of mine-hunting ships."

"Drake was involved in antimine research. That's no big secret."

"You got it. He was on the cutting edge."

"How far did he cut?"

"About as far as he could."

Flagg was annoying me, dropping bits of information for their dramatic effect. "I bet you're going to tell me he developed an Autonomous Untethered Vehicle. An AUV."

Flagg stared at me. He didn't look happy.

"I put two and two together, Flagg. It wasn't very hard."

"I never said you were stupid, Soc. Crazy, maybe, but not stupid. Now you know why I didn't want you poking into this case. You got a big nose, and you know how to use it. Yeah, Drake was working on an AUV. He was leading the pack on research. The Navy's mine countermeasure force, what they call MCM, has been a near-total screw-up. Helicopters and planes are doing fine, but their ship program was a joke. After thirty years of twiddling their thumbs they came out with two ships, the *Avenger* and an air-cushion vessel called the *Cardinal*. They scrapped the *Cardinal* in '86 over design problems and decided to have a mine hunter built in Italy, but that went down the drain. Even Congress had the brains to see it didn't make sense. Navy decided to make a big push on mine countermeasure ships and mine hunters."

"I'm glad to see things are as efficient as they were when I was in government service."

Flagg took an envelope from his jacket pocket. He opened it and pulled out a black-and-white photograph. "The new ships will use hull-mounted sonar to find the mines, then they'll send down this thing to neutralize them."

I studied the picture. "It looks like one of those Japanese minisubs they used at Pearl Harbor, only with a couple of hedge clippers on the front end. What is it?"

"It's called the SLQ-48 Mine Neutralization System. Thing is more than twelve feet long and weighs over a ton. It's got television cameras and sonar on board to find the mine and take a close look at it."

"You're talking about an ROV, something on the end of a tether."

"That's right. When the ship detects a mine, they send this gadget down. It cuts the mine moorings or leaves a little package of explosives to blow them up. Each unit costs around four million dollars."

"Where did Drake's project fit in?"

"He came up with something so much better, the Navy started licking its chops." He tapped the photo with his finger and stuck it back in the envelope. "It made this thing look like a Model T. He called it the Neptune. His machine was far in advance of anything being used now. It was compact, fast, and smart. You could program it to go off on its own to neutralize mines, and when the job was done it would come back to you, just like a puppy fetching a stick."

"So when Drake is killed, and his puppy disappears, you guys, seeing conspiracy everywhere, figure it's a plot."

"Something like that, Soc. Remember, you're the one got shot at the other night."

"I haven't forgotten," I said. "Drake was smart, but he couldn't have been that vital to the work. There were others involved. Navy types, people in his own lab. Couldn't they carry on without him?"

"The work has already resumed."

"So what's the big deal?"

"Drake had built a prototype of his equipment. The prototype is missing. All we have are plans and diagrams."

"You checked the lab?"

"We swarmed over it the night he was killed and hauled out everything that wasn't nailed down."

"I heard there's a Russian research vessel coming into Woods Hole in a few days. You'd better keep an eye on that."

I meant it as a joke, but Flagg looked dead serious. "We plan to. That's why I happened to be in Falmouth when Drake was killed. The Russians have got a stockpile of four hundred thousand mines. You know what we got? We got a few mine countermeasure ships, and choppers, and a bunch of fishing boats we can press into service if we need them. We think the ship's arrival, Drake's death, and the missing prototype are just too convenient."

I shook my head wearily. "The Red Scare's not what it used to be, pal."

"Maybe not," he rejoined. "And if you talked to me off duty, I'd probably say it's just another dumb scheme of the military-industrial complex desperately trying to keep its act together. So maybe we don't have to worry about the russkies, but we've still got plenty of enemies, and even a little country or a bunch of hard-assed terrorists can use something like this to make big trouble. Some Middle East nut could sit in a tent and send this baby out against an aircraft carrier. The IRA could use this gadget to ruin Queen Elizabeth's yachting party. Colombian drug kings could send it against a cruiser while there's a summit meeting going on. All sorts of ways to stir up a fuss. The fact is, somebody took Drake's antimine vehicle, and it's my job to find it."

"Okay, Flagg, what's this thing look like? In case I trip over it. Do you have a picture?"

"Yeah, but I can't let you see it."

"I know," I said. "Security."

He nodded. "You can't miss it. It's about eight feet long by six wide. It looks like an overgrown ROV with a big round thing in the middle."

"It sounds like a commercial washing machine. What's the round thing do? Is that where you put the soap in?"

"It's the eye of the vehicle."

I remembered Ivers's ROV. "A video camera?"

"Much more sophisticated. It sees, but not like any eye we're used to. It's a system of electronic sensors and lasers. The sensors tell the AUV where it is, where it's headed, what's in front of it. Direction. Water temperature. Depth. Obstructions. Whatever. The info goes into a computer. The computer analyzes the input and tells the vehicle what to do so it won't go around chasing schools of fish or dropping explosives under the mother ship. Drake was a genius. He put together a linkage system that's smarter and smaller than anyone before him has been able to do. The only thing better is a dolphin's brain."

"A machine as big as the one you've described wouldn't be easy to hide."

"You wouldn't think so, would you? The thing must weigh half a ton. But I can't find it. Think you can?"

It was a challenge. I picked up the symbolic glove Flagg had thrown down. "Maybe." I thought for a moment. "You talked to Skip Mallowes. He was quite close to Drake. Was he of any help?"

"Nope. He said he just knew Drake from dive trips."

I recalled what the fisherman in the bar had said about

Drake and Skip jockeying equipment around at night. "Do you believe him?"

"No reason not to for now. But we searched his house and boat just to be sure and didn't find a thing."

"What do you think of Drake's assistant, Dan Whipple, as a suspect?"

Flagg made a face. "I talked to that guy. I think he probably drinks too much. Doesn't seem like he'd have the balls to stick a knife in Drake, even drunk. You gotta get real close to the other guy when you do something like that."

"Yeah, but he's got all kinds of motives." I began to tick them off. "He hated Drake because of the way he treated Jane and others, including himself. Drake threatened to ruin him in some way. Whipple would gain monetarily from Drake's death. That takes care of motive; now method. He has the access to the lab. He lures Drake, kills him, spirits the equipment off. Maybe he plans to find it later. His drunk stuff could be an act to throw people off. His alibi isn't especially strong." I looked over at Flagg. "Think my theory will fly?"

He shrugged. "It might get an inch or two off the ground."

"Whipple was real nervous the last time I saw him. Something else just occurred to me. I'll dig around and let you know."

"You do that," Flagg said. "Leave a message at my number anytime. I've got a car phone. They'll patch you through to me fast."

"Okay, Flagg," I said. "I'll keep in touch. That's the most I can promise."

Flagg had drifted off. He was staring out across the water with that heavy-lidded look of his. After a minute he said: "I think this thing has the smell of death."

"What planet did you just arrive from, Flagg? We've got one dead scientist on our hands, and you almost had a dead private cop. That guy out at Drake's place wasn't shooting blanks. And I nearly had my head busted open at Jane Drake's house."

"No, there's something else. I can't put my finger on it." He turned to me. "Look, there's a haunted stream on the Vineyard called Black Brook. Supposedly someone was murdered there years ago and his spirit never left. One day when I was a kid I was passing the brook alone. It was late afternoon and foggy. I was real cocky at first, but the closer I got, the more nervous I got. I tried to bluff it. Walk by at my normal pace. Damned if I was going to run. Then the chills started going up and down my spine. I had the feeling something was waiting in the bushes for me. I thought I heard a noise, took a quick look behind me, and ran like a jackrabbit until I got home. Man, my house never looked so good."

"What did you see?"

"Nothing, Soc. But I could *feel* something. I could *smell* it. Just like I'm doing now. That's what this is like."

He blinked his way out of his trance, which was fine, because it was giving me the creeps. He said, "You were right, calling me an apple."

"Forget it, I was busting your butt for what you said about Annie."

"Naw. I've been losing touch. Maybe the Calvin Klein fumes have gone to my head. I've been thinking like a white man."

"What do you mean?"

"White man goes after a deer. He carries a cannon and goes crashing through the woods. Sometimes he gets a deer, most often not. The Indian way of hunting before we got corrupted, was to listen to the wind. Put yourself in touch with nature. We've lost that. Now we go into the woods carrying a cannon too."

"What's that got to do with Drake?"

"In your way of thinking, Drake is killed. His machine is missing. Therefore he was killed for his machine."

"Logical. It's called a syllogism. All men are mortal. Socrates is a man. Therefore Socrates is a mortal."

"Yeh. But you see the problem. That kind of thinking puts your head in a bucket. It doesn't let your thoughts wander or make outside connections. We set that scenario up and now we're trying to come up with evidence that will support it. Maybe there's something that we're missing. What about the shooting out at Drake's place?" he said doubtfully. "Was that Whipple too?"

"I know what you're saying. That would make Danny Boy a busy fellow."

"Uh-huh."

We got up and started back to our vehicles. "I don't have any answers on that score. If you hear a lead on the wind, pass it along."

"You'll be the first to know," Flagg said.

I drove back to Woods Hole, looked up Whipple's address in the phone book, and found his house down a side road. It was a new captain's house near Quisset Harbor. Big for just one guy. Whipple must have been doing well, or maybe he was just heavily in hock to the bank for his house and car.

Sergeant Gallagher had said Whipple went to the movies and a liquor store the night Drake died. Twenty minutes later I was talking to the guy who ran the liquor store where Whipple had stopped. I showed him my private investigator's license and said I had been hired by Whipple's lawyer. He said Whipple was a regular customer. He bought gin, good stuff, but it was still rotgut. He remembered Whipple coming in that night, just as the cops said. Whipple had asked him the time. Said he didn't have his watch.

The next stop was the movie theater. I gave the manager the same story I had told the liquor man. "We'd like to assure Mr. Whipple that he has no problem," I said. "That he can prove he was in the theater for the whole movie. That he couldn't have left the movie house without being seen."

"That's right," the manager said. He didn't sound convinced himself.

"Of course, when I was a kid"—I laughed—"there was always some way to sneak around a movie theater."

"Yeah," said the manager. "If someone came out and went to the men's room, say, he could wait till the popcorn girl bends down or looks the other way, and sneak right out."

Sharon Prescott had told me Whipple and Drake argued. That Drake threatened to destroy Whipple's reputation if he tried to quit. Drake apparently had something on Whipple. I had an idea what it was. From the movie theater I rode around until I found a pay phone and called Dr. Ivers.

"I know you're probably busy," I said when Ivers came on the line, "but I've got one question. When we first talked about industrial espionage, you said there was a spy in your organization passing on information to Drake and fouling up your project."

"Yes, that was our belief in spite of his denials."

"You mentioned evidence."

"The best kind. Shortly after we fired him, he went to work for Tom Drake."

"What was his name?"

He hesitated. "I suppose there's no harm in telling you. He would deny it if you ever accused him. His name was Whipple. Dan Whipple."

A minute later I was dialing Neptune Technologies Inc. I asked for Whipple and didn't have to wait long. He came on the phone immediately.

"I'm glad you called, Mr. Socarides. I've been thinking about our brief chat outside the Bigelow lab the other day. Sorry I ran off on you like that."

"No problem, you must have a lot on your mind at the lab with Drake gone."

"You're very understanding. But by way of apology, I'd like to give you a demonstration of an advanced ROV model, since you're interested in remote submersibles. I'll be at the Neptune lab tonight until nine o'clock. Can you drop by?"

Why not? It was a good chance to get at Whipple. "Thanks very much for the offer," I said. "I'll be sure to be there."

After I hung up, I thought over what Flagg said about the thing in the bushes at Black Brook and the odor of death. I would never admit it to him, but I smelled it too.

CHAPTER 15

●

About an hour after sunset I parked outside the Neptune lab fence next to Whipple's Saab. The fog had returned with a vengeance. Even a few miles inland, the air was soggy and difficult to see through. The rent-a-cop had gone home or died from boredom. Whipple had left the gate unlocked, and the front door was unlatched as well. The lobby was dark except for the light cast by a small reading lamp on Sharon Prescott's desk. A faint trace of her perfume hung in the room.

I followed a lighted corridor off the lobby. The carpeted hallway passed through a section of offices and ended at a door marked "Testing and Research." The door opened into a room brightly illuminated by rows of fluorescent lights. Set into the concrete floor, and taking up about half the area of the room, was a pool approximately twenty feet by twenty. It looked very deep, but I couldn't really tell from up above. It definitely wasn't the type of pool you'd see outside a Holiday Inn. There was no diving board, and cables with heavy-duty metal hooks at their ends dangled from the high ceiling to within two feet of the water. Bridging the pool was a yard-wide walkway made of steel beams crossed at right angles by wooden slats. I strolled over to the pool and peered into the green water. On the bottom, glowing in the light cast by the round lights lining the pool wall, was a banana-colored blob.

As I watched, the blob stirred with life. It moved, slowly at first in fitful starts and stops, then suddenly darted forward in a yellow shimmer, skittered around the perimeter of the pool as quickly as a sand shark, and rocketed upward in my direction. I stepped back and started to look for the way out. The thing zoomed to within a foot of the surface, then dived in a swirl of bubbles and came to rest again on the bottom. Someone laughed, a humorless drunken laugh. I turned to see Whipple step through a portal that abutted a large darkened glass window. His mouth was distorted in a foolish grin.

"I was watching you from the control room. You looked as if you were going to jump out of your skin," he said. His voice was slurry and I would have bet a six-pack of Old Milwaukee that he'd had a martini or two since I talked to him. In his hands he cradled a black metal box similar to the one Ivers had shown me. His thumbs were on the joysticks.

I pointed into the pool. "Is that one of your doodlebugs?"

"That's right," he said. "She's *my* baby. I designed her. She's a big girl for her age. Four feet long, three feet high, and three hundred pounds. She'll travel at four knots. Has an articulator that can pick up a dime."

"If I had known you had a baby that cute, I would have brought a rubber ducky for her to play with. What's she doing in the pool?"

"She's undergoing reliability tests. We check all the commands, see how the mechanical arms work." He paused, and a sly look crossed his bleary features. "Ivers must have told you about all that procedure."

"He touched on it."

"I'd be surprised if he didn't. He's one smart guy. Knows too much for his own damn good." He frowned, then giggled. "Stay out here. I'll show you what this baby can do."

He stepped back into the control room. The glow of video screens and display panels was visible through the window. I looked at the yellow blob in the water and waited for something to happen, but it stayed where it was on the bottom of the pool. Maybe Whipple had passed out. I walked out into the bridge and crossed to the mid-point where I could have a better view.

Still no motion.

I sqautted and peered into the water waiting for the show to begin.

There was the sound of a footstep behind me. Assuming it was Whipple, I said, "Hey, how deep is this pool?"

The answer was quick in coming; somebody tried to hit a home run with my head. I had just readjusted my body into a kneeling position, so the bat or whatever it was bounced off my shoulders for a bunt instead of a base hit. I tumbled off the walkway and into the cold water. I must have gone down around six feet before I realized I was no longer breathing air. I did a submerged somersault that wouldn't have impressed Esther Williams in the least, kicked my way to the surface, and coughed a couple of gallons of water out of my lungs. The light had gone out in the test room. I probed the darkness, wondering where I could pull myself safely from the water. I decided to strike out for the edge of the pool and take my chances.

I had taken one stroke when the pool lights blinked out. The blackness was now total.

I treaded water a few moments, trying to decide what to do.

Once more I started to swim and once more I stopped.

Twin lights had snapped on in the water below me like a tiger blinking its eyes open. The lights began to prowl in lazy circles, spiraling higher with each circuit until they neared the surface. They caught me in their beam. The

ROV hovered a dozen feet away about a yard below the surface, examining me. I knew it was only a dumb machine, that the eye behind the Plexiglas was transmitting my image to a video screen in the control room, but I felt like a shipwrecked sailor who has just caught the hungry attention of a great white shark. It waited. I waited. I didn't have to wait long. There was an angry whirring of electric motors.

The damned thing was headed straight at me.

I grabbed a quick breath and kicked backward in a surface dive that took me down ten feet. The ROV whirred overhead, made a violent turn, and angled after me.

I dived deeper into the blackness. The machine followed. My hand touched the pool bottom and I spun around. The lights were right there in blindingly close proximity. The ROV zoomed toward my midsection. Its mechanical arm was extended like a spear and the claw was open.

A Lewis Carroll verse danced through my mind.

". . . *and shun the fumious Bandersnatch.*"

I shunned as best I could, but I wasn't quick enough. The claw caught my shirt. The sharp tip scratched my chest just below the left nipple. I jerked my body and the claw disengaged, ripping off a piece of fabric and a few square millimeters of skin.

I swam along the pool bottom. The pool was deep, probably around twenty feet. The vehicle turned and followed. It moved slowly and deliberately at first, then at the last second it accelerated and tried to nail me in a corner. I kicked off, using the bottom as a springboard, and shot toward the surface. There was a sharp metallic scrape as the claw struck the concrete wall.

Only time to grab a quick breath and slip my sneakers off. The ROV recovered from its collision with the wall like a prizefighter shaking off a hard punch. It headed for the surface. The glow from the headlights caught a straight metallic edge a couple of yards away and above me. The walkway. I flailed in that direction. The vehicle saw my move and cut me off before I could hoist myself out. I backstroked toward the side of the pool again. The ROV circled around to block my way, pivoted, and came straight for my groin. I dodged like a bullfighter. The machine spun quickly around and aimed for my head. I ducked. The sled rail caught me a dizzying blow just above the right ear.

The cat-and-mouse game was exhausting me and I knew it could have only one conclusion. I would get tired, the ROV wouldn't. It was coming in low again. I tried to dodge. The claw grabbed my pant leg, hung on, and dragged me down.

I quickly undid my belt and pushed my slacks off. If the damned thing wanted my pants that badly, it could have them. The ROV dropped its catch. The motors buzzed furiously. I looked up. I was nearly under the walkway. Just a few strokes and I could reach up and pull myself out, but the ROV was too fast. It saw my escape route and came at me. I made a sideways feint. As the vehicle sped past I grabbed onto its thick tether. It was like having a tiger by the tail. The ROV wheeled around and came at me.

I reached out of the water and clawed desperately for the edge of the catwalk. Missed. Fell back in.

The ROV gained speed. Another few feet and I'd be impaled on its spear. My stomach muscles tightened involuntarily. Then a shadow dangling above the pool caught my eye.

The machine was almost on me. I needed to buy a few seconds but I didn't have much cash.

I did have the tether, though. I jammed the black rubber cord into the oncoming outstretched claw and gave it a quick jerk and a few wraps around the arm. That's the trouble with an ROV, Ivers had said. It can get tangled up in its tether. The motion diverted the ROV slightly off course, giving me time to do a Statue of Liberty. I flung my arm up and gripped the smooth hard surface of a metal hook hanging from the ceiling. I grabbed on with the other hand and hauled myself out of the water, pulling my bare knees up toward my chest.

Not a moment too soon.

A split second later the claw sliced into the tether carrying electrical power. There was a crackle of white sparks and the hiss of steam. The ROV's lights blinked out.

I began to play Johnny Weissmuller, swinging like Tarzan on the cable, searching the darkness with my outstretched legs. My bare feet brushed something. The walkway. I tried again, got a good swing going, and let go. I hit the walkway surface hard, landing on my knees, and almost splashed back in the pool. But I hung on and caught my breath. Finally, I crawled off the walkway and stood, then felt my way along the walls until I found a switch. An instant later the test room was flooded with light.

I was alone. The knee that had been injured the night before outside Jane's cottage was killing me. I staggered over to the control room, which was still in darkness, stepped inside, and snapped on the light. Whipple lay facedown on the floor. Next to him was the ROV control box. And beyond that was a two-foot-length of lead pipe. Visions of Drake in the seal pool flashed through my brain. I thought Whipple was dead. I ran over, knelt beside him, and turned him over onto his back. There was no blood, but he had an angry welt across his forehead.

"Whipple," I shouted. "Can you hear me?"

He groaned.

I pillowed his head in my hands. His eyes fluttered open.

"What happened?" he said, his voice a croak.

I looked around the control room. A back door was wide open. Someone had exited in a hurry.

"Looks like you were slugged. Maybe with that hunk of pipe."

I helped him stand and guided him into a chair. His glasses lay on the floor. One lens was shattered. I picked up the frames and gave them to him.

"Did you see anyone?" I asked.

Whipple put his glasses on and looked at me through the good lens. "No," he said, talking with effort. "I was getting ready for a test. I heard somebody moving behind me, but I thought it was you. The next thing I know you're shaking me and I've got this splitting headache."

"Do you want to see a doctor?"

"No, I think I'll be fine." He noticed my dripping underwear. "What happened to your clothes?"

"Somebody pushed me into the testing pool. The ROV grabbed my pants, so I had to jettison them. I'm afraid your little baby is slightly damaged."

He shook his head. "Just as long as you're okay."

I examined a six-inch scratch over my ribs and tenderly felt my shoulders where I'd been whacked. "Yeah, I'll live. I'm going to get my stuff, though. Just sit here for a moment."

I went out to the test room and fished the cable out of the water. The claw had done a nice job of slicing the tether and shorting out its power source. I dived down and found my clothes. The ROV was on its side on the bottom. It looked sad, but I didn't feel sorry for it. When I came out I told Whipple in detail how I had put a stop to his rogue machine. He really groaned at that one, but said he would pick the pieces up in the morning.

We left the lab together. I helped him lock up and poured him into his car. He blinked his eyes from time to time, but he appeared able to drive. I got in my truck and headed back to the guest house. I went directly to my room and took a long hot shower, then put on some dry clothes. That took care of the external heating. I needed something for the internal. I was headed out to the bar for a double shot of Wild Turkey when the phone in the hall rang. "Mr. Socarides?" Sharon Prescott said. "I'm so glad I caught up with you. I've been trying to get you for the last hour or so."

"I was taking a bath," I said.

She wasn't listening. "I know this is awful to be calling

on short notice like this, but I remembered you saying, the time you came into the lab after Tom died, that if I ever needed anybody to talk to, you'd lend an ear."

"I meant it, Ms. Prescott."

"Please call me Sharon. I know this is an imposition, but could you come by tonight? I'd really appreciate it. I feel like talking to someone."

I looked at the hand holding the phone. It was trembling, either from hypothermia or delayed terror. I was not in shape for a rendezvous with a troubled and lovely lady. I should get a few pops somewhere, the stronger the better, then go to bed for twelve hours.

"I'll be right over," I said. I've never taken especially good care of my health; why start now?

She sighed with relief and gave me directions to her place. Sharon Prescott lived in a low-slung Cape Cod house a few miles out of Woods Hole on the road to Silver Beach. I parked behind the white BMW convertible in the drive and limped up the flagstone walk. Sharon had been keeping an eye out for me. The front door opened before I rang the bell and she stood there with a smile on her face. She was dressed in a loose-fitting white silk blouse and pleated slacks that were baggy in every place but the right ones.

"Hi," she said. "I saw your headlights through the window and thought I would greet you."

"I've had a tough day at the office, honey. I know the kids have been driving you crazy, but could I have a drink?"

She laughed, a pretty laugh, and told me to have a seat in the living room. I gave her an order for something sweet with vodka in it and sat in a white sofa that wanted to hug me to death. She came in a minute later with two tinkling glasses. She sat at the other end of the sofa. Her crossed legs were angled in my direction.

"I apologize again for dragging you over here. It's just as I said on the phone. I wanted to talk."

I took a sip of the drink. It was cranberry juice and orange juice, sweet. The vodka was Russian and brawnier than the arms on a Volga boatman.

"That's quite all right," I said, examining Sharon. Her hair was pinned back into a bun and held there by a gold figure-eight clip. She had a gold chain around her neck, and the perfume she wore should have been banned as a lethal weapon. It was a late-thirties look. I liked it when Ingrid Bergman and Greta Garbo wore it. And I liked it on Sharon.

There was an awkward little silence. "How is your investigation going?" she said finally.

"A little slow," I said. "It's produced some interesting leads, but nothing solid. I still have no idea where to find Leslie Walther."

"That's too bad," she said.

"What about you? How are things at the lab?"

"They seem to have settled down. The navy contract is on hold for now, so we're concentrating on the commercial work. Dan seems to have a handle on that. He's very happy."

"And you?"

"About how you might expect."

"Any plans?"

"It's time I broke off from this place," she said, as if she were making the decision on the spot. "I think I'll be able to leave the company soon, thanks to Tom."

"Tom Drake? I'm afraid I don't understand."

"It's funny. Tom could be an absolute terror. He didn't care who got in the way when he wanted something. He drove the people who worked for him. He believed in maintaining constant tension. But Tom was a lot more complex than people gave him credit for."

"In what way?"

"He saw working for him as a test. If you let him drive you off, you flunked. But if you stayed, you passed. He didn't care what people thought of him. He had an old-fashioned loyalty to those on the staff crazy enough to stick with him. He set up an employee stock plan to reward that loyalty."

Dr. Drake never ceased to astound. "How did the plan work?"

"Basically it was a simple arrangement. On his death, the ownership of the company would revert to the employees. I wasn't there all that long, but there's a nest egg that will cushion me financially until I figure out what I want to do."

"Was the staff aware of the stock arrangement?"

"No. I did let it slip once to Dan, but I don't think he'd tell anyone. I'm sure he wouldn't."

"How would Whipple fare?"

"He'd be in for a great deal of money. He could take it in cash if he wanted to leave the company. Or keep it in stock if he preferred to stay. I think he plans to remain with the lab, though. There's some sort of employee meeting coming up to reorganize the management."

"Where does Whipple stand to come out in a reorganization?"

"Oh, I'm sure that Dan, with his tenure and stock ownership, will be in line for the chairmanship."

"Miss Prescott."

"Sharon."

"Sharon, then. Pardon me for being blunt, but you seem to be force-feeding me Whipple as a suspect."

"I—I suppose you're right. I should have come out and said it instead of beating around the bush. But please be truthful, what do you think about him?"

"I think it's too early to accuse Whipple or anyone. There isn't enough evidence yet to point the finger in any direction."

"I guess you're right. But I am very grateful to you for coming by tonight."

She uncrossed her legs and moved several inches toward me on the sofa as if she were trying to get more comfortable. It was a subtle move, but one that was the same in every language.

"It was my pleasure," I said. "I enjoy talking to you."

"Do you?" She leaned closer, her silk blouse shifting against her skin as she moved. There was eye contact between us.

This was crazy. An hour ago I was being chased around a pool by a machine that wanted a pound of my flesh. Now I was sitting next to a beautiful woman who wanted something else. Even crazier, I wasn't in the mood for romance. I was beat from my swim. I just wanted to have a quiet drink in a bar and a good night's sleep in a bed, preferably my own. While I was feeling sorry for myself the phone rang. She answered it, said hello, and listened intently.

"Yes," she said impatiently. "I'll come right over." She hung up. "I'm so embarrassed. I really had hoped to talk to you. But could you excuse me? That was my aunt in Hyannis. She's been quite ill and needs a helping hand. I have to go."

"That's quite all right," I said. "Blood is thicker than vodka." I drained my glass. "Thanks for the drink."

She put her hand on my sleeve.

"Please come over again. I'll call you."

"I'd love to chat when we have more time." We shook hands, and a moment later I was back in my truck. I felt as if I had just gone through the revolving door at Jordan Marsh.

It had been an odd visit and I was still wondering about it when I climbed the stairs to my room and stopped. The door was open about three inches. It was shut when I left the guest house; I was sure of that. Chloe's car wasn't out front; she must still be at Cousin Maria's house. I moved fast. I reached my hand around the jamb to the right, switched the light on, and prepared to stick my foot in the way of anybody making a fast exit. No one came charging out with his head down, so I took a chance, opened the door halfway, and peered inside. The room was empty. I stepped inside, checked the bathroom and under the bed, then made an inventory. I looked through the dresser drawers. No one had stolen my underwear, but something was missing from the top of the dresser. The German onionskin papers from Drake's house were gone.

Sharon Prescott.

I slammed my fist into my palm. This had all the makings of a setup. It was just too pat. The phone call. The come-on. The prearranged telephone call from the ailing relative. I was drawn from my place long enough for someone to come in and go through my room. I went downstairs and dialed Sharon's telephone number. After two rings her voice came on the line and said hello. I hung up. Sharon's aunt must have had a speedy recovery. I went back to my room and sat on the edge of my bed wondering who Sharon was working with and why they wanted Drake's papers. I couldn't blame myself for being taken in by Sharon; it was the last thing I expected when she called, but I was still abashed, nonetheless, for doing my thinking with my glands.

I got undressed and threw my clothes on the floor and slipped under the covers. I slept fitfully, dreaming about giant crustaceans wearing bibs with little pictures of people on them. The next morning I made two vows. I resolved never to eat lobster again. Or to answer emergency calls from attractive young women.

CHAPTER 16

●

My sister Chloe laid aside the Life-styles section of the *Boston Globe*. "How's it going?" she asked.

She was sitting across the breakfast table from me at the restaurant overlooking the drawbridge on Water Street. My nose was impolitely buried in the *Globe* sports section. The Red Sox traditionally start off the baseball season in a blaze of glory that stirs the hearts of faithful fans who should know better. Denying the evidence of countless past seasons, we think that maybe the Sox won't go sour the way they always do, and if they can get past their annual summer slump, *this* may be the year for the pennant. The news wasn't good. The Sox weren't going to wait until July to head for the cellar. Boston had been mauled by Detroit in a doubleheader the night before at Fenway. The rest of the season would be like keeping the vigil at the bedside of a patient you knew was terminal.

"Lousy," I replied. "Sox are still taking a beating. I've had more fun reading the obituaries."

"I'm not talking about sports," she said. "The case you're investigating, how is *that* going?"

I looked at her over the top of the newspaper.

"Similarly lousy," I said. "Want to hear about it?"

Chloe nodded vigorously. "I'd love to."

I neatly folded the paper and laid it on a chair. "Okay," I began. "It started with a missing rich girl." I sketched out the highlights of my investigation so far: Drake's death, my suspicions about Whipple. It was an edited version. I glossed over Flagg's secret stuff. I told her about the watcher outside Jane's cottage, but not about my fight with him or my tryst with Jane. I skipped an account of the shoot-out at Drake's house, the tangle with the ROV, and my room being rifled. I didn't want her to worry.

She munched thoughtfully on a slice of whole-wheat toast. Her eyes brightened. "I think I've got it. *Cherchez la femme?*"

I blew air past my lips in a Bronx cheer. "Next you'll be telling me the butler did it. I've *been* looking for the woman, Clo. Her name is Leslie Walther."

"Not her. I'd pick Drake's wife."

"Pick her for what?"

"I think she's hiding something."

Chloe has always been perceptive about people. Since my duel on the dunes with the Gauloise smoker, I had the feeling Jane Drake wasn't coming across with the whole truth. And I had no explanation for Jane suddenly leaving, then returning to the art gallery the night of Drake's murder. That bothered me too.

"Why do you say that?" I said. It was an unenthusiastic query. I wasn't sure I wanted to hear the answer.

Chloe smiled mysteriously. "Woman's intuition." When I wrinkled my nose in response, she added: "I'm kidding, big brother. She just sounds a little weird. Still in love with her husband."

"Lots of people mourn forever," I pointed out.

"Oh, I know that, but there's something else. Why didn't Jane Drake call the cops the first time she thought somebody might be outside her cottage? That just doesn't make sense. She's all by herself on a lonely beach. Anything could have happened out there. Most women I know in that situation would have called the police just to be sure. Unless . . ."

"Unless what?"

"Unless she didn't want the police poking around?"

"Which means what?"

"Which means she's hiding something."

"I'm impressed, Chloe. You have all the makings of a gumshoe."

She smiled her Mona Lisa smile and said, "Now that I've practically solved your case, you can give me some brotherly advice on how to deal with the family and what to do with *my* life."

"With my track record, I'm the last person who should advise you on either score, but I'll do what I can. For starters, I think you should give Ma a call and make up."

"I'm coming to a decision on that. I'm just not ready yet."

"Fair enough," I said. "Well, time to get back to work. Breakfast is on me. Consider it a bribe."

I got up, squeezed her shoulder, and went over to the cash register to pay for my check. I had to wait a few minutes for the cashier. There was a basket of matchbooks on the counter next to the toothpicks and afterdinner mints, and while I waited I idly picked up a pack of matches. The name of the restaurant was printed on the cover. I stared at it, then stuffed the matches in a pocket. I took Chloe back to the Seaside guest house, dropped her off, and said I'd be back in a little while. Then I drove to Leslie Walther's condominium. Her neighbor, Mr. Evans, was at home.

"Why Mr. Socarides, nice to see you again," he said. "Please come in and have some tea. It's my favorite, Earl Grey."

I went into the living room and settled in a wing-backed

chair. Evans clattered around in the kitchen and came out poured the tea and said, "What brings you to our neighborhood, Mr. Socarides?"

"I happened to be in Falmouth. Thought I would stop by to say hello."

"That's very nice of you, Mr. Socarides."

I took some tea. "Mmm. This is good." I paused, then said, "You'll never guess what happened today." Evans smiled. "I ran into Leslie in Woods Hole." It was a lie, of course, an out and out blatant lie. I knew it, and I suspected Mr. Evans knew it too. But I wanted to see what he would say.

The smile vanished. His eyes narrowed. "You know something," he said, sipping his tea, "I never liked these cups. More ornamental than functional. The handles are too darn small for your fingers. I use them for sentimental reasons. They were my wife's favorites."

I waited.

Evans regarded me calmly. "Exactly who are you, Mr. Socarides?"

"First of all, I'm not Leslie's long-lost friend," I said. "In fact, I've never met her. I'm a private detective, Mr. Evans. I've been hired by Leslie's family to find her. And I think you might be able to help."

"What makes you think I know where she is?"

I reached into a pocket, took the book of matches out and tossed them onto the coffee table. "I picked these up this morning at a little place in Woods Hole. You know how it is. You're waiting for your change at the cash register and sometimes there's a basket with these things. So if you smoke or even if you used to smoke, you take the matches out of habit."

"I don't understand."

"How about one of your cigars, Mr. Evans."

He nodded, opened the drawer in the coffee table, and dug out his plastic-tipped cigars. I took the pack from his hand, slipped out a cigar and the matches tucked in the cellophane, and put the matchbook on the table next to mine.

"I still don't get your point," he said.

"Okay, then I'll explain. The first time we talked, you said you hadn't left your apartment in a long time," I said. "Something about a bum leg. Then I lit your cigar with a book of matches. These. They come from a little restaurant on Martha's Vineyard. I've been there a couple of times myself. Place makes a great turkey club sandwich. Only a few matches were missing, so the matchbook could be new. I couldn't figure out how they got here. It made me wonder if you were fibbing when you said you hadn't been out. And whether you would tell another fib or two to protect Leslie."

I sounded like Sherlock Socarides, looking down his nose and saying, elementary, my dear Mr. Evans, boring in, waiting for the suspect to break and confess. But there was steel behind his Casper Milquetoast exterior.

He looked at the matchbook cover, shook his head and smiled. "Well, I'm afraid you may have to go back to detective school. My neighbor left these matches when he stopped by last week. He and his wife had been to the Vineyard. You can talk to him if you don't believe me. His condo is two doors down. Name is George. Nice fellow. Used to be in the computer business."

So much for Sherlock. I tried another tack. Honesty. "Look, Mr. Evans, I told you a couple of fibs myself, and I apologize for it. Sometimes I forget how to tell the truth. So I'll start again. Leslie's father would like to know where she is. He's worried. If you have any knowledge of how to get in touch with her, I'd like you to pass along the message that I'm looking for her. That's all I'm asking."

Evans chewed on the edge of his cigar, practically demolishing the plastic holder between his teeth.

I leaned on him and inserted an escape clause at the same time. "If she doesn't want to talk to me, I won't press it. I won't bother you again. I'll find her eventually,

I think, but I'm basically a lazy person who would much rather be fishing than wasting time asking people questions they don't want to answer."

Evans looked at me over the gray ash of his cigar, the insurance agent again, sizing up a prospect. He was a nice man who was watching out for a friend.

After a moment he said, "There's always the possibility Leslie might call or come by, I suppose."

Mr. Evans leaned back in the sofa, finally lighting a cigar.

"I've been thinking about our Red Sox discussion the other day," he said, savoring a puff. "Well, you know, if we had any sense we would have given up on them years ago. Tell you, though, if I were managing the Sox, this is what I'd do. . . ."

From Evans's place I drove to the Falmouth police station. Gallagher was glad to see me. He smiled, shook my hand and ushered me into his miniature office.

"I've got a few questions about the Drake case," I said, settling into a chair. "You said that before Drake was murdered his car was seen on the Nobska road. Do you have more details?"

Gallagher went into another room. A minute later he returned with a folder. He pawed through the papers inside and pulled one out.

"Here it is, me bucko. Drake's car was spotted around nine-thirty P.M. the night he was killed. The witness worked at the NTI lab, so he knew the car well. There's only one silver Jag around like it, and with the 'Neptune' vanity plate, the ID is pretty solid."

"Exactly where on Nobska road was the car when he saw it?"

"Lessee. Okay. The car was about a half mile east of the lighthouse."

"What direction was it headed in?"

"The witness said the car was going toward Woods Hole from Falmouth Center."

I drew a map on the winding coastal road in my head,

remembering it from my lighthouse rendezvous with Flagg. Falmouth Center was to the east of the lighthouse; Woods Hole to the west. Nobska Point was in between.

"Where do you suppose Drake was coming from, Sergeant?"

Gallagher ran his hand through his thinning hair. "Beats me. He had left the lab around six-thirty, according to the guard, so he wouldn't have been coming from there."

"Don't rule that possibility out entirely. Drake could have left the lab, gone down the road for a snack, then returned and worked at NTI until just before nine-thirty. But I don't think that's what happened."

"Why not?"

"Drake's lab is north of town. He would have been coming into Woods Hole by way of Silver Beach, not Nobska Point."

"Maybe he headed into Falmouth Center to pick up a six-pack or some fast food after he left the lab, and was on his way home from there."

I wagged my head slowly back and forth.

"Naw," Gallagher agreed.

"It's always possible that he did go into Falmouth," I said. "But you know the Nobska road. It's a potholed cow path. The low parts are flooded half the time with huge puddles. You might take it in the daytime as a scenic route, but it's a real pain to drive at night. Drake would have followed the main road home. He wouldn't have wanted to get salt and sand all over the shiny finish of that pretty car of his."

"Maybe he wasn't driving it and the person behind the wheel didn't care about messing it up."

"What are the odds of a guy like Drake letting anyone else drive his car? If you owned one would you let somebody take your $60,000 Jag for a spin?"

"Nope, and I'm a lot nicer guy than Drake. So why was he there?"

"I don't know, Sergeant, but I'd like to find out."

From the police station I followed the Nobska road back

to Woods Hole. I slowed when I passed the drive to Jane's cottage, but kept on going. When I got back to the guest house, I called Flagg and asked if he had seen Whipple.

"I dropped by the NTI lab and talked to him this morning. I would say that by the end of our conversation he had been reduced to a quivering bowl of jelly."

"What did you ask him, Flagg?"

"Suspicions. Innuendos. Rumors. I didn't really say anything. Just hinted that the federal government was very disturbed about Dr. Drake's death and might rethink its position vis-à-vis the Neptune Technologies contract, particularly with the prototype missing."

"Got a new one for you. Whipple was an industrial spy for Drake, who may have held it over his head."

"Another motive?"

"Sounds like one to me. What do you want to do next?"

"Now that I've played bad cop, maybe it's your turn to be the good cop."

"It'll be a tough role, but I'll see what I can do."

A few minutes later I reached Whipple at NTI. He was apoplectic. "What right do you have to go around checking on me?" he raged.

"What makes you think I've been checking on you?"

"I stopped in at the liquor store today. The salesman there described you to a tee, Mr. Socarides."

"Okay, I confess. It was me."

"Goddammit, there are laws against that sort of thing."

"There are laws against murder too."

He was silent. Then he said, "What exactly are you getting at?"

"Simple. You had more motives than anyone to kill Tom Drake."

"I—hold on there. I'm not the only one who wanted that bastard dead."

"That's true, but you probably had better reasons than anybody."

"That's what you think. I didn't kill him."

"But you know who did, don't you?"

"I don't have to answer your questions."

"You're right, but I've heard the feds are nosing around the Drake case. You will have to answer their questions."

There was a deep and agonized sigh at the other end of the line. "Oh God," Whipple moaned. Flagg must have gotten to him.

After a few seconds I said, "Want to talk about it? You might need a friend."

Another pause. Another sigh. Whipple was wrestling with demons. "Okay. Tonight at ten o'clock," he said. "I have a research desk at the Marine Biological Laboratory. Top floor, rear. Be there."

Things were coming together. First Leslie Walther, now Whipple. Maybe I could tie up the whole package within twenty-four hours. In the meantime, there was another loose thread that needed attention. It was just before five o'clock when I parked near the turnoff to the Neptune Technologies Inc. lab. Cars driven by staff people were dribbling out at the end of the workday. After five minutes, Sharon's white BMW pulled out. I watched her car disappear down the road and started the truck, waiting with the engine running.

Twenty minutes after the hour, a faded blue Buick station wagon with a front fender whose rusty ends were bent down into a frown came from the direction of the lab. It stopped before turning onto the main road. I jammed the shift lever into first gear, pulled in parallel to the Buick, and hit my brakes. I beeped the horn and waved. Behind the wheel of the Buick, the gate guard shot me a jaundiced look. I rolled down my window and pointed toward the lab.

"Has Sharon Prescott left yet?"

He acknowledged me, just barely, out of the corner of his eye. Then with a shake of his bulldog jowls, he gripped the wheel and hunched forward as if he were going to floor the gas pedal at the first break in traffic.

"Oh hell," I said. I threw my hands in the air and

grinned. "I guess that means I can knock off early today. You know a place nearby where I can get a cold beer?"

The guard looked at me with new interest. He was almost licking his lips. He hooked a thumb to his right. "Yeah, I know a place," he said. "I was just heading there myself. Follow me."

About three miles down the road he turned into the parking lot of a restaurant lounge. We parked outside and went in together. He headed directly into the bar as if he had been there before.

"Look," I said. "The least I can do is buy you a drink. You just prevented a grown man from going into serious dehydration." He paused, but not too long, and nodded his head. The smoky bar was crowded with tourists and locals. We found a couple of empty stools and ordered two Bud drafts. I took a gratifying sip of foam and said, "You an ex-cop?"

He gazed straight ahead under droopy eyelids as if he wished that I would just pay for his beer and go away or, at the very least, that I would just shut up.

"Yeah Metropolitan District Commission Police. Retired three years ago."

"I thought you had the look." He had the look all right. Potbelly. Tobacco-brown fingernails. "I saw you put your hand on your belt once like somebody used to a holster."

He glanced at me blearily, vaguely intrigued.

"I got you beat, though," I said. "I retired from the Boston PD two years before you did."

He reacted as if I had told him I was J. Edgar Hoover. His mouth dropped open. "You?" he said with disbelief. "A Boston cop?"

I nodded. "Detective when I left." I rattled off a list of cop names. His eyes grew bigger.

"Damn," he said. "I never would a thought it. This calls for a drink on me."

He ordered another round and said that his name was John McCluskey and that he had been an MDC cop thirty-five years when he retired as a sergeant. He remembered the good old days when you could work a guy over without having to worry that the ACLU would bitch about Miranda rights. He would have told me war stories all night, but luckily he had to take a break to go to the men's room. When he came back I caught him before he had a chance to settle in his stool and spin another tale.

"How long have you worked for Neptune?" I asked.

"About a year," McClusky said. "I don't garden or play golf, and my wife and I were getting on each other's nerves. We figured we should both get jobs. She's over at Burger King. Loves working with the high-school kids. We use the money for vacations and to buy presents for the grandchildren. It gives us something to talk about over dinner instead of just staring into space. And it beats playing bridge at the senior-citizens center with a bunch of old poops who sit around talking about their aches and pains. The lab pays me pretty good, but the wife's job was a lot more exciting than mine until last week, about the time you showed up. How'd you get into this mess?"

"I was hired by Leslie Walther's father to find her. That's how I came to be talking to Drake. I hoped he might know something of Leslie's whereabouts."

He nodded, and drained his beer. "Leslie," he said. "I liked her. I thought she was a nice girl. Real pretty too."

"Dr. Drake likes the pretty ones, I guess. That Sharon is a real knockout."

He nodded and gave me a knowing grin. "Oh, you noticed. Yeah, she's okay too. Sometimes when I get bored I call her up on the outside phone and we kid each other about our jobs. How I hang around all day waiting for people to come to the door so she can tell them they can't see anybody."

I took a sip of beer. "I was wondering what her, ah, social situation was these days."

"Save your energy."

"How come? She was involved with Drake. Its unfortunate what happened, but he's not in the picture anymore."

"She may have been going with Drake, but she was

being cute with him. Miss Prescott had an outside interest. Kinda served Drake right, the way he played musical beds. I'm old-fashioned, I guess, but I've been happily married for forty years to the same great lady."

"Congratulations," I said. "That's a disappointment about Sharon. Is she seeing somebody else at NTI?"

"Nope. Dunno the guy's name. I saw them in here once having lunch. I don't usually come by until after work, but it was on the chilly side one morning. I didn't have my long underwear and was nursing a cold, so I decided I needed some medicine to go with my lunch. You know how it is. I came here and sat on the other side of the bar. It's out of sight from the front door and the dining room. I didn't want anybody to see me because I'm not supposed to drink during the workday. But I could see through that crack in the screen. It was like a stakeout from my old cop days. Sharon and her boyfriend were playing kneesy, handsy, footsy, anything they could get away with in a public place."

"Next you're going to say he's better looking than I am, and I'll really cry."

"Naw. Guy was a creep. If I saw a guy like him walking through the high-rent district, like ComAve for instance, I'd run him in on suspicion. Real pale skin, like he'd spent some time in the jug, and black greasy hair. Haven't seen hair like that since Valentino. You're too young to remember him."

"The Sheik?"

"Yeah, that's right. Anyway, they seemed to be getting along real swell. I don't know what she saw in him. Maybe he was loaded with dough."

"Could be. Speaking of loaded, that's what I'll be if I have another beer." I slid off the bar stool and we shook hands. "Let's do it again sometime."

"Fine with me. I'm going to have a few more pops before I go home. Helps me handle all those Burger King stories. Oh yeah, there was one more thing about Sharon's guy."

"Don't tell me. He was really Rudolph Valentino?"

"Not a chance. It was the way he was dressed. All in black, like he was going to a funeral."

I said good-bye and left the bar. On the drive back to Woods Hole I thought about Sharon Prescott's boyfriend. The description McCluskey gave me fit an English chap I had met just a few days before. His name was Winston Prayerly. There was probably a perfectly good explanation for the cozy relationship that apparently existed between Frederick Walther's majordomo and the secretary and paramour of the late Dr. Drake. But I was diverted before I could figure out what it was. Mrs. Stapleton had taped a note to the side of the guest house pay phone. Somebody had called me. Written on my landlady's personalized notepaper was a time, a telephone number, and a name. The name was Leslie Walther.

CHAPTER 17

•

The call from Leslie had come in thirty minutes earlier. I dialed the number and chewed nervously on my lower lip while the phone rang. No one was home. I tried again. No answer. I trudged up to my room and lay impatiently on my bed for twenty minutes, then went back to the phone and tried once more. Nothing. I was on the phone when Chloe came into the hallway from Mrs. Stapleton's kitchen and said we were both invited for supper. The meal was pot roast with gravy, potatoes, and carrots. I might have enjoyed it if I hadn't been leaving the table every fifteen minutes to go to the phone.. Around 9:30 P.M. I gave up on Leslie and called Flagg. He wasn't around, either, but I told his answering service I had set up a meeting with our main man. By then it was time to meet Whipple.

Woods Hole was socked in tight by a bone-chilling fog that smelled of black ocean water and kelp. The murky air was thicker than the *avgalemenos* soup my mother makes with egg and lemon. The beams from my truck headlights didn't travel six inches beyond the bumper before the fog gulped them down. The streets were practically empty. It was a night when sane people stayed home in front of a blazing fire with one hand on a friendly shoulder and the other in a bowl of hot buttered popcorn.

Whipple's turbo SAAB was parked in front of the Lillie Research Building, a brick-and-granite edifice on the corner of Marine Biological Laboratory and Water streets, a block from the aquarium. I left the pickup behind the SAAB, climbed the wide granite steps, and walked through the middle one of three arched doorways into the hushed lobby outside the Lillie Auditorium. The night watchman's desk was empty. He was either on his rounds or taking a nap in the boiler room. I followed an indifferently plastered hallway under exposed pipes, past dark wood doors that had pebbled-glass panels, and climbed the stairs to the library lobby on the second floor. The lobby was deserted except for a young guy using the copy machine. I walked past the card catalog and went through an entryway into the stacks.

It was like stepping into a medieval monastery. I expected to hear the drone of Gregorian chants, but the stacks were so quiet you could hear your eyelids clank when you blinked. Row after row of floor-to-ceiling shelves were crowded with volumes that exhaled a damp musty breath of old paper and vast knowledge. Whipple had said there were 185,000 books in the place. I did a mental computation. You could read one book a day for ten years, skipping the magazines, lunch, and bathroom breaks, without making a dent in the collection. I stopped and glanced through a volume off the shelf. It was an 1839 copy of the British medical journal *Lancet*.

Green metal desks reserved for researchers were set around the perimeter of each room, positioned one behind the other at right angles to the windows along three walls. Each research station had a hardwood chair not made for comfort, a pale blue blotter, and a disk-shaped gooseneck lamp that looked like an art deco flying saucer. Each desk had a brass or wooden plaque attached with a name or names commemorating the generosity of the benefactor who had endowed it.

I went up two more stairways. Here, the shelves were about a yard apart, and even in daylight the space between them would be as dim as a wino's alley. The top floor was dark except for the yellow light slanting through the stacks from the opposite side of the room. I walked past the bookshelves and empty research stations, following the light around the room like a moth, and turned a corner. The sole illumination came from a lamp on Whipple's desk. He was sitting at the desk, silhouetted against the lamp, his back to me. He was bent over the volume on his desk.

I cleared my throat so I wouldn't startle him. Whipple was a nervous guy to begin with, and after being browbeaten by Flagg and me, he sounded as if his stability were on a hair trigger. He didn't turn. I softly called out his name from twenty feet away. Still no reply. Something wasn't right. I trotted over to the desk and gently pulled him upright in his chair. His eyes were open in a dazed expression, like someone who's just learned the IRS has a tax refund for him. The desk blotter was stained dark red. A blond wooden knife handle protruded from his chest.

I touched his neck with my fingertips. His skin was still warm. His killer couldn't have left long before. I searched the stacks with my eyes. My mouth went dry. I didn't like this place. Too many nooks and crannies. I imagined whole gangs of assassins with strangle cords, daggers, and bottles of cyanide lurking behind each row of books. Thinking I heard the scrape of a shoe in the adjoining book room, I jogged over to the entryway and listened. There it was again. I began to go through each row, turning on overhead pull lamps as I went, until the whole room was bathed in light. I was alone.

Even if I had heard somebody moving, he or she could have slipped easily out a side door. I listened. There was only the distant hum of a furnace working deep in the bowels of the building. I sprinted down the stairs to the main level and burst out of the gloomy stacks into the brightly lit area around the book return. The young student was still at the copy machine.

"Where's a phone?" I yelled.

I must have seemed like a wild man. He shook his head, too scared to answer. I ran down a hallway, stopping to give each doorknob a quick twist. All were locked. No time to look for a watchman with a key. I picked one door and threw my weight against it. The door flew open. It was a storeroom. I tried two more doors. On the third I got lucky. I flicked on the light switch, saw a phone, and dialed the operator. I told her to get the police over to the Lillie Building. It was an emergency, I said.

Whipple wasn't going anywhere until the medical examiner arrived, but his killer might still be in the neighborhood, though that possibility was unlikely. Even less likely was the probability of finding a fugitive. The library had five floors of stacks, all more or less identical, with their own exits. Once outside, the murderer could disappear in the soupy fog. By the time the police arrived, he would have had time to stop off for a snack before tucking in for a peaceful night's sleep.

The first cruiser showed up in five minutes. Not bad. I was waiting outside the building when the car squealed to a halt at the curb, its roof lights flashing. I led the two officers upstairs and into the stacks. One of the cops looked familiar. I'd seen him at the aquarium the night Drake died. "Jesus," he muttered, when he saw Whipple's body. "It's a frigging epidemic." I knew how he felt. I was wondering how far my detective career would last if clients learned that making an appointment with me could be hazardous to your health. Tired of life? Call A. Socarides, PI, and put an end to all your problems.

I was sprawled out on a sofa in the reference room when Finch and Gallagher arrived at the scene of the crime about twenty minutes later. I had been thinking about the words on the bell named Mendel in the tower garden on Eel Pond. The inscription says, "I will teach you of life and of life eternal." It was obviously engraved before people started dying violently in Woods Hole within hearing distance of the Angelus.

Finch's mouth was drawn in a tight line. Gallagher's mouth was open for deep breaths. He looked winded. "Stay here with Mr. Socarides," Finch ordered. He charged off into the stacks, officiously trailing a thundering herd of uniforms. Gallagher flopped into a comfortable chair opposite the sofa, a perplexed frown on his plump face.

"What the hell's going on?" he said. "We got another one?"

I nodded. "Dan Whipple from Neptune Technologies."

Gallagher shook his head in bafflement. "I can't believe it. Two murders in one week. That's more than we've had around here in ten years."

I put my feet up on a coffee table where they weren't supposed to be and glanced at the oil paintings of MBL trustees, serious men who looked as if they knew something and didn't like what they knew.

"Consider the bright side, Sergeant. At least you don't have to go chasing victims all over town. Just hang around Woods Hole long enough and someone's bound to keel over with a knife in him."

Finch blew back in a few minutes later with his entourage. I was expecting to have a heart-to-heart talk with him, two cops hashing out an extreme case of felony with the proper dose of black humor and irony. Finch had other ideas.

"Sergeant Gallagher, read Mr. Socarides his rights."

Gallagher's jaw dropped down to his belly button.

"Sergeant," Finch snapped.

"You have the right to remain silent," Gallagher began tentatively, although he didn't sound as if he meant it.

This was silly. "Finch," I growled. "What the hell's going on here?"

Gallagher looked from me to Finch. It was plain he wished he had taken the night off.

"Keep going, Sergeant," Finch said.

Gallagher shrugged and cleared his throat, stalling for time. "You have the right to an attorney."

"Finch!"

"What the hell do you want, Socarides?"

"I want to know what you think you're doing."

"A smart-ass city detective like you ought to be able to figure that out. One corpse plus one suspect equals one arrest. There's nothing I despise more than a cop gone wrong. I'm placing you under arrest for the murder of Daniel Whipple."

I chuckled derisively. "You can't do that," I said.

It wasn't the first time I've been mistaken.

The Falmouth jail wasn't bad as jails go. The room service was on the slow side, the cot was too hard, and I didn't have the key to the liquor cabinet, but I had no trouble reserving accommodations. The only other guest was a drunk in the next cell who had some interesting theories about his incarceration. He was singing "Glory, glory hallelujah," and yelling that he was being held prisoner because of his political beliefs. Not a bad rap. Maybe I should try it. First I would have to attract the attention of the jailer by banging on the bars with a tin cup. Like Jimmy Cagney. I looked around the cell. No tin cup. They were obviously afraid I'd fashion it into a gun.

"Hey, pal," I called. "You got a tin cup I can use?"

"Glory, glory," my next-door neighbor said, and lapsed into sleep, snoring like a buzz saw.

I lay back on the cot and looked at the ceiling. What had Whipple wanted to tell me before he was so impolitely silenced? And who did the silencing? He wasn't a womanizer like his late boss. He didn't seem like the type of guy who would get anyone mad enough to kill him. Kinda squishy. Weak maybe. Drank too much. But I drink too much too. In fact my mouth felt a little on the woolen side. I imagined a six-pack of Bud. I pulled one off the plastic ring, popped the top, and gulped down the contents of the imaginary can. A beer had never tasted this cold and this good.

"Hallelujah," the drunk mumbled.

"You said it, buddy."

A door opened in the cell block and a cop came over with a bunch of keys. He unlocked the cell and motioned for me to get up and out. I followed him to the meeting room where I had talked to the cops the night of Drake's death. Finch was at the table with his arms crossed on his chest. He glared at me when I came in. Sitting across from Finch was Flagg. His expression was carved out of granite as usual. Gallagher stood behind Finch with his back to the wall. He winked. I took courage. Maybe they hadn't sharpened up the guillotine after all.

Finch jerked his head toward a chair. I sat down next to Flagg. Finch pinched his chin and said: "We're going to let you go, Socarides." He almost choked on his words.

"I'm heartbroken, Lieutenant. I haven't stayed in a hotel this good in a long time. Room service could use some improvement, though, and the view's nothing to write home about. But the staff is very congenial."

Finch slammed his palm onto the table. "The only reason we're letting you go is because of Mr. Flagg here. He has assured us, under the pledge of the United States government, that we would not be making a mistake by freeing you on your personal recognizance."

"I would think that's a most wise decision, Lieutenant, particularly where you didn't have grounds to hold me in the first place. I'll overlook it this time."

Finch's face went white with rage. He waggled his finger about an inch from the tip of my nose. "Look, Socarides. This was a peaceful place till now. Family squabbles, crazy drunken college kids in the summer. We've even had an armed robbery and a murder from time to time, so I am under no illusion that this is the quaint little village it used to be. But since you blew into these parts a few days ago I've found the corpses of two respectable scientists on my hands and I'm getting sick and tired of it. I'm sick of hearing the chief asking me when I'm going to have a suspect because the chamber of commerce says it doesn't look good for a resort community to have a killer on the loose just before the tourist season opens. I'm sick of reading my name in the *Falmouth Enterprise*, saying Lieutenant Finch has no solid leads yet. And most of all I am sick of you and your goddamn wisecracks."

I would have felt sorry for Finch if he weren't such a jerk, but I have a low tolerance for idiots who wear badges and use them to toss me in jail. "Really, now, Lieutenant. Do you think I would have called you guys and hung around to show you the body if I had stuck a knife in Whipple?"

"You might have done it to throw us off."

"C'mon, Lieutenant, give me a break. There are a dozen ways to leave that library building. I could have tap-danced 'Swanee River' on the way out and nobody would have seen or heard me. Any prints on that knife?"

He frowned. "Clean. Killer was wearing gloves."

"Is it the same weapon used on Drake?"

"Could be. Plain filleting knife available at any hardware store." His pale face flushed. "*I'm* the one who gets to ask the questions. What the hell were you doing at the library?"

Flagg nudged me with his knee. It might have been a sign of affection, but I took it as a signal to watch my mouth. I fed Finch a little bit of the truth.

"As I explained before you threw me into your dungeon, Lieutenant, Whipple called me and said he had information on the disappearance of Leslie Walther. He wanted me to meet him at the library, and I did. The rest, as they say, is history."

"Do you have any idea what that information was?"

"Sorry, Lieutenant. If I knew Whipple was going to be bumped off, I would have asked him to write me a pre-mortem memo."

Finch let out a sigh of exasperation. Flagg's expression didn't change.

"Okay," he said. "We're releasing you into Mr. Flagg's custody. You're to let us know where we can reach you. I still haven't dismissed you as a suspect or as an accessory before, during, or after the fact."

I stood up to go.

"One more thing," Finch said. "You're going to have to reimburse the MBL for the three door latches you busted."

"That's okay," I said. "But I have a request I'd like to make too."

Finch looked bug-eyed at me. "Go ahead," he said, his voice a low rasp.

"You couldn't fix a couple of parking tickets for me, could you, Lieutenant?"

On the drive back to the library building to retrieve my truck Flagg said, "Dammit, Soc, you've got a big mouth. Hell, I thought that guy was going to throw you back into the cooler despite the awesome power of the U.S. government."

"I guess I owe you and the awesome power another one."

"Naw. This was on the house. That eliminates Whipple as a suspect, though."

"That eliminates Whipple, period."

"Got any more bright ideas?"

I stewed over that question for a minute. This had started out as a missing persons case. Rich girl vanishes. Then it became a murder, and now it was a double homi-cide. If I had been less fleet of foot when someone was shooting at me at Drake's house, or in the dunes outside Jane Drake's place, or in the pool at NTI lab, it would have been a triple murder and the chamber of commerce would *really* have something to worry about. I tried to connect the dots, but gave up when the picture made no sense. Then I looked for a constant, a common denominator, and came back to the missing piece of scientific hardware. A second later I discarded it in favor of Leslie Walther. She disappears, Drake is killed, then Whipple, and Leslie is still missing. There were lots of threads to unravel, but the question was, which one?

I reduced the latest development to essentials. "We were on the right track. Whipple knew something. He was going to come across with some information. We were close. I'm sure that's why he was killed."

"You know anyone else we can put the screws too? Maybe this time keep them alive long enough to talk."

"Why don't we each make a list and compare them in the morning."

"List of what, for Chrissakes? We're supposed to be looking for a murderer."

"Don't get hysterical. A list of suspects. Ideas. Motives. Grocery list. Christmas list. Damn, Flagg, I don't know. I just always make a list when I'm stuck. It helps me organize my thoughts. You got any better ideas?"

"A list," he muttered. He pulled up beside my truck in front of the MBL library and I got out. "Okay. Do me a favor, though."

"What's that, Flagg?"

"Try not to get any more parking tickets."

I reached over and picked the red tag off my truck windshield, holding it with two hands like a businessman posing for a photograph with his first dollar. "Too late," I said.

CHAPTER 18

●

Leslie Walther called me again the next morning.

Mrs. Stapleton knocked on my door and said someone was asking for me on the pay phone. I went downstairs, picked up the phone, and I was talking to Leslie. It was as simple as that.

"Mr. Socarides." "This is Leslie Walther. Mr. Evans said you wanted to talk to me." Her voice was even-toned and cultured.

"Thank you for calling again. I tried to get you yesterday."

"I'm sorry. I was out most of the afternoon and evening. What can I do for you?"

"I'd like to see you, if possible. Your father is very worried about you."

"My *step*father," she corrected.

Hindsight vision is always 20/20 vision, but I can't say the revelation about Frederick Walther floored me. He was just too cold to be the father of the lovely woman in the photograph. It should have made made no difference to me, but I wasn't sorry to hear they weren't related by blood.

"My apologies. Your stepfather then, Miss Walther."

"No apology is necessary; you couldn't have known," she said. "I don't mean to be rude, but I don't see any purpose in meeting you, Mr. Socarides."

It wasn't a flat no. She was saying, "Convince me." So I tried. I told her the truth. What I knew of it. No embellishments, no curveballs. I started with the phone call from Winston Prayerly, told her about my conversation with her stepfather and my brief interview with Tom Drake. She listened without saying a word.

My closing argument was short and sweet.

"Your stepfather hired me to find you. That's the kind of business I'm in. People are always losing themselves, and it's pretty evident when they do that, they don't want to be found for one reason or another. I'd like to know your reason. It's a personal thing with me. I haven't spent any of the money your stepfather paid me. I'll give you the check. If you still don't want him to know where you are after we talk, you can tear it up. I realize that is not a great reassurance, but it's the best I can do outside of swearing on a Bible."

If there is anything I have learned in life, it is the unpredictability of human nature. I expected Leslie to tell me to take my check and stick it in my ear. But she didn't.

"I don't live far," she said, after a moment. "It's nine-fifteen now. You should have time to catch the ten o'clock ferry to Vineyard Haven. When you get off the boat, walk across the street to the seamen's bethel. There will be somebody there waiting for you."

"See you soon," I said, but she had already hung up.

Twenty minutes later I was buying a round-trip ticket to Martha's Vineyard at the bustling Cape Cod, Martha's Vineyard, and Nantucket Steamship Authority. I went on board the black and white ferry and followed the buttery fragrance of English muffins to the cafeteria on the top deck, where I bought a cup of coffee and a plain doughnut that wasn't any harder than a marble paperweight. I took a seat by the window and watched the cars and delivery trucks lined up at the loading ramp as I drank my coffee. I was going back for a second cup when the ferry vibrated with a low guttural roar and pushed slowly off from the dock.

From my seat there was a panoramic view of the brick-and-concrete harborside buildings that housed the Oceanographic Institution, Marine Biological Lab, and the National Marine Fisheries Service. Nobska Light blinked from its perch a half mile down the coast to the east. A minute later Woods Hole vanished, cut off from sight by the offshore fog. The ferry plowed through the mists, warning boats out of their way with foggy blasts of its horn. Halfway across Vineyard Sound the fog cleared and the tan bluffs of West Chop appeared on our starboard side. Forty-five minutes from Woods Hole the ferry rounded the harbor breakwater and edged up to the dock at Vineyard Haven.

As instructed, I got off the ferry and walked over to the gray-shingled Boston Seaman's Society Bethel, a chapel and museum across from the ferry dock. I stood on the corner and waited. Less than a minute later a black Ford pickup truck pulled up to the curb. The back of the truck was loaded with lobster pots, nylon line, and plastic marker buoys. A man got out of the truck and came toward me. He was thirtyish, dark-haired, and an inch taller than my six feet one. He was wearing patched and faded jeans and a paint-splattered work shirt. He came up to me and stuck his beard in my face. It was an aggressive beard, cut so it jutted out at a belligerent angle. "You the guy who's looking for Leslie?" he said.

I smiled and extended my hand. He frowned and didn't take it.

"My name is Bart," he said. "Get in the truck." He turned and walked back to the pickup without waiting to see if I was coming. He had the truck in first gear by the time I had slipped in on the passenger's side. We went through Vineyard Haven and took the cross-island road toward Edgartown. A couple of times I tried to get a conversation going, but if Bart was interested in talking about the weather or how the lobstering was, or even the Red Sox, he didn't show it, and finally I gave up. Fortunately, our destination was only a short drive, and less than fifteen minutes later we were driving down a narrow street through the whitewashed village of Edgartown to the Chappaquiddick ferry landing.

Minutes later the aqua-painted hull of the *On Time Ferry III* nudged the landing and the safety chain dropped with a metallic clatter. Bart drove the pickup onto the open deck. The skipper and crew, who were one and the same, refastened the chain, gunned the engine, and we started across Edgartown Harbor to Chappaquiddick Island. There was room for three vehicles, and benches along the sides, but the truck and its passengers were the only load on this crossing.

Chappaquiddick hangs off the easterly tip of the Vineyard like a huge amoeba, sending sandy tentacles around to enclose Katama Bay on the south and Cape Poge on the north. The island is less than three miles across from any shore point. Back in the 1970s it gained more notoriety than the Town Fathers would have liked when the youngest son of one of America's most prominent political families drove his car off the Dike Road Bridge, killing the young woman he was with and dashing any chance he ever had at the White House. The selectmen had to close the little wooden bridge because it was attracting too many tourists who were cutting off splinters as souvenirs to show the folks back home.

Bart and I stayed in the truck because the island run only takes about thirty seconds. Then he drove off the ferry onto Chappaquiddick Road, a narrow lane that took us past a beach club, and through a woodsy section of scrub oak and pine. A mile from the landing the road forks. The sand-and-gravel road to Dike Bridge went off the left. Bart stayed right at the fork and traveled for nearly another mile through more woods, past a few houses and dirt roads. He turned left at the entrance to a trail made for jeeps and jarred my teeth on the ruts for a quarter of a mile. At the end of the road was a small red-shingled house and a shed with a steep-sloping saltbox roof. The house was surrounded by stacks of wooden and metal lobster traps laid in long parallel rows. A thin plume of blue-gray smoke came out of the chimney and billowed toward the overcast sky.

We got out of the truck. Bart came over and looked at me as if he wanted to tie a buoy line around my neck in a fisherman's knot and throw me over the side for lobster bait. We glared at each other, trying not to blink. My eyes were starting to water when the front door of the house opened and a blond woman appeared at the top of a short stairway.

Leslie Walther.

"Mr. Socarides?" she called. I waved.

"Please come in. It's all right, Bart. I'll be fine."

The lobsterman reluctantly stepped aside to let me pass. "I'll be here if you need anything." He was talking to Leslie, but he was keeping a haddock eye on me.

Leslie shook my hand and led me into the house. The interior was basically one room with a kitchen, living room, and dining room rolled up into a single space and decorated in Salvation Army modern. The kitchen cabinets were unfinished and unpainted. The shag on the living-room rug was only a memory and it was worn in places to tissue-paper thinness. Probably from the more active moments of the two cats and golden retriever who basked in the circle of heat radiating from a Vermont Castings wood stove.

"Please make yourself comfortable," Leslie said. "Bart knows about my stepfather, so he tends to be a bit suspicious and overprotective where my welfare is concerned."

She was smiling, but there was a wariness in the blue eyes. I sat on a sofa covered with cat fur, shifting my weight to evade an attacking spring. One cat jumped onto my lap and milked my stomach. I must have reminded it of its mother. The retriever came over and put his wet muzzle on my knee. I was surrounded. Leslie asked if I wanted a cup of herbal tea, and I said yes. When she put the pot on to boil, I had a chance to compare her with the woman in the photo. She seemed different. Her face was more relaxed, for one thing. The sadness around the mouth that the camera had caught was only faintly notice-able. There was something else that wouldn't have shown in the head-and-shoulders shot. She wore a plaid blouse that hung loose, and the top of her slacks had a U-shaped elastic patch over the front. It was the type of outfit you usually see on women who are pregnant.

She served the tea and sat across from me in an over-stuffed chair that was losing its stuffing. We chatted about inconsequentials. Mostly how we both longed for summer. After we got the preliminaries out of the way, she said: "Well, you didn't come all the way out here to discuss the weather, Mr. Socarides. What is it that you want to know?"

I put my cup down on the floor. The other cat came over and drank out of it, then jumped onto the sofa and fell asleep on my thigh. The first cat glared at it malevo-lently but didn't move.

"I'd like to know why a wealthy, attractive, and intelli-gent woman would leave a good job in a fascinating field and disappear without telling anyone."

"Let me ask you a question first. Do you know who my stepfather is, and what he does?"

"I know that he's a very rich man and that he made a lot of his money in the arms business."

"He's also a very powerful individual who will stop at nothing to get what he wants."

"And what did he want, Miss Walther?"

"He wanted information on the project Tom Drake was working on. He had a buyer who would pay a great deal of money to know what was going on in Tom's lab. He tried his usual methods, bribery, mainly, but he couldn't get past Tom's security. My stepfather doesn't know what the word *failure* means. It became a challenge to him. He had never before been stopped from doing what he wanted. Perhaps he thought he had to prove he hadn't lost his touch. He recruited me to help him."

"He wanted you to be an industrial spy?"

"That's right. My first task was to get a job at the lab. It wasn't too hard. I do have a solid scientific background and Tom liked to have young women around. Next I had to insert myself into the Neptune II project. That was more difficult. Ordinarily, it would have been impossible. But my stepfather, not being a fool, knew I had one valuable asset."

"What was that, Miss Walther?"

She smiled without humor. "You look like a man of the world, Mr. Socarides. I'm sure I don't have to go into detail."

"Pardon my dense skull. I think I understand. You would go that far for your stepfather?"

Sadness had crept back into her eyes, and I was sorry I was the indirect cause, but I had to know more.

"Yes," she said. "As I explained, he is a very powerful man. He had always dominated my life. He never let me forget that I was adopted. I was expected to show my gratitude in every way. *Every* way."

"Are you saying what I think you're saying?"

Leslie nodded. "Ours was not a traditional, nor a healthy father-daughter relationship. It was the reason his wife, my stepmother, left him. She couldn't stand the in-house competition. She loathed him, and with good reason."

So Walther was a dirty old man. That figured. All at once he didn't seem so rich and powerful. He was no different from the raincoat reptiles who hang around big-city bus stations. He just had more money than they did.

"So at your stepfather's request, you moved in on Tom Drake?"

"It wasn't too difficult. Tom tended to wander. Taking him away from his wife wasn't in the plans. I was just supposed to do whatever necessary to pry some information from him. But after a while our relationship changed."

"You fell in love with him."

She cocked her head. "Is it that obvious?"

"Tom was a man that women fell for. That's obvious."

She went on. "You're right. I did fall in love with him. One night I decided to tell him the truth. Why I had come to work at Neptune. What I was supposed to do. The secret was just burning inside me. I had to let it out. It was odd, though. He didn't react with any kind of anger when I told him. Maybe he had suspected something. He simply lay in the bed, staring quietly into the darkness. Then he reached over and put his arm around me and we made love. It was as if I had never said a word."

"Was that the end of it?"

"Oh no. Tom brought the subject up later. Never in an angry way. He said he understood my position and asked me to tell him about my stepfather. I never realized how much I knew until I started talking about it. I told him things I had seen or heard about in the big house over the years. Tom listened to every word. He was especially interested in my stepfather's business dealings."

"Did it ever occur to you that Tom was using you?"

"Yes, almost daily. And I knew our relationship was doomed. That he would never leave his wife, and it was only a matter of time before we parted. He had already begun turning his attention to Sharon Prescott."

"If you knew that, why didn't you leave him earlier?"

"I still loved him. And at the same time, my father was pressuring me to stay. He didn't know I had told Tom about him, of course. Every time I said I wanted out, he would send Winston Prayerly to persuade me to stay at the lab, just a little longer. I was in torment."

"What made you decide to leave?"

She pulled her blouse tight against her swollen stomach. "The ultimate irony, Mr. Socarides. Proof that there is a God, and that He, or She, has a sense of humor. I became pregnant with Tom's child."

"Did he know this?"

"Oh yes. I was deliriously happy when I found out." She shook her head, a slight smile on her face. "I saw my

pregnancy as a way of permanently cementing our relationship. You don't think straight when you're in love."

"What brought you back to the real world?"

She took a deep breath and let it out slowly, as if she
were doing a Lamaze exercise. "I met Tom one day at the
pier after he had come in from a trip with Skip Mallowes.
I told him I was pregnant. I had it all figured out. Tom
would leave his wife, marry me, and with baby making
three, we'd all live happily ever after."

"What was his reaction when you told him?"

"He was angry. He said he didn't care if I had the child
in the gutter. He said it was probably my stepfather's
bastard offspring anyhow. He said if I tried to pin the
paternity on him, he would tell the world what he knew.
That he had enough information to blow my father out of
the water."

"Is that when you decided to run away?"

She nodded. "I went back to my apartment. I was crying so hard it was a wonder I could see to drive. I just
wanted to sink into the earth. I thought of throwing myself
into the harbor like one of those soiled heroines who leap
into the sea in the old Victorian romances."

"I'm happy to see that you didn't," I said. "How did
you end up here on Chappaquiddick?"

"I had known Bart from summer vacations on the Vineyard. We practically grew up together. I called him and
said I needed a place to stay, where I wouldn't be bothered. I wanted to collect my thoughts. Bart said he would
put me up for as long as I wanted. I gave Mr. Evans my
number. He's been like a real father to me and I didn't
want to lose him. Being here is the happiest I've been in
a long time. I plan to stay until the baby is born, maybe
beyond that."

"You could have chosen not to have the baby."

She reflected on that. "Yes, I could have. But I didn't.
I don't know why. Then, when I heard that Tom was
dead, I knew I had made the right decision to go ahead."

"You took a chance having me come out here with so much at stake."

"Maybe not. I knew you'd find me eventually. I wanted you to get the whole picture. I thought that if you heard my story . . . Well, you tell me, did I make a mistake in deciding to see you?"

I gave my eyes a treat. I let them play over Leslie's face, the blue eyes and the strawberry-blond hair, the Giaconda smile. She was going to make a beautiful mother. I considered the consequences to her life if Walther knew where she was. I drank the rest of my tea. It was cold.

"No," I said. "You didn't make a mistake."

Bart was working in the front yard, staying near the house so he could hear Leslie scream for help and come running if I tried to stuff her into a garbage bag and drag her back to the mainland. Leslie told him everything was fine. Bart smiled—I knew he could do it—and clenched my hand in a palm that had calluses as hard as barnacles. He was positively loquacious on the ride back to Vineyard Haven. It was nice to know he could talk, but his chatter about island gossip made it impossible to think, so I didn't.

"If you ever want to do a little fishing on the Vineyard," he said as he left me off at the Woods Hole ferry dock, "give me a call."

"Thanks," I said. "I'll do that."

I headed toward the boat and joined the line of passengers boarding for the trip back to the mainland. I bought a Bud to drink on the trip back and found a seat on the lower deck, where I could sit by the salt-streaked window and think about my talk with Leslie. I should have been elated at tracking her down, but I had a knot in the pit of my stomach that didn't come from the stale doughnuts I had eaten for breakfast.

CHAPTER 19

●

The door to my room was open and Chloe was sitting up on my bed, pillows propped behind her back like a queen awaiting her retainers. She had on a pair of designer-frame glasses and she was reading.

"Hello," she said, rattling the papers in her hand at me. "I brought this stuff back. I hope you weren't looking for it."

I took the papers and looked at them. They were the sheets of onionskin I had taken from Drake's place. The material that had disappeared from my dresser the night I was playing house with Sharon Prescott.

I looked at my sister, dumbfounded. "Chloe, where on earth did you get this stuff?" I asked.

She gave me a sheepish grin. "I was in here the other day looking for shampoo. I saw the papers lying on the dresser. I had them in my hand when Trudie called from downstairs and asked me to see her new curtains. Then I came back to my room and forgot about them. It was rude of me to take something of yours without asking. I hope it wasn't evidence."

"That's okay. This is something I found while I was poking around for a lead."

Chloe relaxed. "I thought you'd be angry. It was a dumb thing to do."

"It's fine, Chloe. But what made you interested in the first place?"

"I took German in college. When I saw the writing I was just curious whether I could still read it."

I shoved a paper at her. "Okay, translate."

She shook her head. "Language is something you have to keep up. It's been a while. I've forgotten all the German I knew except for *Gesundheit!* and *Guten Morgen.*"

My hopes sank. "Then you can't translate it."

"Sorry. But I know somebody who could. Trudie."

"Mrs. Stapleton?"

"She was born in Germany, Soc. Her late husband was an American soldier stationed over there. They moved to the States after they got married."

I grabbed Chloe by the wrist and said, "C'mon." We went downstairs and I knocked on the connecting door between the main house and the guest quarters. Mrs. Stapleton opened the kitchen door a second later and smiled, pleased to see us.

"Hello, Mrs. Stapleton," I said. "Chloe was just telling me you can read German."

"Of course," she said.

I handed over the sheaf of papers. "Do you have a minute to take a look at this?"

She put her reading glasses on and glanced at the onion-skin. "No problem. But first come in and have something to eat."

We went into the kitchen and sat at the table while Mrs. Stapleton served coffee and pastry she had baked that morning. Then we waited as she cleared the dishes and got them washed. She rejoined us at the table, put her reading glasses on, and studied the first sheet on the pile. After a few minutes she pointed to the heavy Gothic-type letterhead. "This is something called the German U-

Boat Archive. The letter is dated earlier this year from a researcher to Dr. Drake, who just died. See, here's his name." She began to translate.

"Dear Dr. Drake:

In response to your inquiry we are able to report the following:

On January 23, 1945, a Type twenty-one submarine, U-2872, left Horton, Norway, for an unknown destination. The submarine last reported its position approximately one hundred miles northeast of the New England coast, USA on February 12, 1945. Data on exact latitude and longitude are not available.

On February 15, 1945, U.S. naval forces detected and pursued a submarine approximately forty miles northeast of Cape Cod, state of Massachusetts. The vessel broke off the engagement. No further messages were received from the U-2872. Evidence to the contrary not being available, it was assumed she sank, possibly as the result of damages.

Our files contain no information as to the U-2872's mission, or cargo, if any. At this phase of the war, records were frequently destroyed, and orders, often oral rather than written, were at times routed outside of regular channels of command.

The U-2872 was built at Böhm and Voss boatyard, Hamburg, Germany, in 1944. The vessel was under the command of Kapitanleutnant Heinrich Küchler, naval class of 1932, a veteran of many cruises, and had a crew of fifty-seven. We will continue to be alert to your interest in this vessel and will notify you if we find additional material."

Mrs. Stapleton looked up from her reading.

"That was wonderful," I said. "Could we go through the rest of this material?"

Pleased at the compliment, she said, "Of *course*." She picked up another piece of paper and scanned it. "This is a letter from someone named Herbert Braun, Frankfurt,

West Germany, to Dr. Drake." She began to read. Braun was an officer aboard the U-2872 who became seriously ill and was yanked off duty from the sub at the last minute, much to his good fortune. The incident understandably made him an instant convert to religion and he talked mostly about his epiphany. But he did say one intriguing thing.

"Before departing, Küchler told me he heard rumors the U-boat would be carrying an important secret cargo. And that he might not return to Germany for a long time. Perhaps never." I asked Mrs. Stapleton to read the sentence three more times.

The other letter had been written to Drake from the widow of the presumed late Kapitanleutnant Küchler. Although she had happily remarried, the former Frau Küchler still had fond memories of her dashing young sub commander. Much of the letter was taken up by her description of the hardships of war, her subsequent life, and the doings of her grown children. But like Braun's letter, it had a tidbit that stuck in my mind.

Frau Küchler said: "On the day he left, my husband told me he was going to make one stop after leaving Norway. He would be told his precise orders by radio once he was at sea."

I shook my head. Drake was interested in an old World War II sub. But why? The fog index surrounding this case increased another notch.

"I don't know what these numbers are," Mrs. Stapleton was saying. She handed over the letter from Frau Küchler. I glanced at the notation on the bottom of the page, then took a second look. It was a series of figures, tightly written in blue ballpoint pen. I recognized them as longitude, latitude, compass headings, and long-range navigation bearings. Drake's writing.

"It looks like some sort of position. I don't have a chart, so I can't plot it."

I thanked Mrs. Stapleton, and Chloe and I went upstairs. Outside her room, she paused and said, "I've done

enough detective work for today. You can figure out what
all this stuff means and tell me later. I've got an appointment with an acupuncturist in Boston. I'll probably stay
up there with friends a day or two. It looks like you're
going to be pretty busy. Maybe we can spend some more
time together later."

That brought me back to reality. "Why are you going
to a pinsticker?"

"He says it will relieve my anxieties, caused, I may add,
by my membership in a crazy family."

As soon as Chloe set off for Boston I headed my truck
out of Woods Hole. I found a marine supply shop in Falmouth, where I bought a National Ocean Service chart of
Cape Cod. Spreading the chart out on the hood of my
pickup, I checked off the navigational figures from the
letter Mrs. Stapleton had translated. With a pencil I circled an area about eight miles southwest of the Cape. I
stared at the circle, thinking, until the depth contours and
numbers began to swim in my vision. Then I got back in
the truck and headed east out of Falmouth on Route 28.

About a half hour later I pulled up next to Lewis Bay
Wharf in Hyannis and walked out on the finger piers to
where a blue-hulled sloop was tied up. The boat had clean
corsair lines, a graceful wineglass transom, and sharp-
edged bow. Neglect had taken a heavy toll, however. The
teak-and-mahogany woodwork needed sanding and varnish. The Pines were frayed. The unprotected sails were
yellowed from the damaging rays of the sun and looked
as if they hadn't been unfurled in years. The sloop had
been painted in spots with colors that didn't match, and
she had the sad air of a once lovely woman, fallen on bad
times, who tries to reclaim her lost beauty with too much
makeup in all the wrong places. I went on board and
yelled down an open hatchway.

"Hey, Mac, you at home?"

"Soc," replied a hoarse whiskey voice. "Is that you? Get
down here, you old son of a seadog."

I went below. Mac pumped my hand and embraced me in a bony bear hug. He smelled of kerosene and booze. He was wearing flannel pants nearly worn through at the knees, a tan turtleneck wool sweater the moths had dined regally on, and a black and battered Greek fisherman's cap on his close-cropped white hair. His crevassed face had a stubble of beard and his skin was as dark as a tanbark sail. He was pushing seventy, and every year he carried must have been a hard one because he looked a decade older than his age.

You can find guys like Mac on every waterfront in the world. Key West. San Diego. Ensenada. St. Thomas. They all look and dress and talk the same. They are men who have grown old before their time. Once they were businessmen or professionals, but something had killed their spirit and their souls. Maybe a wife died or up and left them or a kid had gone wrong. Unlike the urban derelicts who sleep on heating grates, the Macs of the world are drawn to the edge of the sea by happy recollections of good times sailing or fishing or making love within sound of the waves. But their souls are adrift and rudderless. Usually they find only loneliness and they dull their pain with alcohol.

Mac had been a naval officer. He had seen action in World War II and in Korea. And had come through unscathed, physically anyhow. Something had gone terribly awry in his life. He never told me the details and I never asked. Now he lived on his boat in the warm season and during the winter rented a room about a block away. There was a bar in between, so he had the best of both worlds. I brushed away a pile of newspapers and took a seat at the tiny dinette table. The interior of the boat was cluttered with sailing magazines, dirty clothes, and oily tools.

"You came at the right time," he said. "I just got through fixing this damn heater. How are you?"

"I'm fine, Mac, but I could use the benefit of your vast naval knowledge."

A light gleamed in his bloodshot eyes. "You know my

weakness. I will make room in my busy schedule *any*time to talk navy. Hold on, I'll whip up a couple of toddies to take the chill away." Mac half filled two mugs with a brew the texture of crude oil and topped them off with cheap brandy. The bad brandy and worse coffee neutralized each other and the mix wasn't bad as long as you thought of it as a weak sulfuric acid.

I took a tentative sip and got right to the point. "What do you know about a German World War Two submarine named the U-2872?"

Mac had just lit an unfiltered Camel cigarette that precipitated a thirty-second coughing fit.

"Ah, the Cape Cod mystery sub," he said when his lungs cleared out. He took a gulp from his mug that would have grown hair on an entire billiard table. "She was a Type twenty-one vessel, one of the super subs the krauts built near the end of the war."

That was interesting. "What was so super about her, Mac?"

"It was the most advanced type of sub on the face of the earth at the time. And if they had built enough of them fast enough, the Germans could have kept the war going months, maybe years, longer. How's that coffee, by the way? The last batch I made tasted like turpentine."

"You're improving. This tastes like battery acid, but the brandy cuts it."

Mac brightened. "Guess I *am* improving. Might help if I washed the coffeepot occasionally."

"It usually does. But let's get back to the super sub. What was so different about these new U-boats?"

He sloshed more brandy into his mug and took another slug, wiping his mouth with the back of his hand. I leaned forward and listened intently. Mac was a booze-logged old sot, but he knew his warships.

"Let me back up," he said. "The Germans came into the war with a model called the Type seven. It was small, just over two hundred feet long, and its range was limited. Basically nothing more than a modified World War One design, but they could mass-produce it and it was deadly as hell under Admiral Donitz's wolfpack strategy. The Allies lost nearly three thousand warships and merchant vessels to U-boats, most of them 'seven' models or modifications of it. The little bastards swarmed up and down the coast. They sank more than six million tons of shipping in 1942 alone. Then we got smart."

"How was that, Mac?"

"We developed sonar so we could track them down. Then we put together hunter-killer groups of ships that could go after U-boats anywhere in the Atlantic. Donitz scoffed at the idea of planes hunting subs, but we showed him his guys were vulnerable to attack from the air if you had a big enough bang. Then we came up with a mortar system called the hedgehog that could throw a couple of dozen warheads ahead of a ship. Add in the fact that we had broken the German code anyhow, and before long their boats became floating coffins. They lost two-thirds of their subs, and three-quarters of their crews were killed or captured. Donitz's son went down on one sub. Donitz knew he had to do something. He desperately needed a real submarine."

"Wait a minute, I thought we *were* talking about real subs."

Mac lit up a new butt and disappeared momentarily behind a cloud of cigarette smoke.

"Naw. Here's the problem. The term *U-boat* was short for *Unterseeboots,* that is, undersea boats, but no one had built a true submarine. Not us, not the Germans. What both sides had were surface boats that could duck underwater for a little while to attack or run for it. They had to come up for fresh air and to recharge their batteries. Donitz took his case to Hitler."

"Let me guess. Adolf okayed the super sub."

He nodded. "It was called the *Elektroboot* or electric boat. She was around two hundred and fifty feet long, had a range of eleven thousand miles, and could go deeper, faster and farther, and stay under longer than anything up to then. They could cruise underwater at seventeen knots. They had a snorkel that could bring in fresh air. They had six bow torpedo tubes with a hydraulic system that could reload in twelve minutes, the same amount of time it used to take to load *one* torpedo. The diesel engine was a wonder. It didn't need air from the surface to run. Their electronic detectors had a range of fifty miles. They even had a food freezer. The Type twenty-one was a revolutionary machine."

"So why didn't it cause a revolution?"

"It was a case of too little too late. Just like the Germans' jet fighter and the V-2. The Germans used a modular construction. Albert Speer came up with the idea of building the subs in sections and putting them together at the riverside, cutting production time in half. They could fit a sub together in a matter of weeks. But they had design and manufacturing problems and before they could solve them, we bombed the hell out of their factories. Before you knew it, the war was over. Which was lucky for the krauts. The new subs would have kept the ocean war going, and we might have used the Bomb in Europe instead of Japan. Only two super subs were pressed into war service. When we tallied up those two and subtracted from the hundred and twenty-one launched, there was still one unaccounted for."

"The Cape Cod mystery sub."

"Yeah, I've been hearing about her for years. Some people say she's off Plymouth, others swear that she's near Nantucket. North Shore, South Shore, depends on who you talk to. Makes you think the German navy was three times as big as it really was. Some people say she wasn't German at all, but Belgian, and sunk accidentally by the Allies, so they wanted real bad to hush it up. You hear a million stories."

"What kind of stories, Mac?"

"Like the night somebody's brother-in-law got called out to duty at Otis Air Force Base to go after a sub, or some old lady screaming she saw lights of airplanes from the shore. You can hear the same stuff from Maine to Florida, Soc. People were really jittery with all that exposed coastline, and lots of silly stories came out of the war. I don't know how many times I've heard the story about the U-boat crew that broke into the general store in some little podunk town, then rang the church bell. Guess those German boys musta got playful when they run out of Wiener schnitzel."

"So you're saying that the mystery sub is a phony?"

"Oh no. It happened. No doubt about that in my mind. I think we've got a U-boat right off the Cape somewhere and that she's the U-2872 and could be carrying valuable cargo."

I took a swig of the coffee firewater in spite of myself. "What kind of cargo, Mac?"

"Oh, the standard stuff. Depends on who you believe. Let me tell you a story. There's a sub off Block Island, the U-853. She's a long-range model, bigger than the Type seven, but still no super sub. They sank her in 1944 after the commander went after an old U.S. coal ship and brought the furies of hell and the U.S. Navy down on his head. She was the last U-boat kill in U.S. waters. In the 1950s a guy shows up in Newport with blueprints and German documents, flashes a bankroll and hires some divers for big money to go down after the sub, and tells them to keep their mouths shut. He wanted to get into the captain's quarters real bad. You know how hard it is to keep a secret on the shore."

"I know it's damned impossible."

"Right. Before long everyone in the world knew about it. The rumors were flying. There were all sorts of guesses about the sub's cargo: gold bullion, jewels, and U.S. greenbacks the krauts stole out of the American Express office in France. Some people thought the sub was Hitler's getaway boat headed for South America."

"Did this guy find anything?"

"Nope. A lot of dives have been made on her since, but she's clean except for the bones of her crew. Turns out the guy was looking for more than a million bucks in mercury. Supposedly contained in stainless-steel flasks. Seems the Germans were running mercury to Japan to trade for tin, in the last days of the war. Back in '72 some salvagers pulled thirty tons of mercury from a U-boat off Singapore. The stuff was valued at nearly eighteen million bucks, but the West Germans put in a claim and were awarded the salvage rights."

"Doesn't make sense, Mac. If that sub were taking a load of mercury to Japan, what was it doing off the New England coast?"

"Good question. Personally, I don't think she was going to Japan. If she'd been on a secret mission, her torpedo room would have been used for cargo and the commander wouldn't have called attention to himself by going after the coal ship. But your mystery sub is a different story. She might have been on her way to South America when she got in trouble and had to come into enemy territory off our coast. She would have tried like hell to avoid enemy action, but that's easier said than done. She could have been picked up by one of our patrols. Who knows? Maybe they *were* taking Hitler and some negotiable maté-riel to Argentina to set up the Fourth Reich. It wouldn't be a mystery sub if we knew all the answers. Say, what's your interest, Soc? You found her?"

"Nope. But you know me. Always checking out the big score. So you think she went down off the Cape? Any ideas on general location?"

He started to pour me more brandy but I put my hand over the mug, so he gave it to himself. He pulled a book off a shelf, leafed through it, found what he was looking for, and shoved the book under my nose. There was a map of the eastern coast of the United States. It was cut up into numbered grids, in turn marked under larger let-tered designations.

"The Germans used these grid maps to keep track of their subs." Mac tapped the rectangle nearest to Cape Cod. "This square was her last reported position. I think if she had made it to South America where she might have been headed, we would have heard of her by now. A number of guys have tried to find her, but you know what they say. Big sea, little boat."

Mac was paraphrasing the old mariner's prayer. "Lord protect me. Thy sea is so great and my boat is so small."

I borrowed Mac's book and a couple of others and thanked him for the information and the coffee. I spent the rest of the afternoon in a quiet room at the Hyannis Library reading about World War II submarines. Late in the day I looked up and rubbed my eyes. This was nuts. What the hell was I doing reading about periscopes and hydroplane controls? I was involved in a missing person case, and I had found the person who was missing. All I had to do was go to Frederick Walther, hand over his stepdaughter, collect my money, and head for home. But was the case really over? The murderer or murderers of Tom Drake and Dan Whipple were still on the loose. I didn't know who tried to kill me. And don't forget Drake's missing AUV prototype. Which is it, Socarides? Fish or cut bait? I played Hamlet on the drive to Woods Hole, but still hadn't decided what to do when I pulled up to the guest house and saw the LTD parked out front. I had company.

Flagg was pacing the street next to his car, and you didn't have to be a detective to see my old friend was worried. His mocha skin had a gray tinge to it. His brow was furrowed. I was barely out of my truck when he strode over and said, "I've been looking all over for you, Soc. Got a minute?"

"Sure," I said. "We've got to stop meeting like this, though. People are going to talk."

Flagg got right to the point. "We got problems."

"*We*, white man?"

He sucked in his breath. "Do me a favor. Cut the jokes for now. Let's take a walk." We started down the street.

"Okay, Flagg, I can see you've lost your fabulous sense of humor. What kind of problems?"

"Life-and-death ones, man."

He was doing his cloak-and-dagger stuff and it was my turn to be irritated. "You're talking spook talk again, Flagg. Spit it out."

"Drake's missing prototype. We've got to retrieve it. Pronto."

"Don't tell me—the schedule has been moved up on the Russian research ship and Woods Hole is crawling with KGB agents."

"Forget the Russians. The ship got diverted to New York when a crewman came down with appendicitis."

"That should give us more time."

"Just keep listening. I got a call from Washington. They need that AUV fast."

"What's the hurry, Flagg?"

"You know anything about the *Alvin*?"

"Yeah. It's the little deep-sea sub that Woods Hole Oceanographic uses, the one that went down and took those photos of the *Titanic*."

"You got it. A lot of people heard about the *Alvin* a few years ago when she went after a hydrogen bomb from a plane that crashed off the Spanish coast."

"I remember. She made headlines all over the world when she retrieved the bomb."

"What you probably don't know is that there are dozens of other nuclear bombs under the sea. They come off sunk ships, missiles, planes."

"We're awfully careless with our megatonnage."

"Not just us, other countries have been sloppy too. But our government's been taking a lot of heat from environmental groups around the world. Most of the bombs are too deep for anyone to retrieve and too far away for the nuclear stuff to seriously contaminate anything. But it's been an embarrassment internationally. So the navy went out and built another sub like the *Alvin*. She's been working real quiet picking up some of those bombs. They call her the *Rosy*. Short for Retrieval of Ordinance System."

"That's real nice, Flagg. I had a blind date once with a girl named Rosy. That bombed too."

"Stay with me, Soc. I'm not through. The *Rosy's* been working off Bermuda. Nuclear sub sank there a couple of years ago. It's down about a mile. The *Rosy* set down on a deck and the thing caved in. She made it partway out before she got into trouble. Now she's stuck there, she can't come up."

I stopped and turned to Flagg. "Migod. Don't they have an escape system?"

"Yeah. She was built so you can jettison the outer housing, and the sphere that holds the three-man crew will come to the surface. They tried that. But the housing is snagged on some cable. They can't release the sphere. She needs someone to go down and lend a hand."

"What about the *Alvin*? She might be able to do it."

"Yeah, she might. But the *Alvin's* on the other side of the world in the Pacific, and what's worse, her motor's all in pieces. There wouldn't be enough time to get her back here. The French have got a sub that could do it too, but she's in the shop for an overhaul. They tried using an ROV but the damn tether kept getting tangled in the currents and they lost it. They could try it with another ROV, but they think it will just be a waste of time."

I saw what Flagg was getting at. "So that leaves Drake's machine."

"Right, Soc. The Navy's been going over the material. They figure they could program this thing, send it down, and use the mine cable cutters to free the sub. It's a long shot, but they think it's worth it. At least it would give the crew a chance."

We started walking again. I considered the odds. The depth, pressure, currents. "That *is* a hell of a long shot, Flagg."

"It's the only one they've got. There's something else. You'll get a kick out of this. If we find Drake's gadget and it pulls the job off, the Navy's decided to go public with details on the project. They think they'll be able to shake Congress down for more dough if they show that a war machine can be used in a big dramatic rescue. Real funny, huh."

"Yeah, Flagg, a million laughs." I was thinking about the submarine S-4, sunk in one hundred feet of water off Provincetown, and how the thirty-four crewmen aboard watched their lives dwindle with their air supply. About the *Thresher*, whose crew, mercifully, died more quickly when their sub fell to the ocean bottom. Maybe the sea was telling us something, that we had no right to go beyond certain boundaries. I thought of the blackness of the ocean a mile down, and I shivered.

"How long does the crew have?" I asked.

"In about forty-eight hours their air supply will start to run out. They could survive another twelve hours if they don't do any heavy breathing. Of course they might get lucky and freeze to death first."

"Flagg," I said with exasperation, "I don't have a clue where Drake's machine is. Whipple was my best lead and you know what happened to him. How about you?"

"Nothing. I've got my troops out, but I'm not hopeful."

We were at the little garden by the bell tower. I pushed open the gate and we stepped inside behind the hedge. The world seems to stand still in quiet places like this. I pondered the elasticity of time. How would the hours pass for the crew of the *Rosy*?

I said, "I'll try to put something together. Give me a little while and I'll get in touch with you."

"Don't take too long, Soc."

He didn't have to say it; The clock was ticking. He went out the gate and headed back to his car, covering the distance quickly in his big-man's walk. I was alone in the garden. My mind churned with the delicious ironies revealed by Flagg's story. I thought of the letters I had found in Drake's house. I was convinced the forty-year-old war machine lying off the Cape held the key to the deaths of Drake and Whipple. Would it also open the door of life to those who tried to retrieve a war machine even more terrible? I went back to the guest house, called Skip Mallowes, and told him what I wanted to do.

CHAPTER 20

●

Spray slapped the front of the pilothouse as the *Gannet* plowed through the predawn darkness at full throttle. Spanked by unseen seas, the bow rhythmically rose and fell like a school of playful porpoises. Although we were making good time across Buzzards Bay, a nervous impatience gnawed at me, and the boat seemed to crawl.

I turned to Skip and said, "Thanks for doing this on such short notice."

"Hell, it's no problem," he replied with good humor. He was sitting a few feet away, his hands on the wheel, steering the boat on a southwest course out of Woods Hole. His apple-cheeked face glowed green in the light from the compass. "Now that we've left the harbor, mind telling me where we're going?"

I spread out the chart I had marked the day before and pointed to the position circled in pencil. Skip studied the chart briefly and said, "Yeah, I know the area. That spot's around three or four miles southwest of Gay Head. We'll keep on this heading for a bit till we're out of the bay,

then we'll bear left around Devil's Bridge at the tip of
Gay Head. Shouldn't be more than a couple of hours."

"Have you ever dived in those waters?"

Skip squinted into the night as if he'd seen a fire-breath-
ing sea serpent rise directly in front of us. I followed his
gaze but saw nothing. After a moment he said, "Yeah,
I've dived out there. There's an old fishing boat at the
hundred-and-four-foot mark." He tapped the chart with
his forefinger. "This isn't far from there. Water's a hundred-
plus-feet deep, but not too bad. It'll be a little tougher dive
than the one we did the other day. We'll have to keep an
eye on our decompression times. What are we looking for?"

I hadn't told Skip what I hoped to find. I still didn't
feel that I knew him and I wasn't sure how far I could
trust him.

"I've got a couple of answers I could give to that question," I said. "I could tell you what I think is lying out
there and make a fool of myself now. Or I could wait until
we dive on the site, find nothing, then make a fool of
myself. But I'll settle for a middle course. I think there's
a wreck, and it will be one of the most exciting dives
either one of us has ever made. Maybe it will pay you
back for rousting you out so early."

Skip nodded and reached overhead to turn on the radio.
The droning monotone voice of the NOAA weather report
gave a forecast for fair weather, cool but dry, with a light
breeze.

"That's okay," he said, switching the radio off. "Sorry
we couldn't get moving sooner. That fuel pump gives me
trouble every so often."

The sky was beginning to lighten and the long gray
profile of Naushon Island emerged on our right. Naushon
is the biggest island in the Elizabeth chain, a low-lying
and largely barren archipelago that looks on the charts like
the mud dribbles a child makes at the beach. The Eliza-
beths stretch for twenty miles southwest of Woods Hole,
ending in a reef called Sow and Pigs. There's a real ship
catcher called the Graveyard along their southerly shore

where hundreds of captains have lost their vessels, their reputations, and in some instances their lives, when they'd misjudged the tricky current between the rocks of Sow and Pigs and Naushon.

The sun came up as we rounded the westerly tip of the Vineyard. New light sparkled on the glassy wave crests. Cat's whisker clouds streaked the sky. Captain Fitzroy of Darwin's ship *Beagle* would have called it a low dawn, when the sun breaks on the horizon. It was a promise of a good day. Skip reduced speed just enough to maintain headway. We checked our position against the bearings I had supplied and, after some good-natured arguing, agreed that the wreck should be right below us in 106 feet of water. That was easy. The hard part was finding the damn thing. Skip's boat didn't have the kind of sophisticated electronic gear that can help pinpoint a wreck, so we had to resort to a fairly primitive method. We grappled for it. Skip maneuvered the boat while I handled the grapple, a small anchor with four hooks.

We dragged all morning without success. My back and arms were getting weary and my hands sore from throwing the grapple over the side and hauling it in. I was becoming depressed as well. Each throw of the line reminded me of the reason for this fruitless task. Three men were sitting in a minisub a mile down off the island of Bermuda. In a matter of hours their air would run out and they would die. Here I was throwing a hook into the faceless sea, trying to snag a World War II sub that may or may not exist.

Skip suggested a short lunch break. I was reluctant to stop, but I knew I had to knock off or I would be too tired to dive, if and when we did find the wreck. The food made me feel better and raised my spirits. Energized from my rest and sandwich, I went into the pilothouse to look at the depth finder. As a fisherman I've gotten into the habit of checking and rechecking. You're always keeping an eye on your lines, your hauling gear, or your position. I looked at the reading displayed on the long-range

navigation receiver and checked it against my bearings
and the chart. I couldn't believe it. We were about half
a mile off course!

I called Skip into the pilothouse and showed him the
discrepancy.

"Hmm," he said. "We must have drifted. I guess I
shouldn't be doing stuff like this when I haven't had my
normal twelve hours of sleep." He took the wheel and
moved the boat until it was right on the nose. I went back
to grappling. After about a dozen tries I felt a slight tug
of resistance as I hauled on the grapple line. I quickly
reeled it in and grabbed the anchor.

"Hey, Skip," I called. "Look at this."

He came on deck and I showed him the grapple. The
steel tips of two of the four anchor hooks were brownish
red. I wiped a hook with my finger. "Rust?" I said.

His eyes lit up with excitement. I quickly threw the
anchor overboard. After a few more tries the grapple
caught and wouldn't let go. I hauled back on the line,
holding my breath as I gradually increased the pressure
on the rope, afraid at the same time to pull too hard
because it might break away. Even with some muscle
behind it, the hooks held. I cleated the free end of the
line to the boat.

Skip came over and saw the line tugging in the water.
"Looks like you caught yourself a big fish."

"Looks like it," I said. "Let's go down and see what
kind it is."

We started to lay out our dive gear. I unpacked a
wooden spool about two feet long from my gear bag. I
had bribed a hardware-store clerk twenty dollars to put
the spool together for me. Wound around the spindle was
around 150 feet of strong nylon line. Tucked in between
a couple of turns of line was a lift bag I could inflate to take
the line to the surface. Wreck diving can be hazardous to
your health if you don't think ahead. When things go
wrong underwater, they really go wrong. Trouble grows
by geometric proportions. Diving once on an old freighter,

I hooked off my weight belt on a jagged hunk of metal, my unexpected buoyancy slammed me into the ceiling, and I lost my flashlight. All in the space of three seconds.

Normally you'd unwind a safety line as you went deeper into a wreck so you could find your way out. A submarine is essentially a straight tube, though, and I wasn't too worried about getting lost. I was more concerned about the grapple line breaking or the anchor pulling free. It's easy to become disoriented at one hundred feet. A line to the surface marks your position and gives you something to hang on to for decompression stops. Just a little insurance.

I figured my one tank would be good for twenty to twenty-five minutes, so I attached a small air tank divers call a pony bottle onto my main tank. The pony has its own regulator and gives you an emergency supply of air. More insurance.

Skip was suiting up. "You still won't tell me what's down there," he said.

"It could be anything from an unexploded depth charge to a ledge of rock."

"The bottom's sandy here," he said. "No rocks. So it must be a big boomer."

I quickly outlined my plan. I'd lead the way. If there were a wreck below, we would reconnoiter for five minutes. If the inside were readily accessible, I'd make a five-minute exploratory entry while Skip waited outside. That would leave about fifteen minutes, which wasn't long, but would give us time for a four-minute decompression stop and a slight margin for error. I went over the side first, and Skip followed. I had strapped the spool to my back and carried a hand-held halogen light. A smaller flashlight was tucked into a pocket. I grabbed the *Gannet's* anchor line and pulled myself down. Skip was off to my right side, and a yard behind me. Visibility was about twenty feet. Not bad. We would need every inch we could get. Even on a sunny day like today the bottom would be as dim as the lovers' booth in a nightclub.

Halfway down, the outline of a dark shape began to emerge, silhouetted against the sandy bottom. I descended another twenty feet and switched on my light. If the wet suit weren't skintight, every hair on my body would have stood at attention.

I expected a blackened old hulk rusting on the bottom. I never thought I would see a *ghost* ship. Below me was the tapering end of an enormous cigar-shaped object, as big as a skyscraper laid on its side. But it wasn't the size that impressed me at first, it was the color. The thing seemed to glow with a greenish-white spectral energy. Slowly, as I pulled myself deeper along the anchor line, details emerged.

Bingo. There was no doubt about it. I had found my submarine.

As I played the flashlight beam over the sub, I saw that its surface was alive. Literally the weird glow came from thousands of moon-pale sea anemones clinging to the hull, some closed, like bunches of onions, others opened like star-shaped flowers. The growth hadn't taken in some of the rustier areas, so the sub had the mottled skin of a corpse that had been in the water. Silver clouds of baitfish nosed around the wreck in search of plankton.

The grapple prongs were firmly hooked onto a pipe exposed where the wooden deck that covered the pressure hull had rotted away. We were over the stern, looking down at the massive hydroplanes, like the wings of a Lear-jet, and the powerful propellers that could push the U-boat underwater at nearly twenty miles per hour. The sub rested on its keel, listing a few degrees to its portside. I could see about fifty feet of the hull before it faded into the greenish-brown gloom. A tap on the shoulder startled me from my trance. Skip pointed to his air-pressure dial. Five minutes gone. I curled my finger and thumb in the okay sign. Then, swimming side by side, we set off along the length of the sub for a reconnaissance.

When you look at a submarine on the surface, you only see the conning tower and the deck a few feet above the sea. Like an iceberg, most of the vessel is hidden underwater. Not until you view the sub in its entirety do you get the full impact. From a diver's viewpoint, the super sub was a monster. There were more than twenty feet between the keel resting on the bottom and the sub's deck. The massive conning tower on the *Elektroboot* was not open the way it was in the earlier U-boat models. It was enclosed except for a pair of small openings, with turrets for twin antiaircraft guns facing in either direction. The tower would have been protected by a sheetmetal coaming whose streamlined front angled forward in a sharp ridge that slanted down to the deck like the front on an old Prussian helmet. But the coaming had rusted away and only the conning tower itself remained.

The Type XXI was a magnificently brutal machine. Beautiful in its functional design, but ugly in its potential to ambush ships, send them to the bottom and their crews to horrible deaths. It could escape silently and quickly strike again. As we glided over and alongside the hull I picked out some of the features I had read about. The six forward torpedo tubes that could be loaded in a dozen minutes. The bulbous *Balkon Gerät* echo chamber, protruding from just below the bow, that could track multiple targets fifty miles away. I looked for the hull numbers, but they were covered by anemones. I had a good idea of what I would see if I scraped off the marine growth. The designation U-2872. Mac's super sub.

I swam down to the deck hatch forward of the conning tower. Skip followed. Kneeling on either side of the hatch in a slimy bed of anemones, we grabbed the wheel on the hatch cover and put our backs into turning it. I expected the cover to be rusted shut and was surprised when the wheel moved with only a little effort. A minute later we had the hatch open. The cover came up without a rush of bubbles that would have indicated air had been trapped inside the hull. I poked the flashlight into the hatchway, but it had been built at an angle so torpedoes could be loaded into the sub, and I couldn't see much.

I pointed to my chest, then into the sub. Skip nodded and gave me the okay sign. Tucking the gauges hanging from my air tank under my belt, I entered the hatch fins-first. I kept a hand down and the other up so I would have one free in the event I got stuck. Unencumbered, I could have made it in easily. But it was a tight squeeze with my dive gear on, and the air tank noisily bumped against the sides. Skip handed me the light when I was partway in. I inched downward and in a few minutes I had room to spread my arms again. I flicked the flashlight beam around. It bounced off the metal surfaces of long cylindrical shapes. I was in the torpedo room, a cavern with space to hold twenty-three missiles. The compartment was as still as death, but more than forty years ago there would have been the whine of hydraulic lifting gear the *whoosh* of compressed air as sweating crewmen sped each lethal fish on its deadly way.

I probed the darkness with my flashlight and discovered something quite incredible. I couldn't figure it. Conduits and wires hung down, and there was a brownish layer of debris on the floor, but the metal on the tangle of dials and gauges, racks, drums, pipes, and light fixtures touched by the cone of light looked almost new. Time had stopped here. The crew had gone out for a coffee break and never returned. All was ready and waiting for them to come back.

Air must have been trapped in this compartment when the sub sank. If the torpedo room had been flooded, the metal would have been rusted and corroded by salt water. I tried to reconstruct what had happened. Did the sub simply fall to the bottom of the sea? The hull had been built to sustain the pressure of one thousand feet. This depth would have been nothing. Did the men in the compartment die a lingering death thinking of families and fresh air, cursing the fools who had brought them to this place with vain dreams of Glory for the Fatherland? Why didn't they simply flood the compartment and escape with their breathing apparatus?

There was another puzzle. If air had been kept inside long enough to preserve the interior, the hatch would have blown back when we opened it. It didn't. That gave me two options to consider. Either my air-bubble theory was all wet, or somebody had been here before me. I moved the beam along the interior, trying to orient myself. I began to pick out details I hadn't noticed in my excitement, especially in the floor debris, and saw the crew hadn't left after all. I could see a femur. Then an armbone. A half-dozen hollow-eyed skulls stared vacantly at me. I took a deep breath and let it burble out. I was in an undersea charnel house. Dread clung to me like cobwebs. How many men had died here? This was a haunted place. I tried to shake off the chills and moved forward, swimming slowly into the compartment, pulling myself along by my fingertips so as not to dislodge rust from the bulkheads. Moments later I stopped. The skin on my scalp prickled. My pulse accelerated to Mach III.

Something had just grabbed me.

A silent scream echoed through the corridors of my brain. I imagined the white bones of a German seaman rising from the debris and reassembling themselves into a skeleton that reached over with a hold-on-buddy grip. Slowly, I backed up then reluctantly reached over my shoulder, expecting bony fingers to snap around my wrist in a vise grip. I breathed again. A piece of dangling wire had caught on a strap. I carefully unhooked it. Damn! My light slipped out of my hand. I lunged for it. My tank banged against a bulkhead. I was enveloped in a powdery cloud of rust. I let the flash go and pulled the small light out of my pocket and pointed it ahead. The thin beam bounced uselessly off the backscatter from the rust. I swam ahead until I was out of the cloud, moving until I was at the circular pressure door to the next compartment. The door was closed, as it would have been if there had been a sudden flooding. I grabbed the wheel and tried to turn it. It wouldn't budge.

In my mind, I ran over the schematic diagrams I had

seen in Mac's books. The torpedo room took up around a quarter of the sub's length. There would be crew quarters on the other side of the door. Probably more bones. Then the officers' quarters, radio and listening rooms, and just before the control room under the conning tower, would be the commander's cabin. Below would be long ranks of batteries used to power the sub underwater for up to eleven days. If the sub had been carrying a great deal of cargo, torpedoes would have been removed to make space. On the other hand, cargo could have been stowed elsewhere in the sub.

Maybe it was the bones. Maybe it was knowing that my air supply was limited. Or that I was in a steel coffin inches away from thousands of pounds of high explosives in the torpedo warheads. Acute claustrophobia set in. I could taste and smell the decay that surrounded me. I wanted to remove myself from this place of the dead. I'd come back later. For now I had one goal. *Get Out*. I turned and headed back toward the hatch. The rust cloud was starting to settle. The light I had lost was probably buried in the rubble. I didn't have time to spend poking around trying to find it.

I came to the other end of the torpedo room, stopped, and looked up, expecting to see green surface light slanting in from the hatch. There was only blackness. The hatch had disappeared. Had the cover been put back on? I felt a prickle of panic. I was going to drown in this place. The only sound was the metallic intake of the regulator valve and the burbling of each nervous breath, exaggerated by the silence of this grim tomb.

The bubbles from my exhalations bounced against the ceiling and sent down a light rain of dust. I thought my situation through. The ceiling! The sub was listing to one side. I had been looking directly above me for a hatch, forgetting that the sub was at an angle. I was in an *Alice in Wonderland* room where the ceiling was actually a wall. I swam back, looking off to the side, and saw a sliver of emerald. The hatch. One more moment of panic as I squeezed through. Then I was out, my heart thumping, wondering if I would have the guts to go back in. Maybe, if I had live company next time. I looked around for Skip. He was nowhere in sight.

Where the hell was he? Had he become bored and gone off to do some exploring on his own? Maybe he was in trouble. I checked my watch and pressure gauge. I'd been in the sub longer than I planned. I was less than ten minutes away from the end of my air supply. I swam over to the grappling line and got another shock. That was gone too. Quickly I reached over and undid the spool of line. I filled the lift bag with air, held the spool in two hands, and let the line unwind. I swam up to the conning tower and tied the line to a metal projection, then inflated the lift bag from my air tank and let it float to the surface. That would let Skip know my position if he was back on the boat.

A second later I learned I wasn't alone after all.

CHAPTER 21

•

The nebulous smear rose languidly off the U-boat's *Wintergarten*, the deck just aft of the conning tower, shimmering whitely against the dragon-scale green of the water. About twenty-five feet above the deck the apparition stopped and hung like a diaphanous dancer on an invisible Busby Berkeley stage. The sunlight filtering down from the surface was too dim at this depth for me to see exactly what I was looking at. But I could draw some basic conclusions. It wasn't Skip. It wasn't a fish. And I didn't want to be in the same ocean with whatever it was.

I had fewer than ten minutes before my main tank went dry and I had to go to my emergency air supply. Unless I wanted to join the German sailors in their undersea Valhalla, I would do well to get myself topside. I began a slow scissors kick upward. My unidentified companion stirred to life again and began to angle toward me as I ascended. I kicked backward in a sudden ninety-degree turn. The thing accelerated its speed. I stopped. It stopped too.

We hovered a dozen feet apart, facing each other like Doc Holliday and the Claggett brothers at the OK Corral. When Skip and I made our first pass over the sub, I had wondered about the vaguely boxy shape on the deck because the Type twenty-one hull had been designed with no equipment to offer resistance as the U-boat knifed through the water. Using my body as a measure, I estimated the object to be about six feet wide and a couple of feet longer than its width. The edges were rounded off and the part facing me bulged out in an angular convex surface. There was a red sparkle about dead center. As I squinted through my face mask, a blinding white light came on. I moved my head out of the glare and blinked the constellations from my eyes. The light beam reflecting back off the water revealed details in its glow. Below the spotlight was a Plexiglas housing around a foot across. Red sparks danced behind the plastic. My eyes lingered on the two steel arms and the scythelike claws at their tips. There could be no mistake, I was looking at the *Neptune*, Drake's missing Autonomous Untethered Vehicle.

The *Neptune*'s pincers made the claws on Whipple's ROV look like chopsticks. I wasn't going to stick around to see how they worked. I began to swim toward the surface again. The *Neptune* did the same, coming another foot closer. I stopped and swam sideways. The machine switched direction to keep pace, moving with unexpected nimbleness for something built like a home appliance. I swam backward. It came after me. I stopped. It stopped. We were about ten feet apart. The points of the cable cutters looked needle sharp. I sucked my stomach in.

This machine was acting very differently from the ROV. Whipple's baby had been guided by a nasty human intellect. It was aggressive, reacting instantly to my every move, anticipating my strategy, giving me no time to rest. The *Neptune* was a smart machine. But I guessed that in terms of human, or even dolphin intelligence, it was comparatively dumb. At the moment, however, that was no great reassurance. Even a dumb thing can kill. I tried to remember what Ivers had said about the AUV's electronic nervous system. The lasers behind the Plexiglas gathered information and transmitted it to layers of computers. They analyzed the data, made a judgment on what to do, based on the mission program and changing conditions, then transmitted the orders to the computers operating the thrusters, the camera, and navigational systems. And the claws. Don't forget the claws.

My movement qualified as a changing condition. The AUV was responding to it. I had the not-so-funny feeling that the mission programmed into the cold metal circuits behind the plastic facade could be boiled down to a simple equation.

Catch-um and eat-um.

Ivers had compared the AUV's system to a barn owl. The owl uses his acute senses to triangulate a target, swoops in, and *poof*. No more mouse. Terrific. If I twitched, *poof*, no more Soc. As long as I stayed in one place, I would not be owl meat. There was one major problem with this scenario. Time.

I had five minutes of air left. I would drown long before the *Neptune* had to go to the store for new batteries. I stared at the Cyclops' eye. Thinking.

Cyclops.

My mother had practically stuffed me through the university doors with the heel of her shoe to study the ancient classics. It probably never occurred to her that a classical education might some day save my life. It certainly never did to me, or I might have been more diligent with my homework.

With my air supply bottoming out, I had to act quickly. If I thought about it too long, I would be paralyzed. I had to go by instinct. I jackknifed and swam down toward the sub, slid over the rotting deck, then moved along the side of the hull toward the sea bottom. I made a right-angle turn where the hull met the sand and angled back up toward the deck. I coasted over the deck, looking down at the pressure-hull pipes and struts laid open by the deterioration of the wood. Searching for something, anything I could use, but finding nothing.

The *Neptune* could move fast in a straight line, but I was banking on the fact that it wasn't made to take turns like a Maserati, and that its computers would make it follow my course exactly. I was right. The AUV was hot on my trail, but it couldn't put together shortcuts and was having trouble on the sharp turns. It had fallen around thirty feet behind me.

I swam under the bow torpedo tube doors, came up on the other side of the downed sub, then set a course directly for the top of the conning tower. The *Neptune* rounded the bow and was after me, eating up the distance. I made it over the lip of the tower and slipped inside one of the two openings on top, between the gun turrets. *Neptune* skimmed overhead and hovered ten feet above me. It tilted down, its spotlight trying to probe my hide-away. I could just picture the computers saying, Waitaminute, mousie isn't supposed to go into a hidey-hole.

My father used to take me to a restaurant where a retired bookie was a regular customer. Like my father he was from Athens. His name was Jimmy and his white mustache had been turned yellow by exposure to cigar smoke. Pop often left me in Jimmy's custody while he talked politics with his friends. My mother would have been appalled if she knew I was being baby-sat by a nefarious character like Jimmy, but the little bookie taught me two things. One, how to win at checkers. And two, that gambling is for fools. I haven't played checkers in years. I have gambled, and lost, since then. And I was about to make a gamble now, but I didn't have much choice. Sorry, Jimmy, wherever you are.

I used my flashlight to explore the tower housing. The space was big enough to hold a high-school sock hop in. I could pick out the snorkel hood and the base for the periscopes sticking out of the conning-tower room. I was most interested in the junk lying under my fins. I pawed feverishly through the mess, stirring up dirty clouds. My gloved fingers closed on a hard metal shaft. I yanked. It wouldn't budge. I felt another piece next to it. I pulled on that and it came free. The six-foot-long shaft could have been part of the periscope, or maybe a strut or a gun barrel. It was heavily rusted on the outside, covered with green marine growth, and jagged at both ends. I tested it across my knee. The metal was still stiff. Good old German engineering. I hoped it was strong enough for what I had in mind.

I looked up. The AUV was hanging above the tower like a puppy wanting to play. Carrying the pipe in one hand, I eased my body out of the opening and over the rim of the tower, painfully aware that my butt was only a few tempting feet from the points of the mine cable cutters. I hoped my movements might be lost against the metal bulk of the submarine. I floated downward, staying close to the superstructure. The *Neptune*'s sensors were more sensitive than I expected. They picked up my motion. The AUV stirred, then started after me, matching my relaxed pace. I drifted toward the *Wintergarten*. Then I moved around to the starboard side, put my fins against the superstructure, and kicked away from the sub like a rocket.

The AUV hesitated for a second while its computers processed this new development and sent a command to the electric motor, then it came after me. About ten yards from the sub I did a U-turn that would have warmed the heart of a Boston cabdriver, and almost brushed elbows with the AUV on its way out. I slowed. As soon as the *Neptune* made its turn I shot straight toward the sub. I wanted to keep the machine moving until the last possible second. The timing would have to be just right, or I was done. I slammed against the slimy conning tower with my outstretched hand, fended off, and wheeled with my back to the sub.

The *Neptune* was moving toward me, picking up speed.

I jammed one end of the pipe against the side of the tower, looking for purchase in the slippery bed of anenomes and barnacles.

The spotlight grew larger. *Neptune*'s computers hadn't digested the information in time to reverse the thrusters.

I had been inspired to desperation measures. Like Odysseus, trapped in the cave of the Cyclops, his crew reduced by a couple of members whenever the one-eyed giant wanted to nosh. Odysseus had found a mast in the cave, cut off a section to a fathom's length, sharpened it to a point, and poked it into the fire to make it hard. Then he got the Cyclops into a drunken sleep and heated the olive-wood mast to a red-hot point in the ashes.

The AUV was headed right at me.

Even if its reverse propellers cut in now, they couldn't stop its forward motion. The machine weighed nearly half a ton and its momentum would send it slamming into the tower. Or me. Whichever came first.

The words of Odysseus raced through my mind.

When the fierce glow from the olive stake warned me that it was about to catch alight in the flames, green as it was, I withdrew it from the fire . . .

The machine's steel claws were angled at my gut. They were scalpel sharp, made to cut mine cable. They would slice through my neoprene suit, my flesh and bone as if they were air.

. . . and I brought it over to the spot where my men were standing ready.

Even if the claws missed me, I could be crushed if the shaft didn't hold.

Heaven now inspired them with a reckless courage.

I had to concentrate on the circle of plastic where the lasers were. I had to resist the urge to close my eyes. My exertions had used up extra air. I didn't dare risk glancing at the pressure gauge. I didn't have to. It was becoming damn near impossible to breathe.

Seizing the olive pole, they drove its sharpened end into the Cyclops' eye, while I used my weight from above to twist it home. . . .

I clenched my teeth, grasped the shaft in a death grip, and pointed the jagged end toward the midsection of the

oncoming machine, praying that the pipe wouldn't break
or bend. That the Plexiglas wasn't an inch thick. That my
arms wouldn't go rubbery. Dangerous, debilitating thoughts.
I swept them from my mind. I concentrated on the white
mass filling the narrow field of vision allowed by my face
mask, searching for the red laser sparkle under the blinding floodlight. The AUV was a few yards away. I braced
my back against the sub.

Now!

Carrunch.

The *Neptune* slammed into the shaft. My improvised
spear held. The length of pipe shuddered with the impact.
A second later it was wrenched from my hands. I kicked
upward, then off to the side, and looked back.

*He gave a dreadful shriek, which echoed around the
rocky walls, and we backed away from him in terror,
while he pulled the stake from his eye, streaming with
blood.*

The *Neptune* was spinning like a top. No shriek. No
blood. But blinded, nonetheless, by the shaft sticking out
of its electronic eye. I was safe. I would have breathed a
sigh of relief, except for one thing. I had run out of air.

CHAPTER 22

•

Those who have been to hell and back say Hades is a gloomy netherworld where shadows dwell and your worst nightmares come true. It must be something like the bottom of the sea. I was suspended between light and darkness, looking up at the chartreuse surface through the murk, yearning for a taste of the sun. I had to get to the top, and fast. I stuck the regulator from my pony bottle between my teeth and swallowed a full lungful of air. The reserve tank would give me a few more minutes, but I still had a decompression stop ahead of me.

Divers have been getting decompression sickness ever since people began acting like fish. When you breathe pressurized air underwater, your body tissues absorb nitrogen. The gas is released into the blood as you ascend, which is no problem if you take your time. But ascend too quickly and your blood froths like ginger ale newly poured from the bottle. The bubbles collect around the joints in a painful and frequently fatal condition called the bends. The old Greek sponge divers accepted the bends as a fact of life. And death. But in modern times the Navy came up with a system of decompression tables for divers. Just pause on your way up, follow the tables, and the nitrogen leaves your blood at a reasonable pace. It works fine if you have an unlimited supply of air. But I was already into my emergency tank, so there was no time to waste.

I needed a four-minute decompression stop at ten feet. I started up the line I had sent to the surface before my scrape with the *Neptune*. At fifteen feet I halted. Four minutes passed like four days. The sunlight on the water beckoned from a few yards away, almost within reach. I sucked the last dregs of air from the pony bottle. Then breathing became impossible. Shaving a few seconds off the decompression time, I headed up. I was rushing things, but I had no choice.

My head broke the surface. I gasped in the sweet lovely air and looked for the *Gannet*, thinking about the firm dryness of the deck, the bright warmth of the pilothouse. But there were only the unbroken sawtooth lines of endless waves. And me. I was alone, more alone than I have ever felt in my whole life. A lesser man might have panicked immediately in my place. I analyzed my situation first, *then* I panicked. You're in a real pickle this time, Socarides. You are miles from the nearest land. It will be dark soon. There isn't a boat in sight. You're tired from your fight with that floating can opener. The cold ocean water is sapping what strength you have left. Try to talk your way out of this one, big mouth.

My choices were very limited. I could float there for the rest of my life, which would be mercifully short. Cold was already seeping through my neoprene wet suit and into my bones. Soon I would be graced with the chattering teeth and blue skin of a full-blown case of hypothermia. Or I could swim. Maybe I could catch a ride on a passing porpoise. The nearest land was Devil's Bridge, around two miles away. If I swam at two miles per hour, a slow amble of a walk, I should be near land in about an hour, not counting time out for coffee breaks and the push-pull of tides and current. I reminded myself of the old Chinese proverb: *The longest journey begins with a single step.* Then I undid my useless air tanks, checked my compass direction, threw one arm out in front, and took a stroke. Then another. The sun dipped toward the horizon.

As I thrashed away at the interminable ranks of rolling seas I wondered about Skip. Had he simply taken his boat and deserted me? Or was he forced to leave? That was the more charitable view, but I was having a hard time buying it. Someone knew the AUV was hidden in the sub. Someone knew how to activate the machine and sic it onto me. And someone had left me out here to fend for myself.

I swam.

Swimming helped keep me warm. What I really needed was a shot of brandy and an electric blanket. I tried to maintain my usual brainless optimism, but the icy fingers closing around my heart were not just from the chilly waters. I knew that no matter how hard I tried, I was going to die.

I swam some more.

I stopped trying to fight my way up the sides of waves. I'd wait until a wave lifted me and started paddling as I slid down its slope into a water trough. Sometimes, to gain a few minutes of rest, I would flip over onto my back, letting the buoyancy vest keep my head out of water while I kicked with my fins. It was a comfortable position. I could look at the peaceful sky, see the jet trails, and picture the flight attendants moving down the aisle asking the passengers if they wanted a cocktail.

How did those old sea chanteys go? *Blow the man down, boys, we'll blow the man down, give us some time to blow the man down.* I swam in rhythm. Stupid. How the hell do you blow a man down? Turn a fan on in front of him?

Try another. *What should we do with the drunken sailor, what should we do with the drunken sailor, what should we do with the drunken sailor, early in the morning?*

Too fast.

Cape Cod girls they don't have combs, heave-away, heave-away, they comb their hair with codfish bones, heave-away, heave-away.

I stopped singing. It used up energy and was off-key anyhow. Time passed. I had no idea how long I'd been swimming. Had I dozed off? Maybe. Was I any nearer to Devil's Bridge? Who knows?

You know who built Devil's Bridge? Flagg was saying. God, Flagg, where the hell did you come from? He was talking in that arch, Indians-are-so-superior-to-white-men tone of his. No, Flagg, and I don't care. *Well, I'm going to tell you, 'cause you got no choice but to listen.* All right Flagg, go ahead. *Glad to, Soc. Well, Ol' Maushop wanted a bridge so he could walk to the mainland and catch whales by their tails on the way. He filled his apron with boulders, but a crab bit him on the toe and he threw the rocks all over the place jumping around.* I said, Maushop had one eye. *That's what the old-timers say,* Flagg responded. Just like the Cyclops. You know, that reminds me, Flagg, Cyclops was the son of Poseidon, seagod. The Romans called him Neptune. And I put out his son's eye. *Oh gee. Not a good enemy to make in your spot,* Flagg said. The thought of Neptune recalled Drake. I might be seeing him soon. Dr. Drake, I've got some bad news about that invention of yours.

I swam some more.

Flagg drifted off behind me until his voice became one with the slop and slosh of the waves. Good riddance. Let him tell his dumb legends to the fish.

The seas were only a foot high, but each one seemed as tall as Mount Washington. My arms and legs were becoming stiffer. My strokes grew more erratic and my kicks weaker, until they were nothing more than weary flutters. I began to smell fried clams. There was a murmur of friendly voices—Davy Jones's bar and grill. Hello, little mermaid, tresses glowing like emeralds. Come here often? What's your sign. Bet you're a Pisces.

The sun disappeared. Even after it was gone, the light

stayed in the pearly-red sky the way it does on the water long after night falls on the mainland. I thought I could see a gray peak on the horizon. It might have been land or low clouds, or just my imagination grasping for hope.

Dusk fell. The sky turned a deepening purple.

Red sky at night, sailor's delight.

A potbellied moon came out and smiled at me. I smiled back. Hello, moon. Thanks for the company. The moon's face became the faces of all the people living and dead that I had ever known.

I swam, flailing at the ocean. The ocean flailed back. My energy tank was nearing reserve. A traffic cop in my brain screamed at my muscles to stop. Time passed. Minutes. Hours. Days. I couldn't tell. I was losing all reference in the constant tossing of the seas. No up or down. No in or out. No nothing.

I was totally exhausted.

Gong. Ever so faintly.

It was getting hard to keep my mouth and nose out of the water. What the hell. I was beyond caring. My strokes were feeble splashes. It would be so easy to stop, to fall forward on the big water bed, turn the heater up high, wrap the soft down comforter around my aching shoulders, close my eyes, and let the waves rock me to sleep, asleep, asleep in the cradle of the deep.

Gong, gong.

Alarm clock was waking me out of a bad dream. Time to go fishing. Okay, Sam, meet you at the pier. Fire up the coffeepot.

Gong, gong.

I blinked my eyes open, angry at being awakened. I struck out toward the sound, unsure why I bothered. I crested the top of a wave. A green light was blinking. Down into the trough and the light disappeared, but the thought that I wasn't the only thing floating on the ocean had given me an adrenaline rush. I could see the light again, flashing every four seconds. I timed my strokes. One-two-three-four. One-two-three-four.

I was only a few yards away. Looking at a swaying buoy. From water level it was as tall as an oil derrick. It was the most beautiful gong buoy in the world. Uh-oh. There was a merman sitting there, chewing on fish and chips. Green skin, eyes glowing like red coals. Pardon me, sir, is this buoy occupied? Just stopping for a snack, he says, be my guest. Coleslaw's a little soggy anyhow. He slithers off into the waves in foamy whirl of phosphoresence. The buoy was mine, all mine.

The vertical framework of steel struts was about ten feet high and attached to a circular platform around eight feet across. At the top was the light. A bright, friendly Christmas light. Hanging just above the platform a bell was being hit by the four clappers. They clanged like church chimes, drowning out the hiss and roll of the sea. I caught the slippery rim of the rocking platform with two hands and tried to pull myself up. Fell back in. Tried again. Fell. I tried to talk it through. Rest for a minute, think it out, and try again. Use the lift from the waves. I moved around and grabbed one of the metal eyes on the rim of the platform and waited. One minute passed. An hour, a day, a light-year. Time expanding and contracting again.

There it was, a giant palm under my rump. Lifting me. Umph. I simultaneously kicked and pulled myself up by the metal eye. Then I reached over and clutched the edge of the battery compartment cover, a metal plate around a foot across, closer in toward the tower. Fighting to stay with the swaying buoy, I managed to pull my upper body onto the platform and get my leg up and wedged into the green skeleton framework. Finally I jerked my body fully onto the wet metal, grabbed a strut, and hugged the tower like a kid with a teddy bear. After a minute's rest I undid the straps on my vest and reclipped them around a strut to keep me from falling off.

The buoy rocked and rolled with me on it and the bell gonged insanely. It was a wonderful, glorious sound. I didn't care if I went deaf. The moon had disappeared behind a curtain of clouds. I sat there on my hard metal perch and waited, for what I wasn't sure. In time my weary brain succumbed and I fell into a sort of twilight-zone doze. Even the gong couldn't keep me awake.

Morning came. The sun was in my face. I must be back in my bedroom at the boathouse. I opened my eyes. Funny-looking sun. A little white sphere surrounded by darkness. Hallucinating again. I shut my eyes against the brightness and shook my head. A voice came booming out of the night. It must be God.

We're coming to get you, God said. *Do. You. Understand?*

Oh, for godsakes. Excuse me, God. Of course I understand. Swing low, sweet chariot, comin' for to carry me home. I could hear other voices, low and fragmented, other smaller suns flashed in the dark, came closer. Splashes. God yelling directions. Must be angels. The lights were only a few feet away. A hand reached out. There was a rubbery bump against the buoy and a line snaked around the metal framework.

I looked up, and listened carefully to catch those first sweet heavenly words.

"Ho-ly shit," the angel said.

CHAPTER 23

•

One of the young coastguardsmen who plucked me from Gay Head lighted gong buoy 29 off Devil's Bridge brought over another steaming mug of coffee. I was lounging on a bunk at the Woods Hole Group coast guard station, wrapped in a blanket like a Navajo, wearing borrowed jeans, shirt, and sweater. I'd been as cold and salty as a frozen margarita, but after ten minutes under the blistering spray of a very hot shower, my teeth almost stopped chattering.

An ambulance was waiting at the station to take me to Falmouth Hospital. Through numbed lips, I snarled at the driver to dig up another stiff. When the coast guard guys couldn't get rid of me, they poured super-heated chicken soup down my throat and called a doctor. He poked and prodded my aching body and said I might not get pneumonia, but don't count on it. Then he prescribed some antibiotics and said I was a tough old rooster who would live a long life if I moved as far away from the ocean as I could. He said Kansas was nice this time of year.

I was being treated like a celebrity. A living corpse. The

man who wouldn't die. A candidate for Ripley's *Believe it or Not*. Every person on duty at the station had come in to gawk and shake my hand. The guys who rescued me would be able to bore their children and grandchildren for years to come with the story. Ever tell you about the time we picked this guy off a buoy? Well, let me tell you again, kiddies. Half-drowned and froze, he was, and going out of his mind.

The forty-four-foot coast guard boat that found me was on drug patrol. With its long shoreline and protected bays, coves, and harbors, Cape Cod and the islands have been a smuggler's dream since before Prohibition. The coast guard can't stop every vessel on the seas, but sometimes it puts a boat in a traffic lane with orders to halt and search any suspicious craft traveling at night. Just to give drug smugglers something to think about. The coast-guardsmen hate it. Most of the crew are kids in their twenties. When nothing is happening, the duty is incredibly dull. When they do board a boat, it's Sweat City. They know a real drug smuggler can be aggressively protective of his cargo and his freedom. So the kids stand around with cocked M-16s that could go off if somebody sneezes, and pray that the boat is clean.

The patrol boat was near Devil's Bridge when it passed the gong buoy. They threw a spotlight on the buoy and saw a man in a wet suit taking a nap. I didn't have to explain what I was doing out there. What they were doing was looking for my body, thanks to Skip. He couldn't just waltz back to Woods Hole without me. Somebody might have known I was out on the *Gannet*. Questions would be asked. So he covered his fanny with a tall tale. He came in earlier that evening and told the coast guard I was lost. He said we had been diving, which was true, and that I stayed down far beyond my air supply, which was almost true. He said he had tried to find me, which was false, and when it seemed as if I had drowned, which was nearly the case, he attempted to call the coast guard for assistance. But his radio wouldn't work. Imagine that. He steamed to Woods Hole as fast as he could, hoping to stop a fishing vessel to relay the message for help, but didn't come across nary a one. Hours later he burst breathlessly through the front door of the station.

The rulebooks say you should always dive with someone who can help you in case of trouble. It's called the buddy system, but it only works when your buddy sticks around to lend a hand. I asked a Coastguardsman what position Skip gave for our dive and wasn't surprised to see it was the sunken fishing boat he told me about a few miles from the sub. Skip must have figured that by the time the coast guard got a patrol boat out there, I'd be safely dead and it would be just another saga of the sea. Someone from the station called Skip and told him the good news that the patrol boat picked me up. I would have liked to have seen his face when he heard I was still alive. I would have just liked to see his face. Period. So I could punch it.

I phoned Flagg as soon as my lips could move in anything resembling human speech. I told him I had found his missing *Neptune* AUV. I said it was slightly damaged, but didn't go into detail. I gave him the site coordinates as best I remembered them. He said he would get divers on it immediately. I asked him to tell the divers who went down after the AUV to keep their mouths shut about anything else they saw. Then I told him about Skip and his highly suspicious behavior. I suggested that Mallowes may have had something to do with the deaths of Drake and Whipple and that he be found and detained for any reason. Half an hour later, Flagg came over to the coastguard station and we found a private office where we could talk. I laid out the whole story, including the U-boat. Flagg listened for fifteen minutes, responding only with a grunt here and there. When I was through talking he said, "A big steel tomb. I told you this thing had the stink of death."

"Don't get mythical with me, Flagg. Not now."

He gave me a sullen glance. "Why didn't you call me before you went out and got yourself in a big mess?"

There were a couple of answers to that question. The real reason was quite embarrassing, given the outcome of my expedition. I had wanted to solve the case on my own, to show Flagg I was smarter than he was. But he didn't have to know that. I replied, "I wanted to surprise you."

"Huh," he said. "Figures."

I shook the hands of the crewmen who had rescued me and refused their kind offer to stay at the station for the night. It would have been fun to play a few hands of cribbage, but I was afraid a newspaper reporter would find me. I wasn't ready to tell my harrowing story to the whole world. Flagg gave me a ride home. Later I would walk over to get my truck at the fish pier where I'd left it when I went out with Skip. The guest house looked like the Taj Mahal to my weary eyes. It was the wee hours of the morning when I crawled between the sheets I never thought I would see again. I fell asleep almost immediately.

I dreamed I was rocking. I reached out with my hand, expecting to feel the slimy wet surface of the buoy, and mumbled a prayer of thanks when I grabbed a woolly fistful of blanket. The rocking started again. I opened my eyes. Sunlight was streaming through the white cotton curtains. Someone was in my room. I looked toward the foot of the bed. Flagg was standing there shaking the mattress.

"We got it," he said.

I sat up. "The *Neptune*?"

"We got a chopper out there with some divers. They found the AUV just where you said. It's back at Drake's lab right now."

"Great," I said. "When can you get it to Bermuda?"

"They can put it on a plane at Otis air base and fly it there in two hours or less. The only problem is, the machine's busted up."

I lay back on my pillow and groaned. "How soon can you get it working?"

Flagg sat on the sofa and shook his head. "You fixed

that baby real good, Soc. The lasers can be replaced, but the water got into the works. The sensor-computer system is beyond repair. She'll never work again."

I sat up and swung my legs off the bed and onto the floor. I leaned my face against my palms. The news was searing. In disabling the *Neptune*, I had killed the last chance for the three men in the minisub a mile beneath the ocean.

"What's the situation on the *Rosy*?" I wasn't sure I wanted to hear the answer.

"About the same. They're in touch with the surface, but they're trying to conserve their batteries and it's getting chilly down there.'"

"How much time does the crew have?"

"About twenty-four hours if the cold doesn't get to them first. But don't stick your head in the gas oven yet. There's some good news."

I looked at Flagg through my fingers.

He said: "Drake built another sensor system."

"What are you saying, Flagg?"

"We found mention of it when my technical guys went through Drake's papers after he was murdered. He knew this was the most fragile component of his AUV, even without someone smashing it silly with part of an old German sub, so he built a redundant system. The whole thing is contained in an aluminum tube around four feet long. It was made so it could be slipped into place if something went wrong with the original hardware. Trouble is, it's missing."

We locked stares. "Skip," I said. "Any word on him?"

Flagg smiled in spite of himself. "He filled up his boat's gas tank at the fish pier and left Woods Hole sometime during the night. We had the coast guard looking as soon as it turned daylight. Figured he couldn't have gone far."

I got off the bed and started pulling on my clothes. "Dammit, Flagg. Why didn't you wake me up and tell me earlier?"

"Didn't seem much sense to disturb you. Thought I'd let you sleep until something happened. Now it has. I just heard a few minutes ago. Coast guard helicopter has located a boat they think is Skip's. I told them to stay out of sight and not do anything until I arrived and looked things over. Thought you might like to know."

I grabbed my jacket. "You can tell me about it on the way."

Flagg's government ID card was like a magic wand. He simply waved it in front of people and any potential resistance to his wishes melted. The Woods Hole fishing-boat captain we accosted at the pier was about to give us a song and dance when we wanted to hire his boat. In an impressive display of intimidation, Flagg brandished the official laminated card with his picture on it so close to the fisherman's nose he couldn't read the fine print, then tucked it back into his billfold. He said we were Environmental Protection Agency inspectors who had to check out a pollution report near Cuttyhunk Island in a big hurry. Out of the kindess of his heart, he sweetened the pot with two hundred dollars in cash. Within minutes we were cutting a foamy wake out of Woods Hole and heading into Buzzards Bay.

Ecstatic over his windfall, the skipper didn't ask the obvious question. Why hadn't we simply requisitioned a boat from some government agency? I'm sure Flagg would have had an answer for him. We had, in fact, thought of commandeering a coast-guard boat, but quickly dropped the idea. Skip would take flight as soon as a boat with orange hull stripes came within binocular range.

The fishing boat followed a course north of the Eliza-beths between the island chain and the mainland. Flagg leaned against a forward rail, looking out at the treeless, potato-colored mounds passing on our port side. His face was a dusky mask, his eyes half-closed in the drowsy sea stare people get when they look out from a boat. I leaned on the rail beside him and, like Flagg, soon was mesmerized by the dappled surface of the water and the hiss of the bow wash.

After a few minutes Flagg asked, "Ever hear how those islands were formed?"

I could feel another Indian legend coming on. I resisted it. "Yeah. Big glaciers from the north, the same ones that carved Cape Cod out of the ocean. They scooped up the earth and left the islands."

"Naw, that's white man's talk," he said in mock seriousness, waving an arm at the low-lying hills. "Old Maushop did it. Things were in a mess on the mainland, folks fighting and killing themselves. The big guy couldn't stand all that turmoil, so he headed east. He traveled for months, but even a giant can get worn out. He dragged his big toe and it dug a track out of the marsh. The water came in and made the islands. After he had a chance to rest, Maushop dragged his toe again, on purpose this time, and cut the Vineyard off from the mainland so his people would have a peaceful place to live."

"Did it work?"

Flagg looked at me, mischief in his black eyes. "Naw," he said. "Things are still in a mess."

Buzzards Bay can be as cantankerous as the North Sea, especially in the afternoon when the freshening breeze kicks up jagged seas as tall as a basketball player. We were in luck today. The bay was as calm as a bathtub, and the fishing boat made good time. We passed Nawshawena Island and approached Cuttyhunk. One hour after leaving Woods Hole we rounded the north Cuttyhunk jetty and entered the harbor through a channel so narrow you could toss a quahog from one shore to the other. We tied up at the main dock where the shuttle ferry lands after its one-and-a-half-hour trip from New Bedford, the old whaling city that lies fourteen miles across the bay to the north.

I had been to Cuttyhunk a half-dozen times, stopping off at the island on fishing trips. It's the kind of place that can be heaven or hell, depending on your perspective. If traffic is your bag, and noise and congestion, even the floatplane that services the island can't get you back to the real world fast enough. Those who yearn for a simpler and quieter life want to stay there forever. About two dozen of them live on the island year-round. There were three fishermen working on their boats near the pier, but even with Flagg, our boat captain, and myself, people were outnumbered by the sea gulls. Flagg and I told our hired captain to wait for us. We walked over to the red-roofed building that used to be a coast-guard boathouse. It's a warehouse now. A middle-aged man with a friendly face was working inside. Flagg flashed his ID card again. He said we were doing chart survey work for the National Ocean Service and that we needed some transportation. The man said he was using his jeep, but we'd be welcome to take his golf cart.

We pulled out onto the road like a couple of duffers driving along the ninth fairway at the Oyster Harbors Club and headed to the town of Gosnold, less than a quarter mile away. Gosnold was the English explorer who discovered the island in 1602 and went on to name Cape Cod. Except for the cluster of white and gray clapboard-and-shingle houses that tumble down the side of a gentle slope facing toward the habor, the island probably hasn't changed much in the last three hundred years.

It was deathly quiet. Ordinary sounds like the squeak of hinges on a windblown sign or the snap of laundry hanging on a line were stentorian in volume. A cat crossed the street in front of us and I would have sworn I heard the stomp of its paws. We drove through the village center where the island's only store was in the back of someone's house, past the shuttered inn, the one-room schoolhouse, and the white-shingled Methodist church with the striped-bass wind vane on its cupola. A narrow blacktop road bordered by a flagstone wall goes to Lookout Hill, an Everest that soars 150 feet above sea level. We passed four people on the way. I estimated we had seen one third of the island population.

At the top of the hill one of the dozens of deer that run free on the island crashed into the bushes, startled by our arrival. The only other sound was the wind murmuring in the guy wires of a skinny radio tower. Not far from the tower is a huge airplane propeller that looks as if it could lift the whole island if it ever got going. Someone put the thing up a few years ago to produce wind power. Now the cost of hooking it to a generating plant would be too high and nobody knows how to do it anyhow.

We silently climbed an observation platform that over-looked the harbor and Cuttyhunk Pond. Copicut Neck, a low hill to the northwest, was attached to Cutty by a narrow sandy peninsula. When the weather is clear, you can see the reddish bluffs of Gay Head on Martha's Vine-yard, the railroad bridge at the Cape Cod Canal, and the New Bedford mainland. Today they were obscured by a solid wall of fog rolling across Buzzards Bay.

Flagg had lifted a pair of binoculars to his eyes and was peering beyond Copicut at a small barren island with the profile of a Bactrian camel: two low humps separated by a shallow valley. Cuttyhunk looked like a lush tropical forest by comparison. Unlike the sandy Cape, the island had a rocky, unforgiving shoreline that could make mince-meat out of a boat's bottom.

He lowered the binoculars and handed them to me. "Over there," he said. "Near that cove."

I took the glasses and followed the line of his finger. I could see two or three houses and a small pier. At anchor in the inlet was a white fishing vessel.

"Looks like Skip's boat," I said, handing the glasses back. "Penikese Island. Always makes me think of one of those little pug-nose mutts with the bowlegs. I think the state runs a camp on the island for bad boys. Sort of fitting to find Skip there."

"We can send him to camp later. The big question is what we do now."

"We could call in the Sixth Fleet and surround him. Maybe he'd give himself up if we did that."

"What do you think?"

"I think it's a lousy idea. He'd try to make a break for it and you'd have to blow him out of the water. If he's in a mean mood, he might destroy that AUV part or dump it over the side."

"That's what I was thinking. You got any ideas?"

I pointed to the fog bank rolling across the bay. "It's easy. All we have to do is sneak up to the boat in the fog and grab him."

Flagg winced. "Easy, huh. Sneak up and grab him." He cocked his head. "Trouble is, it makes as much sense as anything. Maybe I've been hanging around you too long."

We got back in the golf cart and drove back down the hill to the fish pier on Cuttyhunk Pond. It would have been a great place to set up a canvas and easel and paint the pier, the line of shanties and the workboats, but we had other priorities. We needed water transportation. Five minutes later we found what we were looking for. Drawn up on shore was a Zodiak rubber inflatable boat, the kind favored by Jacques Cousteau and drug smugglers. The Zodiak had a brand new Johnson thirty-horsepower engine.

A lobsterman was scraping the paint off his boat in dry-dock. We said we wanted to rent the Zodiak for a few hours and were looking for the owner. Flagg flourished his badge again. It was National Marine Fisheries Service this time. The lobsterman said he would be glad to rent the boat. Flagg gave him a hundred dollars just so he wouldn't worry. The man said he wasn't worried. The inflatable belonged to his brother-in-law, who lived on the mainland. And even if we wanted to steal the boat, he said we wouldn't get far in the thick fog that was rapidly moving in on Cuttyhunk. He seemed to find the notion amusing.

I took the Zodiak around to the ferry dock while Flagg drove the golf cart back and dismissed our fishing-boat captain. We barely made it out of the harbor before the

Zodiak was caught in the grip of a chill gray cloud that cut visibility down to yards. We stayed on a compass heading that would take us, I hoped, to the westerly end of Penikese. Our plan was to run just offshore. We'd be going into the wind, so the buzz of our motor was less likely to carry. When we neared Skip's boat we would kill the motor and switch to paddle power.

After a half hour we could catch glimpses of the ash-hue shore of Penikese. I pointed the Zodiak more or less parallel to the beach. A few minutes later I shut down the motor. Flagg took a Colt Government Model 9mm automatic from the waterproof bag he carried his binoculars in and checked the action and load.

Eyeing the dull finish on the pistol, I said "I've got a plan, Flagg."

"That would be nice." He sighted down the barrel at an invisible target. "I've got a plan too. We climb aboard, and if the mother doesn't cooperate, we drill him."

That's what I was afraid of. "I was thinking more how I would like to climb aboard and talk to him first."

Flagg slammed the clip into the pistol butt and looked at me, as if I'd just announced my intention to give up drinking beer.

"Dammit, Soc, the guy's a psycho. He's probably killed two people and he tried to kill you. It was just sheer luck you're still alive. What the hell are you going to talk to him about? You going to trade recipes for cooking codfish cheeks?"

"You don't have to get nasty, Flagg. No, I don't want to trade recipes. Okay, turn him into a sieve with that cannon. Suppose the replacement part for the *Neptune* isn't on board. You can say good-bye to those guys trapped in the minisub if you blow him away. I'm interested in the U-boat too. And I haven't forgotten about Drake and Whipple. Look, let me see what I can pry out of him, then you can drill him if you still want to. As you pointed out, I'm the one he tried to kill, so that should give me some say in this."

Flagg showed me he knew how to curse. Then he tucked the pistol inside his windbreaker. "Okay. How do you want to work it?"

"I'll climb aboard, talk to him, and when I get him off guard I'll signal you and we can jump him."

Flagg looked as if he had an upset stomach. "Great. I'll kneel down behind him and you push him down over my back. That's some plan, Soc. That's really a great plan. I can't believe I'm letting you talk me into this." He shook his head in disgust. "What kind of signal?"

"I'll try to get Skip out on the deck. We'll talk, then I'll say something like, 'It's all over, Skip. The clock's run out for you.' " I felt like George Raft in a forties gangster movie.

"That ought to scare the crap out of him. What if I'm not in earshot and can't hear you?"

"Try to get someplace where you can keep an eye on me. I'll cross my arms across my chest."

"I guess that'll have to do," Flagg grumbled. He glanced at his watch. "Just don't get carried away talking over old times."

We began to paddle in quiet, even strokes, just the tips going in the water, pulling back in a clean easy motion, pushing the Zodiak forward a couple of yards at a time, the shore barely visible off to our left. I estimated twenty minutes to Mallowes's boat. The current pushed us along and we were there in half that. The *Gannet*'s bow towered above us. We grabbed the anchor line and held on, listening for movement on the deck. Flagg brought out his pistol and held it on his lap. There was a muffled banging of metal on metal from inside the boat. Flagg leaned forward and whispered in my ear. "Sounds like the guy's working on his engine."

I nodded and pointed toward the stern. We let the Zodiak drift with the current, fending off with our hands, until we had gone the full length of the *Gannet*. I stood up and slipped a line from the inflatable boat around a deck cleat.

"Remember the signals," I said softly. I crossed my arms and mouthed the words, "The clock has run out for you."

Flagg gave me a black look and reached into his bag. He pulled out another pistol and proffered it to me. Unbelievable. The guy was carrying more hardware than the James brothers. I shook my head. I slipped my sneakers off and stretched to where I could peer over the deck. It was deserted. I took a deep breath and I hoisted myself up. A second later I was on Skip's boat.

CHAPTER 24

•

I slithered across the slippery deck like a beached eel, inching toward the shelter of the box used to hold fish on the aft deck. There was a sharp metallic clink from the direction of the engine compartment, forward of the pilot-house. Then a harsh curse. The engine was getting the best of Skip. Seconds later footsteps came toward me. I froze, then relaxed when Skip went down into the galley. In a few minutes the aroma of coffee tickled my nose. I stood, and soft-shoed it to the top of the short companion-way that led below. I peered down into the galley. Skip was facing the stove, his back to me.

"Peekaboo," I said.

Skip whirled around and stared at me fearfully. His mouth, which had been set in a deep frown, dropped open in a guppyish gape.

"Soc," he whispered.

I took a step forward and sat at the top of the stairs. "I was in the neighborhood and thought I would drop by to say hello."

Skip realized he was holding a coffeepot in his hand.

He took a mug out of the sink and filled it, using slow, deliberate movements. He was stalling, focusing on a simple immediate task while he pulled himself together. He took a sip.

"You caught me by surprise, Soc."

"I know it's rude not calling ahead, Skip, but I couldn't find a phone. I hope it's not inconvenient."

"Hell no, not at all. Welcome aboard." His mouth broke into a smile. "I was taking a break. I'm having engine trouble. The fuel pump is acting up again. Just about got it fixed when the wrench slipped and I skinned my knuckles." He showed me the back of his hand. The freckled skin was scraped and bloody. "I almost threw the wrench through the engine block. You know how it is. So I thought I would take a few minutes to calm down, then go back and finish the job."

"There's no big hurry," I said. "You'll need garden shears to cut through the fog. You may have to stay here awhile."

He gave a bemused shake of his head.

"Hell, Soc. A little fog never stopped me," he said disdainfully. "I know these waters better than my front yard. I fished for stripers and blues out here when I was a kid. I'll just take it real slow, use my radar in case there's anybody around who doesn't know what he's doing. Fog's kind of nice. Separates the real sailors from the fair-weather ones. Coffee?"

I nodded.

He filled a second mug and glanced playfully over my head. "Any more company I should pour some coffee for?"

"Not that I know of," I said.

He strolled over nonchalantly and handed the mug to me. I watched his eyes. They would telegraph a move if he were going to make one. The blue orbs looked at me blandly. Skip wasn't ready to act. He was as curious about me as I was about him. He simply said, "Good, let's go up to the pilothouse and have a talk."

"That's what I came for, Skip."

I backed up the stairs to the deck and stepped aside to let Skip pass. He paused and sniffed the damp air like a hound downwind of a rabbit. Then he sauntered along the rail until he came to the stern where the Zodiak was tied. He stopped where I had cleated the Zodiak's line to the *Gannet*.

He looked at me. "Come across from Cuttyhunk?" he said.

"It seemed like a nice day to take a boat ride."

Skip leaned over the side. I tensed, waiting for the blast of Flagg's pistol. Nothing happened. Skip stepped back from the rail.

"Zodiak. I guess they're a nice little runabout. I never liked the idea of floating on a rubber tube, though. Old-fashioned, I guess. I prefer the feel of a solid deck under my boots."

I was half listening. Trying not to let my eyes stray. I wondered where Flagg was hiding.

Skip ambled over to the pilothouse and I followed him inside. He settled into the captain's seat behind the wheel. I leaned against the bulkhead next to the door. He drank his coffee and looked out toward the boat's bow, which was lost in the thickening fog.

After a moment's thought Skip said, "I heard you made it back to Woods Hole without me."

"I had a nice swim and spent some time on the Devil's Bridge gong buoy before a passing coast-guard forty-four-footer picked me up."

"Devil's Bridge. That must have been some trip," Skip said thoughtfully. He pulled a chart off a rack, spread it out, and ran his forefinger from one point to another. He clicked his tongue. "You were darned lucky, Soc. The current was going your way and the water and air temperature has warmed up. A couple of weeks ago you wouldn't have survived more than a few hours."

"Sorry I messed up your plans, Skip."

He turned his friendly blue eyes on me again. "I hope you don't think it was personal, that stuff with the AUV and leaving you out there like that."

"I'm glad to hear it wasn't personal. I was beginning to think you didn't like me."

"Nothing like that. You caught me off guard when you said you wanted to dive on that position, where the submarine was, and I had to improvise. I tried to sneak the boat off site when you weren't looking, but you caught me." He chuckled. "Boy, was I flabbergasted when I learned you knew about the U-boat."

"Finding the sub was just an accident. I came across the chart coordinates in Drake's papers and wanted to take a peek at what was down there."

"Funny. That's how we found the U-boat in the first place. It was pure accident. Dr. Drake and I were running some field tests with the *Neptune*. We wanted to give the vehicle its head in deep water and put her in at the hundred-foot depth contour. The AUV was programmed to fix on any metal anomaly and broadcast pictures back. We were amazed when the vehicle pinpointed the wreck. That *Neptune*'s a sweet piece of machinery, isn't it?"

"Not as agile as the ROV in the lab's test pool," I ventured. "Did you try to make that one bite me too, Skip?"

"You can't blame me for the ROV, Soc, and I'm only partially responsible for the *Neptune*."

"I think you're saying the *Neptune* had a grudge against me."

He laughed casually. "Oh no, nothing like that. It's just a machine. While you were in the U-boat, I took the opportunity to swim back to the boat. There's a control box on board that works off a transponder floating in the water. I simply gave the AUV a computer command to use its articulators on any man-sized object that moved. The vehicle was acting on its own after that. When you were stationary, it watched. When you moved, it followed. I left, assuming that the outcome would be a foregone conclusion. What happened?"

"Your toy got out of hand, so I smashed the laser eye out with a piece of metal from the submarine."

A flicker of pain crossed his face. "That would certainly do it," he said.

"It did. But go on with your story. What happened after you and Drake found the U-boat?"

Skip rolled up the chart he had been looking at, ever the neat sailor, and tucked it in its rack.

"You can imagine how excited I was. I wanted to dive immediately. Dr. Drake insisted on preliminary research before he did a thing. He was very much the scientist in that way. He dug into the files and wrote some people in Germany for background information. I couldn't wait. I went out alone without telling him and dived on the sub. It was supposed to be just a recon dive, to get an idea of what we were dealing with. But when I saw it firsthand there was no stopping. I went back several times and finally pried the hatch open."

"That explains why the cover didn't blow back when we opened it."

"That's right. I had already released the air from inside the torpedo room."

"Did Drake ever dive on the sub? He mentioned he had done some salvage work in Florida."

"Oh yes. He was an experienced diver. In a way, that's what precipitated the problem. When Dr. Drake learned I had gone into the sub without him, he was livid. He accused me of trying to cut him out of any valuable cargo on the U-boat, but he said it didn't matter. He said he was going to go public with news of the U-boat's discovery. He said the West Germans or the rightful owners would claim anything we found."

"So you killed him?"

Skip looked like a kid who'd been wrongly accused of putting his hand in the cookie jar.

"Oh no, Soc. I wouldn't do anything like that. Dr. Drake and I might have been able to work it out. I would have settled for a reasonable division of any treasure. I'm not a greedy man. Besides, we never did get beyond the torpedo room. Maybe there never was anything of value on board. And even if we did find a large cargo of gold, jewels, or mercury, it would have been pretty tough to dispose of without attracting attention. No, the real reason for our falling-out was the *Neptune*'s eye."

"You've lost me, Skip."

"Sorry. Let me explain. It wasn't an eye in the usual sense. It was the computer-sensor system for the *Neptune*, and I was the one who made it work. Drake had hit a wall in his research. The vehicle has to be able to respond to changing conditions. Think of it in human terms. You or I come into a strange room. What we see is contained in a narrow cone of vision, but we have an internal model of the world we live in. We know from experience there are other objects in the room even if we can't see them. Sort of a mind's eye. It keeps us from tripping over chairs. That was the main problem with the *Neptune*, coming up with the model so the machine could function as it absorbed new data."

He opened a drawer and took out a sketchbook similar to the one he showed me on our first dive together. He leafed slowly through the book. The pages were covered with intricate, finely detailed pencil sketches and equations like runic writing.

"Those look like plans for an English garden maze," I said.

"It was like a maze in a way," Skip said. "I have only a limited amount of technical training, but I'm pretty good at creative concepts. I showed Drake how to bridge the gap, to link the sensors and the computers. These are some of the routes I suggested. To his credit, he jumped right in and carried the ball to the production stage."

"But Drake was going to take all the credit for himself."

"Very good, Soc. You *are* a detective."

"You must have known he had a reputation for stealing the work of others."

"I knew that, and obviously I should have been more careful. But he changed the subject whenever I brought it up. He said that I was lucky to be associated with him, and I thought so too. But I still pressed him. He started to avoid me completely. So one night I called saying I had made a very exciting find on the U-boat and that I would meet him at the fish pier to tell him about it."

"Had you found something?"

"Oh no. That was just bait. He seemed to have his mind on other things that night, but he blew his stack when he learned the real reason I wanted to meet him was to discuss my contribution to the success of the Neptune project. He said he would give me no credit whatsoever for the AUV. Sue me, he said. So there was nothing coming to me from my work on the *Neptune*, or on the sub, and it was the AUV, after all, that led to the discovery of the U-boat. It didn't seem fair. Drake would get all the honors, all the attention and money. I would end up with nothing. Nothing," he said desolately.

"So you killed him."

"I didn't plan to, really. Drake had a quick tongue. I tend to be a little slow on the uptake. He told me I had spent too much time in the sun and that my brains were addled," Skip scowled; it was obvious that Drake's taunts still bothered him. "That I was the town buffoon and nobody would ever believe I had a hand in the *Neptune*'s design. That hurt, because I always thought he respected me. He walked away from me. I followed. We stopped at the seal pool. We argued. I had my filleting knife. Well, you know the rest."

"That explains Drake. Why kill Whipple?"

Skip sighed. "Totally unnecessary. Dan just couldn't mind his own business. Dr. Drake and I moved the *Neptune* only at night from its special warehouse at the NTI lab. Whipple had been spying on us. He had seen us take the AUV out a few days before I met the doctor at the seal pool, and he thought I still had it on my boat, but he was wrong. I had put the AUV on the U-boat's deck until I decided what to do with it. I thought its disappearance might divert suspicion."

"It did. The government suspected the Russians had snatched it. The feds were going to stake out the Soviet research vessel when it came into Woods Hole."

He laughed. "Can you imagine? I didn't intend to precipitate an international crisis. I guess that's the kind of world we live in. Anyway, Dan had a vague idea that he'd 'find' the Neptune somehow and this would make him a hero. He suspected me in the doctor's death and suggested that gave him some leverage over me. I went along. Then you came into the picture and he really started to drink. He'd been drinking when he made the rash decision to attack you with the ROV in the test pool and to fake his injuries. It gives you an idea of the muddled state of his mind."

"Why did he want to kill me?"

"Dan thought you were closing in on him. You had been asking him questions, talking to Bert Ivers. He became absolutely paranoid. When you began to put the pressure on, he really popped. He called me in a panic. He said he was going to meet you and tell you to bug out, but I knew better. He was going to spill the whole story. I followed him to the library. He denied it, but he was lying. Well, I had to stop him."

"You forgot your filleting knife."

"I heard footsteps—yours, I guess. I had to leave by a side entrance. Don't worry about the knife," he said emotionlessly, "I'll get another."

"You made a mistake killing Whipple," I said. "I thought he murdered Drake. He had all the motives. And when you come right down to it, Whipple knew very little about you that he could prove."

"He knew I had been working on the Neptune. If that got out, it would draw attention to me. I couldn't take the chance." Skip drained his coffee mug, looking at me over the rim, then put it down on a shelf. "Well, it's been pleasant talking to you again, Soc. Now I've got to tend to that engine and be on my way."

"Where are you going?"

"It's time for a sea change. Someplace warm might be nice. There are a lot of islands in the Caribbean where nobody asks questions."

"There's something you should consider first." Briefly, I told him about the three men trapped in the minisub off Bermuda.

He looked mildly interested in the situation for a second, but only a second. I thought he was going to tell me to go fly a kite. Unexpectedly he said, "Okay. I'll get you the spare part. It's of no use to me. C'mon."

We went out onto the deck where the fog whirled around us. Skip stepped over to a sea chest and opened it. I glanced around. There was a shadow near the stern. Flagg moving into position? Skip reached into the chest and pulled out a harpoon gun. He was just full of little surprises. He quickly cocked the amber-colored rubber sling, wrapped his hand around the pistol grip, and pointed the spear at my chest. My eyes fixated on the needle-sharp barb. I heard the twang of the rubber, saw the spear slide off the black barrel and fly toward me in a silvery blur, felt the steel point slam into my rib cage and puncture my heart, watched the lifeblood spurt from the hole in my chest onto the deck.

"I really am sorry about this," Skip was saying, and he probably meant that too.

I gulped. I'd been playing out my death in my mind. Skip raised the speargun to his shoulder. The dress rehearsal was over. Things were moving too fast. I backed up a few steps, looking for Flagg. He must be waiting for the damned signal.

"I hate to put you in a position where you have to apologize," I said, raising my voice. "So why not change your plans? *The clock's run out for you, Skip.*" The signal.

Skip's jaw muscles tightened. The baby-face expression had vanished and was replaced an uncaring stare. He took a step forward.

"I'm afraid you're the one who's run out of time." He squinted to take aim.

Maybe Flagg didn't hear me. It must be damn obvious it was his turn to get into the act. I tried the visual signal and crossed my arms.

Still no Flagg.

Keep talking. "What about Jane?" I tried in desperation. "You never said anything about her? Isn't that why you really killed Drake? You did it because you were in love with Jane. You didn't like the way Drake treated her. You wanted her for yourself."

Skip lowered the speargun to his chin. The smile came back onto his face. "Jane." He said the name softly, savoring its sound. "You are right about one thing. I loved her. From afar, of course. When they separated I thought there was a hope, although I knew deep in my heart that there wasn't. She still loved him. She'd never let go of that. I suppose in the back of my mind I thought that with him out of the way I might have a chance, but I never actually believed it. Did it enter into my actions?" He mused. "I don't know. Maybe. But it was mostly the *Neptune*."

He raised the speargun again. His finger tightened around the trigger.

I was backed against the fish box on the main deck. I could go no further. Skip was about to play Captain Ahab with me as Moby Dick.

"Help!" I yelled. This was no time to get fancy.

I tried to yell again, but my throat felt full of sawdust. I braced myself for the shock of the spear.

"Freeze!" Flagg's voice, coming from behind me.

Skip's head jerked up and he shifted the speargun onto a new target off to my right.

"Don't try it, Mallowes," Flagg barked. "One twitch of your finger and I shoot."

Skip was going for the big move. There was little chance

he would beat Flagg to the punch, but I don't think he really cared, even if pulling the speargun trigger was the last thing he ever did in this life. I pushed off with my hands from the fish box, came in low, dropped one shoulder, and threw the other into his midsection. The elastic sling went *sprong*. The spear catapulted from the barrel. Skip crashed backward onto the deck. I was on him, knees digging into his chest. He chopped at my face with the speargun handle. I dodged with a boxer's roll of my head and only caught a sideswiping blow to the chin. I hunched forward to get inside Skip's flailing arms and smashed him in the jaw with my right elbow. His head snapped to one side and his eyes lolled. The speargun clattered onto the deck. Skip was out for the long count.

Flagg loomed over me. He was breathing hard.

"What the hell took you so long?" I barked. "He was ready to serve me up as shish kebab. Didn't you get the signals?"

"Yeah, I got the signals," he shot back. "Doing it for your own good. He had that thing pointed at your belly. I was afraid he'd stick you if I just popped up and surprised him." He pinched his thumb and forefinger an inch apart and stared cross eyed at the space in between them. "The sucker missed me by *that* much," he said in disbelief. "That friggin' much."

"What are you complaining about? He missed you."

"Last time I let you talk me into a dumb plan like that," Flagg said. He knelt down and peeled Skip's eyelids back. "Huh. But I have to admit you did a good job sending him to dreamland."

We trussed Skip with line, carried him into the pilothouse, and tucked him in a corner. Flagg found a key ring in Skip's pocket. He went off to search the boat while I called the coast guard on the radio, gave them our position, and told them to stand by. Ten minutes later Flagg was back. He cradled an aluminum tube gingerly in his hands, holding it like a father with a newborn baby.

"Found it in a footlocker under one of the bunks."

Flagg got on the microphone and asked the coast guard to relay a message to a government agency whose name sounded like the letters on an eye chart. Less than half an hour later we heard the thumping wing beat of an approaching helicopter. It circled the *Gannet*, trying to get a fix on us through the fog. We shot up a flare to pinpoint our position. Within minutes the deafening thrash of rotors was directly overhead. A metal basket appeared out of the clouds and descended slowly onto the deck. I radioed the invisible chopper that it was right on target. Ducking low, Flagg dashed in under the downdraft to lay the precious aluminum cylinder in the basket. I gave the helicopter pilot the lift-off signal over the radio. The hovering chopper winched the basket from the deck and moved away. The noise of the whirling blades grew fainter, and before long all was quiet.

CHAPTER 25

•

The Navy divers were real professionals. Eight of them, divided into teams of two, had been cutting their way inward from the U-boat's torpedo room while I impatiently paced the deck of the coast guard cutter, suited up to dive with the next shift. Two heads broke the surface next to the boat and a hand went up in an okay signal. They were through. Now it was my team's turn. We jumped over the side and headed down the anchor line. Moments later we were gliding over the U-boat's submerged deck. I felt a momentary shiver and looked back to make sure the red-eyed *Neptune* wasn't dogging my trail once again with its lethal pincers poised to give me a body trim. There was only the spinachy gloom of the ocean.

One by one we squeezed through the forward hatchway into the torpedo room, where the grinning skulls greeted us in the cryptlike silence. You have to dive on a wreck to know the haunted feeling that comes when you're in a vessel that has taken its crew to the bottom. You can remind yourself that ghosts don't exist, but when you're cut off from the real world, it's as if the crew is still on board. Watching you.

The navy divers led the way to the far end of the torpedo room. The cutting torches had done their work. The pressure door that blocked me on my first dive was open, yawning like a back door to hell. We took turns passing into the crew's quarters. No air bubble had preserved this compartment and here was an overwhelming sense of decay. The overhead pipes and metal rails for the bunk racks were heavy with rust. The brownish-red bones lying in the debris were covered by a dark green marine growth that resembled bread mold. We only paused an instant before swimming forward. The pressure door to the captain's quarters was open. The divers gave me an Alphonse and Gaston sweep of their hands. I could lead the way.

Cautiously I stuck my head through the opening and flashed my light around like Howard Carter peering into King Tut's tomb for the first time. My find was more disappointing. No gold mask or carved sarcophagus. Only more rust and more debris, more marine mold. I pulled myself in by my fingertips, moving ahead with gentle kicks of my fins so as not to stir up a cloud, and looked around. Even the captain's quarters on a submarine were hardly bigger than a walk-in closet. A bunk. A standing locker and a footlocker. A small washstand that doubled as a desk. I swam over to the footlocker. It was about two feet tall and maybe a yard square. An odd shape. I signaled to the divers to center their light beams on it. Maybe it was an ammo box. But why would ammunition be stored in the captain's quarters?

Using a crowbar borrowed from a diver, I inserted one end under the cover and carefully applied pressure. The hinges were gone and the top came off easily. A cloud of rust flew into my face. I explored the contents of the box with my gloved hands. For a second I thought I was into the captain's private hoard of beer. As the rust settled I could see that the box was divided by metal partitions into square spaces. I counted them. There were twelve in all. Inside each space was the top of what appeared to be a cylinder. Mercury was shipped in metal cylinders! You wouldn't need much space to store a good-sized load. I got a grip on the top of one cylinder and pulled, twisting it as I did so. The cylinder slid out easily. I expected it to be heavy, but it only weighed a few pounds. I shook my head. Puzzling. I eased the cylinder all the way out and handed it to one of the other divers.

I went back for more tubes. Each canister was about two feet long and around six inches in diameter. All were light and easy to handle. We transported the canisters back to the torpedo room. One diver went through the hatch and we handed them out to him, then pulled ourselves from the sub. We laid the canisters neatly inside a lift basket lying on the deck and yanked a couple of times on a line leading to the surface. At our signal, the crew on the coast-guard boat hauled on the line and the basket started slowly upward. We followed, guiding the load until we stopped for our four-minute decompression. As soon as we were back on the boat I pulled off my face mask and excitedly knelt next to the basket. The canisters may have been shiny stainless steel once, but after immersion in seawater for more than four decades, they were dark amorphous hunks.

"Let's open these babies and see what's inside," I said.

The two divers who had gone down with me nodded their heads in agreement.

Flagg was standing nearby. "Afraid not," he said, ever the killjoy. "This is a U.S. government operation. We've got to go through the usual bureaucratic channels. There's also the matter of the German government, which might put in a claim for its property. We don't want to offend our allies."

"C'mon, Flagg. Just one of them. We could say the top fell off by accident."

"Sorry. I'm just as anxious as you are to see what's

inside. But aside from the government crap, it might be a good idea to X-ray these things in case there's something that could be damaged if we opened it."

I guess he had a point. I stood up and went over to the leader of the dive team. "Did you find anything on the sub that shows what sunk her?" I asked.

"There's a big rupture in the stern hull plates, probably from an explosion," he said. "The water would have come pouring into the tail. Once it hit the diesel engines, the sub would have stopped, then gone down tailfirst. It happened fast, whatever it was. Standard drill is to lock the pressure doors between compartments to keep them from flooding. That gives some of the crew a chance to get out. So far, the only pressure door we've seen locked is the one in the torpedo room."

"That accounts for the air bubble. But why didn't they escape? Why didn't they just flood the torpedo room and go out the hatch with their breathing gear?"

"I'd venture a guess that seawater got into the batteries that ran the electric motors and produced chlorine in the ventilation system." A grim look came to his eyes. "That torpedo room would have turned into a gas chamber."

"What do you think caused the explosion?"

"We'd have to do more digging to find out for sure. But this reminds me of a Russian sub that went down a few years after the war. They were charging their storage batteries. The hydrogen that was given off wasn't vented properly. There was a malfunction or somebody plain screwed up. Some hydrogen got trapped in the vent system, a spark ignited it. *Bam.* The explosion would have ripped through the hull, and in comes the water, tons of it."

I pondered his words. "Never buy a car that's been built on a Friday or Monday," I said.

"Huh?"

"You know the old story. The guy who's putting the car together is worn-out and thinking about the weekend on Friday, so he makes mistakes. On Monday he's working with a hangover, and he's still doing sloppy work. Either way, he builds a lemon. The Germans were building the sections for these subs in different yards. They could put the sections together and fit the sub out in about a month. That's fast when you consider that they were working under wartime conditions and dealing with new stuff. You don't do your best work building a boat when you're worried a bomb might fall on you or on your family back in town."

"Sounds possible," he said. "I'd guess that the final straw was the depth-charge attack," he said. "They got away but it might have weakened a flawed system."

I looked beyond the diver at the orange plastic sphere bobbing on the waves over the tomb of the fifty-seven crewmen, wondering what the former Frau Küchler was going to say when she learned of her husband's fate.

"You're probably right about the depth charges," I said, "but when you come right down to it, there's only one reason the captain took his ship to the bottom."

"Oh, what would that be, sir?"

"His luck ran out."

CHAPTER 26

•

Jane was sitting on a flotsam log above the seaweed border of the wrack line about fifty yards from her cottage. Rembrandt the Cape Cod black dog splashed in a shallow tidal pool nearby barking harmlessly at a pair of black-capped common terns who wheeled and darted high above his head going *kee-arr, kee-aar* in noisy play. A southeast breeze blew off the sound in cottony puffs and sunlight glittered on the water like melted drops of pure silver. I set off in Jane's direction, walking along the wet hard-packed sand near the water's edge. She saw me coming, looked up from the sketch pad resting on her knees, and waved. When I got closer she sprang off the log and came over to meet me. She wrapped her arms around my waist, pressing her body close to mine.

"Soc, where on earth have you been? I tried calling you at the guest house, but you weren't there."

I traced the outline of her shoulder blades with my fingertips and smelled the scent of her hair, shampoo, and sea spray.

"I'm sorry I haven't called you," I said. "I've been out

on the water a lot in the past few days and wasn't always near a phone."

She locked her arms tighter until I could barely breathe. "That's all right," she said. "You're here. That's what counts. I'm so glad to see you." She tilted her head up and kissed me as if I had been gone for a thousand years. She broke off, a question in her eyes. "Is there something wrong?" she said.

I took her hand, leading her to the log, where we sat and I pulled her close to me. The warmth of her body came through the soft fabric of her blue-hooded sweatshirt and I thought of the night we spent together in her studio. It seemed a long time ago. I began to talk, telling her about Skip Mallowes. How he had killed Tom in a dispute over the U-boat and the *Neptune* design. How he had murdered Whipple to keep his mouth shut.

When I was through she shuddered and pulled herself closer to me. "I can't believe it."

"It's true, Jane. He admitted it to me."

She stared stonily at the sand for a minute, then used her sleeve to wipe away the tears that had started down her cheeks. "I guess that ends it," she said.

"It does as far as the police are concerned, but not for me."

A shadow crossed her face. "What is it, Soc. I don't understand."

"When I talked to Geoff Travers at your opening, he told me you were at the gallery the night Tom was killed. He said somebody called you. You told Geoff the call was important and you had to leave. He said you seemed upset. Coincidentally, Tom was seen on the Nobska road not far from here about the same time you rushed off from the gallery. Jane," I said gently, "who phoned you that night?"

She plunged her hands into the front pocket of her sweatshirt and hunched her shoulders as if fending off a cold wind.

Then she answered. "Tom. He said he had to see me. I told him I was busy. He wouldn't listen."

"What did he want?"

"He wouldn't say, only that it was urgent. He sounded on edge. I told him to come by the cottage and I would meet him here."

"Go on," I pressed. "I want to hear what happened."

She took a deep breath. "Tom said his life was in danger. That Leslie's father was out to get him. I told him to go to the police. He said he could handle it himself."

"You still haven't told me what he wanted from you."

"Tom said Leslie's father would do anything to get a file."

"What kind of file, Jane?"

"Leslie's father had been poking into Tom's navy project. He even tried to bribe a staff member. The man refused Walther's offer and told Tom he'd been approached. Tom wasn't the kind of person who would stand for *anyone* trying to cut into his business. He would pull out all the stops if he had to. He paid a detective agency a great deal of money to look into Walther's background. Tom's file had the results of their investigation, papers about Leslie's father and his business connections."

That figured. I recalled my conversation with Norma after she had started checking into Walther at my request. She had told me she was following in someone's footsteps. Drake's investigators. They would have had an advantage as they probed Walther's dealings. The tips lovingly supplied to Drake by Leslie gave them a broad shovel to dig up the dirt.

"Do you know what Tom learned about Walther?" I asked.

She nodded. "I haven't read the file, but apparently the people Tom hired unearthed information that could cause Walther a great deal of damage. Tom let Walther know what he had. But he knew Walther was the type of man who would stop at nothing to get at him."

"If that's the case, why did Tom suggest that I come by his house that night?"

"Tom had a gun. I . . . I don't think he would have used it." Her voice wavered. "But now I'm not so sure."

I remembered the crafty grin on Drake's face the last time I saw him alive. I could picture the scenario. Drake in one chair, me in another, like Richard Loo and Dana Andrews in one of those old World War II movies. Drake telling me a chain is no stronger than its weakest link. Me looking down the black muzzle of his pistol. Drake's finger nervously twitching on the trigger. Me wondering if I'd see the flash before the bullet hit me. I hate amateurs with guns. A pro will blow you away without thinking about it. You never know what an amateur is going to do.

I said: "What happened to the papers?"

"Tom asked me to keep them until . . . until he came back."

"Did you ever make the connection between the file and the guy who was watching the cottage?"

"Yes, of course. I suspected they were related."

That explained why she didn't go to the police, who would ask too many questions. But it didn't explain why she didn't tell me.

"Why didn't you say something, Jane? I could have helped if I knew what we were dealing with."

"I'm sorry, Soc. I just wasn't sure."

"Not sure about me?"

She nodded.

"Tom stayed here for a couple of hours before he was murdered. You two must have had a lot to talk about."

Jane parted her lips slightly as if she were going to speak, but she changed her mind.

I kept on. "What were you doing to me, Jane?"

She shook her head, uncomprehending. "What do you mean?"

"Let me lay it out for you, then. Tom comes to you, upset about Walther. Then he's murdered and within hours I show up on your doorstep working for Walther. The next thing you know the band is playing waltz music and we're dancing to it. What the hell were you thinking of? Forgive me for asking. I'm just curious why somebody with a powerful reason to fear me would invite me into her life."

She rubbed a charcoal-pencil smudge off her palm with a thumb. "I was confused. After our first meeting I asked the police about you. They said you had an alibi and couldn't have killed Tom, but I thought you might have had something to do with it because you were working for Leslie's father. I just didn't know."

"So you were going to play detective, lure me into your bedroom, and see if you could get me to admit I was involved. Maybe I'd confess to the crime in my sleep or while we were having a pillow talk."

"No, Soc. You weren't what I expected. I wasn't sure of anything."

I tossed a white pebble worn smooth by the sea at a reed sticking out of the sand. I missed. I tossed another one. That missed too. I was stalling. I had another question.

"That night I stayed over," I said. "Was it me you made love with, or Tom?"

Jane turned her head away. I got a cold feeling in the pit of my stomach, as if I had just swallowed an icicle. Nothing was different. Jane and I sat on the weathered log as before, but something had changed, the way the air goes chill when a cloud hides the sun for an instant.

"Jane," I said, "we've only known each other for a few days. It's not as if we had the longest-running love affair of the century. Maybe it had some possibilities, but it was strictly hit-and-run. You know the old story. Two ships passing in the night. It doesn't matter."

She looked at me, anguish in her eyes. "It matters," she whispered. "It matters." And I knew she was right.

I got off the log and said, "Where is the file on Walther? I'd like to see it."

"It's in the studio," she said.

With Rembrandt following, we headed back to the cottage and climbed the stairs to her studio. She pulled a thick brown envelope out of her box of paints and gave it to me. I opened the envelope and scanned the contents. No wonder Walther was upset. Even a quick glance showed I held a package of dynamite.

"I'd like to borrow this for a while, if you don't mind," I told her.

"I don't care what you do with it."

There was an awkward moment when neither one of us knew what to say. I improvised by walking over to her easel and inspecting her latest canvas. "It looks good," I said.

"Yes. Thank you."

"Well," I said. "I should go."

"I know. I'll walk you to the truck," she said.

We went downstairs and around back where I had parked the pickup. As I opened the door to get behind the wheel she took my arm. "Will you call me?"

I bent and kissed her lightly on the lips. "The next time I'm in Woods Hole I'll give you a call and we'll get together."

"Promise?"

"I promise." We both knew I was lying, but it was an acceptable lie because it cut the pain. There would be a hundred lonely nights when I wished I could hold Jane in my arms and feel her warm skin next to mine. I hoped that when I reached for the phone to call her, I would remember our lives had touched for all the wrong reasons. And there was Tom Drake to contend with. Jane was still in love with her dead husband; maybe she always would be. I had no intention of playing second fiddle to a ghost.

The black dog came over and licked my hand. I squatted down and patted his bony head. "Take good care of your mistress, puppy." Then I got into my truck and headed out the sand road. I went back to the guest house, kicked off my sneakers, propped up a pillow, and lay on my bed. I stared at a spot three feet beyond the foot of the bed for a long time. If there were any thoughts in my head, they rambled out as quickly as they came in. I had known Jane a couple of days. No big deal. A split second in terms of a lifetime. In a few weeks I would forget the whole thing. I began to build an imaginary wall around me, brick by brick, neatly layering in the mortar.

The exertions of the past week were catching up with me. I realized how badly I had been battered and bashed since I drifted into this swell little burg looking for a missing woman. Every blunt instrument and sharp-tipped utensil within reach had been flying in my direction and I was sick of it. I had a sore head, sore eyes, and sore mouth. Even my hair hurt. I longed for the sunlit deck of my boathouse. I missed Kojak. I wanted the clean simplicity of a fishing trip with Sam. My eyelids drooped, and I dozed off. I was awakened by a knock at the door. The room was dark. Night had come while I slept. The rapping came again.

"Mr. Socarides? Are you awake?"

I got out of bed and moved in the darkness to the door. Mrs. Stapleton was standing in the hallway.

"Oh, I'm sorry to wake you, dear. It's just that the gentleman on the phone was so insistent. He wants to talk to you and he says it's quite important."

I followed her downstairs, rubbing the sleep from my eyes, wondering why nobody makes *un*important calls anymore. I picked up the phone.

"They got the *Neptune* to Bermuda and sent it down," Flagg said.

"I'm listening." I clutched the phone tighter.

"Those guys in the minisub are up. They're a little green around the gills, but apparently they will be okay. The *Neptune* worked fine with its new eyeball. Thought you would want to know."

"That's good, Flagg, I'm glad to hear it." It wasn't much of a reaction, but I was beat.

"Thanks for your help, Soc."

"Sure, Flagg," I answered. "Any old time."

CHAPTER 27

•

The Walther file was so hot it sizzled. Tom Drake made devastating use of the leads he coaxed out of his lover Leslie. His investigators produced a dossier on Frederick Walther that was well researched, well organized, and in terms of its potential to drag important reputations into the mud, deadly. I sat on my bed with the papers spread out on the quilt, moving them around from time to time like cards in a game of solitaire.

The reports, affidavits, interviews, and money flow-charts in Drake's file drew a seamy portrait of a vast international empire with offices in a dozen cities and served by connections at the highest government levels. With billions of dollars at stake, and just about every country in the world churning out arms, the weapons companies are almost as competitive as the summer T-shirt stores on Cape Cod, and it helps to oil the government machinery with cash. Walther was good at spreading the wealth about. As a subcontracted employee of his, I was in elite company, sharing a payroll that included moonlighting congressman, ambassadors, and cabinet staff. The names were all there, and the documentation to go with it.

I shoved the papers back into the envelope. Twenty minutes later I was dialing Sharon Prescott's telephone number from a pay phone outside a gas station. She recognized my voice and said, "What a nice surprise, Mr. Socarides."

I wasted no time on pleasantries. "Sharon," I said, "I know everything." I paused for a moment and listened to her breathing. "Do you understand? *Every*thing."

I hung up and got into my truck. Sharon lived about a mile away from the gas station. Moments later I drove past her house. The lights were on and the BMW was in the driveway. I parked two hundred feet up the street, where I could watch her front door. Ten minutes later the windows went dark. Headlights flashed on in her driveway, the BMW backed onto the street, and headed away from me. I followed Sharon out of Woods Hole and onto Route 28, heading east from Falmouth. About an hour later we were in Chatham, and Sharon was turning off at a sign pointing to Merrill's Island.

Mists were rising off the salt marsh like spirits of the dead when I drove onto the island causeway and pulled onto the berm at the halfway point. The tide was low and the breeze carried the rank, overripe smell of the flats to my nostrils. As I watched the crimson taillights from her car go up the hill and disappear behind a curve I thought about my conversation with Leslie. Her stepfather was a man who used people. He pushed them around like chess pieces, sacrificed them when he thought it was necessary. Was I the white knight or the pawn? I let the anger build for a few minutes, enjoying the slow burn, tending the fire so it wouldn't get out of control. Then I slipped the truck into gear and drove onto the island.

I parked behind the white BMW, went to the front porch, and rang the bell. A minute later Winston Prayerly answered the door. His pale smooth face was impassive, as usual, like a figure from Madame Toussaud's wax museum. Still he couldn't help raising one thin eyebrow when he saw me. I guess that was something.

"Is Walther in?" I said.

I was setting a tone of impertinence from the start. I wanted no miscommunication.

Prayerly raised the other eyebrow. "Mr. Walther doesn't see anyone without an appointment, Mr. Socarides."

I turned away. "That's too bad. I wanted to tell him I've found his daughter." I shrugged. "On your head be it, my friend."

Prayerly grabbed my sleeve before I got a half a step from the door. I looked at his white-gloved hand. He quickly let go and stepped back into the house. I brushed by, almost mashing on his toes, and waited in the foyer while he went upstairs to announce my arrival. A few minutes later he beckoned from the top of the stairs. I went up to the second floor and he led me to Walther's warroom. Walther was standing by a tall window. His toothy smile wasn't matched by the Nixonish glower in his eyes. Winston must have told him what a saucy lad I was being. I only glanced at Walther. I was more interested in the newest display in the war room. Sharon Prescott. She was sitting stiffly in a chair, smoking a cigarette.

"Hi, Sharon," I said. "Fancy meeting you here. Sorry I was so creepy on the phone." I looked around. "Isn't this cozy? You, me, and Winston. We all work for Mr. Walther over there. Who wants to be in charge of the hot dogs at the company picnic?"

Sharon avoided my eyes. She was looking at Walther. She dragged on her cigarette like a longshoreman, exhaled through her nose in twin streamers of smoke, and immediately sucked down another lungful.

"How nice to have you join us," Walther said. "Won't you have a seat?"

"No thanks, Mr. Walther. I'll just be a few minutes."

"Very well. Winston tells me you have found Leslie. Is that true?"

Prayerly hadn't left the room the way he did on my first visit. He stood near the door. His legs were spread apart and his hands were clasped behind his back.

"I spoke to Leslie just the other day," I said.

Walther walked over and put his hand on my shoulder. He only touched me for an instant, but it made my flesh crawl.

"I don't know why you didn't call sooner, but well done anyhow, Mr. Socarides. I can see Leonard Wilson's faith in your abilities was not misplaced. I knew I could count on you. Winston will draw you a check for the balance of your fee, plus expenses of course, as soon as you deliver the goods." He talked about Leslie as if she were a crate of mortar rounds.

"I'm not delivering the goods, Mr. Walther. Leslie told me she has no interest in coming back."

The cold blue eyes flicked past me to Winston Prayerly. The glance told me Walther was close to putting a lid on my insolence. I looked over at Winston. He had moved away from the door and into the room. His arms were now crossed on his chest.

Walther said: "I'm afraid I don't understand, Mr. Socarides. Is it a question of money? I'm sure we can work something out to your satisfaction."

I reached into my jacket pocket and took out the check Walther had given me. I looked at it, then with great care, folded the check into a paper plane and threw it toward the fireplace. I was never good at making paper planes, even in grammar school. The plane nosed down and fell short of the fire by a couple of yards, but Walther got the point.

"I see," he said. "Did Leslie tell you some lies? She does have quite an imagination. And she's very beautiful. Many people, men in particular, tend to believe anything she has to say."

I grinned a hound-dog grin. "Naw," I said. "It's really very simple, Mr. Walther. I just don't like you."

Walther laughed. "Is *that* all? You wouldn't be the first person to feel that way about me. But be realistic, Mr. Socarides. You must know that ours is merely a temporary arrangement between two parties. You are the vendor, and I am the buyer of services. That's all. Like or dislike shouldn't prevent us from doing business. Unless there is more to it than a mere personality conflict."

"You're right. That's not the only reason."

"Well then, why are you breaching our oral contract?"

"You're the one who breached the agreement first. You didn't tell me the truth."

"And what is the truth, Mr. Socarides?"

"You weren't worried about Leslie. You just wanted me to drag her back here so you could find out what she told Drake and punish her for it."

"You do have an active mind. Why on earth would I do that?"

"You were trying to horn in on Drake's Neptune project. You attempted to bribe one of Drake's guys. But his staff was remarkably loyal. So you sent Leslie in as a spy. It was a tactical error, Mr. Walther. She fell in love with him. She revealed what she was doing at NTI. Even worse, she told him everything about you. Drake started poking into your business. With inside leads from Leslie, it wasn't hard for Drake's investigators to dig up some damaging information. You opened a can of worms when you took on Drake. He put together a file that could bring you and your whole organization down. People don't do that and get away with it, do they?"

Walther walked over to the fireplace and took a meerschaum pipe from a rack on the mantel. I glanced over at Prayerly. He stood as still as a statue, but his arms had dropped down by his sides. I followed Walther to the fireplace and stood elbow to elbow with him. He tapped his pipe bowl with great deliberation and lit the tobacco. He took a puff, blew it in my face, and examined me like an entomologist studying a new species of dung beetle.

"I've heard you have a problem with alcohol, Mr. Socarides. Perhaps that's why you're babbling on about some file."

"Uh-uh. No booze tonight. The dossier is real. I've seen it. It names names, gives times and places. It reads like a best-seller. You're going to be on everyone's reading list, Mr. Walther."

A pause. He drew on the pipe and didn't blow the smoke in my face this time. "You have access to this material?"

"It's in a safe place," I said. If that's what you could call my truck, where the file was stuffed under the front seat amid the clutter of crushed Styrofoam coffee cups, jumper cables, and empty fast-food bags.

Walther nodded pensively. "I'd like my legal staff to examine it. There might be grounds for a libel suit. You can understand my interest. I'd be very happy to pay you for your trouble."

He was trolling for payoff, hoping I'd snap at the bait like a hungry bluefish. "I don't think so. I'm a little miffed at you fellows. I got shot at by someone at Drake's place. Then my knee got worked over outside Jane Drake's cottage. And someone searched my room while I was visiting Miss Prescott."

"What's that got to do with our discussion?" Impatient now.

"I think Winston over there was trying to retrieve the file."

"That's absurd."

"Not really. Drake's death came as a surprise to you, but that didn't end your problems. The file was still out there where it could do you damage. So you had Winston here check Drake's house. I got in the way. Then you decided to stake out Jane Drake's place. I got in the way again. Maybe you thought I had thrown in with Jane, so you decided to search my room."

"I'm not a patient man, Mr. Socarides. Do you intend to turn over the file?"

"*Ohi*, Mr. Walther."

"I don't understand."

"That's Greek for no. *Nada*. Nay. Nope. Do I make myself clear?"

His eyes were locked in a zombie stare. "Very much so, I'm afraid." He motioned to his valet. "It's become painfully apparent to me that you know too much. Winston, please take care of Mr. Socarides."

A pistol appeared in Prayerly's hand. It had the long ugly black snout of a silencer on the muzzle. I stepped behind Walther and grabbed him by the collar, bunching his jacket in my fist, and rammed my knuckles into his spine. It was like holding on to a skeleton, a malevolent bag of bones that talked and walked and hated.

Sharon was out of her chair with her arm around Prayerly. There was fear in her eyes. She wasn't used to the rough stuff.

"Winston, *no*," she pleaded.

I said: "You're in bad company, Sharon. Maybe you didn't know what you were getting into when you decided to be the second-string mole at Drake's lab."

Her mouth slacked open. Nothing came out of it.

"Let me guess. When it looked as if Leslie was a flop as a secret agent, Mr. Walther approached you. He must have offered you a lot of money."

Prayerly ran his fingers through Sharon's hair as if he had done it before. "Not as much as you might think, bloke." Then he pushed Sharon aside and advanced toward me, his mouth set in a grim smile.

"What happened to the Eaton accent, bloke? Gone back to Liverpool?"

He stopped. "I expect so," he said, smiling. "You can't stay there all night, mate."

"How do you know I don't have a gun or a knife tickling your boss's ribs?" I said.

Walther tried to squirm out of my grip. I jerked him back before he got too far, but I was sure Prayerly caught a glimpse of my empty hand because his smile grew wider and he advanced again, more confident. He was right. I couldn't hide behind Walther all night. We could only dance around the room for so long before I'd have my back up against the wall with no place to go. Walther's body was a frail reed to hang on to. A few quick steps and Prayerly

could just swing around him and grab me and shoot me.
He was about six feet away. At this range he could easily
pick me off without hitting his boss. He must have been
thinking the same thing.

He took another step and raised the pistol in both
hands, sighting down the barrel. Walther went stiff as a
fossil. A guttural moan came from his throat.

"Don't worry about a thing, Mr. Walther," Prayerly was
saying.

Sharon saw the move.

"*No*, Winston!" she screamed. She rushed forward again
and grabbed his arm, pulling him back. Prayerly shoved
her aside with a savage sweep of his arm that sent her
sprawling onto the floor. His eyes darted toward her. The
pistol moved off me. Just for a second.

But it was all the time I needed.

I grabbed Walther in a bum's rush with one hand on
his belt and the other on his collar. I took two fast steps
and lifted him off the floor. I handle fish boxes that weigh
more than he did. I threw him at his valet. He sprawled
forward, grabbing on to Prayerly in reflex, and the two of
them went down in a jumble of arms and legs. Prayerly's
pistol angled up at the ceiling. It wouldn't take seconds
for him to recover and stick the gun in my face again.
And I no longer had Walther as a shield.

A *shield.*

The walls were loaded with them. The nearest to me
was a round medieval buckler that had a gold coat of arms
on the front of a stylized and crowned lion standing on its
hind legs in a boxer's stance. I didn't stop to admire the
artwork. I snatched at the shield, but it didn't want to
come off the wall. Winston was extricating himself from
under his boss. I put my foot against the wall and yanked.
The shield gave, pulling the hook with it. I lifted the iron
platter over my head. It weighed a ton. Winston was sitting up, swinging the pistol toward me. I slammed the
shield down. It hit his head with a gong like the doorbell

in a Charlie Chan movie. The gun popped from his limp hand onto the floor.

Walther was a frightened old man, but he had the soul of a snake. He scrambled forward on his hands and knees, his thin fingers groping toward the pistol. They were inches away from the plastic pistol grip. I tossed the shield onto the battle table. Hundreds of tin soldiers flew onto the rug. I kicked the gun out of reach and picked it up and stuffed it under my belt.

I was breathing hard, the anger flowing. "I finally remembered what you said about the phalanx the night you hired me. How one infantryman stepped in when the soldier in the front row fell. Sharon coming in for Leslie. But you forgot something, Mr. Walther. The Roman legions made mincemeat of the Macedonian phalanx."

Walther didn't appreciate the military-history lesson. He sat on the floor and glared at me with malicious eyes.

"You'll be hearing from me, Mr. Socarides. This won't be the last of it."

"I don't intend for it to be, Mr. Walther."

I checked Winston to make sure I hadn't killed him and pulled off one of his gloves. The poison ivy was healing, but his skin still had an ugly rash. Best stay out of the puckerbush, old bloke. I helped Sharon off the floor. The color had drained from her face, but she wasn't hurt.

"Thanks for the help with your boyfriend. He won't be in a good mood when he comes to, so you'd better come with me."

I took her unresisting arm and we walked around the two men on the floor, down the stairs, and out of the house into the night. We stopped next to the BMW.

"That was some mourning act you pulled for Drake," I said. "You had me fooled. I thought you really cared for him."

"I did care for him. It's just that—"

"Yeah, I know. Money talks and love is blind. Tell me

about Whipple. Did your pals back there tell you to set him up for Drake's murder?"

She nodded. "Mr. Walther was trying to get information on the *Neptune* for a rival company that was working on a similar project. If Dan could be made a suspect, the scandal would destroy Neptune Technologies. He was very angry because Dr. Drake was dead and he couldn't get back at him. He wanted to wreck his company for revenge."

I looked up at second-floor windows of the big house. "Figures," I said. I opened the door and stuffed Sharon into her car, advising her to take the money from her employee stock plan and go out of the country on a long vacation. She whispered what may have been a thank-you and started the car engine. When she had gone I put Winston's pistol on the gravel drive and drove over it a few times with my truck. Then I threw the ruined weapon as far as I could into the darkened shrubbery. I drove back to Woods Hole and planted myself on a stool at the friendly Water Street bar. I wanted to tie one on, to obliterate the past few days. I started with beer, and when that didn't do the trick, switched to Sea Breezes, vodka and cranberry and grapefruit juices.

It was an eminently successful binge. I destroyed half a billion brain cells. A batch of gray matter went up in smoke with each swallow. My fingers lost feeling after the first few drinks. Then my head went numb from the shoulders up. Even I know when I've had enough. I tossed a couple of twenties onto the bar and staggered out onto Water Street. I was groping my way along the facade of stores and shops in the general direction of my truck when headlights brushed the back of my head. A car door opened and I heard a voice that had become too damn familiar.

"Thought I might find you here," Flagg said. A hand took my elbow. "C'mon, man. I'll give you a lift."

I got into Flagg's car and he dropped me off at the guest house. I shook off his offer to help me to my room and crawled up the carpeted stairway to the second floor on my hands and knees. I pulled myself onto the bed and closed my eyes. The room began to whirl. I opened my eyes. It skidded to a stop. This was silly. How could I sleep with my eyes open? Somehow I did. More likely, though, I just passed out.

CHAPTER 28

●

When you drink as much as I do, a hangover is not a badge of honor or a sign of manhood. It simply means you drink too much. I awoke the morning after my binge with little hammers pounding at my temples from inside my skull, green nausea, and gale-force turbulence in my stomach. My mouth felt as if I had eaten the contents of a vacuum-cleaner bag. I eased painfully out of bed and washed my face in the bathroom sink. Two maraschino cherries stared at me from the mirror. A shower and shave didn't ease the pain, but they gave me sufficient energy to go downstairs and call Flagg.

"You okay?" he said. "You were under the weather last night."

Flagg was getting positively paternal. "Yeah, I'm fine. I was unwinding after a rough few days. Thanks for the lift."

"No problem," he said. "I was going to call you this morning anyhow. I've requested emergency clearance on the stuff you and the navy divers got from the U-boat the other day. It should only take about ten months."

I groaned. "Aw, jeez. Are you saying I have to wait nearly a year?"

"Nope," Flagg replied. "You deserve better than that. You broke the case. I'd be glad to show you what I've got."

"You're on. I'll meet you at Nobska Point in half an hour."

I had time to stop for a coffee and bagel with cream cheese. The food settled my stomach and gave me the strength to get back in the pickup and face the winding drive up the Nobska road to the lighthouse. Flagg was there ahead of me. He was standing on the promontory across from the lighthouse where a brushy bluff slants down to a monolithic tumble of foam-washed boulders the color of slate. It was the first time I had seen him not wearing a suit. He was dressed in jeans, a soft leather jacket, and buckskin boots and had a daypack on his back.

I looked out over the water at Martha's Vineyard, a blue-green satin ribbon across the sound.

"When was the last time you were home?" I asked.

"Much too long ago. I'm going over for a few days now that this case is done. I need to see Annie and pick up some clay at the cliffs."

Flagg was talking about the Gay Head cliffs, three-hundred-foot-tall wind-chiseled bluffs of rust, moss, and cinnamon colors that stick boldly into the sea like a huge eagle's beak.

"What do you need clay for?" I asked.

"It was something my grandfather taught me. He used to grind the clay to a powder. I can see him now, wrinkled and sunburned from fishing, sitting at the kitchen table for hours, sifting the clay so that it became as fine as talcum. He'd separate the colors and tamp them into bottles one at a time, so there would be layers, black, red, green, and gray, just like on the cliffs. You tilt the bottles and the layers would make real pretty patterns."

"Did he make them as souvenirs for the tourists?"

"Yeah, but mostly he did it just for himself. The old man and his pals would hire us kids to crawl up there and get clay to put in the bottles. They'd pay us a few bucks. The cliffs are a hundred million years old. They are where the Wampanoag got pushed by the white man with our backs to the ocean, where we got the clay to make pots. The cliffs have been the tribe's life. The old-timers like my grandfather were lucky, they knew who they were. It was tougher for us younger guys. The whole world seemed to be conspiring to take your identity away from you. Sometimes I forget what I am and I need to remind myself where I came from."

"You've done well, Flagg. You made it off the island. You've got a good job with Uncle Sam."

He looked me straight in the eye. "I'm glad you brought that up, Soc. You know I worked for the Man, and I'm still doing it. But I never sold out to him, not even way back there in Vietnam. That was a bum rap you hung on me all this time."

I felt the flush of anger in my cheeks. The years rolled away. I could see the army helicopter rising from the jungle clearing, taking my prisoners to their deaths.

"I turned those POWs over to your group," I said. "You tortured them and threw them out of the chopper, Flagg."

"You still believe that." It was a statement, not a question.

"I was *there*, for Chrissakes."

Flagg sneered. "You were nowhere, man. You were out in the field watching that your ass didn't get blown off. You don't know crap about what happened."

"So you were never with Phoenix, Flagg. You never knew that they were a bunch of killers."

"Yeah, I was with Phoenix, all right, but I thought I was helping to save democracy."

"I suppose that makes your hands clean."

"No cleaner than yours, Soc."

"I never threw anyone out of a chopper, Flagg."

"Neither did I."

I paused, confused. "What are you telling me, Flagg?"

"I'm telling you the truth. Something you're not interested in. You didn't want to hear it then, you don't want to hear it now. Not from me. Not from anyone. You're too wrapped up in yourself. If the world doesn't conform to your lousy view of it, you shape things so that it does."

Flagg's salvos were hitting close. "Try me, Flagg."

His black eyes narrowed. "Why the hell should I bother after all these years?"

"I'm not afraid. Are you?" It was a challenge, and Flagg knew it.

He snorted. "Naw." He took a deep breath, let it out slowly, and began to talk. "Phoenix was always on the lookout for guys from the Airborne or Green Berets whose term was up. They came to me with a tempting offer. Good pay, good chance to get back at the people who had killed my buddies. They said I was going to be a *warrior*, man." He laughed ruefully. "I believed them."

"A lot of us believed things like that," I said.

He nodded and went on. "After you turned over the POWs, we took them back to the base for interrogation. I figured they'd be questioned per usual, then offered to work for us as Kit Carsons under Open Arms. These POWs were tough, though. Real pros. The guys in my outfit tried the usual things like pouring water down a guy's throat till he's just about drowned, good stuff like that. They still wouldn't talk, they wouldn't come over. Not even to fake it. They had guts. The more we leaned on them, the more stubborn they got. My group leader got pissed off. He ordered them piled into the chopper for a little ride."

"You knew what was coming?"

"Of course I did. I had heard the stories just like everybody else. They were going to murder these guys."

"Why didn't you try to stop them?"

Flagg raised his voice. "Goddammit, man, I *did* try."

Neither one of us spoke for a moment. Flagg's breathing slowed and he went on.

"First I tried to talk them out of it. When that didn't work I threatened to go over their heads. They just laughed. I got a little rough, and so did they. They got some MPs to grab me, put me in the cooler overnight. Next thing I knew I was on my way back to Saigon. I filed a complaint first chance I got. The brass buried it. They didn't want any more atrocity stories popping up. It would erode public confidence in the war. They kept me on ice for a few months, shuffling papers for the CORDS cover program, then mustered me out of Phoenix and sent me home. Not long after that I got the offer for my current position."

"Sounds like a payoff, Flagg."

"Yeah, I know. Maybe it was. I talked myself into taking the job. Figured I deserved something. Sure, I could go home and pump gas or dig clams on the Vineyard. But I rationalized how it would be letting my people down if I didn't make a success of myself. I couldn't admit that I'd already let them down. I have to live with that."

I shook my head in exasperation. "Why didn't you tell me this before?"

"Get real, Soc. You tried to bend a bar stool over my head at the NCO club. You were in no mood to listen."

"Dammit, you could have tried harder."

"Tried harder at what? I shouldn't have to defend myself to a *friend*. Shit, man, what about you? Maybe you should have tried harder. You knew me, you should have known I wouldn't be wrapped up in anything like murder."

"You let that damn Indian pride get in the way. You were too proud to defend yourself. You let me go all these years hating you because of a lie."

He grabbed the front of my jacket and stuck his face in mine. "Tell me one thing, Soc. Don't bullshit me. Would you have believed me if I told you?"

"No, Flagg," I said. "I wouldn't have believed you. I wouldn't have believed anyone about anything. I didn't know what truth was. I'm still not certain I know what it is."

Flagg let go of my jacket and showed his teeth. "Naw, Soc, you know what it is."

"Maybe. In any case, I'm sorry, Flagg. Sorry I didn't trust you. Sorry I pulled Annie into it."

"Hell, Soc, Annie still thinks you're okay. Don't know why."

"I don't know why either, Flagg." I looked off beyond the surf where the sunlight turned the dappled water into highly polished pewter.

Flagg followed my gaze beyond the breakers. "Fog's cleared up real nice," he said.

"It always does if you wait long enough," I said.

"Well, you didn't come here to discuss old times. I'll show you what was in that U-boat you found." He slipped his pack off and pulled out a packet of stiff off-white papers. He knelt and spread the papers onto the grass, putting rocks down on each corner so the breeze wouldn't take them. I knelt down beside him. The papers were covered with blue-line diagrams. One set showed parts of what looked to be a turbine engine. Another sheet had head-on views and profiles of a stubby winged plane. The explanations were all in German.

"These are unauthorized copies," he said. "I made them before I turned the originals over to the higher-ups. Figured I'd never see them again."

I looked at Flagg. "What is this?"

"This is your treasure, man."

I shook my head, uncomprehending. "These look like plans for a jet plane."

"You got it. With this handy-dandy kit you can build yourself a jet-fighter plane. Back in 1945, you would have had something the Allies couldn't touch. The Germans got a few jet fighters into operation, but fortunately the war ended before they could go into mass production. Like

that super sub in a way. This was an advanced model of
some of the earlier planes. If they'd ever got it into the
air, it would have ripped our bombers out of the sky and
made our fighter planes look silly."

"The other canisters. Did they have plans in them too?"

"Yup. There was a more advanced version of the V-two
rocket on the drawing board. Bigger and longer range,
more explosives. They had a remote-controlled torpedo
that could have made life miserable for a lot of our sailors.
They had some new guns and bombs in the works that
weren't half-bad."

I shook my head. "Does this stuff have any value?"

"Sure, to the Smithsonian Institution, or a war histo-
rian. But all this hardware has been reinvented. It would
have been state-of-the-art then. It's all antiques now. Sort
of like finding plans for a crossbow or a Gatling gun.
We've gotten a lot better at killing ourselves."

"Where was the sub taking this stuff?"

"It was being spirited out of the Fatherland, that's all
we know. Maybe they were going to start a Fourth Reich
in the Andes Mountains and thought all this would come
in handy. Somebody could have been planning to sell
them to the highest bidder or just wanted to use them as
bargaining chips."

We stared at each other. Then I started to giggle. Flagg
chuckled. And we began to roar like a couple of beached
sea lions. The noise startled a flock of sea gulls and they
soared high above us in a white cloud of confetti.

The sobering implications hit me like a sledgehammer.
I stopped laughing. "Those guys who died in the sub. It
was all for nothing, wasn't it? The war was just about over.
They could have called it quits, gone home, got married,
and had kids, except for some bigwig who wanted
insurance."

"You know that's always the way it is, Soc. Maybe the
bigwig was on the U-boat too. That might be some
consolation."

I reached under my jacket and took out an envelope.

"Here's one time we may be able to shake up the big boys," I said.

He took the envelope. "What is this?"

"It's the dirt that Tom Drake dug out on Frederick Walther. Oh, by the way, his valet was the guy I ran into at Tom Drake's house and later outside Jane's cottage. You'll recognize some familiar Washington names. People high up in government who made a few dollars easing the way for Mr. Walther. They won't like to see this information made public. I can see it stirring up congressional committee inquiries, grand jury indictments. Maybe even a special prosecutor à la Watergate."

"Well, now, isn't that interesting." The grin flashed white. "What makes you think I won't sell out to the Washington establishment? I'm part of it, you know."

"I'm not worried, Flagg."

He slid the file into his pack. "Thanks for that," he said. "Well, keep in touch." We shook hands and he went to his car. I watched until the LTD disappeared around a curve, took one last look at the view, then got in my truck and headed back to the guest house. Case closed. Time to go home, take care of Kojak, and catch some fish with Sam.

Chloe had returned from Boston and her car was in front of the guest house. I knocked on the door to the kitchen. "Come in," Mrs. Stapleton sang. Chloe was at the sink, and Mrs. Stapleton was beating eggs in a bowl. Chloe smiled and said, "Sit down, big brother. I'll get you some coffee."

I sat at the table and pulled out my checkbook to pay the rent. Chloe was telling me about her trip to Boston. She had gotten to the part about the acupuncturist when the doorbell rang. Mrs. Stapleton was scrambling eggs in a black cast-iron frying pan. She said, "Mr. Socarides, would you be a dear and answer that. Tell whoever it is to come right in."

I went out to the hallway, opened the door, and saw a hallucination. A woman who looked like my mother stood on the threshold. She was dark and slim just like my mother and wore a black dress the way my mother has been doing since she was born. She smiled and the morning sun glinted off a gold tooth.

"Good morning, Aristotle," she said. She patted my cheek. "You're not eating. I can see it in your face." Hell, this was no figment.

Nothing that had happened to me in the past few days, not the mechanical crabs or the U-boat or being abandoned at sea, could have prepared me for the shock of seeing my mother on Mrs. Stapleton's doorstep. It was as if a slice from one dimension had been pasted onto another.

I croaked: "Hi, Ma. What brings you here?"

She gave an old-world shrug. "Business is a little slow at the bakery. I hear from your cousin in Falmouth that Chloe stays here. So I get George and I say, 'Let's go see your brother and sister on Cape Cod. Especially your sister.'"

I looked past my mother. A white Cadillac Allante with vanity plates that said "Pizza" was parked in front of the guest house. My brother George leaned carelessly against a fender. He was smoking a cigarette. Resignation was written across his handsome features. He waved at me and rolled his eyes. I could smell trouble. Business is never slow at the bakery. My mother doesn't leave her nest on the banks of the Merrimack River and drive two hours on a whim just to say hello to her grown children. There was purpose in those innocent gray eyes.

I shook my suspicions off. My own mother, for god sakes. I put my arm around her shoulders and said, "Come in, Ma, we're just having breakfast. Chloe will be glad to see you."

My sister's face lit up when Ma came into the kitchen. She went over and hugged her. I was ashamed of my own lukewarm reaction, but I knew my mother better than Chloe did.

"Ma," Chloe said. "What a wonderful surprise. I should have called you. But what are you doing here?"

Mother gave her the same fishy explanation. Chloe seemed satisfied and introduced her to Mrs. Stapleton. Everything seemed peachy-keen. I was getting too mistrustful in my old age. Everyone, even my dear, sweet conniving mother, seemed to operate with an ulterior motive. Maybe I'd been spending too much time in the company of nefarious characters and policemen.

"George is outside," she said to Chloe. "Go say hello to your brother."

"I'll tell him to come in," Chloe said. She seemed genuinely pleased. "We can all have breakfast together."

I sat down and tried my coffee again. Chloe was back before I got in my second sip. Her smile had disappeared. Her eyes blazed. Her mouth was set in the square of a passion mask.

"Ma, how *could* you?" she demanded.

"Chloe, listen to your mother," Ma said.

Chloe didn't want to listen. She stormed out of the kitchen and flew up the stairs to her room. With foreboding in my heart, I went to the front door. One of the tinted windows on the Cadillac was rolled down. Peering out was a pudgy fat-cheeked face.

"Hello, Nestor," I called. "Long time no see."

He nodded sadly.

I went back into the kitchen. "Ma, what's going on?"

"Before we leave to come here, I tell George to see if his friend Nestor wants to ride with us. He's a nice boy, Aristotle. Just right for Chloe."

"She doesn't think so."

"She doesn't know what's good for her."

My mother was wrong there. Chloe knew exactly what was good for her. Flight. Her footsteps thumped down the stairs. She burst into the kitchen with a suitcase in her hand. She gave my mother a curt good-bye hug and thanked Mrs. Stapleton for all she had done. Our landlady stood there with a confused look on her face. The scrambled eggs were burning. Chloe paused long enough to kiss me on the cheek and give me a friendly wink.

"Bye, big brother. Thanks for everything. I'll be in touch." She propelled herself out of the kitchen like a rocket-powered projectile.

I followed her to the door. She went over to George and kissed him good-bye too, said hello to Nestor, and got into the red Supra. The engine roared into life and the car shot along the street in a screech of tires. I went down and stood next to George.

He gave an exaggerated shake of his head and lit a cigarette. "I told Ma this was a lousy waste of time, Soc. But you know how it is."

We watched the brakelights flash as the Supra rounded a corner and vanished from sight. I put my hand on his shoulder. "I know exactly how it is, George."

My mother came out of the guest house looking as if nothing had happened. She said, "Come for dinner Sunday, Aristotle. I make something special. Don't worry about Chloe. I know her. She'll be there." She kissed me on the cheek, and a minute later she and George and Nestor were gone. Maybe it was all a bad dream. I rubbed my eyes, looked around at the quiet street, then went inside. Mrs. Stapleton was still shell-shocked at being caught in the cross fire of a Socarides family crisis, but when I explained the situation, she said she was sorry to see Chloe and me go. I think she meant it. The summer rush would be a quiet interlude by comparison.

On the way home I stopped off at Sam's house. He was sporting a Florida tan and he couldn't stop babbling excitedly about Epcot, punctuating every sentence with the words "darnedest thing." I was glad he had a good time, but anxious to go fishing again. I was broker than before I took the case. All I had to show for my stay in Woods Hole were some cuts and bumps and a glove compartment full of parking tickets. In her haste to leave town Chloe had forgotten to pay her rent at the Seaside guest house, and I had to take care of her tab as well as mine. I finally got a word in edgewise and asked Sam if he felt like catching some cod.

"Hell, yes. Don't blame you for wanting to get out on the boat," he said kindly. "Things must have been pretty boring around here while I was away."

"Hell, yes," I said.

ABOUT THE AUTHOR

Before leaving journalism to write mysteries, PAUL KEMPRECOS spent more than twenty years as a reporter and editor on Cape Cod newspapers. During that time he covered every type of sea story, from whale strandings to shipwrecks.

Kemprecos is a first-generation American, son of a Greek immigrant, and he frequently draws on memories of family life in his writing. A certified scuba diver, he prefers to spend his time above water on a sailboat. He lives in a 1930s cottage called the Doghouse on Cape Cod Bay, where he wrote both *Neptune's Eye* and *Cool Blue Tomb*. He is currently completing the third book in the Aristotle Socarides series.

A crackling deep-water suspense novel of violence, passion, and betrayal.

THE COOL BLUE TOMB
by Paul Kemprecos

A 50-million dollar salvage operation. An expert diver dead at the bottom of the sea. An elegant mermaid in a black Porsche -- and an open invitation to dip into the troubled waters of her marriage. Cape Cod's Aristotle "Soc" Socarides, part-time fisherman, part-time private eye, is swimming with the sharks. Only problem is, he's the bait...and blood is beginning to boil to the surface.

Soc didn't think he could get in much deeper, but he'd better think again. A family debt of honor comes due -- a debt only he can settle -- plunging him into the middle of a lethal search for buried treasure. Now Soc's about to discover how deadly the Cape's currents can be. Snarled in a net of smuggling, treachery, and revenge, he's finding out that no matter how far down you go, nothing's harder to salvage than the truth.

The Cool Blue Tomb by Paul Kemprecos. On sale now wherever Bantam Crime Line Books are sold.